for my family, past, present, and future

RADIO BRAZIL

LAWRENCE RUSSELL

THE TERMINAL PRESS

This novel is entirely a work of fiction.
The names, characters and incidents portrayed in it are the work of the
author's imagination. Any resemblance to actual persons, living or dead,
events or localities is entirely coincidental.

Radio Brazil Copyright © Lawrence Russell 2015

Published By
THE TERMINAL PRESS
135 MacPherson Avenue
Toronto, ON M5R 1W9
Canada

First Edition

ISBN: 978-0-9918665-7-1

Book design: Rick McGrath
Typeset in 10pt Minion Pro

RADIO BRAZIL

RADIO BRAZIL

CHAPTER ONE:

THE WAR OF THE WORLDS

AS I CHECK IN, I say to the clerk, "How far is it to Pier 42?"

As to be expected, he knows everything, this guy. "The Moore-McCormack dock? That's on Canal Street. You catching the Southern Cross?"

"I am."

"Five, no more than ten minutes from here. Let us know at check out and we'll arrange a taxi if you like. Luggage?"

"My suitcase is in the Terminal for now."

"Room 438. Enjoy your stay, Mr. Thorsen."

When I get to my room, I take a look out the window. Big office building across the street, which must be 42nd or forty something. It's all windows and you can see the people working, lots of women at desks. One of them looks up and smiles and she isn't half bad, a blonde with specs and a ponytail, and I'm thinking, you know a fella could do o.k. in New York. If he was hanging around, that is. I check the bathroom, then check the bed. I check the bed by dropping onto it and the next thing I know I'm asleep. Bushed. Didn't get much shut-eye on the train from Chicago. Didn't have a sleeping berth, just sat up in the coach. At night the landscape was all lights and different shapes floating out of the dark. We went in a long curve through some part of Milwaukee and there was a big brewery neon: Schlitz, the Beer that made Milwaukee Famous. I was dozing and floating through America in a dream. At one point I got up and staggered to the back of the train where the club car was. I say stagger because that's what you do on a train, even when it's moving slow and easy through the 'burbs. And wouldn't you know it, they didn't have Schlitz, so I settled for a Ballantine instead.

Trains. I like trains. Come to think of it, I like just about anything that moves.

I'm liking the way the pretty waitress is moving about behind the counter. Nice rig, know what I mean? She's tuning the radio set, trying to find some modern music, and she has to stretch to reach the dial.

She knows I'm looking at her, says, "How's that pie?"

"Great," I say. "Blueberry's my favorite."

"I like swing," she says. "You like swing?"

"Sure."

She dials in some orchestra that's nice and throaty, a bit tropical. Could be Artie Shaw but it isn't, guy comes on, says it's Ramon Raquello and his Orchestra performing live from the Meridien Room of the Hotel Park Plaza.

"Joe," says the waitress to the cook who's hidden in his slot at the back. "Where's the Park Plaza?"

"Just around the corner, ain't it?" says Joe, all Brooklyn and bored.

"I never heard of the Meridien Room," says the waitress. She looks at me, says, "You want more coffee?"

I smile and she pours... I sip and she smiles. Radio squawks and a voice breaks in with a special bulletin from some news organization about explosions on Mars and a big one in New Jersey. The only other guy in the place who's sitting a few stools down looks up from his newspaper, looks worried, says, "Another?" When he sees from my expression that I don't know what he's referring to, he adds, "Last year... the Hindenburg."

"The German airship," says the waitress. "It was horrible."

"You see it?" I ask.

"My sister did," she says. "Her boyfriend was one of the ground crew. You know, one of the guys who grabs the ropes, helps pull her in when they cut the engines."

"Good money in that?" I say, thinking I'm cool and witty.

"Not anymore," she says. She picks up my plate, wipes the counter. "You waiting for a train?"

"No," I say. "I came in from Chicago earlier."

"Yeah? You a gangster?"

I laugh, say, "Do I look like a gangster?"

"Nah... you're too pretty," she says. "A wise guy maybe."

With that, she bops off to the music of Ramon Raquello, who has

12

resumed the broadcast. What do you do in New York when you're waiting to catch a boat the next day? Behave, I guess. Earlier, after I had my nap at the hotel, I took a walk around the neighbourhood, made it as far as Broadway, which wasn't much, even though the neon lights were coming on early, this being October and there was a nip in the air. Lots of hustlers, sidewalk hawkers, beggars and crazy people. Madison Avenue has flash, and Times Square kinda interesting. Don't expect they've changed much. In those days it wasn't that clean, as they were always dumping confetti out of the scrappers during the parades, and when you have all those people and cars and trucks, it's crazy. They have cleaning crews working all the time and they hose her down at night, but the place still looks like a pawnshop in a prison when you go sideways for a block or two. They got bars, though. Saloons, taverns. Remember, Prohibition was still in the air, if not in fact. I mean, it was just four years ago since Roosevelt got the damn thing repealed. New law says liquor can only be 3.2% by weight. Guess that's why most of their beer was tasting like piss.

I had a couple, did some window shopping, and when I got back to the Grand Central block, decided to check out the coffee shop right at the entrance to the terminal. Looks like a diner, big window looking at the street, low L-shape counter with spin stools. No booths. It was strictly for quick fixes.

This time of night there's just me and this other guy who looks like a door-to-door salesman. I've seen old barns in better shape. Banged-out suit and shabby raincoat that was all roiled from too much rain and air pollution or sleeping where he had no choice. He looks unshaven, but he's not. You know the type. The only thing between him and a bed in a boxcar is a stool in an all-nighter.

The news bulletins keep coming, breaking up the music, which isn't much anyway.

"Hear that?" says the guy.

"What?" I say.

"Reporter fella says it's a cylinder, a UFO crash."

"UFO?"

"Unidentified Flying Object. Listen—"

Now some expert Professor is putting in his two bits: "For want of a better term, I shall refer to the mysterious weapon as a heat-ray. It's all too evident these creatures have scientific knowledge far in advance of our own."

The waitress comes whistling back with fresh lipstick on her mouth. "What creatures?"

"You heard him," the guy says. "Martians."

13

By now the cook has stepped out to get a better listen. "This is something them Nazis dreamed up," he says.

But there's something about the Professor's voice that's familiar to me. I listen to a lot of radio. Nights back home in Kelowna get awful lonesome without some radio.

"That's Orson Welles," I say.

"Yeah," says the waitress, "that's Orson Welles."

"Nah," says the cook, "that's some guy trying to be Orson Welles."

"Are you saying this is for real?" says the waitress. "I don't believe any of it."

"Sounds like Orson Welles to me," I say.

"Get a microphone and you'd sound like Orson Welles," says the cook. "It's the style."

"Yeah Orson is a dude alright," says the waitress. "The Shadow can lick my ears anytime."

The cook guffaws, slides back to his nest. Two men come in, sit down right beside me. The way their fedoras ride, I'm thinking they could be cops. The way the salesman gets up and splits, he must be thinking the same thing. Keeps his face dropped, limps like he's got blisters or gout.

The waitress coffees them up, the Ramon Raquello Orchestra is back on the radio again, and I'm minding my own business. Of course I'm wondering why they plunked down right beside me when there's like fifteen empty stools and a mile of empty counter. Big cities, you just don't know about some of these guys. They like to get cozy with young flesh, doesn't matter what sex, just so long as it's young.

Both are squatting there like toadstools waiting for the sunrise. I realize they're watching me in the Coke mirror hanging above the soda pump.

"Artie Shaw," says one.

"That ain't Artie," says the other.

They're still looking at me. I look like Artie Shaw, the famous bandleader?

"That's him," says the 1st Toadstool. "He's playing the Blue Room."

"Blue Room?" says the 2nd, the big one who's crowding me.

"Hotel Lincoln," says the 1st.

"It's Latin... that's not Artie."

"Artie does Latin."

"Not like that."

The guy who's crowding me says to me through the mirror: "What do you think?"

I shift one stool away, say, "Think about what?"

The guy turns towards me, gives me the old eyeball shakedown, says, "The rhythm... is that one-three?"

This guy is playing with me. Morse code is one-three. Every schoolboy knows that.

I say, "That's Ramon Raquello doing 4 beats to the bar."

First Toad turns to Second Toad briefly, gets all theatrical, makes a big show, says, "What do you know... this guy's an expert."

I'm thinking I gotta blow this joint or I'm going to be in a fight, and I don't like the odds. I mean, I could handle myself, but two guys? Maybe packing lead pencils in their pockets? In those days I didn't mind getting into a scrap but if they're cops or federal agents, what's the percentage? In a public place like a slot dinner in Grand Central? No thanks.

But there's a big commotion outside on the street, some people running, others dodging to get out of the way, thinking what the hell's going on. Some are looking up like maybe a Zeppelin is doing a night raid over Manhattan or stock brokers are jumping from windows. Some cars are driving crazy, climbing the sidewalk, dodging taxis, running lights. Engines are roaring like elephants smelling fire. It's almost a riot. Well it is a riot. Young negro guy comes in from the station entrance. He's wearing a blue double-breasted pin-stripe suit and a flat top and packing a small beat-up suitcase. He's presentable but he's agitated, says to no one in particular, "What's goin' on, boss?"

Second Toad says, "Shouldn't you be north of Central Park, boy?"

First Toad says, "Forget him, it's Halloween."

You're thinking New York has no segregation, no Jim Crowe in those days, the thirties, and you're mistaken. Most of the blacks were north of Central Park, way up there in Harlem, but I could see a few around, sense that things were changing. Like the song says, how you gonna keep 'em down on the farm after they've seen Paree.

Next thing a guy runs in dressed in some sort of costume—thinks he's Count Dracula, the way his face is painted, or maybe he's wearing a mask—shouts, "The Martians are coming!" Yep. It's time to split that caboose. If this is New York, what is Rio going to be like?

Dracula leaves as fast as he comes in and the black guy disappears too, completely spooked by the action. Meanwhile Orson Welles is back on the radio telling us how many Americans were getting fried by the Martian death rays and even the waitress is looking scared and confused. The Toads are completely baffled. Couple of cop cars pull up outside. One is a Mack wagon, an open top like a chopped fire truck or troop carrier, with four cops wearing gas masks in the back with sub-machine guns. The other is a 38 Ford Coupe, a street racer just like the one my buddy Ross used to have back in Kelowna, British Columbia. The two Toads stand up, slither some change onto the counter, and go outside to confer with two coppers inside the Ford.

The waitress says to me, "You know what's going on?"

The cook has reappeared by now, and says, "Communists one day, Nazis the next, now the goddamn Martians."

The waitress says, "The guy they were looking for left."

The cook says, "The guy who ate the burger and fries?"

The waitress looks at me, smirks, says, "Know what I think? I think he was a spy."

The cook shrugs, says, "As long as he weren't no lousy Martian."

The waitress laughs her giddy laugh, then her face goes to the churchyard when she sees the searchlights suddenly stabbing into the night sky. I'm outta there like a good boy and like a good boy I go straight to my bed at the Carlton. Well maybe not. Maybe I go to the lobby bar, have one or two 3.2 piss beer, write a postcard to my girl back home. Maybe I have a conversation with some lady about life on Mars, etc, New York's like that. You think of one thing, end up doing another, like getting pissed to the gills and waking up the next day with a royal hangover that makes the window look like a door and the door look like a window.

Life—you move through it accidentally, just like music before it's written down as hammers. My father used to play piano, although I never heard him, so it was just another apocryphal anecdote, like most of the stuff I knew about him. Once, during one of his rare visits, he said, I like music because it's accidental… it just happens, like the breeze. He was talking to Uncle Frank, who was also visiting. I don't know what the context was or anything, it was just a thing overheard in passing. Thinking about it now, it's obvious: the man was a fatalist. Guess it was the Great War that did it to him.

So, in 1938 when I get the chance to go south, I take it. A trip to Brazil, courtesy of the local German Club. Why not? 22 years old and flow like the breeze. Mum was German and she brought me up, so that's the connection. The old man was Danish although he was born in Canada like me. Parents were Scandinavian, religious as hell. Not my old man and certainly not me. Thorsen, meaning sometime way back in the mists, we were Norse gods. Mum used to cuff me around when I was young and did something stupid, say, you might be the son of a god but just remember you're also the son of a bitch. Well, she wasn't really. Maybe I was a son-of-a-something from time to time but she wasn't a bitch. She was my lovely mother with the soft hands and the smell of lilac, and why the hell my old man left her is beyond me. Another story, a secret one, one that was withheld from me. The War, I guess. He saw stuff, did stuff, that changed him. Tank commander, one of the first. Battle of Cambria... he was in that and others. Tanks were new science then, although the Mark IV he fought with was a prehistoric looking thing with big exposed caterpillar tracks and artillery guns sticking out of it. It was like they put it in a metal press at the foundry and crushed it to get that rhomboid shape. Not much could stop it, which is why he's still around to tell the story in some bar somewhere.

I figured I might do the army thing too, so I joined the reserves for a couple years, did a bit of this and that, did some studying, had one or two girlfriends, nobody permanent. This was a very exciting time in my life. We were living in British Columbia, in the Okanagan, not far from the border.

So I cross over, go to Spokane which is just a couple of hours away, catch the trans-continental to Chicago. In Chicago I get on another train, travel overnight, come into New York the next morning. Chicago was something but New York's Grand Central Station is something else. Big, like a cathedral, with the light coming in holy slants from the overhead windows. Lots of marble, and it had an echo, a short lag reverb, the sort of sound you sometimes hear listening to short wave radio. All the people, all the movement, the coming and going, everyone dressed like a magazine, suits and fedoras, real big city class. Here I am, just a hick gawking at the fashion models, rich with perfume and high heel locomotion. I was wired—this was action Jackson, and was I ready? Just about. I sit down, take it all in, have the porter drop my luggage right there. Black guy, just like the movies. Porters on the train were black too, first ones I'd ever seen in the flesh. My man is like Sachmo, and you have to forgive me as this was the only reference I had. Give him a tip, guess it wasn't enough, as he stares at the coin in his palm like it's a rare bug. Later, I realize what it was—Canadian two bit coin and these Yankees weren't interested. I got a pocket full of this money, so pretty soon I'm trying to unload it in the gum machine and then the luggage locker. My main case is over a hundred pounds, contains the package the German Club want me to deliver to Brazil. No wonder the porter was pissed off. He had it on his shoulder and his legs were buckling. Well, hell. He grabbed the suitcase, latched on. Bad choice. Hustlers always looking for suckers but sometimes they get suckered themselves.

When I stash the big suitcase, I figure I might as well find my hotel, The Carlton, which is supposed to be just around the corner... although of course, which corner? I go up the stairs and out the main entrance, and the street hits me like a fist. 42nd, running east-west. New York—man, it makes you feel like a bug caught in a herd of elephants. One wrong step and you're road kill. Yes, even then, even in 1938. A hick gets distracted, steps off the curb into a bus or a taxi or some hop head riding an Indian. Look up, you get dizzy. Look down, you get whacked. It's the noise, man—it blinds you.

I turn right, go west onto Madison Avenue. Good choice. My hotel is just across the street. Top class, although the room the Club booked for me was probably the cheapest. Today you'd call this palace art deco. I'm feeling like a dude when I walk into the lobby past all those smiling jockeys looking to mule my luggage and alls I have is my army kit bag with the lone gun essentials slung over the shoulder of my best jacket. At this time, the only hotel of note that I'd ever been in was The Lakeview back in Kelowna, and it was nothing compared to this. It's one thing to be notorious, quite another to be classy. All the Lakeview had was a view and a couple of murders. The police chief shot and killed a pair of lovers in the Lakeview, so they changed the name to The Mayfair to get rid of the smell. It was o.k., sometimes I'd have a beer there, maybe a burger in the cafe. But this New York hotel—I'd be having a beer here. Place like this, they don't change their name because of a couple of bodies in a room.

CHAPTER TWO:

EMBARKATION

THERE'S A SURPRISE waiting for me at Pier 42 when I get there at noon, somewhat the worse for wear, but nonetheless excited and optimistic. After checking out of the hotel, I walk to Grand Central and collect my big suitcase, then grab a taxi to take me to the boat. Pretty sharp machine—a new Chrysler, with big wheels and big engine. So I feel like a prince riding in that big soft back seat, scooting under the elevated subway rails and past the warehouses and the vintage buildings of the dock area. Overcast sky, spitting rain, and all the cabby wants to talk about is Martians.

"You think there's life on Mars?" says the cabbie.

"Be interesting if there was," I say.

"Where you headed?"

"Brazil."

"Now that's Mars to me."

"Me too."

"Where're you from? Out west?"

"British Columbia."

"Where's that? Caribbean?"

Etcetera. Those days, for the average guy from Queens or Brooklyn, the world doesn't extend much further than the Statue of Liberty or the mouth of the Hudson River; for some, Yankee Stadium is far enough. New Jersey is a foreign country and Florida is Indian territory. New York has everything: spics, wops, micks, squareheads, chinks, jews and niggers. All from beyond the horizon at one time but here now. I'm only here 24 hours, yet I've learned more about life than in the previous ten years. It's cosmopolitan, and racism is just a bunch of expletives on the Richter Scale. You just talk the talk without thinking about it much. Free enterprise starts with your mouth, eh. So murder and suicide in the city is about sex, money and racism, often all three at once... routine accidents in the pursuit of business... or should I say, happiness. If I sound cynical, just remember it's 1938.

We have to go slow for a crime scene, cops are fishing a body out of the water. Death is a river waiting to be fed, the cabbie says, nice and poetic the way these New York cabbies are. A cop sitting on a big black horse waves us on and as I look back, see the wrapped body on a gurney being propelled into the back of an ambulance and some diver in a rubber suit lighting a cigarette on the wharf.

"Some chippy whose note came due," says the cabbie.

"You think it's a woman?" I say.

"Mister, the East River sees more bodies than a hooker on a Saturday night," says the cabbie. "Yeah, could be a guy, 'spose. Could be one of them Martians."

He laughs at his own witticism, but me, I'm unsettled. The memory of a drowning I saw back home on Lake Okanagan flickers through my mind, a guy I knew at school. He cramped up or something, and nobody paid any attention to his cries because we were all goofing off that evening, some 80 proof pops down on the beach. Despite the fact that I was in the army reserve and had done some hunting, all in all, I'd lived a pretty sheltered life. This business is like the movies or Dick Tracy, and for the first time in my life I was going to be getting on an ocean liner and even I knew that from time to time these leviathans sank. The Morro Castle—I knew about her. Luxury liner from Havana that caught fire heading for New York, killed all sorts of people. 1934, a mere four years ago. Face it, when someone else is at the wheel, anything can happen.

Big cities. Big buildings, big horses and big women. And big boats.

I get a flash of the liner as we pull up in front of the Moore-McCormack Embarkation terminal which is just a great big shed running the length of the pier. The SS Southern Cross, which used to be called something else until the two Irishmen took advantage of FDR's "good neighbour" policy. Bigger than anything I've seen up close, maybe 800 feet bow to stern. A toy compared to the Queen Mary or the Normandie, of course, but pretty big, pretty exciting for a young fella who's only seen the sea once or twice in Vancouver and who's never been on anything bigger than the SS Sicamous sternwheeler which is only 200 and something feet long and a lake ferry. Still, pretty impressive for the time, you know, very fancy woodwork and all, a classic steamboat and it gave me some idea of what to expect.

I'm not expecting to see my father standing there in the flood of people, all suited up and wearing a Donegal Tweed overcoat. It's a shock. Last time is five, six, seven years ago and then he's just passing through like the breeze. I look like him, no mistake. Tall and lean with blond hair and high cheekbones and blue eyes, a couple of Vikings for sure, although he's starting to go a bit gray. If I'm six-one then he's six and of course got a few pounds on me. He has a bit of a nervous tic, something from the scar on his face, wound from the war. He carries some shrapnel too, bothers him sometimes, but not today. He extends his hand and we shake... not like family but we shake.

Anyway, I'm smiling, either from shock or idiocy, say, "How'd you know I'd be here?"

"Your Aunt Renie," he says.

Renie is his younger sister. Guess she must've sent him a letter about my big adventure.

"I have business in New York," he adds.

That figures. Be an easy hop from Toronto.

"You look pale," he says. "Late night?"

"Yeah, late enough," I say, sort of distracted by all the porters and passengers flowing by, the buzz, the confusion... and the well-dressed women and their flash perfumes.

"I'm thinking you went to the Paramount, did some, ah, what do they call it? Jitterbugging."

"Nah, just had a couple of beer, watched the riot."

"Did you see any Martians?"

"No."

"Good. Let's get you checked in."

In those days there's no screening of luggage like now, no 3rd degree. You just tip the porter and when the suitcase is tagged with your cabin number, you just let the stevedore take it away. Tourist Class for me. I have my ticket, my passport, my Brazilian visa and my medical card showing I'm up to snuff and ready for the mosquitoes. Get my boarding pass, go forward to the waiting room dockside to await the announcement. Guests can come on board, have a drink, take in the view if there's time but my old man isn't inclined.

We're sitting on a wooden bench, the sort of thing that's moulded for your ass yet not all that comfortable. The air is cool enough that you can see your breath if you want. Concrete floor.

The old man says, "Who's paying for this trip? The German Club?"

I say, "Yeah. Great deal."

"Is it?" says the old man sharply. "What's the purpose?"

"Deliver a radio so they can hook up with some German club in Rio."

"Short-wave?"

"Yeah. A Hallicrafter, the latest."

"They haven't got any ham radios in Brazil?"

"Not like a Hallicrafter. I'm supposed to show them the ropes."

At this stage of the game I don't know that private ownership of a transceiver in Brazil is illegal... or maybe I didn't want to know.

"Who's idea was this? Gerwing's?"

Klaus Gerwing is the president of the Okanagan German Friendship Society, or the "Club" as they call it.

"How is your mother?"

I shrug, say, "Living in the past, stuck in the present. Been having dizzy spells. Thin blood."

He nods, says, "So Renie says. Ever see her?"

"Now and then."

"So you dropped out of university."

"Well I might go back."

"You realize you might get called up...."

"What, you think there's gonna be a war?"

"Dollars to donuts, kid. Hitler means it. Germany wants revenge."

"He's got Austria, what more does he want?"

"Anywhere there's a German community, he wants it. Austria, Czechoslovakia, Poland... Lithuania... all the Baltic States... even Denmark. He won't stop."

"Lucky I'm going to Brazil, then."

"Hitler's playing us all for suckers. Believe me, the Führer means war."

A great looking woman comes by and flops down onto the bench just across from us, takes an apple from her pocket, starts chomping on it. Striped fur coat, fancy purse. Crosses her long legs, lets her high heel swing in rhythm with her eating. Wild eyes. Could be 25, but who knows? Could be a kid, could be a lady.

I say, "People around here don't seem to care."

The old man says, "Roosevelt's playing a double game. But Americans are spooked."

"No chance of an invasion here, surely --"

"Here, in the East, they're spooked. If some guy on the radio can cause a panic with a fake Martian invasion, you know there's something else behind it. Hitler's got them rattled."

I want to ask him what he's doing for a living these days—I have the idea, maybe from Aunt Renie or my mother, that he's selling fire extinguishers. In the old days he was a timber cruiser, resumed that for a while after the war but in the twenties left it all behind, including my mother, a German war trophy. Treaty of Versailles. France took the money, we took the women. My history prof back in Vancouver said that and the class thought it was pretty funny; so did I, as I knew it was true.

"German Club paying for everything?"

He's talking to me but of course I'm looking at the babe.

"Yeah... train, hotel, boat, some spending money."

"Return?"

"One way. Figure I might keep going, check out Argentina. Lots of work there, I hear."

"I don't trust Gerwing. Never did. He screwed over Archie."

"Archie McDonald? The guy who shot the lovers at the Lakeview?"

"Yes. Gerwing set him up."

"How so?"

"Long story. Yes, I hear the Argentine is hot."

"Looking for drillers, I hear. I dunno... I'm open."

"Pack of fascists, though. Who's the guy in Brazil? Vargas? Same thing. South America is fascist as hell, so watch out."

"I can handle myself."

He looks me over, says, "I suppose you can at that. What did you do in the Reserves?"

I shrug, play blase: "Oh a bit of this and that. Basic training, lots of forced marches, games."

"Weapons?"

"Sure. Lots of target practice. Rifles, pistols... even got my rocks off with a Thompson."

The old man nods, says, "Who was your C.O.? Kinloss?"

"Yeah, Major Kinloss. Said he knows you."

"We were in France together."

"What was it like... the war, I mean."

"Dangerous. Very dangerous. There's nothing like being within range of a massed artillery attack. Avoid it if you can."

I shiver. Don't know if it's what he's saying or the November chill or the fact that I don't have a fur coat like the babe over there. He takes a flask from his pocket, pours a shot of something in the cap, hands it to me.

"Akvavit," he says. "Viking blood. Shoot 'er back."

I do, and the glow spreads quickly, starts me up like a generator.

He takes a shot too. Akvavit. 80 proof with caraway. Scandinavians everywhere trust it like holy water. It isn't booze, it's medicine.

"I've brought a present for you," he says. "Your Aunt Renie says I should pay more attention to your welfare."

He passes me a package wrapped in brown paper and jute string.

"Thanks," I say, genuinely surprised. "What is it?"

"Open it when you have a private moment... and I mean private. Wait 'til you're on board."

It looks and feels like granny Thorsen's bible, heavy enough for a doorstep, and I'm wondering if the old man has gone Evangelical Lutheran like his mother, who got it so bad she was put in hospital for a while.

"It's a book," he says. "You need something to read on a long voyage."

"Must admit, I don't read as much as I should. Thanks."

I put the book in my bag. The boarding announcement for my cabin deck comes on and passengers start to crowd the exit, start for the gangway. Some guy shows up, collects the babe in the furcoat. Black slick hair and pencil moustache, looks like Mandrake the Magician. In fact, as I later learn, he is a magician. We watch them join the line, disappear through the door.

The old man stands up, takes out his wallet, passes me a couple of C notes. I protest, wonder how the hell he can afford that.

"Young guy needs money," he says. "God knows, I should know."

I get up, shoulder my sling bag.

"Thanks, Dad," I say.

"We can stay in touch through Renie," he says.

We shake hands, and I'm thinking, what do you know, the guy isn't half as bad as my mother says. He seems genuinely concerned about me. Who knows? Maybe we'll see one another again... but then maybe not. Maybe he just gave me my inheritance.

As I turn away he says, "And watch out for women on ocean liners. They have a tendency to act crazy."

I smile over my shoulder, keep going, come out onto the dock, look up at the boat and the people already on board and wandering the decks, watching the action. There is a band, streamers, bullshit. I'm not used to this kind of attention, and flush with dough, I feel like a movie star. I flash my boarding ticket, get a friendly greeting from an officer, start up the gangway all wired up and totally in love with the future, whatever way she's dressed.

WHATEVER MY OLD MAN thinks about the German Club and Klaus Gerwing, they didn't book me into the hold with the cattle, a four berth cabin you share with three strangers and the propeller shaft that runs below the floor and that vibration you're feeling isn't just the ocean. I could've put up with it, but they thoughtfully booked me into the next grade up, a two berth cabin with a porthole and just one stranger. About 240 green gringos one way, which works out at 24 bucks a day and all the grub you can eat. You have to pay for your booze in the bar but it's duty free, so I expect even a hobo like me can afford it.

Whoever I'm sharing with isn't here yet, so I hang a couple of shirts and jacket in the closet, put my ties and shaving kit in a bureau drawer beside the bunk, then check the package the old man passed along. It's a book alright, a big one with a very serious title: *The Decline of the West*, by Oswald Spengler. Never heard of it, of course. Except for a few pages at the beginning, most seem to be stuck together, baked like a brick. Not exactly light reading. How would this help me in Brazil? I dropped out of university because of shit like this. Guess he figures it will help me sleep through rough seas or get smart real slow.

I chuck it on the bed, head out to scope the ship. Up top on the sun deck people are gathering to watch us cast off, pushed by a tug. Just as they are about to pull the gangway, a bunch of monks come running up, a very unlikely late addition to the passenger list. So says a tall gent next to me at the railing, who's wearing a trenchcoat and smoking a cigar. Face like Texas leather. Solid, experienced.

"Monks?" I say.

"Yeah," says the man. "Judging by the hassocks I would say they are of the Teutonic Order... Knights of the Cross."

"Squareheads?" I say.

This just slips out of me, as I'm still a bit rough on the traveller's diplomacy. The man laughs.

"Yes yes, exactly," he says. "By the way, name's Colonel Powell. Retired, of course."

I mumble my name as we shake hands.

"Guess we won't see them in the bar or dancing the rumba," says Powell.

"They got monasteries in Brazil?" I say.

"Sure, it's Catholic," he says. "By the way, are you from Minnesota by any chance? I ask, as you look Scandinavian and there are a lot of them in the Minneapolis area."

"No, I'm from British Columbia," I say. "My family is Danish, though."

"I've been to Denmark," he says. "Spent some time in Europe after the war. Been in B.C. too... hunting. Magnificent place. God's country."

Turns out the Colonel is from Santa Barbara, California. A type I'm already familiar with, even at my young age. A rugged fifty-something who's been all over hell's half-acre and has plenty of stories to tell. Still, I'm sure. Lots of Yanks call themselves Colonel and all they sell is chicken.

"Boat's full of Germans this run," he says. "My guess is most of them are escaping Herr Hitler."

"Even the monks?"

"Especially the monks. Catholic Order, and Hitler has it in for the Catholics."

"I thought it was Jews he didn't like."

"My friend, the Hun doesn't like anyone who isn't a Hun these days. Well, the fact is the monastic orders have money. Gold. And the Nazis are confiscating it from anyone they can, including the Jews and the monks."

I remember my mother is a bit anti-Jewish, never understood why. There aren't any Jews in my home town, let alone monks. To me they're just part of history, guys who live in books like the Bible.

A well-dressed couple a bit further down the railing are waving to someone down on the dock. The man is wearing an overcoat and hat, and to tell the truth, that pussy-mouth moustache makes him look a bit like Hitler. The woman is younger, very pale with dark circles around her eyes and she's shivering even though she has a fur coat and gloves. A flash bulb pops as some guy on the dock with one of those big press cameras takes a picture.

The Colonel lowers his voice, indicates the couple with a slight shift of the head, says, "We have a distinguished author on board."

Again, I look at the couple. Their smiles seem forced.

"Austrian Jews," says the Colonel.

"Who is he?" I say. "Is he famous?"

"Famous indeed. That's Stefan Zion and his wife."

"What does he write about?"

"Love in the modern age. Bit of a poet, not my style. Nevertheless I look forward to engaging him in conversation."

The Colonel is sailing First Class, of course, like the Zs. But sometimes the plebs and the Firsts mix on the decks or in one of the lounges where a party gets going. It only takes a couple of days to get the hang of the protocols on a cruise, the locked doors and those that open. You'd be surprised how fast a group of passengers on a ship form a society, like a small town that's been around for generations. Of course everyone lies about himself to some extent, as fantasies can get out of hand. You can be whoever you want to be on an ocean liner. Strangers when you meet, fools when you leave.

As the ship breaks its moorings and the tug pushes it away from the pier, the Colonel tips his hat, wanders off. The Bridge lets go with the horn—couple of deep roars that echo across the harbour and boom around the scrappers. I hang around long enough to watch the Manhattan skyline light up in the Autumn twilight, feel the engines kick in as the tug peels away and we close on the Statue of Liberty. Some passengers are still waving, even though the distance has reduced all life to an outline. Well, except for the gulls and a few soldiers on Bedloe Island near the big lady. She's impressive in the real. Some of the passengers have tears in their eyes. Americans, I guess. Me, I go looking for the bar.

When I eventually get back to my cabin my roommate is there, dressing for dinner—a bloody German monk. His cassock is lying on the bed and he's stripped to the waist checking out a shirt. Young guy, maybe twenty, twenty-one. Well-built, like he's been chopping wood and hauling dead deer out of the woods, singing the Happy Wanderer, Val da ree ha ha ha. First impressions are often mistaken, however.

"*Guten abend,*" he says. "*Sprechen ze Deutch?*"

For some reason my instinct tells me to keep my half-assed knowledge of that language to myself, play the silent Canadian. He nods at the book on my bunk, says in decent English, "You read Spengler, I see."

"Not yet," I say. "It was a gift."

By now he's got his shirt on and is hanging the black Teutonic cross around his neck.

"Defeatist," he says. "Clever, yes, but defeatist. I read him in my last year at the Academy."

"I'll chuck him in the ocean," I say, motioning at the porthole.

He laughs, offers his hand, says, "Voss... Kurt Voss. I am a member of the Teutonic Order of the Holy Cross."

"Thorsen," I say.

"And what is your profession, Herr Thorsen?"

"Right now I'm looking at possibilities."

He nods as he translates, absorbs. "A tourist."

"More or less," I say. "I hear there's lots of work in South America."

"A young world, lots of possibilities," he says.

"You seem a bit young yourself, Kurt," I say. "You know...."

"To be a monk?" he says. "Good way to avoid military service. I don't like killing."

Makes sense, I think.

"Have you been in the army, Herr Thorsen?"

"Not yet."

"You look like a hunter, someone who lives in the mountains."

I'm wondering if he's casting lines or just being dumb friendly.

"I live by a lake," I say. "Once in a while I hunt."

"My family has a holiday house in the mountains in Bavaria," he says. "My best memories are there."

"Would this be the Black Forest?"

"Nein, nein... the Black Forest is in the south-west. I am the Alps. This is the north-east."

He likes to talk, practice his English.

"Been in the States long?" I say.

"No, we just come from Germany," he says. "The Hamburg-Amerika Line. SS Resolute. This is better, perhaps. We shall see."

He pulls on his jacket. It's tight, too tight for a priest or a monk.

"Now I am ready for dinner," he says.

"Don't you wear the monk suit all the time?" I say.

"Usually, yes," he says. "Our Kommandant says we can dress as civilians for the cruise. I hope it won't be rough."

"You get seasick?"

"Yes. I was sick coming across. We were four to a cabin and two of us were sick."

"So that's why they put you in with me this time."

This puzzles him. I dismiss the lame joke with a flutter of the hand.

Humour is another level in second language skill.

"What I mean is, maybe we can be sick together."

He laughs, sort of. He's younger than me, although there's a formality about him, that German thing that makes them better mechanics than comedians. The steward passes outside our cabin, banging the dinner gong, summoning the hungry. Voss nods, sort of bows, heads off to join his fellow Knights in the dinning room. I hang back as it's obvious I'm not ready for the Lobster a la Newburg and the Mocca Layer Cake just yet. Hell, do they ever feed you up on those boats if you let them. Sugar and peanuts with everything.

I pick up the Spengler, which is still stuck shut, grab a letter opener, ease some of the pages loose... and my god, do I get a big surprise: it springs open to reveal a Colt M1911 automatic.

Sweet beautiful dreams of Christ!

The book had been carved out to accommodate the shape of the gun, an old trick to be sure, but new to me. It's loaded too, seven in the clip. This is one hell of a gun, got twice the range of most of the other pistols out there, good for a 170 feet, standard issue for the Yanks and the Canadian Army, and I'm thinking this was the old man's side arm in the Great War. Now he's passed it along to me... but why? Packing heat across borders isn't cool, could get me in shit real fast. Is Brazil really all that dangerous? No law and order in Rio? I dig the law of succession, his gun, my gun and all that, but the questions just keep coming.

Feels good, though. I sight at the door, then the porthole. I'd fired the 911 on the range during training, of course.

"South America is fascist as hell, so watch out," the old man said. So he gives me a gun, his gun. I can open the porthole and chuck it right now, or I can put it back in its custom cradle and decide later. I remember a cartoon I saw once of the Statue of Liberty and the lady is holding an automatic pistol aloft instead of a torch. Sort of summed up the American way. Not the Canadian way, mind you, but close enough. Law and order is fine and dandy, but is it ever around when you need it? A young man travelling alone across the equator in 1938 needs insurance.

The Decline of the West: good reading so far.

Chapter Four:

HERR Z, COLONEL POWELL AND SOME GERMAN MONKS

BEEN A LONG TIME AGO, all this... yet I remember some of this cruise, this journey, this ship, clearly, because these were times no one forgets if he lived them. 1938. A lot of things happened for the world in 1938 and for myself. As I look back, I think, how did I survive?

It was rough off Cape Hatteras, just wild and we got thrown around pretty good. Don't think SS Southern Cross had stabilizers and if she did, they were smaller than a baby shark's fins. Lots of people were sick. Not me, but lots of people. The monk was sick, sick so bad that as strong a devotee as he was, it had him on his hands and knees with his face in the toilet half the night and half the next day. Passengers were staggering in the corridors, bouncing off the walls, waiters sliding with loaded trays across the floor like Broadway dancers. Hilarious. Some people got hurt falling down stairs or out of their bunks, but I got the hang of it pretty fast. No different than driving drunk on a washback road, pedal to the floor. Roll or get rolled, daddy.

Third day it's clear, and the sailing is smooth enough that your beer sits where you want it. Leastways it does up top in the Stardust Lounge, which has a glass roof for watching those big ocean skies. The only person in there is the writer the Colonel pointed out to me the day we left New York. He has a chess board set up on the low circular drinks table.

"Good morning," he says as I drop into a chair next table over. "Do you play chess, sir?"

"Sorry," I say. "Haven't a clue."

He has a coffee beside the board, one of those small expresso cups. Suppose it is a tad early for a beer, but you know, I'm feeling a bit wild. Could be the smell of the ocean, could be the first real sense of freedom I've experienced. Cheap too. Nickel a glass, dime a bottle.

He speaks with a bit of an accent, an English accent with a Continental whisper... although, to tell the truth, he speaks English a lot better than me.

"I'm hoping someone on board will play," he says, then moves one of the pieces. "For now, I'm playing against myself."

He studies the board and I study the lounge. Some passengers walking on the deck outside, couple of waiters moving stuff around the bar. A young woman passes through wearing green shorts. She has a tag on her blouse. Could be an activities director or a dancer. They have a couple of professionals on board to amuse the passengers, teach the rumba, that sort of thing. She moves through quickly, her heels clicking that sexy high heel click. Smiles faintly, bouncing on my radar.

Z lights his pipe, I light a cigarette.

"You're a writer, aren't you?" I say.

He sighs, says, "I thought I was anonymous."

"A passenger told me," I say. "We saw the press taking photos."

"Yes yes," he says, nodding. "I just finished a book tour. Do you read, sir?"

"Not as much as I should."

"You're young."

"I've read some novels by H.G. Wells."

"His scientific romances?"

"Guess so. *The Time Machine... The War of the Worlds.*"

"I know Wells... reasonably well as a matter of fact. Not in good health these days, but then, are any of us? He visited me once at my home in Salzburg, which had a lot of steps and I think these nearly killed him. A fascinating mind—uncluttered, rational and completely without sentiment. I've been living in London for the past five years, you know. Recently I heard Wells debate George Bernard Shaw. An incredible exchange, poetic and mysterious, with an undercurrent of hostility."

"They didn't like one another?"

"Mmm... that's the thing, they're the best of friends, perfectly civil... but then, the British are like that. Civil, even when speaking to the Devil."

I'm wondering what he means here. Well, I'm out of my depth. What do I know about these people?

I say, "You think there's life on Mars?"

He's staring at his chessboard, working out his phantom opponent's next move.

Eventually he says, "I wonder what Wells will make of what happened in New York the other night."

"It was crazy," I say.

"You see?" he says, looking at me. "The madness isn't just in Europe, it's everywhere."

"I hear people were jumping from windows," I say.

"Yes," he says. "When my wife and I were coming to catch the boat, we saw a body being pulled from the harbour."

"I saw that... a spy, someone said," I say.

"Quite possibly," he says. "When I was in New York, someone accused me of being a German spy."

Was he kidding? I let this go, say. "When you're playing chess against yourself, do you imagine an opponent, a certain person, or is it just another piece of yourself?"

Now Z looks at me with interest. "As a matter of fact, it might be both," he says.

"So you see yourself as another chess player," I say.

"Yes," he says. "Adolf Hitler."

"He plays chess?" I say.

"He certainly does," he says.

"So what's his next move?" I say, thinking of this as no more than a joke.

"If only I knew," says Z thoughtfully. "If only I knew."

But of course he does know. Z could see things in that chessboard of his, yessir. We have a magician on board who's really good with a saw and a beautiful woman but he's clumsy and blind compared to Z. A magic trick is one thing, and raw, strategic intelligence is another.

I carry a worry stone in my pocket, a nice little rock I can work with my fingers, a soother. Not that I'm a fidgety kind of person, but it has a nice feel, keeps me in touch with back home. Piece of basalt with a streak of granite, right off the beach where Indian Creek runs into the lake. As smooth and mysterious as a fine woman's ass... or some other desirable terrain. I'm working it in my pocket as I lean on the railing, look over the big ocean expecting to see land but there's nothing, just water and everything it hides. Supposed to be passing Bermuda but all the waves look like islands to me. Then the dance instructress comes strutting by, slim and business-like in a snug jump suit like she's heading for the engine room to do some oiling. She has a lanyard around her neck with her name, rank and serial number. Don't quite catch any of it as she whistles past, although I know her name is Bobby from the daily activities flyer that some Trojan pushed below the cabin door.

Sort of blonde, maybe 23 or 24, although as the maxim I live by in these days says, distance deceives. She moves fast and she moves real good and my head is twisting like a tight cork in a hot bottle.

She flashes a smile, says, "See you later... the Nautilus Room, 2:30, be there or be square."

Then she's gone, like she's climbed into that lifeboat or that air-conditioning stack further on down. Of course I'm thinking, is she pulling my chain or is she just nice to everybody? We shall see, we shall see.

Various passengers are doing the walk, although most of the fitness types prefer the prom deck below as they can do loops. The middling young crank it up like they're at the start of a marathon, while the old guys just totter along. With all the food they give you, exercise is a good idea. Now and then I find a private place, do a few push-ups, a few Russian squat hops, maybe touch my toes. Don't like the gym—too public, even if there is a punch bag and a set of weights. Apparently the monks think the same way, as there they are, the whole squad in formation doing situps on the bow deck just below where I'm standing. Knights of the Cross? The Bible and solitude doesn't really seem to be their vocation. I'm reminded of the Army Reserve and the fitness discipline I was forced through. Fools, I think. You gave up booze and women for this?

Next thing I know, they've formed a circle and two of them are duelling in the middle.

The Colonel comes wandering up.

"Look at that," I say.

"Interesting," he says. "They keep all the old traditions."

"Wouldn't they be pacifists?"

"Not when they have to liberate Jerusalem from the Mohammedan."

"You mean, like the Crusades? Those days are long gone."

"Tradition, kid, tradition. Just because you wear a crown doesn't mean you have a kingdom, and just because you carry a sword doesn't mean you're a natural born killer."

"Yeah, I get it. Just because I wear a robe doesn't mean I'm a monk either."

The Colonel chuckles. "You remind me of myself at your age, Thorsen. Full of piss and vinegar."

"Just thinking, why be a monk?" I say.

"When you can get married and live happily ever after?"

"You see the blond guy?"

"The fellow who's winning?"

"Is he? Guess he's pretty good. Well he's sharing a cabin with me, name is Kurt Voss. He says he joined the Order to avoid conscription."

"Interesting. Beats driving an ambulance, I suppose. Did he say where they're headed?"

"Might have. Brazil someplace, can't remember exactly."

"Find out, if you can. Just curious."

I nod, look at the sea. The Colonel has a pair of binoculars, is doing a sweep.

"What's our speed, y'think?" I ask.

"Boat like this can cruise at 22 knots."

"Pretty good."

"The Southern Cross is like a big motor yacht. It could enter some of the smaller harbours along the way if it had to."

I see something, could be a piece of debris, way out there to the east.

"What's that?" I say, pointing. "Bermuda?"

The Colonel looks, then passes me the nocs. The object appears and disappears in the roll.

"A ship?" I say. "Maybe it's too small for that."

"I was hoping your young eyes could determine that."

"Seems to be moving."

"Might be a freighter... or a Bermudian fishing boat."

"Beats me. Man, the Atlantic is a big lonely place."

I pass the nocs back after taking a blurry look at the monks and their fencing exercise. Too close to focus, too far to understand. They're using wooden sticks, not the real things, the steel that bends like the Count of Monte Cristo. Mostly it seems to be buffoonery, yet some of these monks have good moves. What next? Mass chanting, bells and incense?

"I understand there are quite a few Germans in Brazil," I say.

"Definitely," says the Colonel. "A favorite immigration destination for the last 50 years or more. Santa Catarina has a million Germans, maybe more, many of them don't speak Portuguese at all, don't need to. Big farming region, almost a country onto itself... in fact, could be."

"Where's that?"

"South of Rio... south of Sao Paulo. It's a province. Santa Catarina. Quite beautiful actually. Wonderful coast, wonderful beaches. Mountains with snow in the winter, valleys with great soil. If they spoke American English, it'd be a great place to get lost."

"You seem to know Brazil quite well, Colonel."

"Big place, so you can never really know it fully. In some ways it's a hundred years behind the United States, especially when you get outside the two big cities. It's a mulatto culture. Mixed blood. Yeah, lots of Europeans in the south and clustered along the coast, but Brazil is like its coffee, coarse, sweet and brown. In some ways Brazil is the future—in a hundred years we'll all be half-caste."

"I had a teacher in high school who said Darwinism guaranteed the white races would absorb all the others and remain white. Survival of the fittest and all that."

"I don't think he understood Darwin."

"Guess not. I don't."

"You religious?"

"Not really... no, guess not."

"Brazil is quite Catholic... but behind a lot of it is the Candomble cult, a black slave religion. It's a derivative of African voodoo. Around Rio they actually call it by another name, Macumba. Witchcraft, pure and simple. The Rio Carnival is just a mass orgy sponsored by the Macumba priests. Fun, though."

"When's that?"

"February. You staying around that long?"

"Don't know. Possibly... probably not."

"Know anyone in Rio?"

"I have a contact... guess I'm on my own."

"You want to bone up on the lingo, kid. Get a few words."

"Matter of fact, I bought myself a phrase book in the gift shop this morning."

I pull it out of my pocket and show him. Green jacket, yellow print. One of the Play a Lingo series, this one Portuguese.

He grunts, sort of chuckles, says, "Oh yes... 'Endorsed by Leading Educators.'"

I point, say, "'See A Picture, Learn A Word.'"

"Better to hear it, I think," he says. "But you'll get by."

"Learn 480 words in a few hours, it says."

"Get yourself a Brazilian girlfriend, kid. Quicker."

The thought tantalizes me for a moment; truth is, this is something I've been thinking about since the deal was first proposed to me back home in Kelowna. I went to the local library and checked an encyclopedia and right away it seemed obvious that Brazil's main domestic product was women—not sugar, not coffee, not rubber, not gold, not leather shoes, but women. Long tanned mysterious women who lie about the beaches all day waiting for tall pale mysterious strangers like me.

Once again, I play the complete dummy. "I've been warned to stay clear... they say the hookers look like normal girls."

The Colonel shakes head slowly. "Who told you that—your mother?"

"Well yeah."

"You'll figure it out. Before you're off this ship, shouldn't doubt."

The monks have dispersed, and some dressy passengers have taken their spot, chatting and taking photos. The Colonel says he met them last night in the First Class lounge, Brazilian big wheels with loads of dough. Coffee, mining, packaged food, big these days and getting bigger. Baking powder, coffee, chewing gum, that sort of thing. The men are wearing linen suits and the women are dressed like they're going to the races. The boss guy has a pen and pad, seems to be posing. A company director, says Powell. The young woman with the camera is his daughter. In that dress she could be a Sunday school teacher. They all have that Latin sun garden look.

"They own a lot of plantations," says Powell. "I've even visited one or two."

"Oh, is that your business?" I say.

"It's one of my interests."

"You have a ranch outside Santa Barbara, didn't you say?"

"Ranch might be an exaggeration," he says. "I own a hundred acres of the coastal sierra, just enough to ride my horse around without scaring the neighbours. You ride?"

I nod. "I used to skid logs once in awhile. Summer work. We used horses for that."

"Drays?"

"Whatever was available. Cattle horses."

"When I was first in the army, I was in the cavalry, learned to ride then. As the training manual says, you can't beat a man with a sabre on a galloping horse to inspire terror. What nonsense that turned out to be."

"They're not completely obsolete," I say confidently. "They still use horses to pull artillery ordnance into tricky places...."

"Oh do they now... would this be the Canadian Army?"

"My father served in the Great War. It's what he says."

"Sure. He's right, but not for much longer. Their only use to the modern military is for horsemeat and glue."

He's scanning with his binoculars again. Me, I'm working my worry stone, thinking of home, now so far away it doesn't exist. The ship is pitching gently as she cuts through the waves. Mild chop, nothing to be worried about, nothing but blue skies ahead.

I SPOT THE GIRL I saw in the embarkation terminal in New York lying back in a deck chair, long as a jaguar, face to the sky, big shades hiding her thoughts. She's wearing a cotton robe that fails to conceal her legs, although that might be the point. One hand hangs limp, her dagger nails almost touching the deck, while the other holds an abandoned book against her stomach. As I wander past, I try not to gawk, feign indifference. Fascinating. A bit older, out of my league. Like those women you see in a magazine modelling nylons, make you want to masturbate. You'd need a course in how to make love to a creature like this, a few language lessons and maybe the approval of a higher authority. She makes me realize that to this stage of my young life I've been bluffing my way, playing with girls, while dreaming of women. I notice an unlit cigarette lying on her chest, like it's fallen from her mouth, which is relaxed and sexy. Must be asleep or made of stone.

I think of my gun, my Oswald Spengler. Would that make a difference?

I don't recognize Mandrake at first because he's shaved off his moustache, now has a baby-face look not unlike Orson Welles. The thought flickers that maybe it is Welles, that maybe he had to get out of Dodge because of his radio fiasco. Word is about that he barely escaped the CBS studio alive and that he's being hunted by the police. Word is that he's gone underground with his mistress, a New York ballerina. But of course it isn't Welles, it's just that way we have of labelling our desires against stars and celebrities... especially on a ship. There are no nobodies.

Everyone is a somebody, if only as a distant relative or an illegitimate child. Didn't take me long to get the hang of what goes down on a cruise. You are who you say you are.

He's walking towards me—or her, should I say. Our eyes lock briefly. His look is cold, like he has me figured and has already dismissed me as an amateur, a lightweight, a boy. All true, of course. I'm not Bulldog Drummond or even Sergeant Dave King of the Royal Canadian Mounted Police. But you never know. I could be worse.

Caught his show last night in the Nautilus lounge but all I remember about it is her. Fantastic figure. Yeah, he's pulling stuff out of hats and making things disappear, doing card tricks and stuff, but the only really good thing he had going was when he sawed her in half. The passengers loved it, although mind you some were fooled, cried out in alarm. It was like he'd cut her right through the belly button. But when he put the two halves of the box back together and she climbed out and walked around the stage on those spike heels, the old guys at the front were licking a different kind of sweat from their lips. Their wives, perhaps remembering their better days, clapped like crazy seals.

He passes, shuffling like a bear with a hangover. I glance back, see him drop into the deck chair beside her, light a cigar. And I'm thinking, what is he to her? Is it all show business or is it something special?

I head for the Nautilus, find about a dozen passengers there getting dance lessons from Bobby and some skinny guy called Eduardo, who wears a tropical shirt and loose strides and a pair of gangster shoes, you know, those slick two tone hoofers that look like a cross between brogues and golf cleats. They're using a Rock Ola jukebox, loaded with all the hits, with a young cabin boy punching in the wooden nickels. Rumba stuff, Dolores del Rio, who's all the rage. I hang back, watch. The old fogies laugh and stumble a lot, but a couple of kids, teenagers, get the hang of it pretty quick. I'm watching Bobby. She certainly knows how to lead. No black footprints on the floor for her.

She spots me, then beckons. I shake my head, but she's insistent.

"You wanna be qualified, don't you?" she says. "Learn the rumba."

"It's the samba I don't know," I say.

"Same deal," she says. "Follow me."

I've never officially danced the rumba but I have no problem at all. She's slim and fits my body like an old familiar suit, loose and light. You just get snakey, move side to side, left first, then right. Or you can move forwards and back, same thing. If you're really cool, you shake your foot twice. You're supposed to keep a bit of distance, keep it polite, although basically there's nothing polite about a rumba.

When the record finishes, I say, "How did I do?"

She says, "You move your shoulders too much."

"You mean, I need more lessons?"

She's smiling, just enough to show some teeth but no gum.

"Just one."

She's not that good looking, although she's not that bad either. Minimal makeup keeps her professional, part of the crew, like a fitness instructor. Pony-tail, pin-ball eyes, meaning they move around. Reminds me of a gym teacher we had in Grade 10, the sort of female who can get you to do another lap even if you're beat.

A new record comes on and away we go again. Then the ship hits a roller and shudders, bow to stern, and we go spinning across the floor, but don't lose our feet. Eduardo has a rough time with his partner, an old babe who's loses it and is left on her knees, clinging to him like she just slid down a pole. Oh, merriment all round and I'm holding onto Bobby tight like a gentleman should.

"Jesus I need a gasper," she says, heads out onto the deck.

I follow, light her cigarette, one for myself too.

"Been doing this long?" I say.

"My fourth trip," she says. "Maybe my last."

"Don't you like it?"

"They told me it was a good way to find a rich husband."

"I thought you were married."

"Eduardo? Be serious, hombre. We work for an agency."

"Wouldn't you fancy being married to a rich plantation dude, live in Rio?"

"Rio's a dump. Bunch of slums really. You getting off there?"

"Yeah."

"Stick to Copacabana and Ipanema—that's where all the action is."

"Everybody says Rio is the most beautiful city in the world... one of them, anyway."

Z and his wife pass by. She's very pale, with midnight eyes, needs supported. He told me she wasn't feeling great, was staying close to their cabin. She's younger than him, maybe forty something. Some men like invalids.

"There goes a famous writer," I say. "He's Austrian."

"That his wife?"

"I think so."

"Bet she has tuberculosis or pleurisy. I've seen that look."

"You think?"

"I've seen that look."

39

"Wouldn't Rio be the wrong place for someone like that?"

"Is that where they're going? The Argentine would be better."

"Better climate?"

"Shore..." she says, stretching the word as she exhales, stubs out her cig. "And they got lots of smart tall guys."

"Yeah? I'm tall."

Eduardo appears at the door, beckons. She starts moving away. "Good. Know what we dancers say --"

I say, "What's that?"

"Never trust a man with short legs."

She's going through the door. I call, "Why's that?"

"Head's too close to his ass."

Normally I don't do jokes, never want to hear them. But I know this Bobby lady likes me, is being easy with me. The question is, how easy? And do I care? Everytime you meet a stranger, you eat a little, get a taste, see how much you want.

We have a daily newspaper on the ship, comes below your cabin door every morning, four pages called The Southern Cross Post. The day's shipboard events like exercise, dance lessons, bingo, south American culture talks, and the theme for the evening festivities... and on the back pages the major news events off the wire or more often than not, culled from the Voice of America hemispheric radio broadcasts.

That week Hungary annexes south Slovakia, to put something between them and Hitler, or Mussolini, I'm thinking at the time. Wrong. They say they're liberating ethnic Hungarians living there, reclaiming territory stolen from them after WW 1. Later someone says it's a frame up by Hitler so he can grab Czechoslovakia. Who knows. You can get a fat headache trying to figure out the politics of Europe, these days. Really, I don't care much at the time. It's all so far away... except, it isn't. This boat is full of experts, some of them refugees. In some of the lounges it's like the Tower of Babel at times, all this monkey talk. They look like humans but when you scramble them all together, sometimes it sounds like animals feeding, like raccoons they way they squabble and fight over a piece of garbage. You see? This sounds racist, doesn't it? But you see, then was then, and now is now, and when you're young, I don't care who you are, then or now, you're full of your own xenophobia. Maybe you keep it private but it's there, these shades of opinion and basic instinct. We call it politics, right? And we're all experts.

The biggest expert is the writer fellow, Z. He doesn't talk much about it to me but he does talk.

"Hitler and the Nazis are intent on world domination and the liquidation of the Jews," he says.

"Surely Hitler will be satisfied now that he has Austria," says the Colonel. "Isn't he Austrian?"

"Yes, alas, he's from Linz," says Z. "He drinks peppermint tea, did you know?"

"The more I hear, the more he sounds like an incredible bore, " says the Colonel. "I had the chance to kill him once. During the Great War. I had him in my sights but he got away."

I know this Z is a smart man, one of these cultured fellows who's a walking encyclopedia, too smart to enjoy life, always a bit melancholy. But now he smiles.

"I can appreciate your humour, Colonel," he says. "The 'Great' War—is it really over?"

"Ah, that's the question, isn't it?" says the Colonel. "Something my fellow countrymen can't grasp."

"I admire American pacifism... if it is pacifism."

"It isn't. Oh, there are pacifists, but isolationism is something else. Most Americans prefer to forget about Europe and its troubles. You're a pacifist, aren't you, Dr. Zion?"

"Yes. As is Bertrand Russell and George Bernard Shaw."

"Indeed. Men of letters aren't always that realistic about how the world works."

"How the world works... you think the war is continuing? I certainly do."

"Here we agree, Doctor. Herr Hitler is unfinished business."

Notice Z has a tic, ripples from his left eye down his cheek now and then.

"Evil is never finished," he says. "My wife and I had to leave Austria because of him. And we're not the only ones."

They're pretending to play chess... or at least the Colonel is, as he told me earlier he didn't like games. It's a way to draw Z out. The Colonel's moves are so careless, Z ends up advising him to reconsider, then advising him what move to make. As he said, he's always playing himself.

He's saying to Powell, "You see, if you do that, it's inevitable you lose, as I will checkmate on the 17th."

Powell says, "I lose?"

Z smiles.

The talk, the smoke, the sound of the ocean, the pitch and yawl, these things are putting me to sleep. I signal the waiter for a cup of coffee. There's a comic book lying on the table. Pick it up, let the pages flicker under my thumb. Dick Tracy. I dig his wrist watch radio. He's trying to figure out if the body in the harbour is from a gangland hit or from that big motor-yacht owned by the plutocrat Fat Desmond. I leaf through it, then see Mandrake enter the lounge with one of the ship's officers, an assistant purser. To my surprise they're speaking in German, too low to understand, but German of some sort. So many accents, regions, with which I'm not familiar. But I think I can read a face. Purser is one of these shadow guys, indeterminate age, bordering on ugly. Polite when he needs to be, like a teller who thinks he's a bank manager. Guess he knows more about everybody than even the Captain as he takes custody of the passengers' passports and any valuables they want to put in the safe. He can cash cheques too—if you're in First Class. As he looks over at Z and the Colonel, his name comes to me: Boettner. American kraut.

Mandrake looks at the chess players, says something to Boettner, who then splits. Mandrake comes over, introduces himself.

"Herr Zion? My name is Kallingram. I understand you are looking for a chess match."

So the magician's real name is Kallingram. What sort of a name is that?

Z says, "Correct, sir. You are German?"

Kallingram says, "I am from Budapest."

Z smiles, says, "Hungarian. Kallingram... the name is elusive. Could be from anywhere."

Kallingram says, "It's Nordic."

The Colonel stands up, says, "Take my seat, sir, and give this man a real match."

Kallingram says, "Finish your game, gentlemen."

The Colonel says, "It's finished."

He moves to another chair, watches.

Z says, "Do you have a color preference?"

Kallingram says, "Why don't I be black? Are we playing for money?"

That drops Z's pipe from his mouth... or almost. "I don't usually."

Kallingram says, "Oh... I was told you were a professional player."

Z says, "No."

Kallingram says, "But you're good, aren't you?"

The Colonel says, "I'll put up the money. A hundred? Two hundred?"

Kallingram grimaces, says, "How about a thousand?"

Z protests, says, "That is not the kind of match I want."

Kallingram looks at the Colonel, shrugs, "Five hundred then."

The Colonel says, "Come on, Z. There's a story in this."

Z says, "I really don't like gambling. My wife would be furious."

The Colonel says, "Nonsense—we're all men, aren't we? Men live by sport."

Z says, "Kallingram here is a professional magician. He knows all kinds of tricks."

Other people have come into the lounge, are picking up on the action. I'm thinking Colonel Powell is going to be picking up bets from a few sporting types before this is all over.

Kallingram says, "Tricks? I'm not Colonel Redl, Herr Z."

Z is wavering, says, "I should hope not. Redl cost us the Empire."

I don't know who this Redl guy is, although later I learn he was the Austrian Kaiser's top spy, sold the army's invasion plans to the Russians and the Serbs. Kiss of death for the Austro-Hungarian Empire, and had a lot to do with the Germans losing the first world war.

The chess match goes on all day and most of the next, ends in a draw, which is too bad as all kinds of people were making bets. Now and then I'd pass through the lounge just to see if it was over, but it just keeps going. Chess: a game for old men and sleeping dogs. I got better things to do. Been meaning to mosey by the radio room, see if I can see what kind of gear they have. Maybe off-limits, dunno. It's on A-deck, not far from the Bridge. Nobody's stopping me except myself, as I see Boettner the Purser, decide to hang back. Boettner goes into the radio room, and a few seconds later the operator comes out alone, ducks behind a lifeboat, lights up a smoke. I wander slowly towards the door, see Boettner's all alone, head phones on, tapping the bug. Interesting. Morse code. As it happens, I know Morse code, know it pretty good.

I'm listening, and looking over the railing at the sea, which is like molten silver. Big wall of cloud way off on the horizon. Balmy and humid, as we're not far from the Caribbean. Then I see that object I saw the other day. No binoculars, so what it is exactly I still don't know. Too small to be a freighter. Must be a fishing boat or maybe a yacht.

I hear incoming international dot-dash. Strong signal. At first I think it's a call sign, then I recognize German. It makes no sense, though, and I'm thinking this is code. When it quits, I scuttle up to the observation deck, watch from there. Boettner leaves the radio room, disappears below. A while later I happen to see him conferring with Kallingram outside the Nautilus, think nothing of it, although it does cross my mind that the Purser maybe has some money on the chess game. Something about these two gents that's as bent as a shot nickel. Jealousy? Could be. The magician's got an act, got a woman, and what have I got?

CHAPTER SIX:

BEGIN THE BEGUINE: UMA

IN THE EVENINGS, the orchestra is playing Artie Shaw's *Begin the Beguine* a lot, or should I say his version. Pure snake oil, although nice snake. Believe Cole Porter wrote it. People are crazy about this tune, especially me. One hundred and twenty bars of continuous melody, enough to make a dead man rise out of his casket, find the nearest lady who can dance. Well rumba, actually. Forty-nine percent foxtrot, forty-nine percent tango, and two percent what you bring to it anyway. So says Bobby, and she's the one who's teaching me. Unofficially.

Sometimes I sit at the bar, sometimes sit with other folks, couple of people from the dinner table, singles usually. Bobby is supposed to socialize but not hang out, as she's considered part of the crew and getting too friendly is verboten. Nonsense far as I can see, judging by a couple of the officers who do a lot of dancing and lingering with the same women every night. So I never drink with Bobby and whatever we've got going is going real slow. It's like rent-a-dance. I'm too shy to hustle anyone else, although I talk big. As it happens Mandrake's assistant is sitting with us. Someone asked her to dance, then brought her back, so here she is, a few feet away all dolled up like an UFA filmstar, drinking scotch like it's apple juice. Has that flapper look—you know, short hair, sparklers on her cheeks, black mask eyes. Short dress for those days and as I said before, her legs are the best.

She's so brazen the way she's looking me over I'm embarrassed. Someone asks her to dance but she blows him off, keeps coming back to me.

"You are Scandinavian, ja?" she says.

Strong accent and if I knew German better, I would've picked up Berlin.

"Canadian," I say.

"Your name," she says.

I tell her.

"Scandinavian," she says. "I am right. Dance with me."

I hesitate. Damned if I know why. Maybe the ship is rolling too much or maybe I'm just afraid of the bitch.

She gets up, starts to totter, so I go to the rescue. She's tall, almost as tall as me. What are we doing—a foxtrot? Dancing on an ocean liner can be hazardous for your health. You try to get the steps in before the floor disappears. Bad enough I'm so self-conscious, so suddenly short of ability. When I was learning to dance as a youth, I'd pick the ugly chicks so I could step on their feet with impunity. Right now we're the only couple on the floor, the only fools willing to make a spectacle of ourselves. She's drunk and I'm not drunk enough.

Everything steadies, like we've reached a sheltered lagoon. We're not really dancing, we're drifting in circles.

> *When we the begin/ the Beguine*
> *It brings back the sound/ of music so tender*
> *It brings back the night/ of tropical splendour*
> *It brings back a memory/ ever so green*

You would never say we were meant for each other based on this. We're lucky to get back to the table as a couple. She flops into her chair, immediately raises her hand for the waiter.

"And what's your name, *fraulein*?" I say.

"Uma," she says.

"Uma," I say. "That's Scandinavian, isn't it?"

"My *mutter*," she says.

But it's impossible to talk. It's too loud with the music and the people yapping and the throb of the ship, which is always behind everything. The drinks keep coming, even after the band stops playing and the older folks head for their cabins. Uma now has her leg against mine below the table. First I think it's accidental, then she's sliding lower in her chair, smiling at me, daring me.

I look back towards the bar. No sign of the magician.

"I want to go for a walk," she says thickly, working her leg against mine.

I try to keep it private, keep it low. "I'm tired."

"Come on, what's the matter? Don't you like me?"

Remember, she's slurring.

I say, "You're too old for me."

Drunk as she is, this Uma's quick as a snake, hisses, throws her drink in my face. Shit, what did I say that for? It just came out of me, all wrong, like I'd spat in the eye of the goddess, only I was the one with the stinging eye. Somebody laughs, and I try to laugh too as I dab my eyes and face with a napkin. Booze is on my shirt and jacket, so I am one wet puppy. They say you're not a man until a woman slaps your face. Guess a high grade scotch counts as a slap. Yet I don't feel like a man. I feel like a student who got slapped by teacher and everyone is thinking what crude smart ass remark did he make. She's on her feet now, tottering, and as she tries to leave, crashes into a chair. A waiter comes to her rescue, hands her off to some opportunist who's only too happy to support a drunken goddess back to her cabin.

Too old for me. By two years, if that. Too cosmopolitan maybe, only that word isn't in my vocab just yet. I've seen drunken women before, fenced their easy love, put them back in the corral. But I'm feeling I failed a test, and that there are bigger tests coming, so how the hell is a chump like me going to handle them if I can't even put a beautiful woman to bed on an ocean liner?

Tough guy, huh? You got a book you never read and a gun you never use.

That night I dream the magician is walking towards me on the deck, a saw in his hand.

Next morning I have a hangover, even though I shouldn't have. I look 10 years older and I cut myself shaving. Guilt can kill you, man, as easily as bad dreams. It comes at you out of nowhere, and you're left wondering what unspeakable crime have you committed. Well this time it's in the laundry—shirt, jacket and tie, which I leave for the steward to take care of. Voss is already up and at it. Hardly ever see the guy, let alone speak to him. The monks keep to themselves, even in the dining room. The gong goes for breakfast but I skip it. You can always get a coffee and a croissant in the Rainbow Cafe, hide behind the Southern Cross Daily. Not much going on, unless you like bingo or deck shuffle. Tomorrow we will be in Trinidad. Last night I saw some lights off starboard and somebody said it was Cuba. Whole mess of islands around here I know nothing about. Haiti. Jamaica. Aruba. The Antilles. And pretty soon we'll be crossing the equator and looking for pink flamingos on the massive mudflats of the Amazon.

Well, that's what the SC Daily says.

As I often do, I encounter Colonel Powell taking his morning stroll. He's wearing a tux, like he spent all night in the casino, forgot to go to bed.

"Who won the chess match?" I say.

"Still in progress," says the Colonel. "They're resuming this morning."

"Is Mandrake any good?" I say.

"You mean Kallingram? He looks very capable to me. Quite possibly I've made a bad investment."

"You could always bet both sides."

"I could. But no risk, no money, y'know?"

"I saw that mystery boat yesterday."

"Yes? Is it a boat?"

"What else can it be?"

"When was this?"

"Just after the chess match got going. Mid afternoon, maybe."

I tell him about the purser and the Morse code transmission.

"It was Morse? Are you sure?" he says.

"Oh yeah," I say. "I know Morse code. I have some training."

"Do you now. What was the communication?"

"Strong signal incoming, so it was close by, coming from another ship, I figure."

"The purser was doing the communicating, you say?"

"Yeah... in German. No surprise maybe—the purser's name is Boettner."

"You know German?"

"Enough. Message was in code, though. No sense to me."

"You remember any of it?"

"It's crap. First I thought it was a call-sign. All I remember is '49 dot B6."

"Did Boettner send this or receive this?"

"He sent something similar... a longer sequence. Just algebra to me."

"Forty-nine dot B six... I don't know what that is. Could be harmless."

"Well it could be. But I was thinking, Colonel, what if that's a submarine out there...."

"What if it was."

"It could be tracking us. Subs do that sort of thing, don't they? Practice."

He's not looking so skeptical now, the Colonel. He's nodding.

"Practice for the next world war, eh. You might be onto something, kid. A lot of vital shipping going up and down this coast. South America is big business for the USA. That's why President Roosevelt has initiated the "Good Neighbour Policy"—this ship is part of that outreach. Last

47

time I went to South America I had to fly, island hop on the clipper. Before, if you wanted to go by boat all the way to the Argentine you had to find a freighter with some passenger accommodations or change ships. Trade is increasing all the time, and more and more shipping is coming and going from South America."

"I can appreciate that, Colonel... even though I've seen only one or two freighters so far."

"Big ocean, kid. They're out there. We didn't build the Panama Canal for nothing."

"Ever been through it?"

"Through it? I was stationed there for three years. Last post before I retired."

"Do old soldiers ever retire?"

He laughs. "You mean, they either get killed or court-martialed? No, I retired. Happy to do so."

"If there's another war, though...."

"Then all bets are off. Say, you'll keep this to yourself for now, won't you? Your idea about the submarine."

"Sure. I got no one to talk to anyway."

"Don't mean to puff myself up, but I do have contacts in Washington. I know people in Foreign Affairs. I'll be checking in with our embassy in Rio."

"Well it could be a U-boat."

"Or it might be one of ours. But... you said there was something German involved?"

"Yeah. I thought it was a telegram, then it went mumbo jumbo."

"Tell me, Thorsen, how do you know Morse code?"

"Boy Scouts. I've always liked radio."

"You mean ham radio?"

I don't tell him I have a radio operator's ticket from the Canadian Armed Forces Reserve or he'll be thinking I'm a bloody spy or something. I've already said too much.

"I was in a club. We would talk to people all over the place."

"Lots of work for radio men down here. Mining companies in remote places. The jungle goes on forever. I can put you in touch with some people if you like."

"Sure. I'm open."

"O.k. I'll be moving along. I'm having my photo taken with the Captain."

"Nice. I wondered about the tuxedo."

"'Dead men wear suits, colonels wear tuxedos, don't you know?'"

He's quite the card, this Colonel Powell. I still remember his line "the pursuit of food is the pursuit of intelligence". How true. If I knew then what I knew later, I'd be a fat man.

CHAPTER SEVEN:

BOBBIE AND FRAU Z

I'M UP TOP NEAR the funnel catching the breeze when someone sneaks up behind, closes her cheeky hands over my eyes.

"Guess who?" a fake throaty voice says.

"Artie Shaw," I say, playing along.

"What a bastardly thing to say!" says Bobby, all giggles. "Can't you tell the difference between a man and a woman?"

I turn around, say, "Yeah, but can a woman tell the difference between a man and his clarinet?"

"You're too funny," she says. "What are you doing up here, anyways?"

"I was lonely," I say. "I was looking for a nice warm smoke-stack."

She's wearing shades and those green shorts again.

"Seems you've come to the right place," she says. "Here, let me show you my secret playhouse."

There's a white metal door, half rounds on the top and bottom, like the sort they use to seal one bulkhead from another. They call it a hatch but it's a door. She pulls it open and we go into this locker which can't be more than eight by eight and there's a lot less room than that as it's full of games gear and other stuff. Even though we're up top, you can really hear those mysterious knocks and engine rhythms that transmit through the hull.

"This is where we keep our records," she says. "Mostly up-to-date. Caribbean, Brazilian music too."

I'm eying the careless pile on the small sorting table and shelf load above.

"Any Duke Ellington?" I say. "He's hip."

"Sure," she says. "We got some Duke."

"Caravan," I say. "You heard that?"

"You betcha," she says. "You know your music."

"I listen to a lotta radio," I say.

She's stretching up for a disc on the shelf but can't quite make it. I close my hands on her small waist, start to lift, but she just relaxes back, her beautiful warm ass against my crotch. My hands find her breasts, my lips her neck. We're in a sexual lock from which there is really no escape. There isn't much light in the locker, not that you need it. Hands don't need light anyway. It's all vertical dancing, as we couldn't go horizontal in that space anyway. We heat up and she's greedy for it. "Be quick," she whispers. "I haven't got much time."

We must've gone at it once or twice a day for the remainder of the trip. Might've missed one or two days for some reason or another. It wasn't love but it wasn't hate either. I got quite good at it by the time of our last dance. She showed me a trick move, the "Gordian knot" as I seem to remember. It was like something a black widow would dream up.

We share a cigarette, agree to meet that night up top on the Lido, check out the starfields and the "cross" that's visible to those who dance the Beguine.

I leave the love locker first, go down some steep metal stairs which happen to take me onto that part of A deck exclusive to First Class passengers. A few of them are at the railing, checking out some porpoises who are running fast with the ship. Looks like fun, the way they're leaping in formation, saluting us or something. But of course it turns out they're on the run from a shark whose dorsal fin is cutting the surface a short ways back. Fortunately the porpoises are faster but this doesn't stop the shark from showing off, doing a barrel roll so's we get a flash of its evil white belly and that double row of reaper teeth. It's just a flash, enough to make the people gasp. The first shark I've ever seen in the real. Now I know for sure that I'm in a new latitude.

Behind me, a woman says, "*Was ist die ganze Aufregung?*"

Middle-aged woman on a deck chair, sun glasses. I think it's Z's wife.

"What's the fuss?" she says.

"A shark," I say. "Big one."

She grunts, scrutinizes me. "The man that women love."

I feel myself going red.

"*Schönling*," she says, smiling. "I've heard about you."

She motions me to sit beside her. I'm thinking I should make an excuse and get out of there, but excuses don't work with the Principal. Yeah, middle aged, looks younger from a distance. Tall, thin, all mugged up in heavy clothes even though it must be 75 degrees F.

"I heard about your incident with *Fraulein* Uma," she says. "A lady at our dinner table was telling us all about it."

"It was a misunderstanding," I say. "The words came out wrong."

"Hmm. Beautiful, isn't she?" she says. "Men become stupid around beauty."

"I sure did."

"My friend says she was very drunk, behaved like a *schlampe*... you know what *schlampe* is?"

"Not nice, I'm sure."

"Hmm... then, men are often to blame."

I must smell of Bobby, and she's picking up on it.

"You don't speak German, *schön*?"

"If I did, maybe I wouldn't have had a drink thrown in my face."

Bobby appears, walks past quickly, slight flick of the eyes, faint smile. Frau Z smiles, shakes her head.

"I saw that," she says.

"What," I say.

"You don't know her? Well, I think she would like to know you."

"Doubt it. I'm just a fool who can't dance or speak German."

She starts to laugh, then has a coughing fit.

"Forgive me," she says. "I'm fighting pneumonia. I picked it up in the United States. It's not contagious."

"Have you seen a doctor?"

"Of course. The ship's doctor is a nice man, but I daresay he's incompetent. No real doctor takes a job on an ocean liner unless he's been struck from the register."

"There's a doctor on board? Haven't seen him."

"He hobnobs with the rich and famous in First Class. You must've have seen him."

"I'm not in First Class."

"I thought not. How did you get here?"

I shrug. "Went up one set of stairs, came down another."

"And voila," she says. "That's how it's usually done. You've met my husband?"

"Yes I have."

"He goes the other way. As much as he loves class, he always goes lower."

"He's a writer, isn't he?"

"Yes. Romances. Take care, you might become one of his characters."

"He doesn't know anything about me."

"But that's the beauty of it. He doesn't need much. He can make it up."

"Are you Austrian too?"

She doesn't answer right away.

"*Nicht mehr*," she says. "No more, nevermore."

"Are things that bad?" I say.

"If you are a Jew, yes."

"The only Jews I know are in the Bible."

"Where are you from?"

I tell her.

"Closest thing to a Jew we have is a Jehovah's Witness," I say. "I think."

This picks her up.

"The Jew as a JW," she says. "I must tell my husband. No, that wouldn't save us. You have to be Lutheran. You have any Lutherans where you live?"

"Sounds familiar," I say. "They eat sauerkraut at Easter?"

This makes her snort. "They eat sauerkraut any day it pleases," she says. "Do you know Adolf Hitler eats spaghetti?"

"I eat it," I say. "And Mackenzie King likes Hitler."

"King? Who is King?"

"He's the Prime Minister of Canada. He likes the same stuff Hitler likes."

"Persecuting Jews and Jehovah Witnesses?"

"Well, don't know about that. I have read that he likes the music of Wagner, like Hitler and all Germans do."

"I don't like Wagner. Do you?"

"Honestly, I don't listen to the old guys. I like jazz, swing."

"Negro music."

"Not anymore. It's democratic."

"Don't you like the symphony? I like the symphony. I like Ravel. My husband knows Maurice Ravel. And Strauss."

"He says he knows H.G. Wells."

"This is true. Wells is another man that women love."

"Don't know if I get your drift."

"Not like you, *Schön*. They love his mind, so they give him children."

Go figure, eh. Guess Wells did it all by some sort of telepathy, could make women pregnant by looking at them. I love science fiction.

"Must be a great life, knowing all these great people," I say.

"Some of them are not so great," she says. "You'd be amazed by how much beautiful art comes from some very ugly people."

"What is art, Frau Zion?" I say. "Can you tell me, 'cause I've never been able to figure out what it is. I mean, what qualifies."

"Don't ask me—I'm just a secretary. I type my husband's stories, that is all."

Somehow I don't think that is all, but it's none of my business. All these people are living on another plateau. They talk the talk, drink champagne, visit museums and sleep real bad. I start to get up, split, when she grabs my arm.

"Tell me, what do you think of this Herr Kallingram? I don't like this game they are playing."

"They still at it?"

"They have agreed to a second game. I am suspicious of this man."

"You think he cheats?"

"I think... I think he is a National Socialist."

"Isn't he Hungarian?"

"He can be anything he wants and a National Socialist."

"What does Dr. Zion think?"

"Zion is suspicious."

"You think he means you harm? What've you got to worry about—you're getting off in Rio, aren't you?"

"Stefan is a great writer... as a chess player, he is human. They play for money, yes?"

"Well I don't know. I haven't spoken to him for a couple of days."

The first is a lie, the second is true. Money is involved, big money by my standards. Other passengers and members of the crew are betting on the game and it's all anyone in the smoking room can talk about. Even the monks are betting on it or so Voss says.

"Would you do me a favour, sir?" she says. "Could you help me?"

"Sure," I say, rising. I assume she wants a lift up.

"*Danke*," she murmurs. "If you could walk with me a little distance to my cabin...."

"Want me to get a steward?"

"No no, just get me to the door and I will be fine. I get a little dizzy, feel like *das alte frau*."

"*Das* what?"

"Old."

"You look young to me, Frau Zion."

"Ah so well-mannered as well. Your mother is Lutheran?"

Is this woman foxing me or am I just too sensitive. If I tell her my mother is German and often goes on rants like a National Socialist, what would she think of me then? No more *schönling*, no more sweet bird of youth and love me 'til I die.

"Must be," I say. "Never goes to church."

"When we have the life boat drill, I saw you and I thought now there is a young man who is willing to help a lady."

Oh oh I'm thinking, what's this? I'm being set up. These European dames can drink your milk, get you weak, then rob you blind.

"I don't carry purses," I say. "Otherwise I'm at your service."

"The divine messenger," she says.

"Hardly," I say.

"No. Herr Kallingram. This is how Zion translates his name."

"Divine messenger... show biz. He's a magician. Probably not his real name."

"Some happy angel of good fortune, who can believe it... I do not. If you find out something about him, please tell me."

"Me? I don't know him."

"*Fraulein* Uma."

"Uma? Uma thinks I'm poison. We won't be talking."

"I think you will. I know her type... I was once one myself."

"I mean, what is she to Kallingram? She his wife, his dolly... or just his assistant? Do you know?"

"She is not a *strayenutte*... possibly they were lovers... I don't know the English word... they try to get advantage."

"Hustle. They're hustlers."

"They are a convenience. Germany was destroyed, you know. People lost everything, so they do what is necessary to live. Perhaps I am a hustler."

"Hustlers don't travel First Class."

"Oh? You think there are no First Class hustlers?"

Don't know if she means this to be funny or not, but I'm laughing anyway. We're at the mahogany and brass swing doors. I shoulder them open, help her across the lip.

"You're very kind," she says. "I think I can manage from here. I would buy you a drink but I need to lie down."

"Thanks, don't need a drink," I say, although I'm thinking I do. "I'll check into the Smoking Room, see how that chess match is going."

"Tell my husband to come home."

"Sure."

She's pale. I dunno. Maybe Brazil will give her some color.

I'm lying on my bunk, scanning a South America information sheet. Talking to myself, the old habit of an only child.

"Brazil is a country of broad ethnic diversity blah blah... the coastline is 4,655 miles long and the landmass accounts for nearly 50% of all of South America blah blah... started as a colony of Portugal in 1500 AD, remained a colony until 1808 when Napoleon invaded Portugal and the colonial ties were broken... dah didi dah dah blah... becomes a republic in 1889 following a military coup... now a federal republic with a bicameral legislature... full of dummies who think it's gotta be their way or no way no doubt... hmm, 26 states... equatorial, tropical, sub-tropical... semi-desert... savannah... temperate... rainforest jungle and lost plateaus... major swamps, big rivers, the biggest being the Amazon... most agreeable climate for living is to be found south of Bahia... lots of birds and wild animals, especially in the north... monkeys pretending to be men and men pretending to be monkeys... yep, got it all. Rio the capital, Sao Paulo the biggest. Current leader is some 'gaucho paulista' with black bushy eyebrows called, um, Getulio Vargas... this Vargas owes his power to the labor unions and the Integralists... bunch of fascists who wear green shirts... the Integralists are funded directly by Hitler and Mussolini... hmm.

"The samba was a way of disguising martial arts training for the black slave population. The elaborate dance choreography hid its true intent, just as the Carnival hid the old voodoo ceremonies...

"Brazil has not been invaded since 1865 during the Paraguayan War... peace-loving, fun-loving, what's not to like?

"Miss Brazil 1938 is the *teuto-brasileiro* Gisele Schaeffer, previously Miss Santa Catarina. Don't suppose you're interested, fella.

"Useful phrases for the traveller include '*onde posso fazer uma merde*'... where can I take a dump... but even I know what merde is, so... Here's another one: '*O seu dinheiro*' which means your money... o.k. '*o seu dinheiro, gringo*'—

Voss comes in, glum look on his face.

"I don't like the sea," he says. "I don't like the heat."

"Five more days," I say. "You can make it."

"Six more days for me," he says. "We leave the ship at Santos."

Santos is the port for Sao Paulo, a day south of Rio.

"Where did you say the mission is?"

"South, near the mountains. We travel by bus. I am not thrilled."

"I thought monks enjoyed hardship."

"They said it was better than national service in the Wehrmacht. I could've just emigrated to Brazil like you."

"I'm not emigrating, I'm just visiting."

"Yes. I forgot. You have a girlfriend back home?"

"Nobody special."

"I have a girl."

"Monks can have girlfriends?"

He shrugs. "I won't be a monk forever."

"You really a monk?"

"Ja. Tattoo as well."

"You got a tattoo? Let's see it."

"Not yet—only when you qualify."

"Oh, you're just a junior monk, like an apprentice."

"Yes, a postulant."

"Aren't you supposed to shave your head or something?"

"Eventually. I will look like a *hirni*."

A Hirni... an idiot. My mother used to call me that.

I say, "What will you do at the mission?"

He's taking his shoes off, groans as he lies back on his bunk. "Work. Hard work. Farm work. Then we pray."

I laugh, say, "Know what? Sounds like the army."

"That's what Trudi said."

"Your girlfriend?"

"Ja. She is training to be a nurse."

"Miss her?"

"Yes... I am Old Shuttehand now."

He sees I don't know what he's talking about, makes a motion with his hand.

"Masturbation?"

"Ja... so many pretty women, so far from home."

"You're gonna make a lousy monk."

"Are you religious, Thorsen?"

"No. Went to Sunday school for a while but that's it."

"What is your education?"

"Two years of university."

"Two years? One day I might go to Heidelberg. My father went to Heidelberg."

"What does he do?"

"He is a lawyer. However, he has been recalled to the army. He was a Captain in the first big War."

"Called up, eh. Does this mean another war is coming?"

"Coming? We Germans are at war. We are in Spain, helping the Nationalists."

"General Franco."

"Ja, Franco. And Hitler wants Czechoslovakia and Poland."

"What for? He got Austria, didn't he?"

"Yes, of course. But you know there are many Germans living in Sudetenland, yes? Parts of Czechoslovakia such as Bohemia and Silesia. Poland too."

"So Hitler wants all Germans united."

"Exactly. The Greater Reich. I fear Russia. My father believes war with Russia is inevitable."

"You like Hitler?"

Voss shrugs. "I have nothing to compare him against. Things are better in Germany. People have a sense of purpose. Before, they felt cheated."

"The Treaty of Versailles."

"Yah, Versailles. The French. Those bastards will pay."

"You think?"

"The French are decadent. They use their women as honey traps."

I laugh, say, "You mean, like Mata Hari?"

"Ja, she was a French agent."

"Maybe she was, maybe she wasn't. French executed her because she was a German spy."

"Double agent, *mein Freund*."

"But she wasn't French, was she? They wouldn't have shot her if she was."

"The French would shoot their mothers if they could profit. They are very decadent."

"Guess that's why they invented the French safe."

"French safe? *Was ist das*?"

"Contraceptive... you know, a rubber."

"No. Fallopius the Italian, he is the man. No, the French are expert in perversion."

"Yeah? I'm going to the wrong country."

"You like sin?"

"What is it... sin, what is it... something the old guys use to control the young guys."

Voss is lying there, looking at the ceiling, hand playing with his cross. At the moment, it's smooth sailing, the ship cutting through the light chop with a soft hiss. Blue skies beyond the porthole. The Caribbean. These days everyone is wearing a banana shirt and shorts, except the old folks and me. Even the monks are jogging around the promenade deck stripped down like soccer players or deck hands loosening up to swab the salt from the nooks and crannies. I'm having fun. Why isn't he?

"You could always jump ship in Rio," I say, sort of *sotto*.

He has a funny look. "Desert? They would shoot me."

"Don't be ridiculous."

"They would hunt me down and shoot me. This is the Teutonic Order. No one leaves without permission."

I scoff. "God doesn't punish deserters."

"I have taken the vow. I must do what I am asked."

"You've still got a girlfriend back home."

"In theory."

"I'll bet that doesn't fit the code."

He's squirming. "I told you, I'm only in the Order because I don't want to be in the army."

"Army's not so bad."

"How would you know?"

My turn to duck and weave. "Two years, isn't it? Not so bad."

"Once in, never out... unless you die before you make 40. They can call you up at any time. Same in Canada, ja?"

"Right now there is no draft."

"Who is your leader?"

"Leader? You mean Prime Minister. Mackenzie King."

"King, yes, I have heard of him. He likes prostitutes."

I scoff. "What crap."

But Voss is insistent. "Yes, yes... we know about him in Germany. He has visited the Führer. My cousin is well placed in Berlin. My cousin visited our family last Christmas with many entertaining stories about diplomatic life in the capital. Ja, King likes prostitutes."

I continue to scoff. "King is a god-fearing Presbyterian."

"Is he married?"

"Dunno. Don't think so."

"Did you vote for him?"

"I don't vote."

"Ah... you are totalitarian."

"Like Commie? I don't think so."

He nods, sighs, has that distant look. "We vote in Germany yet it makes no difference to the outcome."

"Yeah I heard Hitler rigged the results."

"Perhaps... perhaps not. I know something else about your leader... yes, not only does he visit prostitutes, he visits the dead.

"He believes in spiritualism. The leader of our *schutzstaffel* Heinrich Himmler also believes. Himmler arranged a seance for your Herr King when he visited Berlin."

"You're making this up, aren't you?"

"No, believe me, it's all true. My cousin is in the SS."

"What's the SS?"

"*Schutzstaffle...* it's a police unit."

"Why didn't you join it? Inside track and all."

"I considered it. I don't like their uniforms. Anyway, police work is like army work."

All this seems laughable now, looking back. I hadn't a clue what the SS was or what it was about.

I say, "What do you know about President Roosevelt?"

"He is Jew."

"He is?"

"He is Roosen... common Jew name in Germany."

"He's Dutch, isn't he?"

"He modified his name. A common trick in America."

"Maybe, I dunno. There's a Jew on board who's travelling to Rio."

"Ja?"

"Doctor Z. He's a writer."

Voss sits up as eager as a raccoon below the kitchen window. "Z is famous. I haven't read him yet but believe me, he is famous in Germany."

"He's in First Class. He's playing a chess match with the Magician."

"Oh the chess match.... You play, Thorsen?"

"Me? No."

"I could teach you."

"Thanks but no thanks. I got a date with Bobby McGee."

"You have to see someone?"

"Yeah."

"'Bobby McGee.'"

"Date with Bobby McGee—it's a common saying. Like 'slow boat to China.'"

I really have him baffled now. There's a knock on the door and one of the monks sticks his head in. Older guy, maybe thirty, shaven head, looks like that Kraut boxer Max Schmelling, nice and ugly, like he got face-dragged by a horse. Gives me the old suspicious one two, then jerks his head at Voss.

"*Funf minuten,*" he says, deep and dirty, like gravel sliding off a truck.

"*Jawohl,*" says Voss. "*Ich werde da seine.*"

Schmel nods, withdraws. Voss makes a sour face, rolls off the bunk, hunts in his locker, finds his Bible.

"It is so boring *ich konnte kotzen,*" he says. "All this instruction makes me ill."

The monks use an aft lounge for their daily Bible studies and prayer. You sometimes hear their holy moan blending with the groan of the ship.

"What's wrong?" I say. "It's the good book!"

"Ja, it's good," he says without enthusiasm. "Today I sleep."

"Have you tried the library?" I say. "They got a library, you know."

"Yes? I could hide there."

When he leaves, I reflect on how lucky I am, getting a free trip to Rio, meeting women and people way more sophisticated than me. Hey, I'm "the man women love" and what is this poor slob Voss? He's a slave. Even the common deck hands have a better life. The SS Southern Cross is like a prison ship for him, but for me it's like that movie Grand Hotel.

Might be nice to get some sun, I think, darken up my white bones, so I slip on my swimming trunks and go to the pool. The pool is sitting pretty as the ship is smooth and easy on the ocean. Last time I checked it out the sea was so rough the pool was going empty on the deep end with the rolls. It was crazy. Choose a bad moment to dive and you could end up on a stretcher. The afternoon movie in the Nautilus Lounge was a better bet. But right now there's no problem.

I find a lounger, apply some sun lotion to my face, try out the new shades I bought at the gift shop. Woman in the pool doing laps. Excellent figure. Snug one piece suit and rubber bathing cap. She's doing laps like Jane, Queen of the Jungle. Waiter glides by and I order a Pabst Blue Ribbon straight from the ice box, why not. Some fat South American shows up, jumps into the pool holding his nose, knees against his chest, you've seen it, the jackass bomb jump, unloads water onto anyone within ten feet of the perimeter. That's it for sensible swimming. The Queen of the Jungle pulls herself out, takes off her swimming cap which has a magic eye decal, pads past me all wet and dripping.

It's Uma. She doesn't even look at me, although I'm right there. She doesn't even turn around when towelling herself off. I'm glad I have my shades on, play lost. She picks up her stuff, steps into her sandals, leaves quickly. I notice fatso in the pool is watching her, standing up to his neck in the water, like he's been decapitated by beauty, his beady eyes still roaming. Shit. My mouth's dry, even though I'm chugging my beer. For some damn reason I'm still feeling like a boor. Good-looking women can do that to you, even if they're bitches who are always running your tab. Live and learn, fella.

CHAPTER EIGHT

THE DANGER COAST: CHESS MATCH AND RUMBLE ON THE VISTA DECK

THERE'S A REAL KERFUFFLE going on in the Smoking Lounge. The rematch—which lasted two days—has just finished in a draw by mutual agreement of the players. The passengers who'd had a little flutter going weren't happy but I can see from Z's face that he's relieved. Kallingram is sitting on a stool at the bar by himself. He's turned around, one elbow on the counter, like he's listening in to the conversation. Or he might be thinking how he missed his opportunity. You just don't know. Sticks to himself when he's not pulling aces from his sleeve.

I sit down next to Z and the Colonel, near enough that I can tune into some of their talk. The Colonel acknowledges me with a slight nod.

"I had him beaten," says Z. "I know I had him. But this morning, when we resumed the game, he made a strange move... well, it seemed strange at the time as I didn't recognize it for what it was. 49 dot B6."

"What's that?" says the Colonel. "49 what?"

"49 dot B6, the position on the board. Kallingram was two pawns down and his knight was trapped, so the game was as good as mine. Then he moved 49 dot B6... it was what we call a "swindle" in chess. I should've recognized it. *Ich war eingeschlafen*—I was asleep!"

"So he saved himself by forcing a draw," says the Colonel.

"He used a swindle play which resulted in a stalemate. I congratulate him."

"You think he had help?"

Z shrugs. "Does it matter?"

"Just wondering if it could be considered cheating."

"There are no rules on the seven seas, Colonel."

"My sense of it was this Kallingram fellow was making more of this than a friendly game."

"Some people are very competitive."

"Not a very social person… but polite."

"Yes, polite."

Z was uncomfortable with the subject. If Kallingram was a Nazi with a grudge against Jews, perhaps it was too depressing to think about. Here was Z and his wife, thousands of miles from Austria, and the problems of Europe were following them like a bad smell. Maybe he should shave his moustache off. Ever notice how all Austrians with moustaches look like Hitler? Get rid of the moustache, get rid of Hitler.

Z excuses himself, says he needs to check on his wife, take a nap. I notice the Magician follows his exit like a snake tracking a lizard. Silently, hanging from a branch. Then he looks at me. Handsome babyface with no hint of love or basic curiosity.

The Colonel swings past, says, "Feel like a stroll, young fella?"

We hit the deck, go starboard, look west towards the coast which is heaving like a distant mirage above the sparkling water.

"You heard that?" says the Colonel.

"I did," I say. "What do you make of it?"

"No coincidence, that's for sure," says the Colonel.

"Don't suppose it's a crime, though," I say. "So they're using the radio to get some help from an expert."

"49 dot B.6…."

"Greek to me. I was thinking it was someplace on a map. You know, latitude and longitude."

"Well, once again, thanks to these hustlers my wagers have come home flat."

It's hot, but a nice hot, as the breeze keeps us cool. The wake of the ship extends in an easy arc behind us for a mile or more. Some strange sea birds swoop around, looking to see what all that froth turns up.

"What's that coast?" I say. "Is that South America?"

"Guyana. From here to the Amazon it's known as the Danger Coast. Used to be all Dutch, then they did a deal with the British for the northern part. Lot of plantations on the coastal plains made possible by Dutch protection dikes. Fifty, sixty miles inland there's a plateau, all savanna… beyond that impenetrable malarial jungle, broken up in drifts of mountains… some big rivers like the Demerara, which is where you get your sugar."

"So nobody in the jungle but the beasts—"

"Some people live there, maybe you would call them beasts. The Dyukas. Bush negroes, escaped slaves from the first settlements. A secretive people, practice voodoo, speak a kind of bastard English, with lots of African, Indian, Dutch, Portuguese and Spanish grafted in. They travel by canoe mostly, don't like to walk, which has left them with short legs and a large upper body. They have a city that no white man has ever seen, I believe. I certainly never saw it and I've flown over a large part of that jungle."

"Searching for El Dorado?"

"They say it's in there, somewhere. No, looking for timber. They have two important types: greenheart and purple heart. Green for ships, purple for cabinetry."

"Like mahogany."

"Yeah, hard woods. Too bad we're not stopping. Georgetown is worth a look."

I can imagine. Dusty boulevards and crazy palms and moldering government buildings. Planters in white linen suits riding around in pony buggies or chauffeured Packards. Soldiers, brothels, bungalows, rum and mosquitoes... and so many black faces it's dark at noon. Don't know exactly, just thinking ahead like National Geographic.

"The Danger Coast can be a rough place, and I don't mean just for ships," says the Colonel. "Lot of corruption. You can get a gut knife in the liver as easy as a turkey at Christmas. A wise man packs a gun in the Guyanas. Same for Amazonia, northern Brazil, anywhere with no streetlights."

"What do you recommend, Colonel?"

He bites his cigar, spits the stub towards the water, forty feet below, flowing off the hull at 20 knots.

"For a strong young man like you? You'll be o.k. in Rio, just as long as you stay out of the *favelas*."

"*Favelas*, what's that."

"Slums... mostly up on the hills. Any big city close to the equator in South or Central America attracts thousands of squatters. They set up these shanty towns where anything goes. This is the thing you'll notice, the dramatic disparity between the rich and the poor. People with money live in villas with gardens that look like Eden, while the poor live in hellholes."

"There's no in-between?"

"Middle class? Sure there's a middle-class, mostly European immigrants, and that's what you'll see in the suburbs... like Niteroi. The *ricos* are old Portuguese and European. But there are a lot of poor people, believe me."

"Easy to get a gun in Rio?"

"Real easy, I'd say. But also it would be real easy to end up in the municipal jail, because you could be buying from an X-9. And from there, next stop the Black Cathedral."

"The what?"

"It's a penitentiary that you don't want to know. They call it the Black Cathedral because it looks like a church from the outside. Stick to the beach."

"I'm not really a beach person."

"Son, women out-number men 6 to 4 in Rio. You'll like the beach."

"O.K, I'll case the beach. But you said something about an X-9."

"That's what they call an informant. Damn near everyone on the street is an informant. You sell what you've got in Rio. Don't talk politics with strangers."

"I'll keep that in mind, although I know nuthin' about nuthin'."

"Get yourself a gold chain and a cross. Look humble."

"You're kidding me, right?"

"Sure. You'll have a great time...."

We get a whiff of something and it isn't tonight's dinner.

"Christ," I say, "who died?"

"Get used to it," says the Colonel. "They'll dump tonight when we're all asleep."

Sometimes shit smells like vinegar, sweet and sour at the same time. As I came to realize, it was a sure way to tell when you were in the tropics. Shit, it's everywhere in the air, your shit, their shit, everybody's shit, especially downwind. You wouldn't want to be a napping fisherman whenever an ocean liner dumps its tanks. The SS Southern Cross might be sleek and white with a mustard smoke stack and cut a fine figure as it passes Zero and heads for Capricorn, but inside, its guts are just like any sewer below any hotel.

"Guess it's the heat," I say, pressing a hanky against my face.

"Time to take cover," says the Colonel. "We'll talk more later."

Night on a tropical ocean is something else. The sky is big and deep and full of starfields everywhere you look, merges with the water so there's no horizon. The water sparkles with the starlight, and the ship's channel sparkles with plankton. The air is balmy, and maybe you lose your sense of up and down, feel like you're hanging off the edge of the earth. Out-of-body experience? Can be and you don't need to be drunk or roofed either. It's nice when you're with someone warm with the right hooks to hang onto. Alone, the experience can be eternal, and you might even allow yourself to fall over the side. I'm thinking that's what happens sometimes when a passenger goes missing. They go up on the observation deck, see the southern cross, let themselves swoon, drop into the eternal.

I'm with Bobby, arm-in-arm, sitting on a bench in a sheltered spot near the funnel. It's real quiet, the diesel engines on glide, just the hiss of the surf and the odd knock, those mystery sounds that big ships have. It's dark, real dark, except for the odd pool of light near the lifeboat bays and the navigation lights up on the bridge. We're port side, looking south, maybe south-east and the cross is low and bright, slanted like an axe. There's no mistaking it, even if you've never seen it before.

"Latinos call it the Crux," says Bobby.

"The Crux," I say, measuring the word out like a dummy.

"Just another word for cross," she says. "You know, like 'the crux of the matter.'"

"The crux of the matter, eh," I say. "Now I know what Begin the Beguine is all about."

"I think you knew all along, darlin'," she says.

"No, I thought it was a name for the Orient," I say.

"The Beguine is a dance," she says. "A sexy form of the rumba."

"That makes more sense than, uh, 'the cross of the matter.'"

"The cross of the matter? The 'heart' of the matter, you."

"Know what I think? The Crux is a woman...."

"How you figure that?"

"A certain part of a woman."

I slide my hand below her dress, run along her nylons and garters, get real intimate, work for her pleasure. We kiss, exchange tongues.

"You must be right," she murmurs. "You must... you must...."

So much for the mysticism of the moment. We go at it right there. That's the thing about sex—it's always best someplace unexpected. Well, maybe this wasn't exactly unexpected.

Cigarettes follow.

"You have a nice figure," I say. "So alert."

She sighs. "You're not so bad yourself."

"Me?"

"Yeah, you. If you don't have a good body, sex is a criminal act," she says.

"Who says?"

"I say. Don't tell me you don't know you're attractive."

I'm thinking, I am?

"Men can only measure women," I say.

"Bull," she says. "Women sure as hell measure other women."

66

"Maybe so," I say. "I don't have a clue about guys."

"You got it and you know it," she says. "I could rent you out."

"Rent me out?"

"Yeah, rent you out. Few old babes on this ship who could use a thrill."

"Hey, I'm not into crime."

"That's a pity. I was hoping you could steal a few ashtrays for me."

"The ones with the cool company logo?"

"They are cool, aren't they? Friends back in New York are always after me to get them one."

Yeah, we're bantering like lovers in love with anything but reality. I didn't know anything about this woman. It was like a rendezvous in a dream. You come and you go and who knows why.

"What's that scent?" I say.

"You like it?" she says. "It's called Gaucho. Bought it in the duty free in Buenos Aires."

"Smells like mint," I say.

"That's 'cause I'm quietly sucking on a Polo," she says, sticking her tongue out, the Polo mint impaled on the tip. "Want one?"

"Sure," I say... and we exchange in a kiss.

I did find out some things about her. Not much, but some things, like she was married but considered herself separated.

"How come," I say.

"He's a sadist," she says. "We met when he was in the military in North Carolina."

"Got any kids?"

"Obviously not."

"Maybe you'll get back together."

"We're done. What about you?"

"What about me."

"Got a girl? Hey, it doesn't matter. I just borrowed you, mister."

I shake my head, although I'm thinking maybe there's someone, maybe the girl down the street. Nothing said, maybe a look or two, a bookmark for the future. Some people you're not quite ready for. You gotta get out there and practice.

"I'll never forget the Southern Cross," I say.

"The ship or the constellation?" she says.

"Neither," I say. "The woman."

She giggles. "I should hope not," she says. "Rio's three days away."

We linger for a while, see a couple of shooting stars, make a wish. I get my hand on the cross again, just a friendly fondle. She moans or sighs or both. Someone passes by quietly, pays no attention to us, crew member probably. We talk some more, bite and lick, go our separate ways. Her stairs go one way, mine another.

I must've been asleep, as I wasn't ready for what happened next. Was just starting down when someone dropped a boot into my spine, sent me crashing down the 50 degree stairs to the next deck. The attack knocked me out, goddamn. Hit my head or something. Bounced down the last few stringers like a barrel cut loose from a load, lay there pissing myself as the staves start popping. I could see somebody up there but whoever or whatever was just fudge. Then the lights went out.

Was I rumbled or what? It was still dark when I came to, and I figured my leg was broken and maybe my left arm. My head was cut, left side, maybe on impact, maybe as I dragged against the wall. Couldn't recall if I'd any money on me or not. Nothing seemed to be missing. I got myself to my feet, started to think maybe I just stumbled and fell... because I'm thinking, why? When you're with a stranger woman, anything can happen. Could be she has another lover, a member of the crew. The other dance queen, Eduardo... or maybe one of the monks getting real moral about me. Boettner, the purser, a real slimy double act if ever there was one. What about the Magician, Kallingram? If anyone could come out of the dark, it could be him. Hell, it could even be the Captain. No messin' with the crew, no messin' with the hired help. And then, it could be someone I don't even know, someone who's been watching me with cool unsympathetic eyes like a bloody Martian.

I get myself back to my cabin, clean myself up, skip breakfast, lunch and dinner.

CHAPTER NINE

MAGIC IN THE NAUTILUS ROOM

THAT EVENING I'M NURSING a drink at the back of the Nautilus Room, mad as hell, trying to calm myself down. Moments I get so mad I could pistol whip the first person who looks snake eyes at me and crazy as it sounds I got Oswald with me, tucked behind my belt above my ass, concealed by my sports jacket hanging loose and easy. No more ambushes, man. What was I thinking? My old man as good as warned me. I got soft and easy, let my guard down, thinking I was travelling with sophisticated folks, high rollers and bon vivants when in fact this boat is full of sickos. Goddamn. Etcetera.

Actually I am in the Nautilus but Oswald is still glued shut and hidden in my cabin. I just run this movie in my head to soothe the bells. Guess I'm mad at myself for being a chump. No need to start acting like a cowboy. You gotta be cool, alert and psychic. Don't let it happen again, and if it does happen, at least get a piece of the action.

It's another theme night, Pirates of the Spanish Main this time and I really don't need to dress up because I got the wounds and I walk with a limp and my lefty is like a hook anyway. Still, I've got a little black mask that I bought in the gift shop. My jacket isn't exactly zoot but close enough. Might be I look like one of those guys in a casino movie playing roulette or blackjack or more likely an enforcer told to dress the part and blend in. I'm drinking rum. It's very good. Morgan's Special Reserve. Not too sweet with a nice coffee flavour. I drink and I watch. Bit of a variety show out there on the floor. The orchestra plays a set, people dance, trip the light fantastic in their nutty costumes. Some ladies look like sluts, which I guess is the point. They can paint themselves any color they want and wear whatever risque outfit comes to mind. The guys aren't much better. Earrings, daggers and swords and plenty of fake beards, although of course some can't be fake. Most of them don't bother, though. Like me they just bought a plastic hook and an eye patch and ditched them after the third or fourth drink.

Much to my surprise, Voss comes in, stands near the door like an usher. Undershirt and shorts. I motion him over.

"Ulrich," I say. "Here's your chance—have a drink."

I motion to the barman. "A beer for my friend."

Voss looks at me, says, "I didn't recognize you."

"My own mother wouldn't recognize me," I say. "What's up? You skip class?"

"No, I do laps."

"Laps? This time of night?"

"I'll just take a look, I can't stay."

Barman drops a couple of Red Stripes, cold and wet from the ice box. Fancy glasses too.

Voss shakes his head. "No," he says. "Verboten."

"Verboten my ass," I say. "It's a diplomatic necessity."

I pass him the beer. He looks back at the door, then takes a sip, then a swig, and then chugs about half the bottle.

"I hear you groaning last night," he says. "You dream?"

"No I fell down the fucking stairs," I say. "See the cut?"

He nods, then smiles. "Ah—a smite."

"A smite?"

"Ja, a *mensur*, my friend. The badge of honour, you understand."

He makes a slicing motion with his finger.

"Duelling," I say.

"Yes, duelling. A smite."

I nod, smile. Starting to feel better. Better about it, better about that, and better about what might come next.

Voss jerks his head towards the dancers, says, "Your girl here?"

What's this—did I tell him about Bobby? I don't think so.

"If had a girlfriend," I say, "you and me wouldn't be sharing a cabin."

He nods, no smile, just the sad face of a guy who is doomed to find his fun through the eyes of others. He kills his beer, fades back with a thank you wave. I look around, see Bobby coincidentally. We haven't talked since last night. She struts past disguised as herself—tight ass skirt, tight rack blouse, gold high heels, crazy lipstick and a set of shades with one lens missing just to make it all kinky. A pirate, sure, but not a classic pirate. Don't know if she sees me or not. Occasions like this, she has to socialize a bit, make the feet get restless, the bones spin. Some of the old guys like to dance with her, especially the Yankees and the south americans. Business men with wives who look like they should be running a bake sale or a brothel, nothing in between. The guy she's dancing with now, he's wearing a fez, supposed to be a Turkish pirate, I guess, and he's got a dirty pirate hand, always moving up and down her back to her ass... excuse me, I'm just trying to catch the rhythm, y'all. Am I jealous? Nah. Amused, because his wife sure as hell is jealous. She's a madame smoking Strikes, sucking them so hard she's spitting 'bacco. When the tune finishes, Bobby moves on and the guy returns to his table, flops down grinning like a jackass and the wife leans into his ear, gives it to him. He reaches for his drink but by now there's nuthin' left but a smell.

Along the wall, beside the big mural of the Greek gods and the sea horses, someone is beckoning me. Mrs Z. I hesitate, look around to see if she's summoning somebody else. Nope. She's with her husband, not exactly a party boy, but then on this particular evening I'm not exactly one myself. Slide off the stool, stick to the perimeter, wiggle my way through the melee to their table.

"Sit, sit," says Mrs. Z. "Join us please."

Z rises from his seat, bows, the way these old world guys do. Neither are in costume, unless you consider a tuxedo and a cocktail dress as fancy dress.

"We're here for the magic show," she says. "Is it ten yet?"

I glance at my watch but it's on yesterday time or the day before. I don't even know what day it is, let alone the hour. I've been slipping through zones and falling down ladders like a clown.

"I must thank you for helping my wife," says Z. "Lotte and I are most grateful."

I nod, smile a little.

"You've injured yourself!" exclaims Mrs. Z. "See, Stefan?"

"It's nothing," I say. "I clipped a bulkhead."

"Ships can be dangerous," says Z. "Obstacles everywhere."

"Hope you're feeling better, Mrs. Z," I say.

"She actually went to the dining room tonight," says Z. "*Sei ab wei ein Pferd.*"

She's amused. "He calls me a horse."

"Just an English saying, Lotte," says Z.

"Then say it in English," says Mrs. Z.

"She eats like a horse," says Z.

"You see? He insults me."

Just banter, eh. Clearly in better spirits, both of them. They're sharing a bottle of white wine. I order another beer.

"I hear you're still the champion," I say to Z.

"Champion?" he says, puzzled.

"Undefeated," I say.

He thinks about this, then says, "I didn't win, and I didn't lose, yet I feel I lost."

"Sounds familiar," I say. "Who said it?"

"I don't know," says Z. "Sometimes I seem to be acting out someone else's life."

"Know what you mean," I say. "Sometimes I hear stuff on the radio, forget about it, then start talking like the words are all mine."

"Stefan is always writing," says Mrs Z. "He'll probably write a story about the chess match."

"No no," says Z. "In Brazil I will only read and dream."

"Dream, of course," says Mrs Z. "He thinks he saw a submarine."

"I did see it," says Z. "It had the profile of a U-boat."

"When was this?" I say.

"Last night, just before dark," says Z. "Going south, same as us."

"Stalking, y'think?" I say.

"Can't say... more as if it was sailing with us," says Z. "Then it disappeared."

"You think it's German?" I say. "Could be American or British... maybe Brazilian."

"Brazilian navy doesn't have submarines," says Z. "I wrote a book about Brazil."

"Not about their military," says Mrs Z. "You're a poet, *mein* Mann."

"The Portuguese have one," I say. "The Golfino."

"You see?" says Mrs Z. "It could be anyone. You think we're that important? You think Hitler would send a submarine to kill us?"

Z chuckles nervously, tries to soothe her in German. This couple is really strung out, no question. My introduction to the European horror, something that's coming, something very few people this side of the pond have a true inkling of. I didn't. I'm just a boy looking for new toys.

"Enough of this depressing talk," says Z. "I'm sure Herr Thorsen is interested in other things."

"I know he is," says Mrs Z a bit sharp. She looks at me, smiles, like, we share a secret, don't we?

"Do you have any hobbies?" says Z.

"Yeah, radio," I say.

"You listen to foreign broadcasts?"

"Whatever I can pick up."

"How does that work?"

"The signals bounce off the ionosphere, and you pick up the bounce."

"This would be short-wave...."

"Any wave, but short wave, sure."

"Fascinating. Radio is such a strange invention. I often think it's like listening to the dead."

"Yeah, and you can talk to them too."

"This is legal where you come from? Canada, isn't it?"

"Yes and yes. So long as you stick to the right frequencies, don't mess with the military or commercial channels for aircraft... boats... police."

Z reflects, then says, "The next war will be fought with radio."

"Yes it will," I say. "Because it's wireless. The Great War was all about telegraph and semaphore signalling. They did have some radio. Radio doesn't need wires or lights, works anytime, day or night... just about anywhere."

"Interesting," says Z. "Have you ever spoken to Brazil?"

"As a matter of fact...," I say, start saying, think the better of it. Mrs Z breaks in, says, "Enough of the boy talk. We have a request to make, Herr Thorsen."

Z looks a bit doubtful, says, "Is this the time, Lotte?"

She ignores him, says, "It concerns a small object we need delivered in Rio. Very small. Naturally we don't expect you to do this for nothing."

"What is it?" I ask. "Is it illegal?"

Z's reaction raises flags for me, the trembling laugh, the uneasy shifting in his chair.

"A small objet d'art," says Mrs Z smoothly. "Very small. You can carry it in your trouser pocket."

Do I look like a mule? Do I look like a sucker?

"We need it delivered to a certain address," says Z. "Believe me, we'd be very grateful."

"Very grateful," says Mrs Z.

"What about customs?" I say. "Won't they be a hassle?"

"It's a chess piece, a Queen," says Mrs Z. "No value to anyone but us."

No value to anyone but us. I notice Z has his right hand in the right pocket of his tux jacket, like he's got a worry stone in there.

"Part of a set?" I say, thinking it might be from the recent match with Kallingram.

"One of a kind," says Z. "Been in my family for a long time."

"You'll think about it?" says Mrs Z.

Oh I'm thinking alright. I'm thinking how can I duck out of this without looking like a jerk.

"Two hundred dollars," says Mrs Z. "We would need it delivered within, oh, two weeks."

"Yes, two weeks," says Z. "After you get settled."

"I'll think about it," I say. "Because you know I have business in Rio. It's not just a holiday."

At this point Bobby swings past, drops a beer on the table for me. "Wanna see the Cross?" she murmurs, just low enough for my ear only. She doesn't wait for an answer, just glides on into the festivity. I haven't talked to her since last night... and we do need to talk.

Mrs Z smiles, has my eyes in hers, says, "*Schön*."

"She gives me lessons," I say.

Kind of lame and why do I have to justify myself? Old enough to be cool, young enough to be guilty.

"Then why aren't you dancing?" says Mrs Z.

"Kind of gimped tonight," I say. "Fell down some stairs."

"You walked into a lifeboat, you say?" says Z.

"He says he fell down some stairs," says Mrs Z. "Pushed by a woman, ja?"

We all have a laugh at that one. It's like my ridiculous adventures have become a decoy for something more serious.

"Excuse me for asking," I say. "But why don't you just deliver this chess piece yourselves?"

They exchange looks. Z hesitates.

"Tell him," says his wife.

"Someone broke into our cabin yesterday," says Z. "Perhaps we left it unlocked, I can't remember. Whoever it was went through our luggage, although nothing was taken."

"The steward?" I say. "Might be innocent."

"We can't take that chance," says Z. He adds: "We didn't report it."

"You think they were looking for the chess piece?"

"We don't know... and we can't take that chance," says Z.

"Huh. Must be really special," I say. "Must belong to Adolf or something."

I laugh. Z looks a bit choked. "Just kidding," I say. "Valuable?"

"It is, it is," says Z. "It would be safer with someone else."

Bound to be another reason, some other agenda, I guess. We don't get into it, as right then the Magic Show starts, and there's Uma walking across the stage like a cabaret model from some kinky Berlin after hours club. The only "magic" I want to watch, naturally. Funny how being a lover for a few days on an ocean liner can give you confidence. If we meet now, goddess, things will be different. I'll let my hands do the talking instead of my mouth. No point in trying to be a gentleman if you're just a peasant. Like the Greeks say, two bodies, one soul.

The show is more or less a repeat of the other night, with the sawing-the-woman-in-half trick getting the people flipped out once again. They are happier with the disappearing act, the one where Uma is wheeled out in a large throne chair, then put in a bag and disappears. Next Kallingram wraps the throne in a sheet and then opens the bag, shows everyone that it's empty, where O where has the beautiful assistant gone? When he pulls the sheet from the throne, well, there she is, lovelier than ever. Magic.

Kallingram bows left and right as Uma spins around, like an Egyptian Queen returning from the dead. I light a cigarette, wonder why. I'm smoking too much. Can't suck these damn things and stay in shape. In fact, before I started on this journey, I didn't smoke that much at all. Guess I have the idea that cool sophisticated people smoke. It's like engine coolant—if you're gonna run with the pack, you gotta stay cool.

Kallingram closes out the act with the Magic Stone trick, a variation of one of those common tricks I've seen carneys do whenever they blow into town with the circus, hustle a few bucks outside the tent.

"Ladies and gentlemen... *madames et monsieurs... senoras y senors... mein damen und herren*," he says in his stagey baritone, "I have in my hand the Sorcerer's Stone, an object so powerful it can divine the secrets of the universe."

He holds up the stone for all to see, although it's too small for me to recognize at this distance.

"Yes, it looks like a common pebble," he continues. "Something from the beach or your driveway at home, perhaps. Yet appearance means nothing. This simple stone is the essence of magic."

Uma sets three jars on the table.

"Does anyone have a dollar bill? If someone would be so kind...."

As usual, some joker steps forward, opens his wallet, forks over a bill. Kallingram displays it, gives it a good snap, reads out the serial number. Uma writes it down.

"You agree, sir, this is the correct serial number?"

The man checks the number against the one Uma is showing on the note card, nods, then hands the bill back. Of course somewhere along the line a switcharama has happened but the dummies don't see this. Kallingram turns his back to the audience, crumples the bill, tosses it over his shoulder. Uma collects it and then, at the prompting of the audience, puts the crumpled bill in one of the jars, unseen by the magician who still has his back to us. You know the rest—he makes a show of passing the Magic Stone over the jars and when the ancient crystals start acting up, he picks the right one and holy cow, the serial number is the one and only. Corny. But I guess corny is what the people want when they get on an ocean liner that could sink any old time and leave them like floating husks, good for nuthin' 'cept shark food.

But Kallingram hasn't finished with us just yet. He holds up the stone once again.

"I'm glad you enjoyed our magic show," he booms. "Truth is, magic is often about illusion, and my confession is that this Sorcerer's Stone is indeed a common pebble... some quartz, some basalt... oh, it might be a precious stone to someone, a passenger, one of you I expect for it was found below the observation deck. If the owner is here, and would like to claim it...."

Sonofabitch. My worry stone—he has my worry stone!

"Excuse me," I say to the Zs, head for the stage.

The Magician sees me coming, a faint smile on his baby face, his glossy eyes black and malevolent. Or so I think, maybe because I'm full of malevolence. But I'm trying to be cool.

He hands it over: "Your stone, sir?"

"Thanks," I say. "Thanks for finding it."

"Oh I didn't find it," he says, as smooth and posh as a movie villain. "My assistant Uma did."

I look at Uma. She's been watching me, but as soon as I start to speak, she turns away.

"My lucky rock," I say.

Kallingram nods, says, "Then let us hope your luck continues."

Get it? He's one of these guys who's always in innuendo mode. No compadre with this dude, the Divine Messenger. Yeah, he could've kicked me down the stairs. Uma, I don't know. Her drink in my stupid face should be enough, you'd think.

Chapter Ten

THE COAST OF BRAZIL

BOBBY SAYS I MUST SEE the doc, get some stitches. Guess it is pretty bad and the plaster I stuck on it is only making it worse. She arranges it, even though it's dang near midnight and the doctor is playing poker with some officers. He turns us over to his nurse, who really was asleep in bed, goes back to his game. Not so bad. Three stitches, maybe four, and some cream for my bruises.

"You'll have to get these stitches removed in Rio," the nurse says.

She's so sulky with sleep, it's a wonder she didn't stitch my eye shut as well.

I check myself in the mirror. "Call me Frank."

"Frank?" says Bobby.

"Yeah, Frankenstein," I say.

Even the nurse gets a giggle from this. She fixes a plaster on the wound, which tidies it up, so I look legit again. She winks at Bobby, says, "Good as new, Frank. Next time you're out at night, take off your sunglasses."

Bobby takes me for a turn around the promenade deck, which is pretty quiet, except for the odd passenger sitting on a bench having a smoke or relieving the sweat. It's moist and balmy, like the Amazon jungle is exhaling its juices. Can't see it, although I know we're passing the estuary tonight. Big mouth, 150 miles wide, the black boss, they call it... El Jefe Negro, from the old god of fertility. A lot of water comes down those channels all the way from Peru. As I would later discover for myself, even the forests are flooded, vast swamps they call varzeas which might be beautiful to the eye but are full of easy death. They have a saying in Brazil, something like "the man who finds El Jefe is El Jefe" which means he who finds the source is a god. I didn't know it then or even care but there is a source. An old volcano in the Andes and an icy cliff that's marked with an icy white cross. Not something I learned from Colonel Powell. No sir. He was only part of my education. The source is something you have to find for yourself.

Maybe it's in the air, the Amazon sweat, but right then and there I have an intuition that something big is coming down. It's a feeling without a face, just one of those vibes like radio noise trying to focus. Nothing paranoid about it, just a strong feeling. When I was a kid I went to a revival meeting with another kid I knew at school from a family of "Dippers" as we called them. Real old time religion. A travelling preacher with a tent and a harmonium and after a bit of singing and praying, people were invited to step forward and "bear witness". Some of them did, lurching out like zombies, speaking tongues. Some just used it as a form of confession but others were the real deal, completely gone. It scared me, and I never went back.

Now I'm feeling like I want to "bear witness".

"What's wrong, Mr. Thorsen?" says Bobby. "You alright?"

"Feel like I'm having a stroke," I say. "Just need to sit down."

She steers me to a bench and we get comfortable. A bunch of movies pass through real fast and then it's gone, whatever it was. Fortunately I have my worry stone in one hand, Bobby in the other.

"You sure your husband isn't on this boat?" I say.

"You're left-footed," says Bobby. "I noticed that right away."

"I am?"

"You probably stumbled in the dark. Real easy to do."

"But I'm right-handed...."

"You see? You led with the wrong foot."

"Hmm, think I know when I've been kicked in the back."

"That would be attempted murder, and who would want to murder you?"

"That's what I'm trying to figure."

"You got a secret?"

"Like what?"

Maybe I'm a bit sharp in my reply. Technically, I have no secrets... except maybe a couple of small items that are nobody's business but mine.

"What do you know about the Magician?" I say.

"Not much," says Bobby. "First time I've seen him. The Company

78

often hires different entertainment for one cruise, usually down and back. I think he's just doing the Rio leg. I haven't spoken with him or her."

"They married, you think?"

"Doubt it. I heard she got skunk drunk second night out, threw a drink at some guy."

"Yeah? You ever done that?"

"Not on this ship. If I did, I'd lose my job."

"I was the guy."

"You? No way. What a bitch."

"She was drunk, figured I insulted her or something. A language issue. She's German."

Bobby's intuition dials in the situation like a radio soap opera.

"You think maybe she was spying on us? Or him?"

"I dunno, Bobby. I mean, we're strangers. I don't know these people." We sit with our own thoughts for a while. In a way I wish this gal was getting off in Rio with me. In a way... but then, do I need a woman to slow me down? Just when I'm getting ready for take-off?

"Have you ever spied on, um, someone doing it?" she says.

"I don't spy," I say.

"Not even accidentally?"

I wouldn't call Bobby an exhibitionist just because she likes to dance and take modest risks, but I was beginning to sense that maybe she was a bit more ruthless than the average chick. Who was I but a stand-in for a missing husband. Once married, you get used to regular nooky, so I guess I was just a rental for this particular trip. Depressing? Unfair? Sometimes conversation can lead you straight into a box canyon.

"No," I say. "I don't spy... not even accidentally."

A lie, of course, although at the time, at the moment, I thought it was true.

Normally I'm as horny as a fresh egg in a frying pan but tonight I'm as neurotic as a monk. You know what that means. A lonely bed and a big moon swaying in the porthole.

Beautiful morning, smooth sailing, somewhere off Bahia, the north coast of Brazil. I'm looking for the Colonel, and I see him in the Rainbow, talking with Lotte Z. I'm trying to avoid her, sort of. Still haven't made up my mind if I want to be part of her chess game, although her offer of 200 bucks to deliver the Queen is nothing to sneeze at. I grab a coffee and a copy of the SC News, slip into an alcove unnoticed. News, news... Franco seems to be getting the upper hand in Spain... Turkish President Ataturk croaks... Nazis go nuts in Germany, attack Jews, smash a lot of windows, torch a few temples... 'Homicide Hank' Armstrong agrees to a rematch with Lou Ambers for the World Lightweight title... Leo da Silva a.k.a 'the Black Diamond' says he's heart-broken by Brazil's loss to Italy in the World Cup soccer semi... yep yep, everyone seems to be going nuts. Like they say, if you chop wood, chips fly.

P.A. in the Rainbow Room is playing a little Brazilian radio, some station in Salvador, I guess. Mostly samba, which seems to be all the rage. Bobby told me Carmen Miranda was the big star and I should expect to hear a lot of her in Rio, tunes like *Sambista de Cinelandia* and the new hit *Carmisa*, although Artie Shaw is top of the charts right now with Beguine. Nice to know what to expect. No dead European church music, know what I mean? Let's stay loose.

Can't help but overhear a little conversation too.

"I was in the opera," says Lotte Z. "Not a soloist, just part of the chorus."

"This was in Vienna?" says the Colonel. "I once attended a production by Bruno Walter at the State Opera."

"Oh really? Possibly I was in it."

"Wagner, can't remember which piece. I'm a philistine in regards to opera, I'm afraid."

"Walter is a marvellous conductor. He was lucky to escape the purge."

"Guess you mean the Nazification...."

"Ja, all the Jews were dismissed from the orchestra right after the *anschluss*. Stagehands, office workers, students. It was becoming unpleasant well before that, and I left earlier because Stefan said we should move to England."

"How did you like England?"

"We liked it as much as can be expected. We liked it until their Prime Minister came back from Munich, declared 'peace in our time'."

"You don't believe it?"

"Do you, Colonel Powell?"

"No."

"The news this morning is very bad. Attacks all over Germany. Do you know what Hitler said? 'If you want to wear a gas mask, don't wear a beard.' He has made his intention very clear. He has built a concentration camp for us. Ja, Mauthausen. Several people we know have already been sent there. Imagine, successful citizens whose only crime is being Jewish thrown in with vicious criminals and prostitutes. To work in the quarries, leased from the City of Vienna, to work as slave labourers to mine granite so Hitler can build his Reich for his so-called Master Race!"

She's really worked herself up, has a small coughing fit. Right out of key with the samba in the background. I didn't know what to make of it. Exaggeration? Why would anyone give a damn what religion someone was? These Jews must be right out of step somehow, like the crazy Doukhobors we got back in B.C. The Sons of Freedom. Not only did the Douks burn the houses in their own community, they torched a bunch of public buildings and schools. Bunch of crazy Russians so high on their religion the only authority they recognize is God. Pacifists supposedly, yet every once and a while they go nuts. Their idea of a peaceful protest is to strip down and walk through town stark naked, all of them, men, women and children. Their leader got assassinated by a bomb in 1924 when I was a kid. Inside job. Peter Verigin. His son who was also called Peter Verigin came from Russia to succeed him and I hear he's a bit more flexible, so he didn't get bombed even though the faithful lose it now and then, are the cause of a few unsolved murders. I always wondered what "Doukhobor" meant, so one day I went to the library and looked it up. Russian for "spirit wrestler", whatever that is. Could be like the Indian thing, you know, wrestling demons coming from the 'other side' or it could be plain old ha ha ha lunacy. "Jew"—wonder what that means? I didn't stay in Sunday school long enough to know.

"Where will you be living in Rio?" says the Colonel.

"A place called Petropolis," says Mrs Z. "It's 70 kilometers to the west of Rio. Stefan says it's lovely."

"So I've heard," says the Colonel. "They call it the Imperial City."

"The summer home of the old Emperor, I understand. Agreeable climate, which is important for me. We have a small house arranged."

"Believe there's a German community there, so you'll feel at home."

"I hope so. Stefan says it's a favorite spot for artists and writers."

"Perfect."

"I hope so. And you, Colonel, where will you be staying?"

"Oh I have a friend at the American embassy. Then I'll be travelling north for a couple of weeks."

"Will you drive?"

"Fly. I'll take the clipper to Salvador."

"Aren't we passing Salvador now?"

"We are."

"Pity we aren't stopping."

"Well I have business in Rio anyway. Say, you play chess as well?"

Blah blah. I'm thinking, Jesus, what a life. To have the dough and the time to glide around the world just as you please, First Class all the way. I'm getting to like it myself and I'm just budget Tourist.

I'm surprised by Z who slips in unnoticed and sits beside me.

81

"My friend," he says softly. "Tomorrow we disembark in Rio. Have you made a decision?"

I don't know what to say, although I'm tipping... 200 bucks. He sees my hesitation, pulls the chess piece from his pocket, sets it on the table. It's black and shiny, like a fancy salt shaker, no big deal. I pick it up, get a feel of it, nod, slip it into my pocket.

"To be honest, I can use the money," I say.

His voice is a low, husky slur: "I have written the address on this card. Do you need the money now?"

I shrug, say, "Later is o.k."

"We are most grateful, Herr Thorsen," he says. "I will leave the money at the Purser's Office in your name. Thank you."

Z collects his wife, and they head for the deck to catch the sun and the sea breeze. She's still a bit uneasy on her feet, so he's got his arm around her just the way I remember my grandfather and grandmother towards the end, although the Zs are a lot younger. Won't be long before she's in a wheel-chair, I'm thinking. My hand closes around the Queen in my pocket. Feels good. Feels like black gold. Feels like enough dough to keep me going for a month if there should be a problem with my assignment in Rio. And I have enough for a couple of months anyway, and didn't the Colonel say he could put me in touch with some work?

I samba my way out of the Rainbow Room, catch up with the man.

The Colonel likes to walk, and he likes to talk, and I don't mind listening. He reminds me of Teddy Roosevelt, a leader of men and animals. Roosevelt fought in Cuba with the Rough Riders and he even explored the Amazon. "Speak softly and carry a big stick," said Teddy. Powell is like that, easy with words and good advice. Educated, worldly, bit of an old school adventurer, a slouch hat kind of dude, only today he's wearing a wide brimmed Panama.

So I ask him about the Cuban war, the one between the Spaniards and the Americans in 1898.

"Oh yes," says the Colonel. "That war. Two things: the machine gun and malaria. We won it because of the machine gun, and we nearly lost it because of malaria."

"Thought so, which is why I'm asking is malaria still a problem in South America."

"It certainly is. We still don't have an effective antidote, a magic pill for it. In the Cuban campaign it took a terrible toll on the American troops... dysentery and yellow fever too, although malaria was the real killer, was killing men even after they returned stateside. A plug of cotton in the nostrils just wasn't good enough, especially in the rainy season.

Government recruited a lot of blacks from the South, figuring they'd be immune to the hot weather diseases... they were called the 'Immunes' but hell, 30 percent went yellow or malarial. Mosquitoes. If you happen to be in the jungle, kid, stay under cover at sunset."

"What started that war?"

"You mean 'who' don't you? William Randolph Hearst and that other agitator, Pulitzer. They stirred the people up. Some say Hearst arranged the sinking of the USS Maine in Havana harbour. Who knows? Was it just an excuse for an intervention on behalf of the rebels so that we could continue on and get Puerto Rico and the Philippines from Spain? Who knows... America always backs the rebels."

"America didn't back the Nazis...."

"Outside our sphere of influence. Besides, that was an internal putsch. It has to be a colonial or foreign occupier holding down the local population."

Like the way we do to the Indians, I think, but keep the thought to myself, because the Colonel is no international socialist.

"No malaria in Rio, is there?" I say.

The Colonel chuckles, says, "You'll be o.k. Just remember to wash your hands. And cross yourself."

I fall in with his humor: "I will, I will. And get a gold chain...."

"Especially a gold chain."

"But you know, there was malaria in Rio... a hundred years ago when Charles Darwin visited, three crew members of the Beagle got malaria and died. I know about this because I wrote an essay on Darwin, last one I wrote before I dropped out of university."

"University? Where was this?"

"Vancouver."

"Wanted to see the world, eh? I don't think there's any malaria there now. Swamps have all been drained."

"Darwin was very angry at the way the locals treated their slaves."

"Not a problem now, been so much inter-marriage. Still, you never know. The slums are full of angry blacks."

"Think there'll ever be racial harmony in this world?"

"Hope so, otherwise we're doomed. Some English writer whose name I forget said the future is the half-caste. If that's true, then the future is right here in Brazil."

"That writer Zion has written a book on Brazil."

"Has he? Wonder if it's in the ship's library...."

"Did I tell you? He says he saw a submarine."

"Zion says he saw a sub?"

"Yeah, although his wife thinks he's jumpin' at shadows."

"Maybe not, maybe not... he's a famous writer, a Jew, could be he's been proscribed."

"Proscribed?"

"Marked for assassination. He's said some unkind things about the National Socialists."

"Is he worth a submarine? A tad extreme, should think."

"You learn about the Lusitania in your history class? Torpedoed off the south coast of Ireland, spring of 1915. Terrible loss of life, over a thousand people. All because the Germans thought she was carrying somebody and something they didn't like."

"Yes, but England and Germany were at war. There's no such war now. The Southern Cross is an American ship too."

"You're very trusting, Thorsen."

I hesitate, say, "You're making me nervous, Colonel."

"Why? You see the sub again?"

"Not since we discussed it."

"You can relax. If it was going to happen, it would've happened off the Danger Coast."

"Why there?"

"Middle of the night, low probability of a witness, little chance of rescue."

"Christ, you're serious, aren't you?"

"Not really, kid... actually, I thought the odds were higher that we might get hijacked."

I'm laughing, although maybe I shouldn't be. Imagine: hijacked like we're some bootlegger truck running the Canadian border into the US.

The Colonel looks at his watch. "Well, got a poker game in five minutes. How about you? Another fight, maybe?"

Haven't mentioned the stairs incident to him. Maybe Mrs. Z said something.

"A ping pong game," I say. "Maybe a movie this afternoon."

"There you go, that's what I like to see: a young man staying fit. No boxing, mind you—"

I feel like a delinquent school kid. "I leave that to the monks."

He tips his hat, moves along. I wasn't kidding about the monks. They box. Saw them going at it up top on the basketball practice court yesterday. Court's like a big cage, and they were taking turns at slugging it out, urged on by that ugly bastard I call Schmel. I watched Koss square off with another kid, and he wasn't bad, although frankly I could take either of them. Lots of hopping, lousy penetration. Genuflecting instead of punching. Saw that purser Boettner watching from the other side, like a lizard looking through a crack in the rocks. Guess he likes to practice his German although I can't imagine him talking about the Holy Spirit or transubstantiation. He's only there briefly, then disappears. I like lizards. But if he was a mosquito, I'd kill him.

A rain squall comes on, warm and fast. I move under cover, look at the big coastal map that's on the wall, figure we must be close to a city called Bahia. Remember somebody said it was a bit of a dump, dockside anyway, dirty and not much going on except religion, cocoa and sand. Sometimes the SS Southern Cross stops here, but not today. See a fishing boat, a primitive looking thing with a sail and no gunnels, just a wooden raft like the *jangadeiros* use. The rain passes as quickly as it comes, and I head down four decks to the purser's office, see if my 200 is ready. Boettner is there, messing around in the back office, so fortunately I don't have to deal with him. Don't like the dude no way Jose. When you're young, you're 90 percent instinct, and instinct tells me stay clear. Money's there in a fat brown envelope with my name on it. Flash my cabin key to the skinny kid in the loose uniform, sign on the dotted line. I count it as I head for the gift shop. Stuff is supposed to be duty free. Have these sleek Zippo lighters with a cool company logo on them, a big black enamel letter "S" cutting through a small white letter "C" in the middle. Steel like polished silver. The other side has a porthole with the bow of a liner coming right at you. Nice. Gotta have it.

Pass the time by watching the matinee, an Errol Flynn double feature, a real lightweight the ladies think is great. His latest, *Robin Hood*, strictly for kids but I guess we can all laugh along... and another new one, *The Dawn Patrol*, a WW 1 flier flick. During the intermission I step outside for a smoke, encounter Bobby travelling between "duties" (as she says), and we share a "gasper" (as she says). Promises to come back later, find me on the Dawn Patrol, which she does. We watch a bit, then start making our own movies. We slip out, head up top to the playroom.

We were in there a long time or so it seemed. First one was on the table but that wasn't enough, so the second was on the floor... and I think the third was standing up as we shared a cig. Outrageous woman, especially in the dark. Always moving, even when she wasn't.

Think that was the last time I saw Bobby. Don't remember saying goodbye, although maybe the ashtray I gave her was goodbye. Guess I thought I might see her again if I rebooked a passage back on the Southern Cross. But right then I wasn't going back anywhere, just moving forward somewhere.

Wake up before dawn to sound of a heavy engine throttling up and down. Take a look through the porthole. Big launch trying to sit close enough so's the Pilot and the Immigration people can catch the ladder. Coastal lights twinkling not far off.

I hear Voss stirring. "*Was is das*?"

"Looks like the Rio pilot," I say.

"Uh... you leave us today."

"Yeah."

"You finish Spengler? I think not."

"Nah. Too busy to read."

"You leave it behind, I can practice my English."

Maybe you should leave it behind, Thorsen, I say to myself. Especially if you don't wanna end up in the Black Cathedral.

"I recommend the phrase book they're selling in the gift shop," I say. "Forty essential obscenities."

"Uh?"

"Forget it. Listen, I have to go get a coffee and deal with immigration. If I don't see you before I leave, *auf wiedersehen*, mate."

The coffee is good, like a slap in the face from your first woman. Check my passport and visa—all a waste of time if my bags don't get through. Of course I can always play the dummy, these things are perfectly legit in my country, we all pack guns and short wave radios, so lighten up, folks. My man back home, Klaus Gerwing, assured me everything had been greased, I would be met and taken care of by some guy called Alfredo X. Fine. But what if I don't make it through the declaration? What if they do a search? This is a new experience. I've taken chances before, like when I lay on the railway tracks in Myra Canyon and had to hang from the trestle when the train came rolling by. Or a similar stunt in Basic when I dove below a Mark II Matilda tank and lived to be here now. But this was just cowboys and indians stuff, not like this. This is poker and you gotta have a poker face.

Look at my passport photo. No smiles allowed. Handsome, yes, but I sure look like a prick. Passport says my eyes are blue, but the picture doesn't show it. Says my hair is blond, same thing. Says I'm a student, but am I? My ass gets tight and I sigh with a nervous shiver. These guys are like apes, and apes hate humans.

Other passengers are gathering, waiting for the call to go down to C Deck where the Brazilians will check our documents. They're set up in a little room with no windows, the sort of place the crew hang out to play cards. Two tables, two lines. One for returning citizens, which is short compared to the other, which is for the visitors. Interestingly, a couple of male officers do the returnees, while we get two women.

When my turn comes, the older one looks at my documents, while the younger one stares at me boldly. They're not beauties, but kinda exotic anyway, something different than the 49th Parallel. *Pardos* is what they call them, or *morenos*.

"You're a student?"

"Yes."

"And what is it you study?"

"History."

"*Voce fala portugues*? You speak Portuguese?"

"*Em breve, senhora*. I want to learn."

"Good. In Rio we speak a special kind of Portuguese. Your visa is for three months. Do you intend to stay three months?"

"Yes... perhaps longer if I can find work."

She murmurs to her colleague *possival imigrante*. The young chick writes this down.

"Good. We need men. The ones we have are useless."

Both of them laugh, set their boobs jumping. The older one stamps my passport, slips the visa inside as she hands it back to me, big smile, big teeth.

"Welcome to Brazil, *Senhor* Thorsen. Enjoy your stay."

Great start.

Chapter Eleven:

RIO

THE EARLY MORNING SUN is a rosy pink on the hills and mountains of Rio de Janeiro. Lots of mist or should I say steam rolling across the water of Guanabara Bay and through the gullies and valleys of the city some folks say is the most beautiful in the world. Sun is flashing like heliograph signals off the distant windows of the hotel towers and commercial buildings. Very modern along the beachfront, yet almost like a painting of Jerusalem in the background and if not Jerusalem, then one of those Mediterranean cities from the old travel books. It doesn't disappoint. There's magic here, I can feel it. Portside Sugar Loaf mountain is sliding into view girdled in mist, like a breaching whale, and away in the distance on another peak, there he is, Jesus Christ, the big statue that looks like a cross at this distance. Passengers are shielding their eyes, pointing.

The cameras are out... the usual Kodak Bantams with the folding lens, and I see an American couple with the latest Super Six-20, costs a bundle, first camera with auto exposure. Beauty. Krauts have Leicas and Agfas of course. I looked at a couple of cameras in the gift shop, but passed. Cheapo Wonderflex for 10 bucks, and a much better 35 mm Argus C2 a.k.a. "the Brick", a real solid bugger way out of my budget, natch. What I want is a movie camera. I see a woman panning around with one of those compact Kodak 16s, lucky bitch. And... what's this? My friend the Colonel up ahead with a very professional looking unit.

"A Keystone 16 millimeter," I say as I come up behind him.

"No," he says as he continues filming, finishes his shot.

"A Filmo?" I say. "A Bell and Howell news reeler? I mean, that's a serious camera you've got there."

He lets me take a look. It's rugged, with a three lens turret and an oval body with a large spool capacity, spring winder on the side. Camouflage green.

"You won't find this on the market anywhere," he says. "Just yet."

"You got friends in Hollywood?"

"Yeah, I have friends."

"How long does it shoot?"

"Three minutes. Actually, it's useful for my survey work."

My survey work. Agriculture. Plantations, I think he said. Of course he could be surveying for something else, like possible airfields maybe. Just a thought. You pose as a tourist or a consultant, travel around, shoot some film, take some photos... who knows. You're just a gringo with lots of money and lots of time. *Bem-vindo ao meu pais, senhor.*

A flying boat passes overhead, the engines popping as she throttles back for landing. A weird looking bird, like a flying catamaran, dual fuselages that act as pontoons, although the cockpit is in the wing meld, dead centre below the engines which are in-line, one puller, one pusher on stilts. I recognize it right away, the famous Italian Savoia-Marchetti S.55, on all the aircraft silhouette I.D. charts for military Reservists. The story is well known. The Brazilian navy acquired this one for a few sacks of coffee beans when Francesco de Pinedo flew it from Dakar to Brazil in 1927. Ever see the H.G. Wells movie, "Things To Come?" The big flying wings the Airmen use? The technocratic super race from the Mediterranean? The S.55 is a bit like one of those. Prehistoric birds fitted out like small ocean liners. Unforgettable. The Italian fascist airman Italo Balbo led a formation of 12 of them to the Chicago World's Fair in 1933, all the way from Italy to Lake Michigan which got everybody talking, even us kids in school back home in sleepy old B.C. He gave a speech to a bunch of Italians in New York, said, "Mussolini has ended the era of humiliations." Guess a few S.55s help. Guess the Brazilian Navy thinks so. Guess I do, sort of.

The Colonel looks up, grunts, says, "Brazilians like to buy their weapons from the fascists."

"Bit of a dinosaur, isn't it?"

"A lot of Italians in Brazil. More than the Germans even, second only to the Portuguese. Sao Paulo? Millions of Italianos there. Japs too. So recognize what you're heading into here, young fella."

Then, about two hundred yards away, a submarine emerges from the surface mist like a phantom. It's sailing with us, but diverging. There's no mistaking the swastika.

"I think I do now," I murmur, pointing.

"Well how about that," says the Colonel.

He swings his camera around, dials in the long lens, takes a shot before the submarine disappears into the foggy blur. "Yeah, Mocangue Island, just off Niteroi. Navy Base."

"Think it's the same one that's been riding shotgun?"

"Dunno. Subs don't have the speed. Even the new Krupp Type VII C can't do better than 18 knots on the surface."

"Helluva coincidence all the same."

The Colonel nods, says, "Well, son, that's what life is all about... a series of coincidences."

I try to laugh, but I'm feeling a bit wired.

"What do you think of Rio so far?" says the Colonel.

"Beautiful," I say. "Peachy weather."

"You want to get in touch with me, leave a message at the US Embassy. I'll be in and out of town for the next couple of months. Know where you're staying?"

"Not sure. Someone is supposed to be meeting me. Friend of a friend back home."

"You'll be checking in with the Canadian Consulate, of course."

"We don't have one yet. British handle our needs, I believe."

He nods, offers his hand, and we shake.

"Nice to have met you, my Canadian friend. Enjoyed our conversations. Maybe we'll talk again soon."

"Thanks, Colonel. *Ate logo.*"

He smiles. "You been studying that book—see you later too, *amigo. Ate logo.*"

I linger, keep taking in the sights. Overhear a passenger saying, "Next part's the one I dread. Last time we were here it took us 5 hours to clear customs... and we had nothing of any value, except 4 cartons of Camels I bought on board for 15 cents a pack... these cariocas, they're very slow." And someone else says, "Don't argue with them or they'll make you open everything." This one almost destroys the view for me, but then a female says, "I always carry chalk... just put an X on your case and it'll pass right through, no problem." Chalk. Why the hell didn't I think of that?

Lots of small islands, just rocks with white scars. Cocks crow... palms flow. It's like a song, the dawn sharpening the mountains, the whole vista they call *os gigantes adormecidos*, the sleeping giants. The vapors, the smells... the stevies grabbing the mooring ropes... the long dock and the embarkation sheds, the white colonial customs house, all kinda shabby the way it is in the tropics, like they're too sleepy and narced out to give a shit. Ficar legal, man. Stay cool. I'm picking up the vibe before I even head down the gangway.

But when all is said and done, Rio is a face. I'm looking at some local beauty who seems to be there to meet someone when this less than pretty hombre in a customs uniform directs me to empty my kit bag onto his section of the long table where the passengers are getting the 3rd. What a buzz. It's a real zoo, lots of yapping and shouting and things going bang. I was hoping for the Queen of Hearts, and I draw a Spade.

This guy looks like Valentino's distant cousin, the one who shows up at the parties to pick your pocket. Shades and a skinny moustache and acne scars like he got dusted by a shotgun when he was a teenage punk. Put his face on a billboard and he could pass for a banana republic dictator.

I undo the tie, let my possessions slide out for examination.

Customs guy has a stick, taps the bottle of scotch. I have two but this one is primo Oban Highland Single Malt. Excellent bribe if needed.

"One bottle only, *senhor,*" he says, as his free hand extends.

I'm thinking he wants money, but he snaps his fingers, so I hand over my documents.

He looks at my passport like he's asleep on his feet. Maybe he is. Maybe he's been looking at too many gringos, they all look the same, arrogant pricks who come here to sneer at our waiters and steal our women.

"*Senhor* Thorsen," he says, contralto, a boy in a beast's body. "You have a suitcase?"

"Yes," I say.

"Do you see it?"

I'm looking. It's not on the table and I don't see it on the floor.

"It's green," I say. "It was in the hold. Should be here."

He nods, seems to be looking around, although this turns out to be show.

"I'm afraid I have to tell you that your suitcase is missing... possibly stolen. If this is so, then you can apply for compensation. We will wait for a few days, see if it turns up. Can you live without it?"

Can I live without it blah blah. I guess so, although that suitcase is the reason I'm in Rio.

"Stolen," I say. "Are you sure?"

"I am sure," he says softly, while he uses his stick to lift the cover of my big Oswald Spengler book. It's sort of experimental, like picking his nose while thinking of something else. Maybe he's toying with me, maybe he's waiting for my wallet.

I'm sweating. Things have gone to hell here real fast, just like the distant siren that's maybe coming for me. But what do you know, a couple of guys show up, both in suits, one Euro and one Latino, who's shorter and more casual. The Latino whispers in Valentino's ear, passes him a fat envelope. Valentino is looking back at me but he's hard to read behind those shades. But another customs guy is pushing my stuff quickly back into my kit bag… all, except the primo Scotch.

"If you wish to pay the duty…."

I dunno who's saying this, it's just a voice. I shake my head, and Valentino hands me back my passport.

"*Bem-vindo au Brazil, Senhor,*" he says.

"What about my suitcase?" I say.

Valentino is ushering me away.

"*Mach dir keine Sorgen, Herr* Thorsen," says the Euro in German. "Don't worry, we'll find it later."

This is my contact guy, Alfredo. Slender, wears glasses, looks like he's never done a day's work in his life. Not one of your thin-lipped Krauts, got a slouch mouth like a woman who's just come from the dentist. When Klaus Gerwing said things would be greased at the Rio end, he wasn't kidding. Don't worry about it, he says. And he's right, 'cause they've got the goddamn suitcase in the trunk of their car which is parked on the street less than a block from the security gate. Signed, sealed and delivered with a chalk mark, no less. Aces, baby.

"We can thank Eddie," says Alfredo, switching to English. "Eddie has friends."

Eddie smiles, offers his hand. We shake, just a whisper, not a commitment.

I let my kit bag slip from my shoulder into the trunk. Eddie slams it shut, pumps it to make sure it's secure.

"Alfredo Van Rottingen," says Alfredo.

His handshake is automatic. Again, no commitment.

"Dutch?" I say.

"Ja," he says. "But really German. How was your journey?"

"Pretty good," I say. "So this is Rio."

Seems to be Eddie's car. Don't know what it is, could be European, not very big but big enough. I get in the back and Alfredo gets in the front with Eddie, who's driving. Not a lot of talking. Fine with me, as I'm looking around, checking out the natives. We seem to be heading into the thick of the city, as the talent is looking good, all shapes, all sizes, all colors. Everybody jay-walks, and not just the good-lookers, and the guys are hanging off the sides of the trams like secret service agents. Shit, this is so crazy, so foreign it's like Buck Rogers on the planet Mongo.

"Your family is German?" asks Alfredo, without turning around.

"My mother," I say.

"Been to the old country?"

"Me? No."

"We have a big community here. Very vital."

"So you're a friend of Klaus Gerwing...."

"We correspond. I represent the Greater Germany Cultural Association, so we... we correspond."

"The radio should make it easier."

"That is the objective."

"Been in Brazil long?"

"A long time? No."

I notice some soldiers sitting in a truck armed with rifles, one with a sub-machine gun, probably an officer. A little further along, see another truck, same thing. Seems to be a traffic jam, 'cause we're slowing down. Alfredo and Eddie are talking in Portuguese, assessing the situation. Seems there's a parade going on, a bunch of paramilitaries in green shirts marching down El Centro like they've just won the war or are heading off to storm the Presidential Palace. Integralists, or in the local parlance, *Integralistas*. At the intersection there's another group coming, very rowdy, some wearing red armbands, clenched fists extended, and waving sticks. Doesn't look good.

Eddie pulls over, grins at me as he gets out, says, "See you later, *amigo*."

He heads off at a trot towards the action just as some more soldiers show up, swerve into the middle of the street, block the traffic with their jeep. Alfredo slides behind the wheel, reverses into an alley and we're outta there. He threads a few back streets, pulls over at a public park or maybe it's a grave yard, lots of trees and crazy plants and a few old guys snoozing on benches. Big aqueduct with white arches just above, with a yellow tram moving slowly across it. I'd be thinking it's a postcard if there wasn't a riot going on a couple of blocks away.

"You can get in the front," says Alfredo. "You know how to drive? I have no license."

I thought he was a bit unsure of himself on the shifts. I get behind the wheel.

"What was that all about?" I say.

"Communists," says Alfredo. "The bastards are having a conference. The Comintern. People from all over the country... the unions and other party members. Foreigners too."

"And the guys in the green shirts—friends of Eddie's?"

He nods, says, "Just follow that bus and then take the first left.

We can go the fast way by the Botanical Gardens, or the slow way by Copacabana."

"Slow way sounds good. Unless we're in a rush."

"No rush. I have an apartment in the South Zone, in Ipanema."

"This radio work?"

"Believe it does, yes."

"Unusual to see a radio in a car."

"Eddie likes to listen to the police."

"Huh, 30-40 megahertz range, I guess. No music."

"You like music?"

"Love it."

We're passing through an industrial area with some glimpses of the sea. On our left, high above the Botafuga district, the famous Corcovada with the statue of the Navigator, now free of morning mist. Soon we're on a street called Isabel which connects with Atlantic Avenue and the hotel strip that runs the length of Copacabana, fun beach of babes and penniless hustlers, except for those sections cordoned off by the best hotels for the pleasure of their flush guests. A mile, could be two. What they call a *balneario*, what we call a resort. Hard to keep my eyes on the road. Place is vibrating—could be the heat, could be the color, could be the surf, could be last night's insomnia wearing off.

"See this building?" says Alfredo. "The Copacabana Palace, most famous in Rio, maybe in the world. You know Carmen Miranda? She has a suite here."

"Yeah," I say. "I've heard of her. The samba queen."

"Latina bimbo," says Alfredo. "*Mist.*"

"Crap? Really?"

"This is a very crude country, Thorsen. Beautiful, certainly. But crude."

Nothing crude about the Palace. I could do a suite in there nicely. Alls I need is a white linen suit and a box of cigars.

"So how come you're Alfredo and not Alfred?" I say.

"I am Alfred... when in Rome, yes?"

"Right, I get it. Blend."

But it doesn't sound to me like Alfredo is doing much blending. Seems tight-assed.

"They just started calling me Fredo at work, so I became Alfredo."

"What sort of work?"

"I'm an engineer."

"Yeah? So, uh, why didn't you just build a radio?"

"Because it's illegal for a private citizen to own and operate a short wave radio in Brazil, Thorsen."

94

"You could buy the components and build one... or two."

"Not so easy. The radio retailers are required to report any unusual purchases."

"Really? That tight, huh."

"This is the Novo Estado. This government was established by a military coup in '37 and Getulio Vargas is a dictator. You must remain silent about your business here, Thorsen. Secure, confidential. You... we must be vigilant."

Man, this isn't exactly how Klaus described the situation to me. Strictly fun and games, with a bit of cash to play the ponies and the gals. Of course Major Kinloss knew different. "Watch your back," he said. "They say they have no capital punishment, but y'know, it's a military dictatorship and the military just shoot people they don't like." This shitty political conversation is making me miss the babes on the beach, and believe me, there are babes, 'cause I'm catching them in the flicker. What did Colonel Powell say? They outnumber men ten to one or something?

"Alfred," I say. "You don't mind if I call you Alfred?"

"I prefer it," he says. "Wouldn't you?"

"When did you come to Rio?"

"A year ago. I came on the last crossing of the Hindenburg, as a matter of fact."

"The Zeppelin? How was that?"

"Good."

He's staring through the windshield like he's double-focaled, not really seeing what's happening. He adds: "It was the greatest experience of my life."

This guy's a Nazi, I'm thinking. I don't know much about it but I know they're thrilled by technology, especially German technology.

"Shame what happened," I say. "As a matter of fact I was talking to a witness in New York. Well, someone who knew a witness."

"Sabotage," says Alfredo. "It is a superb piece of engineering."

"Superb, sure. But dangerous."

"Life is dangerous."

"Only for dummies."

He turns his head, looks at me like I'm a bug about to be extinct.

"This car," I say. "It's a piece."

"It's a German car," he says.

"Pieca shit nonetheless. You hear the transmission? The shifting is all wrong. The throw is all wrong."

"You're a mechanic? I understood you are a radio expert."

"I know about cars. Where I come from, you have to. You gotta be self-reliant."

"No division of labour?"

"Sure there is. But no socialism."

He grunts, pleased about that no doubt. He reminds me of a preacher with no religion, just the attitude, and I just want to get up his nose. However, it's a beautiful day and the beauty just keeps coming. Atlantico becomes Vieira Souta at Ipanema, which is another resort zone, bit more sleepy, sand a little less white than Copa. But it's nice, maybe easier to handle. Can see a set of twin peaks on the range.

"*Dois Immaos,*" says Alfredo. "The Two Brothers."

"Abbot and Costello? I know, I know, they're not brothers."

"Keep driving until we reach the Garden of Allah."

The Garden of Allah is a plaza located in a big gulch that separates Ipanema from a ritzy area called Leblon. One time the gulch was a river connecting the big tropical lagoon behind Ipanema with the sea. Bit smelly now but the vegetation is rich, rich enough to hide the odd turtle and alligator and dope dealer and a homeless migrant or two from El Norte. We hang a right, then double back for a couple of blocks. Alfredo's apartment is in an older neighbourhood but looks o.k. and is an easy walk to the beach. As directed, I pull into the kerb, cut the ignition. The engine coughs on for a few seconds.

"Timing," I say. "Easily fixed."

"Eddie's problem," says Alfredo. "Let's leave the suitcase in the trunk, bring it in when it's dark."

"Snoopy neighbours?"

"Just a precaution."

Lots of shade trees, some of them making a tunnel. Street's narrow, buildings low and colonial, stucco with wild colors, some with decorative railings and low walls just to separate them from the sidewalk. Fredo's got a place on the second floor of a building that looks like it was painted with hot dog mustard. Tiled floor in the entrance, something I'm not used to. Still, you could get lost here if you wanted. Hear the ocean but not see it. Get the early sun without being blinded. Go to sleep without drunks in the street... or just those few who, um, get lost.

Can really smell the lead in the air, now that the heat's coming up, and of course the odd whiff of septic. No wonder they use so much perfume and smoke so much, although evidently Alfredo doesn't smoke.

I'm just about to light up when he raises his hand, says, "No smoking in the apartment, please. I have asthma."

"Sure," I say, pocket my Zippo, slip the fag behind an ear. *Can I take a piss or is that forbidden too.*

Bathroom is like any other, except its got one of those French douche bowls and looks like a woman is around, as there's a pair of panties and a slip hanging from the bathtub rail. Is there a Mrs. Van Rot? Don't recall him saying.

"You can sleep here. One week only, then you must have another arrangement."

No surprise. I already know this and I certainly don't want to be around... but I can handle Ipanema for a few days. Job is a job. That's right—I have two bosses, but sure as hell this Fredo isn't one of them.

"Sure. When am I going to get paid?"

"I'll have some money for you in a day or two."

"A day or two? You knew I was coming, didn't you?"

"Are you short of cash?"

"I can always sell the radio."

"Don't be silly. I'll have your money for you tomorrow."

"How much?"

"A hundred dollars to start. Brazilian currency of course."

"Are you kidding? A hundred bucks? You think I came all this way for a hundred bucks?"

"Just a start, Thorsen. This is for a greater cause."

"A greater cause what—"

"The Fatherland."

I'm about to say Fatherland fuck off, but then I think, you don't milk a cow by insulting it. Stroke it, baby.

"Alright o.k.," I say. "*Deutchland uber alles*. I came here because of my mother and my mother loves Germany, and whatever my mother loves, I love too."

"Good. You won't regret this."

Oh one of us will and I'm hoping it won't be me, tight-ass. I'm clutching my worry stone in my pocket, giving it a good squeeze.

"Someplace around here I can get something to eat?" I say. "I was up real early, didn't get much."

He takes his glasses off, cleans them against his jacket.

"I can't join you," he says. "Have to go back to work for the afternoon."

"Fine. Expect I can find a place."

"All sorts along the beach. You might try the Cafe Louco Azul."

He goes into the kitchen, comes back with a key. "You'll be sleeping in the back room. Table in there where you can set up the gear when the time comes. I won't be back until after six. Ida might be here. She knows you're expected."

CHAPTER TWELVE:

BAD RECEPTION IN IPANEMA

FEELS GREAT BEING OUT and about in Ipanema on my own. Great, because I'm a stranger and haven't a clue what's around the next corner. Don't head for the beach right away as I might see a For Rent sign, see what the neighbourhood is like, see the shops and cafes, the shape and size of the locals. No agenda, just scope the place. Maybe I want to be somewhere else. We'll see.

Turn the block and there's like a little commercial district and there's a shop with some cool shirts in the window, a little more tropical than what I have. Small place, one guy who looks like Coco the Clown, only he's dressed like a bank teller and smells like something from a ladies' dresser. He gets it right away that I don't know much of the lingo yet.

"*Quanta*?" I say, pointing at the shirt I like. Charcoal, with some blue zulu ripples.

He takes his tape, measures my neck, pulls one from a drawer, lays it on the counter. Feels good. I pull out my wallet, show him some Franklins. He grunts, takes a pencil, does some math on a notepad. 3.5? He then writes 4 and circles it. I give him a five and he gives me some change, some coins that are as light as bottle caps and maybe worth just about as much. But we're happy, he's smiling, and I'm smiling. He tries to hustle a pair of slacks but I wave him off. It's a real pantomime but he gets the drift, bags the shirt and I'm heading for the door. "*Ate logo, senhor*," I say as I exit, and he waves.

Feel like I'm initiated now, in the flow. Head for the beach and the golden glow. People everywhere, on the street, on the beach, in the sea. Buses, cars, bicycles, people walking the dog. I enjoy the way some women are just wearing bathing suits and short robes. This is as close to a nudist colony as it gets for me. Not that there aren't suits and people in working clothes, but there aren't any overcoats around here, y'know? Plenty of cafes with tables on the sidewalk and there doesn't seem to be much difference between a bar and a cafe, leastways here on the strip. Not like back home. None of this men one side of the fence, ladies and escorts on the other nonsense. These guys are civilized. No prohibition, no inhibition, mister it's an exhibition, as Mae West says. Well I could sit anywhere and ogle the *cariocas*, but I see the Cafe Crazy Blue, figure I'll give it a try.

Sit down outside, just beside the entrance which is wide open as if maybe there is no door. There's a blue canopy for shade and a great view of the action, coming and going. Waiter comes past, wipes the table, and I order a beer. *Cerveja*. One of the first Portuguese words I learned. Cervay-ha. Dead easy and damn useful. Waiter thoughtfully brings a little dish of nuts as well. Beer is a Bavaria, although it's made locally. Tastes a bit light for Kraut brew but I'm not complaining, as I'm ready to adapt. Jukebox is playing samba, of course. Not too loud, cause some old guys are playing chess between cigarettes and coffees, and they need space to think. Chess. This reminds me of the Zs and the delivery they want me to make. Even though I've just left the ship this morning, all this seems like a month ago, stuff I read about in a magazine. Look over the water, half expecting to see the Southern Cross out there, but of course I know it's leaving this evening. Santos, Montevideo, then Buenos Aires. At least half the passengers got off in Rio, so the party will be a bit more subdued the rest of the way.

I check out the jukebox. It's loaded with Carmen Miranda, and I see Artie's Begin the Beguine. I try some of my bottle caps and the box seems to like them, as the disc drops and Artie comes on. All nostalgia for me now. Bobby... Uma... the others. Like a movie you see once, don't remember the ending. Maybe there is no ending. Sometimes paths cross. Sometimes they cross and you don't know it, but I think I'd know Bobby if I crossed her again, and I certainly would know Uma.

But Ipanema is full of babes. I got eyes.

I order another beer and some tapas. I know about tapas because we had a Latin Night on the ship, a theme prep for the south. Chunks of fish, olives, onions, other stuff in a float of olive oil and vinegar. Goes with anything, beer or wine, or even a shot between the eyes. Like these women drifting past, their eyes locking and unlocking, sometimes smiling as if they know you or maybe the monkey hanging on the pole behind your head. There's only one language on the street: telepathy. I could sit here and be telepathic all day but figure maybe I should look around some more, then head back to Fredo's, take a nap. I put all my Brazilian change on the table. It isn't enough, and when I add a dollar to the pile, the waiter looks at it supiciously and shakes his head. I add another and he's a little less suspicious and looks like he's expecting more. Look I know beer is no more than 30 cents a bottle, and coffee is less than 20 cents a pound, as I made enquiries before leaving the ship, so I get up and let him swifty sweep it all into his left hand. "Sa ood," he says.

I'm thinking I have to get some local currency, so the first bank I see I slip in and exchange fifty US. Fortunately I have my passport in my hip pocket. Called the Real and if you're getting a bunch, Reais, and you get about 15 of them for a buck US. The notes look like dollars, except they got this old Don Quixote guy with a goatee in the middle. Nice blue tint but don't snap 'em too hard or they'll separate like toilet paper.

Now this is interesting. I walk down the strip as far as the Garden of Allah, that gulch that marks the start of the ritzy neighbour called Leblon and I'm thinking I might take a stroll through there just to mark it on my map. I'm walking along when out of nowhere this kid comes running past and whips the bag with my new shirt in it right out of my hand, takes off down into the Garden. He's all in red, so he's visible, and I'm after him like a bullet. Sonofabitch is fast and he knows the terrain but I'm no old man myself and have quite a bit of obstacle training, first in the Cadets, then in the Reserves. Better footwear would help, though. Better footwear and a gun because just when I think the little prick has pulled a muscle, is slowing with a limp, this black guy who looks like a headhunter steps out of the bushes with a pistol aimed right at me. The kid has stopped and is looking real pleased with himself, and me, I'm just a dumb gringo who fell into their trap like a drunken sailor. The Headhunter is snapping the fingers of his free hand, jabbing at me with the pistol, snarling mumbo and I'm thinking where the fuck is Oswald now that I need him? In my kit bag in the back of Eddie's car is where, goddamnit.

"Take it easy," I say. "You want money? I got money."

The kid is already modelling my new shirt, open and loose like he's the man, even if it's way too big for his skinny body. I pull some dollars from my trouser pocket, some loose shit, don't know how much. Could be a fiver or a tenner in there. Guy snaps it from my fingers like an animal in a zoo cage. I'm bigger than this guy, and obviously a lot better fed. He looks like he's been sleeping in trees, definitely missed out on school, because he doesn't know what the hell this money is. Can you believe it? Even a flippin' monkey knows an American dollar when he sees it. I'm just thinking about going for him when someone somewhere blows a whistle and this scares him off. He drops the money and he and the kid bolt into the brush. I don't know who blew the whistle, the cops or some citizen from one of those lush looking properties that border the Garden of Allah. I don't know who blew the whistle or why or if that gun was real but it looked real.

I need a piss. I pull behind a palm tree and let her go, what the hell, this is just a sewer anyway. Very annoying, could've been worse. I lost my shirt, but I didn't lose my fortune.

Must have been tired, really tired after that chase in the gulch because after I got back to Alfredo's apartment I didn't even bother to snoop around, just crashed on the davenport that was supposed to be my bed while I worked on our project. Been a long day, which really started the day before as I didn't get much sleep on the ship, worrying about customs and the hassle of landing in Rio. So I slept deep and would've still been asleep if Fredo hadn't woken me up.

"Have you seen Ida?" he says, making no apologies.

"Haven't seen anyone," I say, sitting up. I could see it was dark outside or almost. "Christ, what time is it?"

"Just after seven," he says. "We have the radio."

I can see Eddie through the door in the living room standing beside the green suitcase.

"What about my kitbag?"

"The *seesack*? Ja, we have it."

"Thanks. My extras are in it. Toothbrush and stuff."

"Where is Ida, I wonder... business in Sao Paulo. Perhaps the bus is delayed or her mother still needs her."

"Dunno. All I've seen is a kid and a guy with a gun. Clowns tried to rob me. Well they did."

Alfredo looks back at Eddie, who comes to the door.

"Where was this?"

"That gulch... what do you call it, Garden of Allah?"

"*Mata Machado*," says Eddie. "Punks."

"Machado—what's that?"

"*Favela* in the Tijuca Forest," says Eddie. "Tree planters who think bandits are *manifestantes*."

"Rif-raff from the hill slum," says Alfredo. "They usually don't cause trouble during the day. They take your money?"

"Just a new shirt I bought," I say. "Doesn't matter. Won't happen again."

"Welcome to Rio," says Eddie. "You should get a gun."

This advice rankles Alfredo. "He doesn't need a gun! I don't have a gun!"

Eddie looks at me, grins as if to say Fredo got no sense of humour. I wonder, though. I wonder if Eddie's packing. I look for a bulge in his jacket. Maybe, maybe not. He could have it on his ass or above his ankle if he's a real cowboy.

"Gentlemen, can we get started?" says Alfredo.

"Water any good for drinking?" I say, getting to my feet.

Alfredo nods, runs me a glass at the kitchen sink. Still trying to get used to the heat. Tastes like something, not sure. Lead maybe.

Eddie picks up the suitcase, staggers into my room, tries to heave it onto the table.

"No, let's open it on the floor," I say. "Easier that way."

Radio is heavy, at least 40 kilos. Steel chassis and case. Heavy, but I get it onto the table.

"What's the voltage in Brazil?" I say.

"One ten 60 cycle," says Alfredo.

"What do you know," I say. "Same as Canada. Plug?"

"Flat pin, looks the same," says Alfredo.

I see the wall socket below the table, plug in the radio, but leave it unswitched. Hunt for the Morse Code key, then get it connected. Then I get down to business.

"Before we go any further, Alfred, where's my money?"

He goes to his bedroom where, I hope, he has my money. Meanwhile I'm thinking how we can string the antennae wire. Realistically it needs to be strung on the roof like a fifty foot clothesline but right now that's not an option.

"This is military equipment, yes?" says Eddie, touching the radio softly like it's a dangerous dog.

"Similar," I say. "200 watts, lots of power."

"You can communicate with Canada?"

"We'll see."

"Mexico?"

"If there's anyone listening."

"Buenos Aires?"

"Should think so."

Germany?"

I shrug, say, "Depends... the antenna, the elevation, the weather... and by weather I mean the solar photosphere. Evening is best."

Alfredo returns with a wad of new American bills.

"Two hundred," he says. "If you're successful, we can negotiate a monthly retainer."

As I run the bills past my nose, I say, "What—you got other stations?"

"Neighbouring Associations would like to be in the... the network. They will need instruction, naturally."

"All amateur."

"Naturally."

I'm holding one of the bills up, wondering where the hell Fredo would get brand new 20s.

"Something wrong?" says Alfredo. "You can exchange it, any bank."

"These are brand new notes," I say. "You got a printing press at work, Alfred?"

"Be serious, *senhor*," says Eddie. "Alfredo is an honest *maluco*."

"Are we ready?" says Alfredo.

I stuff the wad in my hip pocket. "The antenna wire," I say. "Can we hang it out the window? Not the best, as it should be strung horizontally. Am I right when I say no one wants to go up on the roof tonight and do it? I thought not."

"We have to be quiet," says Alfredo. "The owner lives downstairs."

"She's worse than Rosa fucking Luxemburg," says Eddie. "I know her."

"Can't we run it around the ceiling?" says Alfredo.

"No good," I say. "We'll hang it out the window into the courtyard. Should get 30, 40 feet. We're just testing anyway. Klaus isn't expecting contact until November 13.

Fortunately there's a small balcony which makes the job easier. Fredo insists we turn out the lights while I drop the wire over the hand rail, and use a small reading light to work by. I power up the radio and put on the headphones. Takes the tubes 15, 20 seconds to get hot. I jump to Band 3 right away but there isn't much going on but Band 4 is something else. At 10 megahertz I'm picking up some close and prescient Morse stabbing like a jagged nail into the middle of my skull.

I pass the headphones to Alfredo, say, "Check this."

He puts them on for a moment, says, "What is it?"

"You know some Morse?"

"Ja, but—"

I look at Eddie. "You?"

Eddie shakes his head.

"German," I say.

"You're receiving Germany?" says Alfredo, obviously impressed.

"No, this is close by. Gentlemen, we have a U-boat in town."

Now this is just a guess on my part but I know a sub is in the area and I know the frequencies the German navy likes to transmit on. This is hot noise and the encryption is pure Kraut. Fredo and Eddie exchange looks, look very uncomfortable, like I've walked in on them having sex.

"How do you know? Do you understand the message?"

"No I don't. It's in code. I suppose I could copy it down and waste a month trying to figure it out but that's not what I'm here for."

Eddie says, "Senhor, you can break this code?"

I say, "What's the matter? You think I'm a spy or something?"

Alfredo says, "I was led to believe you were a skilled amateur. Where did you get your training?"

I say, "Cadets."

"Cadets...."

"Yeah. Like your Hitler Youth."

Alfredo nods, says, "So you have military training."

"Sure. Don't you?"

Alfredo chooses to skip this, but Eddie likes to express his macho credentials, says, "I was in the Brazilian army, a Lieutenant. I was part of the force that ensured the removal of President Luis and installed our current leader President Vargas and the enlightenment, Estado Novo."

Well, this was the only real success this night, and we could've picked up the sub with a wrist watch or a pair of false teeth, as it was only a few miles away. Alfredo had some frequencies and call signs written down, but all we got was noise, like fried eggs dancing on the sun. "Diego" in Buenos Aires. Noise. "Condor" in Chile. Noise. "Pancho" in Mexico. Noise. We didn't bother with Canada or the USA, although it wasn't clear to me if there were stations in any of these places, or if this was just some frequency fishing by Alfredo.

Around 10 pm I state the obvious: the radio needs to be located on higher ground.

We decide to walk to the Crazy Blue, have something to eat and drink, discuss the plan. The sea is rolling in the darkness, dropping heavy on the beach. For a second I can feel the sidewalk move, like I'm still on the ship. Still balmy out, but we choose to sit inside near the bar.

"There's a large cultural resource in Hamburg," says Alfredo. "It's essential that we establish contact."

"You mean, like a library?" I say.

"Yes, exactly," says Alfredo. "The Fatherland is proud to invest in Cultural Associations overseas."

That's it, money. We're all interested in money. Even I could listen to Wagner for money.

I notice that Eddie is using some spanking new dollars, has no trouble cashing them at the bar, maybe because the manager obviously knows Senhor Eddie or because Yankee dollars are worth more than bottle caps or bullets.

"I can find a house," says Eddie

"No neighbours would be good," I say.

Alfredo nods. He and Eddie fall into Portuguese, discuss the budget. I guess.

"I have been lobbying some friends in the Ministry to make amateur radio broadcasting legal in Brazil," says Eddie.

"How's that coming?" I say,

"For individuals, no, but for legitimate organizations, it might happen."

Beer tastes good, nice smell of cooking too. Guess I'm hungry, although I thought I might have to fast for a few days after all that rich eating on the ship. Tough to dial back.

"You married, Eddie?"

"Once I come close... then she fly away."

"How about you, Alfred?"

Alfredo shakes his head. Eddie seems to be smiling to himself at the thought. I was eating something called *feijoada completa*, which is beans and chicken, tastes pretty good for my first real domestic grub. The beer helps too, these big bottles like stick grenades. Place is hopping for ten at night but then these cariocas like to eat late, fart later. Guess that's the way it is in these hot countries. You wait for the sun to go down, then start cookin'.

"Who's Ida?" I say.

"My housekeeper," says Alfredo.

"Really," I say. "I don't see any house to keep."

"It's the custom in Brazil," says Eddie. "Everyone has a maid."

"Even if you don't need one?"

Eddie wiggles his shoulders, smiles, says, "People might think you're *veado*."

"Yeah? What's that?"

"You know, like a young deer."

"A deer?"

Alfredo doesn't seem very hungry. He's drawing circles in his beans.

"He means homosexual... don't you, Eddie?" says Alfredo.

"The *senhor* asks, I tell," says Eddie.

"You got any guys who dress up as women in Brazil?" I say.

"We shoot them," says Eddie. "Sometimes we make mistakes, ay caramba."

"Eddie exaggerates," says Alfredo. "Brazil is decadent. It tolerates."

"Like Berlin?" I say hopefully. "I hear anything goes in Berlin."

"No longer," says Eddie. "The Gestapo has purified Berlin."

"*Senhor* Eddie has never been to Berlin," says Alfredo. "Have you, *mein freund*?"

The hoods on Eddie's eyes drop like a lizard pleased with its position in the sun. He sighs, cigarette smoke exhaling from his nose and mouth like rolling fog. Fredo winces.

"As it happens, I receive an invitation today," says Eddie. "Berlin wants me."

Alfredo doesn't buy it. Me, I have no idea.

"Who wants you?" says Alfredo. "What for?"

"And Rome," says Eddie. "You know how it is. The movement in Brazil has a lot to offer."

"Who wants you?"

"It's a cultural matter, Alfredo. You know we have to be discreet."

"I should be kept informed, Eddie."

"Eh, you have been informed. Don't sweat, amigo."

"I want to know... we have ah, ah... a project underway."

If Eddie had a tail, it'd be thwacking right now. Yeah, he does look like a happy lizard.

"They send a submarine for me," says Eddie. "It's here now. You hear it yourself, thanks to our Canadian amigo."

Finally Fredo cracks a smile, although it's anything but happy. It's what he does with his face when he's close to losing it. Eddie's laughing though and I'm laughing because he's laughing.

Eddie swivels in his chair, shouts "*Cervajo!*", waves three fingers.

"Not for me," says Alfredo. "Work tomorrow, and I need to sleep."

"Work?" says Eddie dubiously, then looks at me.

I look at Alfredo and he says, "Thorsen has a key."

The waiter comes with the grenades, the big sweaty bottles from the ice box. Alfredo's already on his feet, so the waiter looks askance at Eddie, who just nods, two, three, just keep 'em coming. I'm glad to see Alfredo go. If he's what it's like to be 30, then I don't want to make 30. If he's German, then maybe I want to be Brazilian.

When Fredo leaves, so does the tension. I say, "So, Eddie, what was that riot about today? Who are the guys in the green shirts?"

Of course I know who they are but I just want to hear his ideas.

"*Integralistas*," he says proudly. "My Party."

"Tell me about it," I say. "What's the situation?"

"You have a Party?"

"Me? No, I ride alone."

"Hmm. Integralism is about the New Man, you know what that is? No more humiliation. The New Man stands strong, has balls, 'as the will to succeed. You hear about Salgado? No? Plinio Salgado, an inspirational person for us in Brazil. A Paulista."

"Paulista, what's that?"

"Paulista is someone who comes from Sao Paulo, our biggest city. Salgado was a journalist in Paulo, a writer, novelist, art critic. A very sensitive man, amigo. First he forms the Green-Yellow movement, believers in Brazil, believers in the *mestizo* identity."

"What do you mean, *mestizo* identity."

"This means the soul of Brazil is the mixed race person."

"So no racial purity like Adolf Hitler and the Nazis talk about."

"Take a look around you, amigo. Adolf Hitler would have to kill 50% of the population, maybe more."

That's a crazy thought, worth a laugh. Eddie nods in the direction of a couple tall dark-skinned beauties dancing near the juke box. "Put these ladies in a concentration camp? Ay caramba I think not."

I wonder if Eddie is just squaring a circle. These nationalist groups can always dress for the occasion.

"I thought Integralism was just Brazilian fascism."

"Hmm. We take some ideas from the Italians. But Salgado is a sensitive man. Our symbol is the Greek letter Sigma—nice, si? 'You are my brother.'"

"The Sigma symbol means you are my brother?"

"The salute, amigo. Like Julius Caesar. You stand erect, click, salute, say '*Anuae*.'"

"*Anuae*... that Greek too? Or Portuguese."

"Brazilian. Tupi, the language of the Indians... you know the Amazon? The Rio Negro? That is where they speak Tupi."

"*Anuae*—'You are my brother.'"

"Exactly."

"So Vargas is sympathetic to the Integralists?"

Eddie's eyes go lizard again, but not so happy.

"There is some friction, unfortunately. We supported the revolution of 1930. We had hopes for Vargas, although Salgado is the man to lead the new Brazil. I mean, we help Vargas with the communists and that bastard Prestes. We fight the bastards in the streets and continue to do so. Bolshevism is cancer. Are they any fun? I say no. They take all your money and it rain all the time. However, this is not the issue with Vargas and Salgado. January of this year, we supported the Vargas coup d'etat and the

Estado Novo. Yes, the Integralistas supported Vargas. I myself take part in this coup... at the street level, *claro*. And then, how does Vargas repay his friends? He bans our Party and forces our leader into exile. Unbelievable. Vargas promise to make Salgado a minister in his new government in return for our support and respect. We believe Integralism will be the ideology of the Estado Novo, of the new regime... but he fuck us over, *maluco*."

Nice to get the raw story, although it's kinda domestic and unreal for an outsider like myself. I just want to find out how Alfredo fits into the puzzle, and myself for that matter. I like history, but daily politics bore the ass off me. Find it hard to follow the names, the issues, the cultural noise. For me the only real politics is tits and ass, all else is theatre. Oswald Spengler, The Hour of Decision.

"No longer in the army, are you, Eddie?"

"No. I am a retainer for the Ministry of Culture."

"What's that mean? You beat people up?"

Eddie laughs and when Eddie laughs he's like a leaking head gasket. Hiss, choke and smoke. For a sophisticated guy, he's noisy.

"And you, *Senhor* Thorsen, you are a university man?"

"I'm a university dropout."

"Dropout? This means...?"

"I had a failed romance and quit."

"Ah... a woman. I understand completely."

"I don't want to talk about me. I want local education. Tell me about Alfredo."

Eddie's drinking from the bottle now. I like that. A man who drinks from the neck is o.k. in my experience.

"Alfredo has lots of money," says Eddie. "He must have a very good job."

"What does he do? Told me he was an engineer."

"Deutsche Electric."

"So he's an electrical engineer?"

"Possibly. His real work is German culture in Brazil. We have Germans, you know."

"So he's a sort of administrator."

"Yes, he's a sort of engineer, sort of administrator."

Eddie knows exactly what Alfredo is but this is all I'm gonna get right now. There's curious, there's nosy, then there's stupid. Besides, I got manners. Maybe Eddie has a sister.

"Where's the action around here?"

"You like to dance, *senhor*?"

"Sure."

"You can dance anywhere in Rio... here, the *Zona Sul...* or *El Centro.* Lots of clubs, cafes, places."

"Hotel Copa?"

"*Claro...* if you are rich like President Vargas or Alfredo."

"Fredo dances? I don't believe it."

"Maybe he does, maybe he doesn't... but Fredo is rich. He has a big bag of money."

"What... he got a problem with banks?"

"Eh, you keep it in the bank, the bank knows and pretty soon every bitch in Brazil knows."

"Sure. Tell me something, though: right now, is Brazil a police state?"

"Some say yes."

"What do you say?"

Eddie shrugs, says, "I say join the police... there are many kinds of police in Brazil... just talk softly and carry a big stick."

That figures. Guess that's why he has a police band radio in his car.

There's a park or a plaza in the Ipanema strip, about half way and a couple of blocks west towards the big lagoon, known locally as Hot Rodrigo on account of the fact that some guy back in ancient times had his balls chewed by an alligator. This plaza—Osorio I think it's called—has shops and bars that are wide open to the street the way they do it in the tropics. Happening place. Bit grubby, lots of crap on the sidewalks and gutters but what the hell, the gals look good, walking along sucking on nectars, talking that samba talk whether they're heading to work or to the beach, no difference, it's in the air. There are guys too but I pay no attention to them *claro...* which means "of course". Three days and I've picked that up, a utility word. I'm sitting on a bench beneath the boulevard trees waiting for a number 49 bus, take me into El Centro, when who do I see on the sidewalk heading this way but the kid and he's wearing my shirt. He's soliciting pedestrians, even cars as they pass. Takes me a minute to figure out his act. Selling cigarettes, packs, but mostly singles. Stolen, I guess, so he discounts. Some people are biting.

See my bus coming, so I have a choice to make: miss it, grab the little prick and get my shirt back or stick to schedule. But hey, what's the percentage? He's around, I'll see him again. I have business in town. Maybe I feel sorry for him. But when I think of his partner with the gun, maybe I don't feel too sorry, just sorry enough to put justice on hold. Even as I get on the bus, he's making a sale. That shirt makes him look legitimate, a dude.

I'm just about the only white guy on the bus and when we go through the tunnel, I am. Gets me where I need to go, where I need to check in, let them know a citizen is in town, see if there's any mail: the Embassy. Meaning the British Embassy as we're part of the Empire and just because we have a half-dozen prospectors out there in the Mato Grosso and one or two hustlers in the Amazon basin, Ottawa can't justify the expense for a separate consulate. There's a reading room where you can catch up on the news back home although, claro, the papers are all a week or more out-of-date, so I skip the news. I already know about Kristallnacht, Hungary grabbing southern Slovakia (wherever that is), the mid-term US elections, Barcelona about to fall to Franco, interventionist paranoia in South America and Mackenzie King seeking spiritual advice from ladies in dark alleys. Last night I was listening to the Voice of America, so I'm up-to-date. And here's a letter for me from Major Kinloss.

I go into the reading room, sit down, write a couple of postcards, one to my mother, one to my Aunt Renie. "*Saudocoes do Rio*" (Greetings from Rio), same card for both of them, same hugs and kisses. Nice space. Ceiling fans and orchestra palms and mahogany everywhere and enough leather armchairs to refit the Titanic. And you can smoke while you read and listen to the discreet chatter of the typewriters in reception. The big portrait of George VI, the guy who had to take over from his brother Ed last year, the Nazi who got pussy whipped by the American divorcee... which reminds me these guys are even more German than me. I'm only half and these blokes are full throttle German, the Wettins, and they changed that to Windsor during the Great War. Guess George thinks he's English, just like I think I'm Scandinavian.

The message from Kinloss is simple: a name and an address to contact a.s.a.p. Guess this is my official or semi-official cipher in Rio. Some fellow by the name of Alexander McKenzie, or "Al Mac" for short. Run it as "almac" and it's a callsign, I'm thinking. Not too subtle, but has a nice feel.

The address is in Santa Teresa, the old town above the viaduct, the Arcos da Lapa, steep narrow streets and great views if you're not stuck in an alley. Took a taxi. Driver could speak English, told me he'd been a merchant seaman for a few years, mostly up and down the coast, in and around the Caribbean. His wife is from Jamaica, half-English he claims. Soccer. That's his thing. Tells me he could run me to Ipanema for three bucks if I want him to stick around. Or he could show me "the real Rio" for five. Get the impression this includes a woman. Tempted to ask him if he knows where I can get some 12 millimeter bullets for my 911.

Al Mac wasn't answering the door but an old lady who was watering her flower baskets across the street pointed a few doors down, says "bar".

See two old guys sitting outside an open door playing dominos, big beers and cigarettes on the table, so I figure I might as well check it out. He's in there, sitting by himself reading a newspaper. Late forties, early fifties, well into middle age, gringo from head to toe. Boy, does he seems familiar, like I know him already. He's got a Brazilian nicotine tan yet somehow he's *deja vu*.

I step back from the door, signal the taxi driver with my hand, fingers and thumb all spread, gimme five. Al Mac sees me coming, pushes a chair out with his foot.

"Thorsen?" he says.

I nod, sit down. "Alexander McKenzie I presume."

"Yeah. Look, before we start, I have to ask you a couple of questions, o.k.?"

"Fine."

"Where's Myra Canyon?"

"South Okanagan."

"So if you know that, you know how many trestles they got between Myra and June Springs."

"Well I might might not. Let's say eighteen."

"Just askin'. I've read your file but that doesn't mean dick."

"Sure, Mr. McKenzie... but that cuts two ways."

"Yeah?"

"You might be somebody else."

"I am somebody else, fuck's sake. McKenzie is just a name."

"Kinloss says they call you Al Mac."

"That's right."

He's a big man, with meat hooks like a cop, like someone used to breaking up brawls and throwing drunks in the tank. Now it comes to me, like the Divine Messenger is whispering in my ear.

"You're Archie MacDonald."

"That so."

"You're Archie MacDonald, the Kelowna police chief."

Not sure if that look is derision or the executioner's smile. I blunder on.

"You shot the girl and the guy in the Lakeview Hotel, then you committed suicide... supposedly."

"Committed suicide, eh."

"That's what the papers said. That's what people said. That's what my old man said."

"Your old man, eh. Sig Thorsen? Sure. You're his kid."

I shrug. "Am I wrong?"

The waitress comes over.

Al Mac says, "You want something?"

"They got coffee?"

She fetches a coffee for me and whiskey for him. Guess a dead man needs a shot when he finds out he's alive after all, even if it's only 11 am.

"Am I wrong?"

"Yeah. I didn't shoot the guy."

He's letting me figure it out.

"So your suicide was staged... officially or unofficially, I wonder."

"Sort of both, actually."

"So you just came to Brazil and got lost."

"I like it here."

"But somehow you're working for Canadian Military Intelligence."

"No such thing, kiddo. Not officially anyway. We're just setting the hooks. You and me, we're just islands in the stream."

"Me? I'm no spy!"

"Let me guess," he says. "You get a chance for a working holiday courtesy of that Nazi asshole Klaus Gerwing, and your C.O. Major Kinloss says go ahead, but keep me fully informed, your duty as a patriotic citizen. You're not active, right?"

"Not at the moment."

"You're active, Sergeant Thorsen. You're just not getting paid."

"Right about that. So what am I?"

"A canary."

"You mean my balls are on the line?"

"See something took a piece of your head. Get that in the line of duty?"

"Come to think of it, maybe I did. I just don't know."

"So... you want to cut and run?"

That's exactly what I'm thinking, get out of Dodge... although did I really have no clue? The whole setup was bent right from the start. And when my old man showed up in New York and gave me the gun, I should've realized he was still tied in to the military, some Special Operations unit working out of Ottawa. Low budget, just warming up for the next big war and the Fifth Columns that could be anywhere, even British Columbia. When our Reserve unit was doing those forced marches and combat drills in the Monashee Mountains we used to sit around the campfire at night, speculate about the Japs coming off submarines into the rain forest on Vancouver Island or up one of the lonely uninhabited fiords on the mainland. The Yellow Peril. And the Krauts, well hell, they were everywhere. They could just rise up in the middle of the night and Canada be goners.

My taxi man comes looking for me, and I send him away, tell him to return in an hour. Al Mac signals the waitress, says, "You need a real drink, Thorsen."

"Just a beer. I'm stupid enough already."

So I tell him what's been going on. Naturally he knows all about it.

"Alfredo? That ain't his real name, boy. His name is Anton Vanderzalm, and he's an Abwehr agent."

"He told me he was Dutch-German."

"Well he might have some Dutch in him, but his allegiance is to the Third Reich. He works for German Military Intelligence."

"So he's a 100% spy."

"Damn rights. He's part of what they call the Amtsgruppe Ausland..."

"Foreign Intelligence."

"That's right, Division 1 of the Abwehr."

"Is he really an engineer? Told me he works for Deutsche Electric."

"Might be an engineer, I dunno. But his job is bullshit, a cover. He was sent here by Canaris to set up a network in Brazil with links to other South American substations."

"So this means Klaus Gerwing is also a German agent."

"I think so. But he might be a dupe. Haven't made up my mind about that yet. If you hang in there, we'll find out."

"So who is this Canaris?"

"The head honcho of the Abwehr. Admiral Canaris, been involved with spying since the Great War. Remember that exotic dancer the French shot? Mata Hari? They say she was one of his ponies. He's experienced. The Germans are aggressively expanding their networks right now. Brazil is up for grabs... hell, all South America."

"Alfredo strikes me as a wimp."

"Oh you think? Let me tell you something. Before he was here, he was in Spain doing stuff for the Condor Brigade."

"Hard to believe. But his buddy Eddie says he has a big sack of dough."

"Yeah, sure. As it happens, I tailed him yesterday. Had a tip off. Took the ferry over to Niteroi where he rode a launch to Mocangue Island—Brats got a navy dock there—and he met up with an officer off a U-boat that's in town. I have a very powerful pair of binoculars... watched them do the drop at the security gate. One fat attache case with some operating dough for Alfredo to play with, my guess. You get any?"

"Chump change."

"You're a wireless expert, aren't you?"

"Don't know about expert, but yeah, I can tune a dial, dial a tune."

Pull my wallet, show him one of the twenties.

"New Uncle Sam," says Al Mac.

"Is it counterfeit?" I say.

"We happen to know a large pallet of German money that was frozen in a New York bank was released by the State Department on the condition that it go through Brazil. It went to the Caribbean, and dollars to donuts this sub couriered it to Rio. I wouldn't be lighting my cigars with it."

"I'm happy to hear that. Met a man on the ship coming down who said Hitler was fond of printing dollars and pounds, any foreign currency he thinks he needs."

"No question. But Hitler is real good at getting our governments to give him whatever money he wants. The British just gave him 23 tons of Czech gold, fer chrissakes. When he marches into Prague—and believe me, he will very soon—the gold will be waiting for him in the Reichbank's London account. The fix is in. Munich, couple of months ago. Peace at any price."

"You're well-informed."

"In this business, you gotta be."

"As I said, I met a man on the boat, an American, who was really well-informed. A Colonel Powell. Name mean anything?"

"Powell? I know Powell."

"He got off in Rio."

"He's a canary for the Joint Committee in Washington. He's very well connected."

"So he's a spy..."

Al Mac groans hard enough to make the heels of his chair squeak.

"We don't use that term, fuck sakes. He's a tourist or he's a business man or he's a diplomat, anything but a spy."

"Sounds like 'argument of the beard' to me, Al."

"The beard? What the hell is that?"

"Argument of the beard—when is a beard a beard or when are you just unshaven."

"Gee, that's good. You go to university by any chance?"

"I tried."

"No kidding. Well sometimes Powell has a beard and sometimes he's growing one."

"Right. Guess it comes down to when he's getting paid for the job."

"You got it."

"You think Ottawa might pay me?"

"Depends whether you're in or out."

"I'm in. And where can I get some ammo for my 911?"

"Shit. You're full of surprises. I can see why they picked you."

"Who? Who picked me?"

He studies me for a sec, like he's tuning brain waves.

"That's just it, isn't it... lederhosen Klaus or the boss. You're like a Bowie knife, kid, can cut both ways."

"Hey, I'm no Fifth Column, Al—"

"Yes, and your mother isn't German."

He's got a point but he's pissing me off.

"My head look square to you?" I say. "You fuggin tell me, old man."

He's a big bastard, make no mistake, and it looks like he's swelling up to go for me.

"I'm a Captain, Sergeant," he growls. "That's my pay scale. Better remember it."

"Rank means nuthin' here," I say.

"Kid, you report to me," he says. "And if you breath a word about me or any of this business, you're dead meat."

We take a minute to cool. He picks up his newspaper, gets into something. Meanwhile I sip the dregs of my beer, think things over. Man I don't like being told what to do by a stranger, let alone manipulated. Former cop from my home town, goddamn, and a killer to boot who's getting paid by the King to pass along... what? Gossip about Brazil and its ridiculous politics? I'm choked. Don't think I like this guy any better than Alfredo. Can he run a wireless? Can he break a code, never mind write one? We know he can use a gun, so we're probably equal there. He's just a fat cop who faded into the sunset on a pension, and still a bully.

"You're the boss, Al," I say as sweetly two-faced as I can muster.

He looks at me over the top of his newspaper. Nearly bald, freckled, bushy eyebrows, eyes like drills going backwards. He grunts, says, "There's a big cat on the loose. Scared the shit outta someone in the Tijuca Forest, which is down your direction in the Zona Sul."

I say, "What kind?"

"Jaguar. They usually stay north, but they can go long range. Hmm... seems to be fully grown. Very dangerous. Stalk and ambush, very opportunistic. Reminds a person just how dangerous a place old Rio can be."

I scoff. "You think it wants to hang around the beach, find a woman?"

"Jesus Christ Thorsen you're a mouthy pup! Let me tell you something, there are places in this city where you can wake up in the morning with a snake on the bed. Guess you haven't had time yet to step back from *a doce vida* to see how most of the people really live around here. Windows without glass, shitters without toilets. Pretty cute around here, nice view of the Hunchback and the millionaires down on the Copa, but go 10 kilometers out of town, and you can't tell the difference between the people and the animals."

Woa... that helped, let him get steamy.

"I'm aware of the *favelas*," I say. "I know not all shit finds a hole."

He's looking at me incredulously, the newspaper crunching as his hands go stiff. "Not all shit...."

"Gimme a chance, Al," I say. "Only been here four days. However, I have made contact with Germany."

Not strictly true, but it gets his attention.

"You been talking to Germany?"

"No, just receiving... the Abwehr foreign intel station in Hamburg."

"The hell you say. Would this be Alfredo's handler?"

"Yeah, must be. He said it's a cultural facility, like a Voice of Deutchland or something. But our transmitter has to be on higher ground to start sending and receiving properly. We're looking for a new place tomorrow, me and this guy Eddie."

"That would be Eduardo da Silva, Alfredo's local pigeon."

"Seems like a nice guy for a fascist."

"Listen to me, you have to be very careful here. There are no nice fascists. He could be counter-intelligence."

"You mean a Vargas agent?"

"Could be, as not long ago he was in the Brazilian army. Could be they know Alfredo is a German V-mann, so they set him up with da Silva. Maybe not, but you gotta play the possibility. These Integs are a problem for Vargas. Sometimes he needs 'em like you need nitro. Handle with caution. They're not always just about theatre... some are unstable, capable of anything. You got a gun?"

"I wouldn't want ammo if I didn't."

"Colt 911?"

"Yeah."

"Let's walk next door to my place."

Al Mac has a couple of big rooms upstairs. Man they like loud colors in this country, maybe to blind you against the reality. The plaster has been painted so many times the color is off the spectrum. Basic furniture and the bed doesn't look like the sort a woman might sleep in. Straw pillow, although I guess that's basic in this town. Couple of small comic books lying on the table, and a pile of them in a box. Quick glance, look kinda racy for a cop but maybe not for a disgraced cop hiding in Rio. Open door to the small balcony. Nice views, even if a few terra-cottas and cupolas get in the way. Can see Corcovado if you lean south off the balcony, which is what I'm doing when he hands me a box of ammo.

"Twenty rounds," he says. "I'll take one of those new twenties."

"Thanks," I say. "Thought I was on the payroll now."

"Next time you report in, I'll let you know. Now don't be wasting these on tin cans, kiddo, or go shootin' up some bar down on the Copa or you'll end up saying prayers in a *catedral negra*."

"Yeah yeah... what kinda insurance you got, Al?"

He's moving around like the daddy bear in Goldilocks, moving dirty dishes from the table into the sink, which looks like something he's been pissing in. Big shoulders, bit of a belly. Guess that's why he needs those red braces to keep his pants up.

I hand him an Alfredo twenty.

"You don't need to know," he says, slipping it in his trouser pocket. "Get picked up, they might give you the 3rd degree."

Torture. I go cold at the thought.

He chuckles, says, "Let's just say if I had to rob a bank, I could rob a bank."

Believe him. He just robbed me. Buck a bullet, a tad excessive methinks, especially as we're supposed to be on the same side.

"How do you pass the time, Al?" I say. "When you're not tailing guys and casing banks."

"I draw," he says.

"You're an artist?" I say.

He shrugs. "What's art? I draw for myself."

Look around, don't see any pictures on the walls. Oh well, he doodles. Passes the time, shapes time.

There isn't much more to be said. We agree to meet in a week at a different location, then I go downstairs to the sunny street, look for my taxi.

CHAPTER THIRTEEN:

A GOOD *INTEGRALISTA*

WHATEVER DAY IT IS, Eddie comes around nice and early and I'm waiting in the street outside Alfredo's, ready for the tour. Before we go anywhere, though, I reset the timing on his car engine. No big deal. He has a tool kit, pops the hood, and I loosen the distributor and dial 'er in, don't even have to take the fag outta my mouth. You just have to listen to the revs, the pitch, get her sweet. I nod, he shuts the motor off, I tighten the nut, throw the wrench back in the kit. Do I get my hands dirty? Not really. Back home I've done this so often it's just part of the procedure.

"Is she ready?" says Eddie.

"Cat's in the bag, bag's in the river," I say.

Eddie is one grateful cowboy and shows it by driving like a lunatic for the first few blocks.

"You make it new again," says Eddie. "Now I drive like the Baron, eh?"

"Which Baron?"

"Manuel de Teffe... you don't know him? Brazil's greatest racer? He always wins the Rio Grand Prix... every year he wins Rio... Sao Paulo, Buenos Aires, Tripoli, Naples, Milano... he win them all. Seriously, you don't know the Baron?"

We're speeding past the lagoon or the *lagoa* as they call it. It's a swamp and smells like one. Lots of color: green, yellow, blue, black and the unknown. Lots of birds. Pure Brazil.

I point at the small radio below the dash: "Isn't this illegal?"

Eddie smiles. He forgot to shave this morning, hangover shadow like a happy bullfighter.

"You like music, amigo?"

"This isn't for music," I say.

"I get music."

"How come you rate this?"

"A good *Integralista* has many friends, even police friends, and I am a good *Integralista*."

"So you like to listen in on the police."

"*Muito necessario*...." He leans forward, throws a switch. "Check it out, amigo—Radio Brazil."

I start scanning and she's popping in seconds. Portuguese of course. Staccato voice like lightning burning through metal. "What's this?" I say.

"They find a body in the Tijuca," says Eddie.

"Murder?"

Eddie shrugs, says, "Possibly. Every day they find a body somewhere in Rio."

The officer is talking to a woman, probably a dispatcher. Eddie drops his speed so's he can pay attention.

"*Ay caramba* this one is ugly... the head is almost ripped from the body. Sounds personal to me, amigo... very personal."

"It's a man?"

"They wonder. It could be a boy. Eh, some kid from the *favela*, some *veado* murder maybe. These faggots enjoy messy death."

Wonderful. Great music. And the day seemed so promising. Eddie shuts the radio off, points. "We go past the Planetario... then the Catholic University," he says. "Good neighbourhood and, as you can see, the houses are private."

"Is this Leblon?"

"Close, but not really. This Gavea. Cheaper than Leblon."

He takes us up a steep street where all the houses are walled in, so all you see are the roofs and the bushes that hang over the walls. Water running down the low side, almost enough to be a stream. He stops outside the last one on this stretch.

"This for rent?" I say as we get out.

"Expensive," says Eddie. "But no problem, Alfredo has a bag of money."

As I find out, the door in the wall is locked. Eddie steps forward with a key. The door opens into a courtyard that's big enough to park a car or catch the sun and watch the butterflies which seem to be all over the flowers. House is a shabby gray stucco, almost German in style except for the roof, which is the common red terra-cotta you see lots of in Rio. Steep too, or steep enough so's I don't really be wanting to go up, string an antenna. I go around the side to the back, which isn't bad, leastways for our purposes. Big, with the wall all the way around and beyond that some waste ground before you get to the trees, which cover the side of the mountain or morro as they say. The property is past its prime, obviously a good rental.

We take a look inside. Big, at least a dozen rooms up and down and the windows have blinds. Some furniture, basic, enough for our needs. I check the fuse box. Seems o.k. Wiring seems to be the standard knob and tube, not great for grounding, but I can fix that. Neighbour to the north is close, but hidden by the wall and the vegetation. Same goes for across the street and there's nobody to the south. It's quiet, it's high, just as Eddie said.

We're in one of the back rooms.

"What do you think?" says Eddie.

"We could set up here," I say. "Could even put the radio in that closet, big enough, just push the table and gear right in there, keep the dust off it. The antenna can go through the window here, maybe to that tree or the wall. Hell, we can hang clothes on it during the day if there's anyone looking. When can we get it?"

"Now," says Eddie. "The owner lives in Paulo."

It's a strange place, the way silent empty houses are, like the ghosts are taking a nap. The previous occupants left some stuff lying around, like they left in a hurry. Maybe students—books, magazines, some 78s and even a thirsty looking plant in the hall. You know, the light in Rio is usually very bright, even if there are clouds rolling about, but this place is all shadow, inside and out. Perfect for a nest of spies, I guess.

Check the upstairs bathroom, note that I can see Corcovado from the small window. That's the thing about Rio. You can always tell where you are, even at night, 'cause they have the big statue all lit up. They don't call him the Redeemer for nothing. If you can't see him, you're either upside down or pissed or both.

There's a clinic in the Praca Osorio where I drop in, get my stitches removed. Should've been done a couple of days ago as they're starting to ingrow like rebar in concrete, hurt like hell when the nurse snips and yanks. I'm a novelty act, Frank's monster, can only point and grunt. She likes me though. Dark, like milk chocolate, smells just as good. Takes my pulse, combs my hair, little extras. Less than ten reais.

Eddie's waiting outside, ass on the fender, reading the late edition of O Globo. He holds it up, shows me the photo. Gruesome closeup of a body.

"*Yaguarete*," he says. "Jaguar attack. Messy, huh?"

"Is this what we heard on the radio this morning?"

"*Sim sim*. The Jaguar rip his head off... it always goes for the head, cracks the skull, pierces the brain."

I'm looking, and I think I recognize that shirt.

"Who is it? I say. "A student?"

"Nobody, amigo. Just a punk from the *favela*. Machado. Live in the jungle, die in the jungle."

Damn, I'm thinking, if that's what you get for wearing that shirt, I'm glad it got nicked. Justice? Seems a tad excessive.

"They get the cat?" I say. "They shoot it?"

"No *senhor*. The *gato* is free to kill again."

"There a bounty?"

"What, you hunt?"

"I've done a little hunting, yeah."

"You have big cats in Canada?"

"Mountain lions. We call them cougars."

"Well I tell you, we are relaxed about this sort of thing in Rio. When a punk gets killed by a wild animal, it's population control. If the *yaguarete* kill a racehorse, then the army is looking for it. Eh, it's just natural subtraction."

"You mean natural selection, don't you?"

"No no, natural subtraction."

Well if it works for Eddie, guess it works for me. I say nothing about my connection to this unfortunate event. It's too mystical to get into, never mind embarrassing.

We drive to Alfredo's, start packing up the gear. I'm taking all my stuff because I'll be living in the new digs, not something I'm really looking forward to because up on the morro it's a bit out of it and I'm getting to like the Ipanema stroll. We've just got the radio locked in the case when Ida shows up. It has to be Ida 'cause she has a key and just walks right in with a little suitcase of her own. She's all in black like a nun but she's not a nun, cause she's got a figure and knows it. No makeup, like a warden from a girl's reformatory but that's not it, not that hard looking. Teacher maybe, but then why would she be a housekeeper? Older than me, obviously. Women who are half-way between me and my mother confuse me. I just can't place them.

"Ola, Ida," says Eddie. "*Como vai? Como vai a sua viagem*?"

"*Tudi traquilo*, Eduardo," she says, looking past him at me. "*Onde esta Alfredo*?"

Blah blah. Then they're talking about me.

"This is the gringo?"

"Yeah."

"German?"

"No, I think he's Scandinavian. From Canada."

"He's very young."

"Is he? He just looks young."

"What does he know? He's just a child."

"Eh, what do you know, Ida? *Senhor* Thorsen is an accomplished *maluco*."

She steps towards me, starts speaking some pretty fair German. "So, Herr Thorsen," she says. "*Lesen Sie Deutsch Literatur?*"

"*Ja naturlich,*" I say smoothly. "Spengler."

"Spengler?" she says, surprised. She looks at Eddie, who shrugs, hasn't got a clue.

"*Er ist dekadent,*" I say. "*Aber...*"

I'm about to follow up with Stefan Z, another guy I haven't read, but she shifts into English. "What do you know about Rio?"

"Darwin's favorite city."

"Darwin? He's your Prime Minister?"

"No, I mean Charles Darwin, the naturalist. He lived in Tijuca. He liked Rio."

"Do you?"

Eddie says, "Ida is engaged to Alfredo. Imagine."

Ida snorts, "What nonsense! There is no such arrangement."

Eddie says, "Alfredo is a mess without you, dear Ida. Every day he say where is Ida, why isn't she back? True, Thorsen?"

I nod, sure, what the hell.

Eddie is relentless: "*A fruta proibida e a mais apetecida...* forbidden fruit is the most desired... correct, Thorsen?"

Sure.

Ida hisses: "*A morte nao escolhe idades, menino!*"

Eddie gets theatrical, says to me, "You hear that, amigo? She call me a little boy, threaten death. I think Ida is touchy about something... what can it be now... oh, *claro*, you have a lover in Sao Paulo."

Ida says, "You know very well I went to Paulo to attend to my mother, Eduardo."

Eddie says, "Ah *sim sim*, the doves coo when mummy sleeps."

Ida ignores him, points at the radio case, says, "Are you leaving, *senhor*? So soon?"

I say, "Yes... Alfredo likes his privacy."

She looks askance at Eddie, who says, "A house in Gavea... more suitable for our work. So you have Alfredo for yourself, Ida."

They drop into Portuguese again, argue. He's pulling her chain, hey, don't know why. The setup is beyond me. She's coming on more like a boss rather than a servant.

Anyway we quit the banter and lug the gear outta there, get on with the mission. Can see her at the window watching us as we put the stuff in the car. The lady downstairs is doing the same thing, so you got these two birds on different branches spying on the spies. What a laugh, eh. If only they knew.

Chapter Fourteen:

AMAZON AVENUE

AROUND 6PM it's especially quiet up there on the morro as I string the antenna wire, measured best I can to avoid the accursed half waves, catch a good signal load. Hundred seven feet, hooked to an insulator I drive into a tree. Also lock a ground onto an iron pipe that's running up the back wall, bathroom breather probably. Should work. Actually I'm quite excited. No one around to bug me, no Alfredo with his slide rule mind, and his no smoking shit. Eddie is wherever Eddie is... expect I'll see them soon enough but in the meantime I can dial the world.

It's a known fact that it's easier to send and receive north-south/south-north than latitudinally, say west-east like North America to Europe, for example. If for no other reason Brazil would be a good hub location to route messages between North and South America and the Fatherland. I get the picture with Brazil—it's playing both sides until it sees which way the wind blows. Right now it's blowing Germany's way so maybe they'll tolerate some free-lance wireless but if the USA decides to get active who knows what happens then. These guys are setting up agents and right now Deutschland is ahead. It's all about a bunch of dummies and canaries with one or two professional zoo keepers. Cultural exchanges... you get a lot of strategic info from a little bit of cultural noise. Ship and aircraft movements, cargo manifests, resources, gossip, politics and just about anything useful for fighting a war.

Which gets me to thinking about Klaus back home in good old Kelowna by the lake, just exactly what his game is. I know he's trying to hustle my mother. Her business, I guess. Seems to me he was in Brazil before he emigrated to Canada, or maybe it was the Argentine. Anyway he's got a sentimental spot for South America, especially Krauts in South America. Yet if his idea of a wireless network is just an innocent hookup for homesick exiles, why the hell was I met by a guy like Alfredo who's only been in Brazil for a year and turns out to be an Abwehr agent? It means Klaus is either a zoo keeper or a dummy because honestly I was expecting to be met by some German who'd been here for years. I remember when Klaus told me about Germania, the colony in Paraguay on the southern border of Brazil. Paraguay in fact is the last country Brazil had a serious war with, all kinds of people killed, vicious stuff, depopulated the region so badly that it needed lots of new immigrants to get going again and a bunch of Germans took the opportunity in 1886 or thereabouts.

The story is kinda crazy, although typical of the colonizing I've read about. Nuevo Germania was set up by Nietzsche's sister and her husband as a place to get away from the Jews, grow cotton and eat bananas. The husband couldn't cut it, though, so he committed suicide and Nietzsche's sister eventually drifted back to Deutschland, left the colonists to sink or swim by themselves. She died two or three years ago, 1935 maybe, and Hitler gave her a state funeral or something grandiose, as the Nazis love Freddie Nietzsche. Bit of a fiasco, really, yet none of this bothered Klaus. Far as he's concerned, South America is German, just like North America is English. The fact that they're speaking Spanish and Portuguese is just transitional, a temporary condition to be tolerated until the cultural *anschluss* kicks in. *Liebensraum* is more than just a few aryans with ploughs and 5 round strip-clip Mauser 98s, it's cultural communication and right now this means wireless.

I finish my cigarette as the radio tubes light up, get warm. Got a notebook and a pencil beside the Morse key or the bug as we military hep cats like to call 'em. Got a microphone too in case I get a chance to recite a poem to "Halle" in Hamburg.

It's noisy out there, ships and aircraft, maybe some of it military. Antenna seems to be working well, lots of traffic from the USA. I tap out a callsign to Klaus, see if he's in his office at the Association clubhouse, receiver running. "T-cub" to "T-papa" which is a play on tragen, the German word for "bear", something we dreamed up before I left town. Seven hours difference, so it's noon with him and he's probably at work. I try several times but don't hear anything back.

I'm getting Hamburg, though, pretty good signal. The Abwehr probably have some damn good Telefunken gear in that old house and hundred foot antenna masts strong enough to tie a Zeppelin to. Some

German voice messages flying around, some of them coded like modern poetry, no rhyme or reason if you don't have the decryption. Some of it seems too close to be the Fatherland. Brazil has an island or two way out in the Atlantic, Trinidade Sul, just rocks I believe, but useful for a radio relay and if I had an RDF loop antenna I could tell for sure. It's one of these RDF loops that the local authorities will use if they want to flush our little setup here, so that's why transmissions have to be kept short and to the point, so no horsing around for me. I can listen, but sending is strictly by the playbook.

I'm looking at a map, tracing the old flight path of the airships that used to fly between Germany and South America until the Hindenburg disaster, see the Cape Verde Islands off Africa, think yeah, they must have radio stations still in place along the way. The (LZ 127) Graf Zeppelin used a 140 watt transmitter for its low freq messages, telegrams and weather reports and the like. Must have been something, a trip on that. I dial to 3 megahertz as if I'm expecting one of its messages, a lost transmission that's been circling the ionosphere for the last 2 years since its final SA flight. I catch something alright: an S.O.S.

Alfredo and Eddie show up just as I'm trying to figure out what's what.

"It's working?" says Alfredo. "*Gut*."

"Great location," I say to Eddie, who smiles.

"What's this... S.O.S?" says Alfredo.

"Yeah," I say. "Think it's an airplane."

I turn up the speaker and we listen for a moment. Desperate voice comes on. Portuguese. Eddie and Alfredo know what it is.

"Flying boat," says Eddie. "Ditched in the sea."

"Got a position?" I say.

"Brazilian navy," says Eddie. "One of ours."

"Unfortunate," says Alfredo. "But not our problem."

"Could be my amigos," says Eddie. "This is bad."

"Got a position?" I say again.

"Somewhere east of Santos," says Eddie. "I should make a call."

"Not our problem," says Alfredo, a bit testy.

"If it was German, you would make a call, 'fredo," says Eddie.

"I wouldn't," says Alfredo.

Me, I'm just the diplomat: "Eddie, if we can hear it, others can too, don't worry."

"Forget this," says Alfredo. "Let's get on with business, shall we?"

"Oh you mean some kultur?" sneers Eddie.

"Haven't you forgotten? Culture is money," says Alfredo.

"The dead don't need money," says Eddie, whatever he means by that.

These guys are close to taking some swings or worse. Eddie's burly enough, could take a coaster like Fredo, but who knows what Fredo's got in his pocket? I know what I've got, although I'm not ready for show and tell just yet.

There's some snap, crackle and pop in-coming. I flipped frequencies but Eddie doesn't know that.

"Hear it?" I say. "The coastguard are onto it. Don't worry, Eddie."

Alfredo's looking at me with new respect. Don't know if he knows what I did or not but whatever whichway he can see Eduardo is more relaxado. Maybe Eddie doesn't quite buy it but he's letting it go, thinking percentages.

Alfredo smooths a piece of paper on the table. "Can you send this for me?" he says.

It's a paragraph of mumbo in German, a coded message obviously. Later learn that's a page of German literature where the words and phrases are given numbers hitched to the lines. It could be page six of such and such an edition of Grimm's Fairy Tales or Mein Kampf, you just reduce the words to numbers, sequence them, whatever way you want. Mind you, it's a bit more complicated than this, as dummy numbers and dummy paragraphs are stuck in there to hide the meat and potatoes, so it looks like a bunch of bad typing, drive you nuts. Basic Abwehr spy talk.

"Callsign?" I say.

"Halle in Hamburg," says Alfredo. "You know the frequency, I believe."

"Sure, but what's our Callsign? You need one," I say.

"*Kultur*," says Eddie sarcastically.

"*Lagoa*," says Alfredo.

Portuguese word for "lagoon". Good enough, I suppose. I Morse the message, sign it Lagoa, and what do you know, we get an acknowledgment within a couple of minutes. Hamburg never sleeps.

Over the next few days "Lagoa" is in touch with the other stations: "Diego" in Buenos Aires, "Bolivar" someplace up country, "Condor" in Santiago, "Pancho" in Mexico City, "Jose" in Panama, "Jack" somewhere in the States, and of course "Traben" a.k.a. "T-papa" in Canada. I'm thinking there isn't much more use for me here and I'm bored as hell in this house up on the hill on Amazon Avenue. Do I give a damn about these incomprehensible messages? No way Jose. I miss Ipanema. It's a 20 minute walk to the nearest food and then, hate to say it, there's the warden. Second day I wake and there's someone in the house. It's Ida. Seems Alfredo thinks I need a housekeeper... only the thing is, Ida doesn't do any housekeeping, she's a flippin' warden, there solely to keep an eye on me.

Certain times of the day she wants the radio on, even if there's nuthin' on it, pete's sake. I'm supposed to keep a log of any calls from any of the stations and she gives me the third degree if I leave the house to take a walk or take a shit. It's ridiculous. I notice she has snacks and a cosy little room set up, but cook a meal for me, the slave? Forget it. Don't know what she does all day when she isn't spying on me or the invisible neighbours. Well she reads... she sits in her room or sits in the front patio and reads, always dressed black, or mostly black. Maybe because the butterflies are yellow and blue and stay clear of black, dunno. I suppose I could handle all this except she smells of garlic and I hate garlic. Not strong, not real noticeable, unless she's close, and then it can hit you like a poison dart. Be worse if she wore lipstick, I guess.

"You're lazy," she says. "You don't even read. That book you have has never been opened."

This makes me sit up. No shirt but at least I've got my pants on.

"You've been going through my stuff?"

"I should cut the pages for you."

"Stay away from my personal stuff. Have you no manners?"

"Manners? Look at you—is Rio too hot for you, *senhor*?"

"I didn't ask you to come into my room, lady."

"Only *campones* walk around without a shirt."

Well I don't know what a *campones* is but I do know the beaches around here are full of them. But I guess she never leaves her shadow long enough to notice.

And then there's the day the radio is picking up some medium wave, some local happy music and I'm practicing my rumba steps and she shows up, insists I turn it off.

"Are you stupid? You want the neighbours to phone the police?" she says.

"What's wrong with you?" I say. "Isn't this kinda normal behaviour around this town?"

She stalks over to the radio and of course she doesn't know a switch from a nob and I'm thinking if she puts her paws on it, she'll screw it up and the Abwehr will be wanting their money back. Her paranoia is preposterous, but I hustle over there, shut the music off. I even try to be nice to her.

"You want a cigarette, Ida? I got Luckys...."

"You're a child… you lack ideology and discipline."

Don't know what she's talking about. I got discipline. I wake up with a hard-on every morning.

"Ida, do you understand Morse Code? No? You want to learn it?"

This throws her. "You think you can teach me? You?"

"Well do you know it or not?"

She raises her head like a proud contessa about to spit.

"I know you're clever, Ida. I know you could learn to use the bug."

Her mouth is moving with a nervous twitch. She's thinking about it. I tap a little samba on the key, a few dots and dashes.

"You can talk to a lot of people in faraway places with this… Italy, for example."

"Why would I want to talk to Italy?"

"Your folks are from Italy, aren't they? Culture, Ida, culture."

But just when I think she's softening, she says, "You should take a shower."

Bloody hell. Three or four days of this and I'm just about ready to vanish, grab a plane for Buenos Aires, but then Eddie drops by and I'm able to escape for a beer. He takes me to some classy joint on the main drag, back of Leblon, not far away but far enough.

"Eddie," I say. "Ida is driving me nuts."

"Eh *senhor*, you know what to do," he says, clenching his fist, pumping his wrist. "You make her obey."

"She's spying on me."

"You see? She likes you."

"She's old enough to be my mother, man."

"Ah but she isn't your mother, amigo. Make her happy."

I groan. What the hell is it with these guys who think every problem in life can be fixed by a roll in the sack? My stomach tightens. Hunger. I feel like a steak. I order one and more beer. Been losing weight. The heat, the lack of sleep and a square meal and those long walks down the hill to the mercado have left me as skinny as a marathon runner.

Eddie says, "The reason I see you is to invite you to a party tomorrow evening."

I say, "Party? What sort of party?"

"You will see how the rich in Rio live. Sound good?"

I grunt, nod.

"A very wealthy business man called Manuelo Barasso who is an important patron of our political movement is having a party at his house. Some people from the government and the armed forces will be there as well."

"Sounds stiff, Eddie. I dunno—what about women?"

"Eh, I don't bullshit when I say some of the most beautiful *gatinahs* in Rio will be there. These are crazy women, amigo. No hang ups."

"They're looking for guys with dough. They don't want a gringo like me."

"They have guys with money... they always on the look out for a boy toy."

"Hey I'm no gigolo. I dunno. The fuzz make me nervous."

"*Os homi* are human too... I'm a sort of a cop, si? Hey, I want you to come."

"Won't I need a suit?"

"Clean pants, nice shirt, man. If you want, I'll swing past tomorrow and we can buy new shirts. I want you to meet my girlfriend."

"Alright, you talked me into it. Anyway, I gotta get away from that bitch Ida."

"Bring her as your date, amigo."

"Are you kidding?"

And so on. Beginning to think Ida is Eddie's pony, his way of controlling the situation. While Alfredo thinks he's the boss, in reality Eddie is just playing him... and me, *claro*. Alfredo is supplied with the name of a sympathetic contact in Rio who turns out to be Eddie, who in turn supplies a "housekeeper" to make things look legit. Me? I'm just a tourist with a short-wave radio. I start out as a dummy, become a canary, and then what next I don't know. Let's hope it isn't a dead man.

"Is Alfredo coming to this party?" I say.

"Not invited," says Eddie. "Fredo doesn't know how to dance."

Interesting. I'm wondering what the fix is here, what's really going on. Know I'm supposed to feel privileged and all, that I got an inside with the natives, and when Eddie picks up the bill, I'm wondering if we're really pals or if I'm working for him now.

Chapter Fifteen

PARTY WITH THE BARASSOS

I THINK YOU GUESSED I bought the same shirt I had before, the blue one with the black zulu stripes and the ivory buttons, short sleeves, very sporty and tropicalismo. Never got to wear the first one, and even though the guy who did wear it ended up dead, I'm just not that superstitious. Couple of weeks in Rio and I've got a bit of that carioca tan so I don't look so much the crazy Viking raider just off the boat or a pale Nazi on holiday. I'm starting to blend, easy loose like samba. Homesick? Not me. Got a feeling something good is coming my way.

Eddie's wearing a white suit and chewing on a cigarillo and his girl Bebe has a great set of knockers below that red dress and an ass that could melt the stone lid on a pharaoh's coffin. She's short but she's loaded, got all the extras. Stagger heels, slave bracelets, molten lipstick, dangerous smile, nose like a dagger. I thought Eddie was married but this is no wife. Bebe is a weapon, and I'm starting to see how Eddie operates. She's hands on right away. Yes, I know. She doesn't speak English.

Barosso's villa isn't a basic street step-up, with iron bars on the windows and wonky flagstones for the portico and orange peels for stucco. This is like a palace set in a botanical garden, albeit protected by a ten foot wall with broken glass baked into the crust like a reptile's tail and a gateway guarded by a big black guy wearing white gloves and steel-toed boots polished to look like shoes. He checks Eddie's invitation card, then salutes as he waves us through. As we glide below the palms and the trailing lotus vines to the parking area, I'm thinking how come this country is supposed to be poor? Doesn't look poor to me. Ponds and terraces and flower beds that glow in the dark and a house that looks like a planetarium. Big, not exactly modern, not exactly old. Maybe it's the colonnades, arches and all the marble and the orchestra playing in the ballroom that's open to the terrace that make me think it's more grandiose than it really is, or maybe it's the people, all that nervous energy, severely sober or severely pissed, don't matter. Some ways it's like the ocean liner, except here no one's falling down as the ground moves. Yet.

Might be 70, 80 people here, not sure as there are a lot of rooms and a lot of servants or retainers who look like guests. Lot of the men huddle, especially the older guys. I mean, this is a generational party, more like a reception, although who the honoured guest might be is hard to figure. Could be he'll come over the wall at midnight, scare the shit out of everyone. If I knew the lingo, maybe I'd know. Eddie and his girl start dancing and I drift towards the bar, get myself a shot, try one of the courtesy cigarettes they got piled up on a gold plate. Turkish. Heavy reek. Not to my taste, so after a couple of drags I discreetly ditch it in an exotic plant pot and keep moving, case the joint. Since all the big sun doors are open to the night, you can move through the rooms and courtyards easy as a bird. Don't try to engage, just peck and explore. The entrance hall is something, big as a church with a set of stairs that might take a week to climb.

I'm looking, see this young babe descending. She's young, seventeen, eighteen, but painted up to look like a full throttle woman. Blonde, green dress, yellow buttons all the way down the front, nothing flashy, has the Latin look although is pretty pale, definitely old Euro stock. Almost skipping down the steps, no hip swivel like some movie queen making a grand entrance. She heads straight for me.

"Hi," she says. "I know you!"

Perfect North American English. Nice mouth, nice eyes, nicer figure.

"Saw you on the Southern Cross coming down," she says. "You probably didn't notice me."

Well I didn't, unless maybe she was the pretty young gal who was having her photo taken that day on the deck. The Rio business man and his family.

"Were you in First Class?" I say.

"Yes we were, and it wasn't exactly ring-a-ding-ding. Pretty stuffy."

"So are you American?"

"No *senhor*—I went to school in the USA. Just graduated. Now I'm home."

"You live in Rio?"

Big, teasing smile. "Yes I do. What's your name?"

"Thorsen."

"Sure you are. You look perfectly Scandinavian. Actually you look like Charles Lindbergh, only better. Are you a flyer by any chance?"

"No, afraid not."

"I'm Lucy... short for Lucinda, which was my grandmother's name."

"Got a boyfriend?"

"Me? I don't rate."

"Oh yeah? Don't rate? You're a kidder, Lucy Rio. Bet you're here with a sweet 250 lb football player."

"Mmm... we don't play that kind of football in Brazil."

We're moving, don't know why, unless we're following each other. We end up on the main terrace where most people seem to be, either standing or sitting at tables, eating and drinking, yapping and laughing like they won the lottery or the government has fallen. Eyes flicker our direction.

Lucy slips her hand in mine, says in a throaty whisper, "Pretend we are in love."

Well, that might not be too difficult, but I'm wondering, for whose benefit is this? Me, her, or that priest over there wearing the black vaquero hat. Actually there's a clutch of them and they look like heat— cops, military, business and death. I class the priest as death. They're all dressed as civilians but, *senhors y senhoras*, do civilians usually wear sunglasses at night? Not all of them are flying blind, mind you. Maybe three, and the others could be benevolent middle-aged civil servants and assorted *comerciantes*. Man these guys like moustaches. Pancho Stalin or Rudolpho Hitler, take your pick. I don't get it. Some guys grow them to look older, others to look younger, but to me they make the line between classy and criminal awful slim. Notice a couple of banners—one Brazilian, green with the planet and stars, and the other Integralist, green with the Sigma symbol. With those little spotlights, they sure dress the place up like Buck Rogers.

"You know any of these people?" I say.

"I know them all," says Lucy. "Only it's the names I forget. Guess you're a gate crasher."

"You think I came over the wall?" I say. "You don't get past that big guy at the gate any other way."

"Hey, you got a nail for me?"

"You're too young to smoke."

"Light me or I'll have you thrown out."

"Oh yeah? Who'd listen to you, doll?"

I flip her a Lucky, one for myself. She's trying to be the fast chick but I know she's putting on a show. First drag she coughs.

"What's upstairs?" I say. "The ladies cloakroom?"

"I'll show you," she says. "But first, dance with me... or am I too young for that as well, *senhor*?"

She pushes me towards the ballroom, then grabs my hand and next thing I know we're whirling around in a foxtrot or something similar. The orchestra then drops into a rumba and everybody is yelping yi yi yi and shaking their hips. Nothing vulgar, mind you. This crowd is too midtown for that, except for Bebe, Eddie's date who's dancing with some flathead who looks like he's been taking lessons in Africa. I would say she's doing the Beguine the way she's rolling the beat. No sign of Eddie. Guess he can't bear to watch or maybe he's seen it before. Well we dance and we dance and then we escape outside, get some air, drinks from the terrace bar. Lucy just takes a sip, then excuses herself, says she has to see someone. Fine. The orchestra is taking a break anyway.

Somebody's talking in German, couple of guys below, shadows, just out of sight. Naturally I eavesdrop.

"Propaganda is just another form of poetry," says one guy.

His German is edged with something else, another dialect, another nationality.

The other guy laughs. "It certainly is in this country," says the second guy. "What did Reichmarshal Goering say recently? 'Every time I hear the word kultur I reach for my pistol' or words to that effect?"

More laughing. First guy says, "Si si, the fat one is always good for a bon mot."

Si si... Brazilian? Maybe, although the voice has more of a lilt to it, like one of those Italian opera dudes.

He continues: "So Berlin is investing?"

First guy says, "Heavily... Prinz-Albrecht-Strasse has made Brazil a priority."

Second guy says, "I'm surprised the Gestapo has an interest here, though. I thought this would be Canaris' sector."

First guy says, "It is Admirald Canaris' *sektor* but Heydrich has been promoting his interests with the Brazilian special police."

Second guy says, "The Brazilians have a Gestapo unit?"

"Yes. Military. Very amateur but I think we can shape them up. Henrique Holl. Have you met him?"

"Don't think so. You're enjoying your visit?"

"Indeed."

"The women?"

"Like a visit to the zoo."

Bit more laughing, then the first guy says, "How did you cross?"

"By boat. Very enjoyable. You?"

"Oh I flew. My brother-in-law arranged it all."

"The Count?"

"Si. Italy wants to establish regular flights between Rome and Rio."

"Well Suckert, that's very nice."

"Yes, it is very nice. And it's nice to discover some of my books are available in this country."

"Ah... the writer who never sleeps. You know, Suckert, some people consider you an agent provocateur."

"Mussolini? Of course he does."

"Others too, *mein freund*."

"Berlin?"

"Ja, certain individuals have no sense of humour. You still hold a commission?"

"I do, sir. Captain in the Fifth Alpine."

"Very nice."

"It opens doors."

"Doors are always open for you, I imagine. Where are you staying?"

"The Copacabana. I tell you, my heart sings when I enter the lobby of a grand hotel."

More laughing. What a couple of toads, I'm thinking. Free holidays, titles and great salaries to boot. And I'm also thinking there's something familiar about the voice of the real Kraut, like I've heard him on the radio or someplace.

Eddie is at my shoulder. "Where've you been, amigo?" he says. "I want to introduce you to the host."

"Barasso?" I say. "Would he care?"

Eddie sniggers, says, "*Senhor* Barasso cares about any man who dances the rumba with his daughter."

"Lucy is his daughter? Heck, I wondered about that."

"I notice your wandering hands, Thorsen...."

"*Sacana*... wandering is for old men."

"Hey Lucinda is nice *buceta* and she likes gringos. But I think, *senhor*, it would be wise to have a formal introduction."

"Just a dance, man. I won't be seeing her again."

"*Sempre di devagar para um funeral, manoluco.*"

"Uh?"

"It means, 'always go slow for a funeral'. Hey, what do I know?"

Eddie, what a diplomat. Laugh on, man. Know he's just pulling my chain. I can see Senhor Barasso holding court with the heavies near the Integralista banner. Assume it's him as he's the man I saw getting photographed with Lucy on the ship. About fifty, maybe older. No moustache, and the more handsome for it. Bit of a paunch, some gold on his wrist. Linen jacket, tropical shirt. People listen to him.

A couple of waiters are circulating with trays of champagne and people are taking a glass even if they have a drink in hand. Something's coming down. The babble dies off as Barasso raises his voice, addresses the guests on the terrace. Portuguese, so I don't know what he's saying. Eddie murmurs in my ear: "A few words about the brave aviators who died." Guess he's talking about the distress call we heard the other night. Apparently the seaplane broke up on impact and sank. No survivors.

Barasso raises his glass, looks around, nods. "I toast the brave men who lost their lives the other evening," he says grandly. "*Senhors, senhoras*—to the crew of the flying boat Santa Teresa! *Saude!*"

Saude! echoes as the crowd picks it up. Barasso continues speaking. Eddie murmurs, "That fucking *filho da puta* Alfredo... one phone call from the *mercado*. I could've made a difference."

I say, "You knew some of the crew?"

"One guy—we went to school together. He go navy, I go army."

"Eddie, no one could've got to them in time."

"What do I say to his widow? What?"

"You say nothing."

Eddie's drinking fast now, anything within reach, keeps muttering filho da puta son of a whore. Barasso is still eulogizing when, out of the blackness, there's a godawful scream, a woman's scream, somewhere out there in the garden. Several young guys run down the steps to investigate. Bit of shouting, then Eddie and I follow, not sure what to expect. Soon clear enough, however, when we reach the pergola with the fountain, see the body of a mangled white woman lying on the ground beside a headless statue like she's a sacrifice. What a sight—her head a bloody mutilated mess, almost ripped from her shoulders just like that kid in the Tijuca and this property borders the Tijuca. Her bloomers are around her ankles but if you get attacked by a predator, guess that's what happens.

Amazing how many pistols appear when death visits a party, especially in Rio. Better than nuthin', I suppose, but not really adequate for hunting a bush crazy jaguar. Even Barasso knows this. When he arrives and sees what he sees, he immediately dispatches a servant back to the house for something more serious. An M1 Garand, eight clip semi, a weapon I've certainly used on the range but not for hunting. As rifles go, it's good enough. Barasso looks around, says, "Who knows how to use this?" I'm thinking Eddie's going to step forward but he's not interested and it's looks like these other pretty boys haven't got a clue.

What the hell. I step forward.

Barasso looks at me, says, "You, *senhor*?"

I say, "Si si... I know."

He hands me the rifle and I check the gas plug, then the clip. The servant hands me some extra ammo.

"Couple of flashlights be good," I say.

Barasso snaps his fingers, barks, "*Lanterna!*"

The woman had been dragged for a ways and I could see the pugmarks where the cat started its run, so, figuring it retreated the way it came, I head into the deep gloom of the tropical garden. Eddie and Barasso follow with the flashlights and pistols. Have to say this Barasso has balls. He's got plenty of retainers he could send out as bait, but no, it's his party and his guest who got killed, so he's gonna be in the cohort. We hear a whimper in the bushes, and I'm just about to start blasting when the flashlights reveal this guy with no pants and crazy eyes standing frozen with fear. White tux jacket and black dickie bow. Mulatto, reminds me of the singer in the orchestra. Alright, one and one makes two, but where is three?

"*Onde esta o gato?*" says Barasso roughly.

This man has been struck dumb, like God has given him a concussion. I conclude the victim is not his wife but maybe someone else's. I level the rifle at him and this gets him babbling and pointing.

Takes ten eternities or more to find the cat. I was thinking it had gone up a tree and hopped the wall into the forest but it was just up the tree. Could hear it mewing and coughing, like it was sick and wanted a nice warm home. A black panther, one of the rare ones where you can't see the spots because of the skin mutation. Some ladies like them as pets or cigarette lighters. As dangerous as we know dangerous. Two hundred and fifty pounds and fast, and if you don't stalk it, it'll stalk you. Cat like this can carry your scent for years and still come looking. Solitary and certainly doesn't think of humans as divine. We're meat, maybe inferior meat, but meat whatever way you cut it.

It's thirty, forty feet away and not a clear shot. If it charges, there's no guarantee Eddie and Barasso will hold their ground, keep the lights on it. Never shot a big cat before. Shot a bear once, don't know why, except it was expected of us young lads back home if you wanted to be a man. Shot quite a few dummies on the range, but that's not quite the same, is it? They don't move, and they don't come looking for you if you miss.

"What you gonna do, man?" whispers Eddie.

"Gimme your flashlight," I say. "And *Senhor* Barasso, keep yours on the cat, please."

Take my belt, strap the flashlight to the forward stock, snug to the barrel. Yep, the old pit lamping trick. I move in slowly, rifle raised, finger on the trigger, light on its eyes. It stares right at me, them old demon slits, then shifts position, and I think it's either going to come for me or run. What am I, twenty feet away? It opens its mouth, emits that ungodly piercing owww cats do when warning you off or preparing for combat. It's all I need. I fire, and the cat crashes to the ground. One bullet, lights out.

Barasso comes up, looks, then thumps my shoulder. "Magnificent," he says. "First rate shooting."

Bullet hole's in the chest, just below the throat. It's coming for me now: the old post-mortem shakes. Need a cig, but can't find one. Eddie knows. He lights a cigarette, puts it in my mouth. Barasso crouches down, brushes his pistol across the cat's face, lifts an eyelid. It's dead.

When we get back to the house, the guests burst into applause, or what's left of the guests cause maybe the shooting spooked them and for sure the ambulance that came for the victim did. Everyone wants to shake my hand or get me a drink, although Barasso insists that I have a shot of some 200 year old whiskey he has, so smooth it tastes like pussy. Eddie's words, not mine. Goddamn, suddenly everyone is speaking English or anyone who wants to speak. There you go, boy—shake hands with the Colonel, the Captain, *Senhor* So and So, his wife, his daughter, his mistress. I see Lucy in the background with another woman, maybe her mother. Don't know if they're pleased or not.

"*Senhor* Thorsen," says Barasso, "allow me to introduce you to Major Kallingram of the German SS."

Jesus Christ, it's the Divine Messenger. Does he recognize me? He nods, not so much a movement but telepathy. Instinctively my hand goes to my pocket, feels for my worry stone. It's there.

"And Captain Erich Suckert of the Italian 5th Alpine Regiment. Captain Suckert is a famous writer in the Latin world."

Suckert gives me a friendly nod but by now I'm looking around, wondering if Uma is here. Lots of pretty women and if she's around, she's lost in the crowd.

Captain Suckert says, "Americano?"

I say, "Canadian."

Notice he's using a cigarette holder which no doubt marks him as an officer.

"No one is really Canadian," he says. "English?"

"Danish."

"Ah. Half-caste myself. My father is German, lucky for me. You hunt, of course."

"Not much... but, yeah."

"I look at you and I say, this man is a soldier."

"What makes you say that, sir?"

"Who else could use an American M1 rifle so expeditiously?"

"It's Canadian. Garand is a French Canadian."

"Ah... I learn something. If so, why doesn't the Canadian Army use the M1?"

"They do."

"Oh. I thought the Canadians use the British Lee Enfield rifle."

"That also."

Suckert turns to Kallingram, says, "Have you ever fired the M1? It's an amazing weapon. Never go to war with America."

Kallingram dismisses this notion with a shrug, keeps his trap shut, his eyes roaming. Reckon the 36 inch rip-tooth handsaw is his weapon of choice.

"Pity about the jaguar," says Suckert. "Such an elegant creature."

"Just natural subtraction," I say.

"Subtraction?" says Barasso. "Eh, I like that."

"Anyone know who the victim is?" I say.

"Gate crasher," Barasso says. "I hope to God, otherwise the newspapers will invent a scandal."

The ambulance is drawing away, no lights, silent as a hearse. Couple of cops want to talk to Barasso, so I just fade into the ballroom where Bebe ambushes me with the hippy hippy shake. The last samba. What the hell, eh. Death has come and gone and the survivors can just keep on dancing. So we dance and we dance and pretty soon I'm dead sober and I don't see any of the women I love. But I'll tell you, it's damn weird to arrive as a stranger, then leave the party famous.

Chapter Sixteen

BAD VOODOO:
GRINGO SHOOTS BIG CAT

ANOTHER BEAUTIFUL DAY IN RIO, and I'm wondering if it ever rains in this city, although they tell me it does. Haven't been here long enough to pick up the rhythm. I bring rain with me, expect it, but it's not happening despite the morning mists on the morro and in the distant valleys of los *gigantes*. Damn good storm would be useful, clear away some of this tension. Guess I'm restless.

Ida is watching me with her police eyes and alls I'm doing is shuffling a deck of cards, playing blackjack with myself. I'm hitting 21s so easy I'm thinking I should head for the casino in the Copacabana.

"Thanks for leaving the light on for me last night," I say. "This is one dark neighbourhood."

"The light?" she says. "What light?"

"The three candles on the sidewalk... well, the cobblestones as there is no sidewalk, is there?"

"Three candles... where?"

"You didn't put them there?"

"Outside this house? No. Someone is fooling with you, *senhor*."

"Right outside the yard door. Well, close."

"Did Eduardo see this?"

"Nah, he dropped me off, bottom of the hill. Figured a car that time of night might be suspicious."

"Did you see anyone?"

"No. The candles were set as a triangle. What's that all about?"

140

She's thinking this over. "It's unusual to see this in a neighbourhood like this. Were the candles black or white?"

"Just candles, I dunno. What's the matter? Someone sending a message?"

"Perhaps. Perhaps someone thinks this is an ile."

"An ill-ee? What's that?"

"An *ile* is a Santeria temple. The black people bring this nonsense from Africa."

"You know, Ida, you look like a priestess."

"Huh. You make fun, but I warn you, *senhor*, many people in Rio take this nonsense seriously. Have you offended anyone?"

"Just you, Ida. Or so it seems."

She ignores this, just gets up and leaves the room. Hear the front door open and her going outside. I draw another card, blow my hand, dealer wins. Enough of this. Start building a house, just passing the time as I wait for her return. Truth is I've never been any good at fooling around with cards, even as a kid. Lousy at dealing, lousy at cheating. I can bluff, but that's not always enough.

When she returns I say, "Nothing left now, *claro*."

"I believe you," she says. "Possibly it was meant for the house next door."

"Is Alfredo expected this evening?"

"Don't you know?"

You see, that's the thing, I should know, but since Ida was installed here on Amazon Avenue, Fredo's been keeping his distance.

"He didn't say. I thought you had a schedule."

"Schedule?"

"Timetable."

A slow shake of the head. "*Nein*," she says. We're speaking in German, as she's easier with it than English.

"You mean 'negative.'"

She doesn't know what I'm talking about.

"Radio talk, Ida. 'Nein' sounds like the number nine in English, so you say 'negative' instead. Comprende?"

She nods, says, "What is 'yes' then?"

"You would say 'affirmative'. Understand that English is the lingua franca of the radio world for ships and aircraft, so lots of foreign words clash, cause confusion. For example, even 'affirmative' can cause a problem in a broken transmission. The receiver might only catch the last part of the word affirmative so it sounds like 'negative'—understand? So some operators prefer to say 'affirm' instead of 'affirmative.'"

"But the grammar is wrong."

"What's grammar? Grammar is just a way of dressing an expediency, right?"

She looks doubtful, like all the rules she learned in the convent have just been exposed as bull.

"Clarity is the essence—right, Ida? *Klaheit is das Wesen.* Didn't Spengler say that?"

For the first time, maybe a smile, just a softening in the eyes, the mouth.

"What is the protocol for Morse?" she says.

"Oh, you want to learn a little Morse code?" I say. "Take a seat."

Open the closet door, pull the radio table out, set up a couple of cozy chairs. Don't smell any garlic today.

"You see radio waves move at different speeds, sit in different places in the spectrum," I say. "Short waves—Kurzwelle or KW for short—move quickly in the 100 to 1000 megahertz range... like fish in the ocean, some swim fast, others just cruise nice and slow."

I flip on the transceiver, wait for the tubes to get warm. "*Wer ist deine Mutter*?" says Ida.

"My mother? She's German."

"Does she live alone?"

"She does."

"My mother is alone."

"Sao Paulo, isn't it? What's it like?"

"Not like here. It's modern, skyscrapers like Chicago."

"So, Ida, are you an Integralist?"

"What I am, and what I am not, is private."

"Just trying to get a handle on what these things are, is all. You said I lacked ideology and I'm just trying to figure out what you mean. Eddie's an Integ and I don't know what he stands for."

"Eduardo is a passenger."

"Passenger? What does that mean—he's just along for the ride?"

"Did you meet any *Integralistas* at the party? Or was it all just drinking and dancing."

"What's wrong with that? Party, isn't it? Yeah, I met people. I met the host, *Senhor* Barasso."

"You met *Senhor* Manuelo Barasso? I don't believe you."

"It's true, Ida. We had a long conversation."

"He was just being polite."

"Don't think so. He wants me to marry his daughter."

"You see? You're still a child. Everything is a joke. I won't say you are a liar. I will say you are a comedian."

"Hey, I was right about the candles, wasn't I?"

An odd thing happens right then—Klaus Gerwing's voice is on the radio, old T-Bear. He's drifting in and out but he's there, doing a loop with the callsigns.

"That's Traben," I say to Ida. "Finally."

Guess she's wondering why anyone would call himself a bear.

"The station in Canada," I say. "Let's see if we can hook up."

We're flying in fragments but he gets enough of me to know I'm picking him up. Lots of fried eggs and cross-drift. He switches to German, seems to be talking about *die unbegetenen Gast* which means "the uninvited guest", whoever or whatever that is. A warning? I just don't know.

"I suppose it makes sense to you, *senhor*," says Ida.

"Perfectly," I say. "Alfredo will be pleased."

Alfredo shows up just as it's getting dark and he isn't pleased. He's got a newspaper with him, some tabloid that's published with the favelas in mind, meaning it's big on pictures and cartoons and very simple headlines, like this one, *GRINGO ATIRA GATO GRANDE*, or to put it in crude English, *GRINGO SHOOTS BIG CAT*.

"It's well that they don't have your name," says Alfredo. "Yet."

"Wonder how they got the picture of the cat?"

"That doesn't matter. It's your picture we need to be concerned about."

"They won't get it from me."

"If someone knocks, don't answer the door."

"You know, Alfredo, I'm not stupid. I actually thought I'd done something good here. Barasso was very grateful."

"Tomorrow the big dailies will be onto it and they'll be looking for you."

"They won't find me, and if they do, I'll deal with it. Hey, I'm just a tourist."

"It's not that simple, *mein freund*. The article says a voodoo priest is calling for revenge. He considers the jaguar you shot as sacred."

"Sacred? Why?"

"Because it was black."

"That makes it special? I don't believe this. It killed people... it killed one of theirs, fuck sakes, the kid in the Tijuca."

"These are superstitious people, you have no idea... if this priest says it's sacred, then it's sacred."

"Oh what's he gonna do? Stick pins in a doll? Hey, I got plenty more bullets."

That was unwise. Now Alfredo knows for sure I know how to use a gun, he might be thinking I'm packin' right now.

"Explain to me how this happened. Explain to me how you were the man of the hour."

"Didn't Eddie tell you?"

"I haven't seen Eddie."

So I tell him what happened, just the basics. A party full of fascists without the balls to take care of business. A lady had her head ripped off and I had to shoot the cat. End of story. I omit the encounter with *Sturmbannführer* Kallingram and *Kapitan* Suckert. For now.

"We made contact with Traben a little while ago," I say. "Two way."

This picks him up.

"You spoke with Traben? What did he say?" says Alfredo.

"Not much. Bad noise, lots of drift... but I heard him, and he heard me."

"Well, the essential thing is we know it can be done, and Traben can be part of the network."

"Got anything you want sent to Hamburg?"

"Not today. I just came to warn you."

He goes off to the kitchen to confer with Ida. She'll tell him about the candles and he'll assume they're onto me, so I start packing. Put on the jacket I was wearing most nights on the ship, slip Oswald into the inside pocket. Everything I have is in the sling bag, so I'm ready to vamoose. Just as well, as Alfredo is back fast.

"You didn't tell me about the candles," he says.

"Now you know," I say.

"You must've been followed."

"Possibly. Guess I should find another place to camp."

He nods.

"Just drop me off at the beach," I say. "Maybe I should sleep in a hotel tonight. What about your place?"

"Hotel would be better."

"We got an expense account for this?"

He opens his wallet, pulls out some *conto de reais* or Vargas Royals.

"Two nights," he says. "Stay low, then we'll see."

"Will I be coming back here?"

"We'll see."

I start to follow him through the door, but he stops.

"I'll send Eddie for you."

So he's on foot, I think. Must take a taxi to and from the *mercado* down the hill, disguise his tracks. I actually think about following him but as my old pal Ross used to say, never walk behind anyone with a flat ass or you might lose your way.

Copacabana used to be a fishing village, then someone blasted a tunnel (*Real Grandeza*) from Botafogo, so Copa became part of Rio. Between the avenue and the beach there's a wide promenade, some of it made of black and white tiles that swerve like waves, but they're still working on it, just like the lifeguard tower at the south end that everyone swears is there until they try and find it. Behind the strip, there're empty lots, piles of sand really, some of them with concrete footings and stalks of rusting rebar, projects abandoned when the money ran out in '32. Vagrants sleep there with the toucans. But hey, no problem. Beach faces south, so it gets the sun all day. Over two miles long, and if it wasn't for the odd sewer outfall here and there, it'd be the best beach anywhere, although that really doesn't matter as lots of people have their own swimming pools anyway.

I'd like to say I'm booked into the Copacabana Palace Hotel but of course I'm not. Not far away but not the Palace, not within eyeshot of Carmen Miranda. My place doesn't even look like a hotel. No sign, no grand entrance, and you have to go up the stairs to the second floor to find reception, and when you find it, chances are there's nobody behind the desk. It's not a dump, even if there are bars on the windows rather than glass. Some nice tiles mind you and the room always has a fresh bowl of fruit on the table. No toilet, just a jug of water and a hand basin. Bathroom is a few doors along. No tub, just a shower and a museum toilet, meaning, it doesn't always flush. It's an old hotel, with a courtyard and all sorts of plants, the sort of place that might've been a hacienda for some Portuguese explorer. Could be, as it's called the Cabral, and Cabral is the guy who discovered Brazil, isn't he?

Cheap. I'll make a profit out of this, as it's about half as much as Alfredo gave me for a per diem. Registered under a phony name—Eddie's idea, although I dropped the hint when he brought me here. William Hertz. Fits the face, the hand, eh. Don't know if voodoo priests can read anyways or even if they know my name but if they knew where to set the hex, they probably have my name. When I look around Copa, I have the feeling that a lotta people are hanging around here under an alias. Lot of theatre, lot of putting on the Ritz.

Plenty of flashy metal around too, the sort of chariots people with dough drive. I'm sitting in a little cafe, don't know what it's called, just easy, with tables on the sidewalk patio, finishing up a glass of *chopp* and a little plate of *refeicao* when this bomb deluxe pulls up just across the street. Never seen anything like it before, looks like something dreamed up by a rocket engineer. Whoever drives this is no *favelado*. Big coupe with wire racing wheels and sweeping fenders. No bumpers to mess up the flow. Skirts on the back with chrome flashings. Two door. Long and low like a cheetah stretched out for speed—even when it's parked. You got to have bucks for one of these, maybe own a plantation or an aircraft factory. Talking about aircraft—the windshield is split in two like the cockpit window of a DC 2 and the wipers are hinged from the roof. Italian speed art, I'm thinking. Classic streamline era design, just like those magazine ads where everything is just an impression, a blur, stuff that just plays on your mind. Desire on wheels, man.

Later learn it's a 1936 Bugatti Type 57S Atlantic. Some car... some women.

Lucy Barasso, and maybe her mother. I'm so mesmerized by the car I almost miss the real show, the Milano clothes and the bitch legs that swing from the shadow of the bitch mobile like a movie routine. Almost call out, but that would entail removing the fag from my mouth, so I just drop some money on the table, slither across the *rua*, follow. They go straight into the Copa Palace by a side door, as this certainly isn't the lobby entrance, but of course rich cariocas would never use the front door. I'm thinking I'm going to get hassled by some suitcase jockey, but then, what the hell, am I not a handsome gringo, so why wouldn't I have business at the Palace? Can smell their perfume even when I lose sight of them in the twists and curves, the ascents and descents. They're moving with a purpose, like they're late for an important date.

This is certainly a grand hotel, grander than anything I've ever visited, except in pictures. Sure, it has the usual colonnades, vaulted ceilings, hardwood floors, dead air carpets, potted ferns, crystal chandeliers... marble here, marble there... Roman arches and Greek stairways, just like the pictures in my old school encyclopedia of the ancient world... I'm hard on their tail when they go into a restaurant, the one with the bamboo furniture and the potted orchestra palms, extends onto the terrace with a view of the beach and Sugarloaf. Not that busy, but I've already eaten lunch, and well, I'd be the uninvited guest. Maybe I can ambush Lucy on the way out, accidentally on purpose.

I'm just stepping back when I see a familiar statuesque figure. My heart jolts, no lie. Uma. She's going into the pergola by a different door, don't know if she's seen me or not. She intersects with Lucy and her mother and they embrace the way glamorous women do, kisses and excited chatter. My mouth goes dry. How is it possible that I've held two of these women in my arms, made love to neither? Sense of inferiority, lack of confidence or maybe I just don't give a damn. Or maybe I just don't know how to play the game. Dishonesty between men is to be expected, but with women it's verboten. My mother. Must be my mother, for sure as hell I can be a two-faced sonofabitch.

There's a waiter at my shoulder with a menu.

I say, "Where's the bar?"

The waiter points to an elevated area which he says is the entrance to the lounge. Good. Can order a beer and maybe watch the women, take in the atmosphere. The lounge is long and narrow, with a hardwood runway and carpet on the sides where the tables line the walls, which are mostly windows you can't see through, fancy leaded glass. Tough to get a view without being obvious. Just one or two people in there, as most are outside.

There's a black guy looking at me. He's not real black yet he's not Teuto-Brasiliero either, some white guy with a tan. One of his eyes is a bit twisted, just enough to make him look like he doesn't give a shit for the Ten Commandments. Medium build and I'm wondering how long his arms are, if he can throw a straight punch, or if he doesn't bother with fisticuffs, has other ways of neutralizing someone he considers an enemy. Hope not. The Copa Palace isn't the sort of place I want to use Oswald to settle a homicidal maniac. Maybe he thinks I'm Hollywood and he's running movies in his mind and then again, maybe he isn't really looking at me at all. We'll see.

A beer, some peanuts... ten times what it costs across the street.

Put my hand in my pocket. The Queen. Had forgotten all about her. I put the chess piece on the table. I'd promised the Zs I'd make the delivery, yet somehow it seems no big deal. Spin her around in my fingers, just like a salt shaker. Must be an heirloom, a thing of sentimental affection because I can't see any other value. Was this the Queen that was on the board when Kallingram made his big comeback? The swindle? Don't know, wasn't watching.

I'm just trying to get Uma into focus when a man with a military haircut joins Cyclops, who's still giving me the one good rude eye he has. The new man is big—too big for his suit—and wearing shades. He doesn't sit down. He and Cyclops exchange a few words and then they amble over and sit down at my table, one on each side so's I'm trapped.

Shades snaps his fingers, says, "Documents."

I say, "Excuse me... who are you?"

This fellow with the shades is certainly sullen. He's like one of them bad Buddhas, all pout and no smile.

Cyclops says, "You have a passport?"

I reach into my inside pocket; it's right there, nice and snug behind Oswald. I'm thinking do I just play this out or what. I try the passport. Cyclops checks it out.

"Russian?" he says.

"I'm a Canadian," I say.

"Communist?" he says.

"I'm a tourist," I say. "You can see I have a legitimate entry stamp."

Cyclops passes my passport to Shades, says, "*O que voce acha?*"

Shades holds it close to his nose, sniffs. "*Cheira a merda.*"

Cyclops says, "You're a guest at this hotel?"

I say, "I'm having a beer, is what. Who are you? Hotel security?"

Shades hisses, says, "You're a fucking communist asshole."

Cyclops nods, tosses my passport onto the table. "This is a forgery," he says. "You're Russian."

"No, amigo," I say. "I am not Russian."

"You look like a Russian," says Cyclops. "Who are you? Why are you in Rio de Janeiro?"

"Heard it was beautiful," I say. "It is."

Cyclops says to Shades, "*Eh, ele vem aqui para as mulheres.*"

Shades is lining me up like an artillery gun, dead eyes for death. Cyclops has one good eye on me, the other on Sugarloaf. I casually reach out, recover my passport, leave my hand close to Oswald. Cyclops meanwhile picks up the chess piece, looks it over.

"You play chess, *senhor comunista*?" he says.

His voice is high, has a female squeak about it, like he's in drag and doesn't know it.

"Sure I do," I say. "You want a game?"

"Artists play chess," he says. "You a communist artist?"

This is left-field, don't know what he's digging for. Shake my head, say, "I'm not an artist."

Now Shades is inspecting the chess piece. He sniggers, says, "*Uma ficha para seu cu.*"

No reaction from me, so Cyclops says, "What's the problem, *senhor*? You don't speak Brazilian? I'll tell you what the Sergeant says... he says your Queen is a plug for your asshole. Now why would he say that?"

I shrug, say, "Guess he's used one before."

Cyclops says to Shades, "*Ele diz que e precio um para conhecer um...* how about that? A funny communist?"

I reach for the chess piece, drop it in the side pocket of my jacket, say, "Gentlemen, I think I'll just move along. I know when I'm not welcome."

At this point Cyclops drops a comic book on the table. Looks familiar but then all comics look familiar. This one is pretty crude.

"You draw this?" says Cyclops. "You bring this filth to our country?"

"What are you talking about?" I say.

"You are '*Senhor Prolific*,'" he says. "You are the artist."

'*Senhor Prolific*'—don't have a clue what this blind ape is talkin' about. They're bent cops and they're trying to frame me up for something. Incredible... well maybe not so incredible except for the fact that we're in the Copacabana Palace Hotel and you'd think this would be considered sacred ground second only to the Saint Sebastion Cathedral and you'd think they'd save this sort of shit for the street or the rubber room. I stand up, try to look indignant while calculating a fast exit. To be caught with a chess piece is one thing but with a Colt 911 is quite another.

By now we're definitely drawing the attention of others. We're all on our feet now and it doesn't look like they're going to let me go quietly. And then who shows up but Lucinda and her mother.

"What is the trouble here?" says Mrs. Barasso with the natural authority of those with power. "Why are you bothering our friend?"

"Your friend?" says Cyclops.

"Yes, *senhor*, our friend and our guest," says Mrs. Barasso. "Who are you? What are you? *Policia Federal* or *Policia Civil*? Neither? Municipal? Do you have some identification?"

Both apes reach for their bully tags, flash their metal. "I am 1st Lieutenant Jorge Horace Repo. And you, *senhora*?"

"I am *Senhora* Leonora Barasso... I'm sure you know who I am."

Cyclops would like to smile but the occasion isn't yet ripe for grovelling.

"Repo, Repo... I've heard of you," says Mrs. Barasso. "They call you Horus, *corrigir*?"

"I don't know who calls me that," says Cyclops. "We all have nicknames, I guess."

"Well Horus isn't as bad as the Angel of Death, Lieutenant," says Mrs. Barasso. "You know, it's really outrageous to carry on this sort of harassment in our most esteemed hotel. Now Lieutenant Repo, listen closely: I know the owner, and I know the Chief of Police... and I also know the Minister in charge of all police in the country... and I do have occasion to speak with all of these people. But I suppose this is just a misunderstanding...."

"I have orders, *senhora*," says Cyclops. "It concerns foreigners."

"Foreigners?"

"Communists. As we know, the Comintern has been active recently in our city."

"Does our guest look like a communist? Or should I say, would *Senhor* Barasso and I have a guest who is a communist?"

Cyclops nods slowly, but he isn't willing to let it go.

"No, *senhora*... but you might have a guest who is an artist, *sim*?"

"You mean, because I am an artist, Lieutenant? What of it?"

"Perhaps you've heard of *Senhor Prolific*—"

Lucy speaks up: "He draws the dirty comics, mama."

Mrs. Barasso looks down at the comic book on the table.

"Is this one? Let me have a look at that."

Cyclops passes it to her, says, "I warn you, *senhora*..."

Mrs. Barasso flicks a couple of pages. "Who's this supposed to be? President Vargas?"

Cyclops says, "It's filth."

Mrs. Barasso smiles, says, "It might be filth, it might not be filth... it might even be erotic art. But whatever it is, *Senhor* Prolific writes in Portuguese and our guest does not speak Portuguese, so therefore our guest cannot be '*Senhor Prolific*'—*corrigir*?"

"Perhaps... but there are those who speak who cannot write, and those who write who cannot speak."

"Beautifully said, Lieutenant... perhaps you can be a poet when you retire."

Now Cyclops backs off. That twisted eye is almost where it should be, parallel and contrite.

"Perhaps our information is incorrect."

"It is incorrect. Our city owes this young gentleman a debt of gratitude, as he is the man who shot the wild *gato* that held us all in terror. You read about it in the newspapers, claro."

Boy, I wish she hadn't said that, as I think these two apes could easily be apostles of the old religion. They want their mitts on me and while I'm not sure if they really think I'm *Senhor Prolific*, I'm sure they want to get me in their temple. However, we're done for now, and I walk away with the women like an old time gallant. We leave by the same route as we entered.

When we get to the car, both women start to laugh.

"*Senhor Prolific*!" says Lucy. "Imagine!"

"Who is this *Senhor Prolific*?" I say.

"The *Senhor* is the author and perhaps the illustrator of the Mexican Bible," says Mrs. Barasso.

"Salacious comics," says Lucy. "They say they come from Mexico."

"I'd never seen one before," says Mrs. Barasso. "Manuelo would have a fit. This one has Vargas intimately engaged with Carmen Miranda.

These two policemen are Federal, so the President is obviously trying to hunt down the perpetrators. It was different, of course, when the stories featured soccer players and film stars. He and all our other men lined up happily at the tobacconist's to buy a copy from under the counter and laugh their heads off at the club or in the barracks... but now, eh, this is different. *A cobra mordo o rabo*—the snake bites its tail."

"I can assure you I'm not *Senhor Prolific, Senhora* Barasso," I say. "And I've never seen that comic book before."

"Please... you can call me Leonora... I know we missed being introduced the other evening. Lucy has told me all about you."

"Oh... but what does she know?"

"I know you're a smashing dancer," says Lucy.

"And you're a damn good shot," says Mrs. Barasso. "Although it's a shame about that beautiful cat."

"Thorsen didn't really mean it, did you?" says Lucy. "He loves animals."

"Really Lucy," says Mrs. Barasso. "You're sense of humour is like an American teenager's."

"What's that exactly, mother?" says Lucy.

"Sarcastic, sick, and impolite," says Mrs. Barasso. "Remember, *Senhor* Thorsen, Lucy is just seventeen."

"Eighteen," says Lucy. "Soon."

"You must join us for dinner tonight," says Mrs. Barasso. "We're all alone. Manuelo is in Sao Paulo on business. Say, seven o'clock?"

"Very kind of you, senhora."

"Where are you staying? I'll send a car for you."

"The Cabral."

"The Cabral...?"

"I know it," says Lucy.

She looks at me and winks.

CHAPTER SEVENTEEN:

EVERYONE WANTS TO BE A NAZI

SENHORA BARASSO speaks better English than I do, and I suppose that's because she is English, was born there, English father, Spanish mother. She tells me some of this herself, and Lucy fills in the dots when mama isn't around. Lucy's the one who comes for me in the Bugatti. What a car, what a ride. Don't know why the old man lets her drive it, but if he's not around, guess she can play. Nice dash, nice instruments. Must be what it's like to fly some hep plane, like a Lockheed Electra. When she steps on the gas, it feels like we're about to lift off.

When I was a student in Vancouver I briefly dated a rich gal but I never set foot in her West End mansion, let alone met her parents. I wasn't looking for a meal ticket then and I'm not now, although Barasso might have something for me beyond entertaining his daughter. Just hedging my bets, y'know? Alfredo seems like a dead end, although if Mac and the boys back in Ottawa want me to keep stroking Fredo, guess that's what I'll do. But we don't get along and instinct tells me I'm not in the Abwehr's future plans. If I want to be smoking Cohibas and chowing scotch seared steak, I have to be thinking ahead.

"How come you're a friend of Eduardo's?" says Lucy.

"Met him by accident," I say. "First day in town. He found me a place to stay. He seems to be well-connected."

"He is."

"Works for some government ministry, doesn't he?"

"Eduardo? No way. He works for my dad."

"Your dad? What does Eddie do for your dad?"

"I don't know. He makes things happen. My dad has all sorts of people working for him, doing stuff. Guess Eddie is a manager."

"Nice... but what does he manage?"

"I don't know. People. Politics, real square stuff. And maybe some mean stuff."

"Mean stuff?"

"My dad's business needs lots of security."

"I can understand that... but, um, how come all that security couldn't take care of a hungry cat the other night?"

"Maybe they like cats."

"Oh really? When a lady gets killed, how much love can there be? Maybe they're into voodoo."

"Don't be silly."

We're pulling through the gateway without stopping for the gatekeeper's blessing. Guess he recognizes a Bugatti when he sees one. Then again, maybe he lets everything through.

"How come Hercules there couldn't stop the cat coming in?" I say. "He's got eyes, a nose, plenty of muscle."

"The wall is two or three kilometers long. Boy, you're really obsessed with that gato."

"I shot it, didn't I? Forget it... say, do you know where this address is?"

She kills the motor, takes a look. "Not Rio," she says. "That's a Petropolis address."

"Where's that?"

"In the mountains... not far."

"What's 'not far'—can I walk it?"

She giggles. "No *Senhor* Prolific, it's 60 kilometers. You will need a car."

"Hmm... know anyone with a car?"

"If you're a nice boy, I might drive you. But I won't drive *Senhor* Prolific...."

"Tomorrow?"

"*Sim.* Who do you know in Petro?"

"Someone I met on the Southern Cross."

"Not another Nazi, I hope. Everyone wants to be a Nazi these days but they're so boring, doncha think? No? Who is she?"

"*Fraulein* Uma."

"Such a liar! Uma is staying at the Copa and you know so."

"I didn't, until I saw you guys earlier."

"You've met her? Beautiful, yes? Don't lie."

"She's o.k. Married, though, isn't she?"

"She's not married. She's a model and you know what models are like."

"No, I don't know."

"What were you doing at the Copa anyway? Hoping to run into her?"

My laugh is kinda phony. Not true, of course, but could be. Want to pump Lucy some more about Uma but this is when her mother shows up, raps on the car window like we've been necking. You know, Leonora might use a paint brush but she also uses a leash, I'm thinking. Fine. I don't want to be accused of reckless behaviour even if her daughter is playing me for practice. Women are always trying to be friendly with animals and some animals are always trying to be friendly with women. We sort of play around in the reckless middle ground, don't we? Thing is, you have to start out with a code even if at the end of it all the only code you have left is around your ankles.

We have dinner in a small room just off the kitchen. Big long windows that look out over the garden. Couple of servants, black of course. It feels quite different from the dining experience on the ship, even though it's sort of the same. It's formal, and you should know how to use a knife and fork, even if you don't know what the hell the food is. Fish, I think. It's mushed in some sort of vegetable sauce, so I'm thinking a spoon might work, but hot damn it tastes good whatever which way you shovel the gumbo. The women don't eat much, they just like talking.

"University?" says Lucy. "I'd rather travel. The Calistros are sending Mia to Europe."

"But you don't like Mia," says Mrs. Barasso. "Anyway, your father wants you to go to university."

"You went to Europe."

"That was different. I grew up in London, and you could travel overnight to Paris."

"You ran away, mama. You did what you liked."

"I did what I had to do to stay alive."

"Is that what you call it? Mama was an artist's model."

My mouth is full, so all I can do is nod. Mrs. B seems amused.

"Yes," she says. "I'm hanging in some famous galleries, although you would never recognize me."

"Modern art," says Lucy. "People look like cartoons."

"Sure," I say. "It's decorative. I like some of it."

"Have you studied art, Mr. Thorsen?" says Mrs. Barasso.

"Not at all," I say. "A camera seems easier."

Mrs. Barasso laughs. "*Claro*—why use a bow and arrow if you can use a gun?"

She's an easy lady to be around, rich or not. Don't think I've ever met any female like her, except maybe Lotte Z. Women without sons, except for the men they live with. They look at you a different way than most mothers do, maybe as a memory of someone left in a ditch or with the gypsies. Truthfully, I'm starting to find her more interesting than her daughter, although maybe it's the package. Guys are always saying, hey, want to see the future, look at the mother.

We close out with coffee and cigarettes, although Lucy refuses my offer of a fag, no doubt because she knows mama won't allow it. I tell them a bit about Canada. Leave a lot out, natch. I find I do better with a bit of mystery attached.

I say, "It was interesting to meet Major Kallingram at your party."

Mrs. Barasso says, "Major who? I don't think we met."

"German, officer with one of those Nazi police units. Remember the Southern Cross? The magician?"

"I remember the magician... Uma let him cut her in two."

"Well he's really a major in the German SS."

Mrs. B looks at Lucy, says, "Was the magician at our party?"

Lucy says, "I didn't see him. Was he in uniform?"

I say, "Your dad introduced him to me. Him and that Italian guy, a Captain in one of their Alpine regiments."

"Well I know him," says Mrs. Barasso. "Captain Suckert. He gave me one of his books. Very interesting man. Surrealist."

Lucy says, "You're kidding about the magician guy, aren't you?"

I say, "Same name, same face."

Lucy says, "This is crazy. Does this mean because he's a magician he can be anyone he wants?"

Mrs. Barasso starts laughing, then Lucy. "Just imagine," says Mrs. B, spluttering, "just imagine if everybody at the party was pretending to be someone else! Now that's surrealism."

"Yeah, just a bunch of *favelados* in costumes," says Lucy.

"Maybe I dreamed it," I say. "Same name, same face."

"Wouldn't the magician have stayed on the boat?" says Mrs. Barasso.

"Isn't he part of the entertainment?"

I shrug. "Ask *Fraulein* Uma."

"I'll ask my husband when he comes back from Paulo," says Mrs. Barasso. "Now, sir, would you like to see some more of the house?"

There's plenty to see, although rooms are just rooms to me, and pictures of ancestors just mess up the walls, give the spiders somewhere to hide. Lucy probably thinks the same as she excuses herself, disappears somewhere. Lots of mahogany and marble, church glass and big vases, ceiling fans, dead clocks, flies and other weird insects. Lucky the ceilings are high. Somewhere I hear a piano, a bit of Eddie Duchin or something similar. Duchin sounds like a lot of people, so a lot people can sound like him. Pop jazz. I'm interested but Leonora Barasso is steering me towards her studio.

She's using a stick. Sometimes she needs it, sometimes not, she says. Hip. Blames high heels, the weather, the stress, the big party the other night. Far as I can see, she moves pretty good. Maybe that stick is for something else, like me.

Studio is at the north end of the house. Yellow door with a clown painted on it, a motif, not a portrait. She stops, hand on the door nob. Her eyes are gray and I remember Lucy's are brown. Sometimes she needs glasses, and she keeps her hair tied back and clamped but I bet it's Lucy-similar, like her rack... a bit more mature, claro, but similar. Women. They're more like sisters than mother and daughter. I wonder.

"What do you think of this new invention, television, Thorsen?" says Mrs. B. "Should I be worried?"

"I've never seen it," I say.

"I saw a demonstration in New York. We have a friend here in Rio who owns a few newspapers and radio stations, and he says it will replace everything... art will be television or not art at all."

"Just radio with a picture. One megahertz band."

"Oh, so you do know something about it. One day you should meet our friend... Assis Chateaubriand. An art lover, despite his brutal ways."

"Brutal? You mean he steps on insects?"

"Yes. Insects, people, institutions... Chato will not be denied. Anyway he wants to bring television to Brazil."

"Most people have radio sets here?"

"Goodness, no. So who would be able to buy television?"

"Could be used in theatres."

"You mean replace the movies?"

"TV pictures aren't big enough for that. Businesses could use them... cafes, bars. I wouldn't worry. Comic books are here to stay."

She chuckles. "You mean *Senhor* Prolific will continue in business?"

We go into her studio. Big, messy, full of junk is the first impression, but then I guess I know nothing about art and artists. Stacks of canvases and a few unframed paintings on the walls, all modern stuff, all kid's stuff except it's a bit too slick for kids, maybe. There's a big old camera, the accordion type with a brass lens, the sort of gear some guy with a horse and a Winchester 73 photographed the Old West with, or maybe the Panama Canal dig. Other cameras too, newer.

Big old camera, big old couch. I flop down, let myself sink to shape, say, "So how did you learn all this stuff? Paint, photograph, I mean..."

"I learned in Paris. I went there with an older man, a German artist I met in London. I was also a model for the surrealist photographer Bix Photon—not his actual name, claro—so I learned a lot about experimental methods from him... darkroom manipulation, mostly."

"What a life..."

"Yes. What a life. Would you care for something to drink? A beer?"

"Sure, if it's no trouble, *Senhora*."

She bangs her foot on a lumpy area of the carpet. This is an old time bell ringer back to the kitchen pantry or the *despensa* as they call it. Minute or two later one of the servants shows up and what do you know, in short order I have my beer and Mrs. B. her gin and tonic. Easy to be an artist in this sort of world. I wonder how she did it, how she hooked up with Manuelo Barasso, millionaire Brazilian business man.

"Skoal," I say, raising my glass.

"Skoal," she says.

She's fumbling to light a cigarette. I whip out the nifty Southern Cross flamer I picked up on the ship, get her burning. She settles back, puts her beams on me.

"I'm looking for a model," she purrs. "Two, actually."

"Lots of beauties in Rio," I say.

"Oh I have the female," she says. "It's the male I need. Interested?"

"Me?"

"Want to make some money? I pay my models, unlike most artists."

This is a strange proposition, something I've never considered in my wildest dreams. A model? Would I end up as a statue in a garden with no head and no cock, just something for the birds to shit on?

"Would I have to take my clothes off?"

"That wouldn't bother you, would it?"

"You'd be surprised. My parents are Lutheran."

"Oh... God fearing people, are they?"

I laugh. "Hardly. They don't even live together."

"Well, think about it."

I nod. It's hard to refuse a lady, especially when she's dangling her daughter.

"Tomorrow I got to make a quick trip to Petropolis. Lucy says she'll drive me... if that's alright with you."

"It is… as long as you don't take your clothes off."

To this, I don't say a damn thing, even laugh, despite her amused expression. Can hear the piano faintly which reminds me that real beauty is often in the distance. I'm fed up playing radio man on Amazon Avenue, but is this any better? Feel like a flamingo who's always sucking up to women while messing with their hair in the salon.

"I can write you a cheque," says Mrs. B. "A young man always needs some *grana*."

"I'll think about it," I say.

CHAPTER EIGHTEEN

DEATH IN PETROPOLIS

I CAN SEE WHY Z chose Petropolis rather than Rio because it's in the mountain rainforest, cooler, more like Alpine Austria and less than two hours from Rio anyway, although we make it in just over one hour, even with a stop to take in the view. Valleys, mist, smell of rain. Guess we go up about 6000 feet by the time we get to town.

Quaint. Got a palace and a fancy museum and a bunch of canals to feed the jungles they call gardens. All sorts of houses, sizes and styles. Lot of modified Kraut, sort of Mediterranean Survivalist. Steep roofs, verandas, yards that blend with the forest. Lucy tells me the last Emperor of Brazil, Don Pedro and his wife Dona Isabel, had their summer palace built here and in fact they're buried here too. You can check all this out at the Imperial Museum if you have the time and you can see the small bachelor house of Santos-Dumont the famous Brazilian aviator. A coffee millionaire, just like Lucy's dad, and a lot more interesting than Don Pedro because he moved to Paris and started making airships so he could fly along the boulevards instead of walking. Brazilians consider him to be the real pioneer of aviation, not the Wright Brothers, but of course they would. They say he hung himself in '32, others say he was murdered. Depressed by what Vargas and the gaucho cabal were up to. He was big news for a while, although I had no idea he lived in Petropolis, anymore than I knew Petropolis existed before I met the Zs.

We're not in the Bugatti. Good thing too, as it turns out, as the Buga draws attention. We're in Eddie's heap, the one with the cop radio. Lucy says she doesn't want to risk banging up her dad's car but I think mama put her foot down. The fact that Lucy showed up in Eddie's car confirms what she said about him working for Senhor Barasso. Too bad in one way as I was hoping to get a chance to drive the Bugatti, but it doesn't matter, car is a car... especially when you've got a nice looking young babe as a navigator. I'm looking forward to seeing the Zs, to handing off the chess piece, showing off Lucinda. Assuming, that is, they'll be home.

House is easy enough to find, sits on the hill above the street, veranda and big windows facing south. Shallow pitch red roof. Some people might call it a bungalow. Looks quiet... what time is it? Going 11:30 am, warm out, pockets of mist hanging in the cloud forest. Large bird circling, wings extended, gliding on the thermals. Nice spot. Pause on the top step to check the view. House is not unlike many of those back home in Kelowna, where folks sit watching the lake, waiting for the postman, rain, or some stranger with a different story to tell. I know. I was always waiting, bored out of my mind.

"No car," says Lucy. "Do they have a car?"

"Don't know," I say. "Doubt it, somehow."

I try ringing the doorbell, try knocking. Try looking in the window. Try holding my breath and listening. Then I try the door but it's locked.

"What do you want to do?" says Lucy.

"Let's wait in the car for a bit, see if they show up," I say.

Have a weird feeling. It's in the air, in the silence. The car feels more secure. Lucy snuggles in close, murmurs, "We could go someplace private."

I turn on the radio, roll the condenser. Right away there's a voice transmission, loud, real close. Portuguese.

"What's this?" I say. "Understand any of it, Lucy?"

"*Os homi*... the cops, I think," she says. "They're talking about a car... two people, a man, a woman... huh."

We keep listening. Frankly I'm surprised these hicks would have a radio. Military, more like.

"*Esperrado*... what does that mean?"

"Means 'suspicious'. Say, are we being watched?"

Check the rear view mirror, look up and down the street. Dead. Some light traffic flicking past at the junction but nothing moving around here except the guy working in his yard couple of doors down. Lady and her dog in the distance coming this way but no cops that I can see. Transmission stops. Again, that weird silence which isn't really silence.

"Hang tough," I say to Lucy. "I'm going to take another look."

Try the front door again, then walk the veranda, even the back.

160

Nothing. I'm wondering if this is even the right address. When I get back to the car, Lucy is talking to the lady with the dog. The lady looks like she's just come from the cathedral and a few unanswered prayers.

"*Suicidio,*" she says, looking from Lucy to me.

"Suicide two days ago," says Lucy. "The German *senhor y senhora.*" Austrian, I think, although the technicality hardly matters. The news should be a shock, yet somehow it isn't.

"Is there a relative or a friend around?" I say.

"*Que eles tem familia... ou um amigo quie vive em Petro?*"

The lady turns, jerks her head towards the man who's still working on something while keeping an eye on us.

"*Perguntar ao Senhor Cabanas,*" she says.

Ask the man. I nod, say, "Who found them?" Lucy translates. The lady gets flustered, like she just got groped by the priest.

"Noela," she says.

"Her dog," says Lucy. Dog is real ugly, one of those stunted toy bulls with no tail and a face like a 100 year old baby.

"The lady see the bodies herself?"

Lucy asks the question and the lady just jerks her head towards the man she calls Cabanas. "*Perguntar-lhe,*" she says.

Yeah, I know: talk to the guy. We thank the lady, then take a stroll across the street. The man is peeling dead fronds off his tropicals. Looks about 60. Cabanas... that's his name, really? Red face, timid belly. Looks old country German to me. Guess it's the little burgomeister hat and the leather mittens.

"*Guten Tag,*" I say. "*Wir kommen zu spat.*"

"Too late?" he says. "Ja. A tragedy."

"We met Herr Zion and his wife on the ship from New York recently."

"You're German?"

"Danish."

"You speak German well."

"And you, sir, are from the old country?"

"Ja... distantly. I was in Argentina for many years, and I've been here for many more. Yes, yes... a tragedy."

"The lady says they committed suicide."

Now he looks grim, real grim. Mouth tightens, bends.

"You found them?" I say.

He nods. "The dog was barking. Seems Herr Zion would give it a biscuit every morning, so Noela liked to visit. I went over because she just wouldn't stop barking."

"Must have been a shock...."

"Ja. It was a shock."

"You know Herr Zion was a famous writer?"

"So it is said."

"Jewish."

"He was? I didn't know. He looked normal."

"How, ah... was it pills? Did they take pills?"

He glazes over.

"I knew she was ill," I say. "But suicide? Both of them?"

"It wasn't suicide," he says quietly. "They were murdered."

I look at Lucy, but of course she doesn't understand German, is smiling politely.

"Murdered?" I say. "How? Why? Nothing about this in the Rio papers."

"The police are keeping it wrapped," he says. "I was told to say nothing. *Mund geschlossen!*"

"Was it a robbery?"

"No, no... it was butchery."

And this is all I can get out of him, as he clams right up.

"No suspect?" I say.

He just shakes his head, looks faraway. "The dog wouldn't stop barking," is all he says.

We were being watched, of course. Watched and tailed. We're within sight of the Crystal Palace when we're flagged down by a couple of motorcycle cops. Damn near run them down, as Lucy is chattering away about the Palace, how it was a big greenhouse built by the French to grow orchids and somehow it got dismantled, ended up here in Petropolis. A Ford pulls in behind us and a couple of suits get out.

I roll down the window. Young guy. Baby fat face. Heavy glasses. Shoulder holster. Looks at me, looks at her.

"*Credenciais, por favor,*" he says.

Lucy opens her purse, gets her license, although I'm the one behind the wheel. I have my passport, though. He checks our stuff quickly, confers with his partner.

"*Siga os oficiais, por favor.*"

Lucy nods, says to me, "They want us to follow them."

I say, "Figures."

Lucy says to the cop, "*Qual e o problema?*"

They want to ask us some questions, what else. Notice he doesn't give us back our I.D. The two motorcycle cops jump start their bikes, roar off. We follow, and the suits follow us. Somehow it doesn't feel like El Presidente's motorcade.

"What is with these jerks?" says Lucy.

"Guess we're suspects," I say.

"Suspects for what?" says Lucy. "We didn't do anything."

"I know, doll," I say. "But somebody did. That German I talked to says the Zs were murdered."

"Wonderful," says Lucy. "This mean we won't be back for dinner?"

"Sorry."

She fidgets in her seat, then of all things, tries to wipe the lipstick from her mouth with the hem of her blouse. "I'm afraid, Thorsen," she says. "They'll try and implicate us. Brazil isn't the USA."

"You've got nothing to worry about... once they realize who you are, you'll be o.k."

"I've never known anyone who was actually murdered. People my parents know, sure... but I don't know them. Who would want to murder these *pessoas*? There are no *favelados* in Petro. This is a nice place. People are normal."

Remember back on the ship Z talking about Hitler and his hate for the Jews. I'm wondering if the problems of the old country caught up with Z and his wife, that Brazil was no sanctuary after all. For sure this damn chess piece has something to do with it. But what? Starting to feel like a mouse who's so busy with the cheese he doesn't see the trap.

Actually Lucy has nothing to be concerned about at all. A name is a name and Barasso is a name these folks recognize. Coffee and pastries for her, the interrogation room for me. Picture of what looks like President Vargas on the wall. I'm offered a smoke—it's strong, definitely local.

"How do you like Brazil? Nice beaches, yes?"

"Yes."

"But too hot, yes?"

Is he practicing his English? Put on a uniform and these guys start making a game out of most situations. He's the boss, though. Captain somebody. Pancho moustache but no Pancho belly. Gold tooth, gold ring.

"Petro isn't hot," he says. "Petro has a friendly climate. Is this why you visit?"

"I came to see *Senhor* Zion."

"Claro. You are friends?"

"Met him on the ship from New York, couple of weeks ago. He and his wife invited me to visit them."

The Captain is nodding, seems satisfied. Bangs his hand on the table, stands up. "Come with me please."

We go down to the basement. Definitely cooler here, although you wouldn't want to keep too many stiffs waiting without ice. There's a smell, could be anything. Gas, chemical, decay, anything... something. Hate these places. However, my host doesn't waste any time.

"Is this the man you know as Stefan Zion?"

Dead man is unshaven, otherwise unmarked. Hair continues to grow, even after everything else has quit. All I can do is nod.

"You are certain, *Senhor*...."

Been holding my breath, feel real tight. I let it go.

"What happened to him?" I say. "The neighbours mentioned suicide."

The Captain pulls the sheet lower. Christ! The body is separated at the navel, like he's been pushed through a buzz saw, except this is a clean cut... if you can call this sort of butchery clean. The upper torso and the lower pelvic area are a bit out of alignment, like the way you coax a puzzle into position. First thought is this is some sort of ugly autopsy manoeuver.

"This look like suicide to you, *Senhor*?"

What can I say? I'm looking, but by now I'm going blind.

"They do the same thing to his wife."

"Why?"

"We don't know why. Murder is one thing, but to murder like this is another. Political, yes?"

If by "political" the Captain means sending a message, I guess Z's death is political. But I dunno—was Jack the Ripper political?

We go back upstairs. When you've just seen something like this, yeah, maybe you're dizzy, maybe you can't get your breath, and maybe the world is a blur, your memory scrubbed like you been clubbed. Thank God he didn't ask me to look at Mrs. Z.

"So, *Senhor* Thorsen, I take it you can account for your whereabouts two nights ago?"

"Yes. I was at a party given by *Senhor* Manuelo Barasso."

"Ah... would you be the pessoa who shot the jaguar?"

I nod. "It killed a woman... a guest."

"*Muito bom, muito bom...* I read about this in O Mundo. Imagine—a jaguar killing people in Rio. Is this your first jaguar kill?"

"Yes."

"What brings you to Rio? We don't see many Canadians here."

"I was on my way to Buenos Aires. Thought I might get work in the oil fields. Might end up there eventually."

"Yes. Once you master the samba, the tango is easy."

He's not pitching this as a joke. It's like he's remembering an old mistress or a holiday in Aires... or both.

164

"You met Miss Barasso on the ship?"

"Yeah... the romance carried over."

"Very good. Just as long as you aren't some Red Casanova, *Senhor.*"

'Red Casanova'—what's he suggesting? I'm a Soviet honeybee?

"Where are you staying?"

"Hotel Cabral."

"Have you registered with your embassy?"

"Yes."

"This is an ugly business. People will think there is a maniac on the loose. I caution you to say nothing to anyone about this matter for now."

That's it. He actually reaches out, shakes my hand. What does this mean? Goodbye for now, or forever? As we drive back to Rio, the mountains of the Serra Fluminense are very pretty.

I FIND MAC ALL ALONE in the Reading Room deep into a copy of the London *Illustrated News*. Months old, but it's the photos of the Red attack on the pocket-battleship Deutschland anchored in the harbour at Ibiza and the reprisal shelling of the Spanish port city of Almeria that has him interested.

"I'm askin' you," he says. "Who's this war really between? The Republicans and the Nationalists, or the Soviets and the Nazis? I think we know, eh. I was just talking to an attache fresh from London and he says Great Britain is starting a National Register for conscription, starting December 1... just a matter of days."

I sit down, smell the leather. He looks me over, says, "What's up? What've you got for me?"

"Am I on the blackboard yet?"

"Yeah, you're on. Fed checks into an account at the Bank of Commerce. What've you got for me?"

I plunk the Queen on the fat arm of my chair. He's not impressed.

"You been playing chess?"

Tell him the story of the Z's, how I met them on the SS Southern Cross, how I went to Petropolis yesterday, found they'd been murdered.

"And they gave you that chess piece to... what? Clear customs? Must be worth something."

"You tell me."

He takes a look. "Maybe there's something inside."

"Don't think so. Looks and feels solid to me."

Mac turns it over, examines it closely.

"You try unscrewing the crown?"

"I tried everything."

"It could be a key to unlock something, or could be it's got a secret chamber. They could have diamonds in this."

"That's what I thought, but shake it, you hear nuthin'."

"You have to ask yourself, what were they afraid of losing? And is this why they were murdered?"

"Been asking myself that question all night, all day since I got back."

"You look all shook up, kid."

"Why cut 'em in two?" I say.

"Disposal, transportation. You can stack the body parts easier."

"Yeah, sure... possibly. But they weren't transported anyplace."

"Maybe the killer was interrupted."

"But why would the killer bother transporting them? If he was sending a message?"

"A disappearance is a lot cleaner."

"Yeah but that's just it, isn't it? So, were these killings meant to be clean or just plain dirty? The cuts I saw were real clean, not the sort of thing a guy who hunts deer could do."

"Part of the autopsy? Surgeon could do it."

"My first thought, Mac. I know next to nothing about autopsies but don't they just usually open 'em up, y'know, strategically?"

"Didn't the police say?"

"I didn't ask."

"And they're keeping it out of the papers..."

"I was told to keep my mouth shut. Same with the neighbours."

"This chap Z had an enemy. Wonder who."

I pick up the chess piece, juggle it. I'm thinking about Kallingram, have been thinking about him on and off since leaving Petro. The connection is obvious in one way, but distant in another. Sure, he likes using a saw, playing chess, dressing up... but murder? What for?

"Could this chess piece really have anything to do with it?" I say.

"Let me see it again --"

I pass it to Mac, who shakes it, gives it a couple of twists.

"I tried all that," I say.

"So this guy Z gives this to you on the ship, asks you to carry it through customs, then deliver it to him in Petropolis?"

"Yep. First I thought the address was for someone else, someone here in Rio... which makes it all the more weird. Why didn't he carry it through himself? Just a chess piece."

"Was he a chess player?"

"Yes he was... like I said."

"I say we cut 'er open, kid. Right through the middle."

"Wreck it?"

"Right through the middle... real careful."

I'm thinking, might as well, no harm now. Yet I'm loath to give up the Queen. "I'll get a hack-saw blade," I say.

"I got one at my place," says Mac. "I'll go back, do it right now."

I put my hand out. "I want to be there, Mac."

He looks a bit pissed, like, who is this kid? But he hands back the chess piece. He leaves first, after depositing a fart in his chair. He doesn't joke or apologize or maybe even notice. Guess living alone in Rio as a secret agent allows him to be rude and crude, or maybe he's just getting old. It's like the way he dresses, those loud shirts, buttoned all wrong like the Leaning Tower of Pisa—he just bends and blends.

I hang around for an hour, enough time to clear some space in case we're being watched, which I don't think we are. I write a couple of letters, one to my mother, the other to Aunt Renie. Say nothing about the murders, although I do mention shooting the big cat at the party. Enclose a news clipping. Won't be able to understand the lingo but they'll appreciate it anyway. Bit of excitement, eh. The boy does good.

Hop the tram for Santa Teresa, one of those buggies with no sides that the locals call a *bonde*. Electric. Fun, if you don't suffer from vertigo going over the Carioca Aqueduct. Black guys just hang onto the sides, ride for free. Women too... kids... even the bloody lizards. Get your pocket picked real easy, so you got to be alert, even if the passengers sitting down look asleep, just sway with the bump and grind like zombies dressed for the gig. Lanky black guy running behind the tram like he missed it or maybe he just likes running. Get off on the morro or the Two Brothers hill, which is Santa T. View is spectacular but after a couple of visits, you don't even notice.

I could hang out here. It's older, a bit more real than the Zona Sul, less middle-class. Cigarettes are cheaper, beer too. Maybe the chicks aren't premium, but how many does a guy need?

Don't know if I like the soldiers hanging around the junctions, the so-called military police. More of them about than you see in the Zona Sul. Last revolution was six years ago, so you'd think it was time to relax.

I go in, back door, unlocked, as arranged. He's got a little blade, low buzz, fine cut. He snaps his fingers impatiently, and I hand over the chess piece. He lays it on its side on the kitchen table, starts sawing gently.

"By the way, you shoot that panther?" he says. "Don't deny it."

"I had no choice, Mac. His ears went back and he started hissing and batting his paws in the air at me."

"So it weren't just some drunken fuckin' around."

"No way. Here's the thing: some voodoo guys from the *favela* are on my tail. Cat was their pet or something."

"You been threatened?"

"Not sure. Let's say this: I checked into a hotel under an alias for a couple of nights."

He stops sawing. "She's hollow, for sure—see? There's the sleeve. Probably a tube, a capsule, some sort of chamber."

He continues sawing, rotating the chess piece a little at a time.

"The oldest trick in the world," he says. "If a spy has a wooden leg, chances are it's hollow."

"You think Z was a spy?"

"Probably not... let's see, what have we got here?"

What we have is a small metal tube, a sleeve capped at both ends. Mac pops one with his thumb, shakes the tube, and small roll of microfilm drops onto his open palm. Looks like 16 millimeter, like the size you use in a small movie camera.

"Does this answer your question, boy? Does it? Let's see!"

He unspools the film carefully. Might be four frames... five, six.

"How do we read this?" I say, naive fellow that I am.

He goes to a drawer, comes back with what looks like a hefty wrist watch.

"What's that?" I say.

"Live and learn," he says. "This is a Dargon wrist watch, which is just a lens for reading micro-film."

He flips the glass open, and sure enough, you can load the film and read the frames one by one. He's looking, but he's stumped.

"Is this German?" he says.

I take a look, start reading: "*Inhalts-verzeichnis... Führer Spitzenreiter Richtlinie Anzal 49...* bloody hell, man, listen to this: Führer Directive Number 49 B July 18 1938... says, as I translate it, '*Following the occupation of the Iberian peninsula and the capture of Gibraltar, the Straits must be closed, the English to be prevented from gaining a footing on any of the Iberian islands, especially the Canaries and the Cape Verde Islands, and those in the deep Atlantic, including the Azores and Trinidad South, as these will assume additional naval importance after the operations for Gibraltar for both the British and for ourselves. Furthermore, the Cape Verde Islands and the Azores are vital for our Amerika project.*' "

"Sonofabitch," says Mac. "Hitler's intentions in his own words... let's look at the other frames."

He advances the film. Frame 2, more stuff from Führer Directive 49, including the implications for Brazil if the Germans seize Trinidad South and Fernando de Noronha to the north.

"Sonofabitch," says Mac, like he's muttering a mantra. "Everybody wants to get his hands on Fernando de Noronha... easy hop between the Verdes and Noronha. If he wants to launch an attack on the USA, sonofabitch this is the way to do it, goddamnit."

"For the *Amerika* project," I say. "Whatever that is."

"Could be, could be," says Mac.

"What was Z doing with this stuff?" I say.

"Jew, you say?" says Mac. "Maybe he thought it was insurance."

"More like a death sentence," I say.

"Probably acting as a courier," says Mac. "Maybe he didn't know what was sealed inside the chess piece."

Frankly Stefan Zion didn't strike me as being that naive. He was a very nervous man. "What do we do with this?" I say. "Kick it up the chain?"

"We've hit the jackpot here, laddie," says Mac. "I've been sitting in Rio fer five years and no intel like this has ever crossed my path. Visits by submarines and vacationing fascists are small potatoes compared to this."

"Sure, if it's legit." This thought puts sand in his motor.

"You mean, it's fake? Twisted?"

"I admit it looks legit but y'know, Stefan Z was a writer, and these writers are always making things up."

"Sure. Could be. So maybe it isn't purloined. We got experts who can say for sure."

"Like who?"

"Brits have ciphers at the Embassy. We work with them."

Do I trust this guy just because he's a fellow Canadian, from my home town? But just as I'm wondering about him, he's wondering about me.

"You tell the cops about the chess piece?"

"Of course not," I say. "Think I'm a chump?"

He's playing it through, like jazz. Can almost hear the wheels spinning inside his clock.

"The cop says to you, he says, why did you come to Petropolis to visit this guy Z... the cop, he wants a reason. A social call is bullshit, he won't accept that... he'll think this gringo is here for a reason because he's not a relative... and the Austrian and his wife, new in town, have been cut in two, new in town, here a couple of weeks, cut in two, new in town... and you're saying you didn't tell him the real reason for your visit, Thorsen? The cop was either a goddamn idiot or you're not being straight with me."

"I'm telling you, I didn't tell him. I was with a beautiful young chick, the daughter of a Rio millionaire, a hot shit *Integralista* who gets respect, and anybody dating his daughter gets respect, so the Captain accepted that this was a simple social call. It's not impossible, you know. We met on the ship, they asked me to look them up. Nice people, friendly people."

True story, of course, but not the complete story. I don't tell him about my run-in with the two flat-feet at the Copacabana Palace, that Lieutenant Cyclops actually fondled the Queen while telling me I was a faggot.

"Nice friendly people," says Mac, mocking me. "You were used, sonny."

"Sure," I say. "I've been used from the day I was offered a free trip to Rio."

"Yeah, well, victims usually like being victims in my experience. I'll take this to the Embassy."

He reinserts the microfilm into the tube, scoops the two halves of the chess piece, goes into what he calls a bedroom to stash it all. I notice the box he keeps his 'art' in, take a look. Porno comics, like the last time, only this time they're new. Stack must have a hundred copies, baled with string the way you see them being dropped off at a news seller. Same edition Cyclops laid on me at the Copa, the Getulio Vargas-Carmen Miranda spread. Interesting. Mac must be selling them.

When he returns, I say, "How's the art going?"

He doesn't know what I'm talking about.

I say, "You told me you did some painting to pass the time."

He collects himself, says, "That's just a cover, y'know?"

I say, "You wouldn't be *Senhor* Prolific, would you?"

"What do you know about *Senhor* Prolific?"

"I know you've got an awful lot of Mexican Bibles in that box over there."

"So? Part of my professional duty."

"Porno? You're kidding me. You're a dirty old man."

"Get educated, kid. It's called disinformation."

So he's passing himself off as an *agent provocateur*... what bullshit. He's selling them.

"Gee, Mac—you might bring down the Estado Novo, maybe the entire government with these."

"Don't get smart with me. I know what I'm doing."

"Fine. Guess I'll go someplace, have a beer."

"Hold on: what about Alfredo? What's going on there?"

I fill him in. Radio network is running, contacts made, even "Traben" is linked.

Mac laughs. "That clown has been picked up," he says.

"They arrested Gerwing?" I say. "Then who am I talking to?"

"A ghost responder we set up in the Caribbean."

Cute. Now the Abwehr is talking to Canadian and British Intelligence and doesn't know it. What a day, what a day. Knew there was a change in the weather coming. There was a brief, warm shower this morning when I woke up in Copa, so who knows, could be a storm brewing.

Having a beer in this bar below the hill, somewhere near *O Centro*, old Rio. Actually I'm having more than just a beer, I'm having several because... because things have gotten a bit too crazy. News of the Z murders has broken and it isn't pretty. Headlines like "Jack the Ripper in Rio" [*Jack O Estripador No Rio*] and "Famous Foreign Writer Found Murdered in Petropolis"... [with a sub-header, "Nazis Suspected"]. Seems some relative showed up and there was no way to keep the lid on it. No mention of me and Lucy, fortunately, although I wouldn't be surprised if the cops come looking with a few more questions I can't answer. Be real easy for me to end up as a patsy, especially if they find out about the chess piece.

How can I keep this from Alfredo? More or less impossible, as Eddie knows. Lucy told her parents about our adventure, and of course we used Eddie's car and he works for Lucy's dad. I don't need any more publicity. Alfredo's already jumpy, so maybe it's time for me to retire from the radio business.

There's a dog sleeping on the floor right at the open door. A mongrel, brown, a bit of white. Old enough so's he doesn't give a damn. Like the old freckled guys playing draughts who let their cigarettes smolder in the ashtray, their beers go flat. Sometimes they're looking at the board, sometimes they're looking into space. Me, I'm smoking too many cigarettes. Supposed to be good for your throat but I don't believe it. Aunt Renie always warned me off, told me not to get started but I got started. Just as the sun is starting to slant, send long ones through the smoke, guy comes in, trips on the dog, curses. Mulatto. Young, bit older than me maybe. No jacket but fairly well dressed, not slick but slick enough. Goes to the bar, chats with the barman, looks around. Has a beer, drinks from the neck. His eyes keep finding me, so after a while he wanders over, big smile like we're old buddies.

"*Ola amigo*," he says, then slips into English. "You a sailor?"

I shake my head.

"I was a sailor once," he says. "British Merchant Marine. I'm from Guyana. First time in Rio?"

"Yeah."

He drags a chair back with his foot, sits down. "Five years ago I jumped ship here... nice little piece of pussy. Everytime I try to leave, uh, there's another pussy."

He laughs, and I just keep smiling.

"My name is Paul," he says. "Bet you're Johnny. You look like Johnny Weissmuller."

Tarzan? I look like flippin' Tarzan?

"William," I say.

"Sure... William, so they call you Bill, right?"

"Nine times out of ten."

"You looking for action, Bill? Sailors are always looking for action."

I shrug. I'm just loaded enough to hear him out.

"You wanna smoke some *maconha*? Sure, let's smoke some crazy stick."

"I like beer, man."

He nods, rocks in his chair. "Sure sure," he says. "Beer is good, let's have beer."

He waves to the barman, the skinny old lizard with the crazy gray hair and beard, paunch and limp rollie in his mouth. He ambles over with a couple of grenades and yeah, I pay.

I'm making contact with the natives, and I don't mean the coffee millionaires who live behind castle walls or in caged villas at the beach. Real people. People without aliases, people who don't cheat, rob and steal to make it through the day. So I'm thinking anyway, getting happy with the beer. Imagine my surprise when Paul asks me if I know how to use a gun.

"We can make some easy paper," says Paul. "I need a partner."

"What for?" I say. "Anyone can boost a drunk in an alley."

He waves this aside, cause he's a big operator or wants to be. Real fast off the mark, but then, maybe he's all movie talk.

"True," he says. "Let's get loaded instead. You like music?"

"Yeah, I like music."

"You like cha cha cha? You like jungle?"

Yeah he's a hustler, but I figure he knows this town a lot better than I do. I'm bigger than him, could take him easy, just as long as he doesn't come at me when I'm asleep. Wish I had my silent partner with me though, but I left Oswald back in my room at the Cabral.

He takes me to a real dive not far from here, a few alleys, a few steps

173

and cobblestone switches. Edge of downtown, can't be far from where I got off the ship weeks ago. Less than a mile, more than a mile. Noisy, everyone getting drunk as a skunk. Small, with a bunch of whores dancing to a radio. Some of them don't look half-bad half-naked, although I guess it depends on how drunk you are. Cockfight going on at the back. Ugly stuff. Bets placed, blood on the floor. Guess this is a workers' bar, a place to gamble, fight and fuck, more or less in that order. It ain't white, it's shades of piss, just like the bottles of booze stacked behind the bar. Paul seems to know a lot of the candies, so maybe he's a pimp, or on a recruiting drive for a housekeeper. He smiles, he strokes, he purrs in many tongues although in the end it's all just one language. But we don't sit down, linger, just find a view spot at the end of the bar.

"You don't want these putas," says Paul. "They have no spiritual integrity."

No spiritual integrity. I laugh so hard it burns.

"My father was a Presbyterian minister," he says. "Full of *desgreta* like that."

"Guyana, you say?"

"Yeah. Georgetown. Know it?"

"No. So you're from the Danger Coast, eh."

He smiles the old crooked smile, says, "I walk with danger, *senhor.*"

This guy must have finished Bible School or something as he speaks really well for a spook without a wallet.

"I'm looking for a fellow," he says. "He's supposed to be here by now. He owes me."

"Wouldn't mind hearing some local music," I say. "Guys who don't wear suits."

"I know just the place," he says. "Could you lend me a few *reais*?"

Knew this was coming but I'm a mug when half-pissed. Besides, everything's so cheap in the skids you can live forever on shrapnel. So I give him some paper, couple of hundred maybe... 10 bucks in real money, chump change. Hey, you gotta pay the clown.

"I owe you," he says, immediately signals for a couple of shots.

It's brown. I take a sniff. "Rum?" I say.

"Yes, Guarana," he says. "Cut with a special bean from the Amazon. *Saude!*"

We knock 'em back. Bit sweet, but with the beer, tastes real nice. Don't get stupid either. This is second plateau stuff, mind reader shit. Woa! Paul is laughing. Woa! We're brothers now. Black guy sitting by himself in a recess by the arch, several bottles on his table, having his own party. Lanky, receding hairline, big forehead, big eyes. Looks familiar.

Paul nudges me. "*O Angolano*," he says.

"Yeah?" I say, thinking he must be a hood.

"Yeah," he says. "The Angolan. Brazil's best long distance runner."

"Drinks a lot for a runner, doesn't he?"

"Twenty beers a day... more sometimes... one for every kilometer he runs."

Makes sense. Guess he sweats them. Now I remember: he was the guy who was running behind the tram earlier.

"Cariocas have big hopes for him, next Olympic Games."

"Was he in Berlin?"

"No, *senhor*. But he will be in Tokyo, Japan next year."

1939? Don't think so. Tokyo, summer 1940... if the Angolan can stay sober. Notice the ladies don't bother with him. I say, "You know him?"

Paul makes a face, wiggles his hand so so. "The Angolan isn't an easy *pessoa* to talk to."

"Lots of spiritual integrity, eh."

Paul laughs. "Hey Bill you're a funny *janota*. I think we're going to have fun tonight."

And so it goes. We have a couple more. Notice Paul keeps looking at his watch. Interesting, cause I don't usually wear a watch unless I'm working or going to church, and Paul doesn't strike me as a dude who does either. Waiting for the man, I guess.

And the man shows eventually. Short, sweaty, brown beard all the way ear to ear. He's carrying a cage with a red cock, steel daggers clipped to its claws. He tries to slide by without Paul seeing him but Paul grabs his shirt. "*Voce tem o meu dinheiro*?" says Paul urgently. Portuguese, of course, but by now even I know *dinheiro* means money. Guess the man doesn't have it, as they argue. Man looks at me, and what it gets down to is he's suggesting that the gringo bets a wad on his red rooster and we'll all be rich.

Paul turns to me, says, "What can I do? How can I get my money back?"

The man, this guy with the fighting cock, has the eyes of a fanatic, eyes that roll heavenward even when he's looking at you. His smile is pure Judas, can be bought for 30 pieces of silver or maybe a back rub in a dark alley.

"How good is the bird?" I say.

I'm not slurring my words. Remember, I'm on the second plateau. "Never lost a fight," says Paul.

I'm looking at the cock, this skinny killer that looks even crazier than its owner. That beak, those Lutheran eyes. Suddenly I'm an expert. "Put yer on money him," I say carelessly.

"Ah if only," says Paul softly. "I don't have enough cash."

"The odds," I say. "What's the bookie paying?"

Turns out the bookie is a gimped Italian called Giuseppi. He sits at a modified school desk on a small stage above the pit, which is just a circle of chicken wire on the floor, back of the bar. It's a mad scene—blood, feathers, shit and a bunch of raving drunks. Usually this stuff bores me but I've been sucked in, and you know here I am forking over just about all the dough I have on me. Giuseppe demands an entry fee, just for the privilege of putting Red in the ring for 5 to 1 odds, but Paul ponys up for that... with the money I loaned him, natch. My sign language doesn't seem to work with Giuseppe, so Paul helps with that too. What I don't know is Paul takes my money and puts it on Whitey, so when Red gets ripped apart by Whitey, I figure we've lost everything. I mean, what a fiasco. Our bird was all showbiz, had no moves at all, couldn't even get out of the way. Doped, stunned, or a goddamn avian pacifist, whatever, it's murder in the lst degree.

You see? See how it works? Make friends, then sucker the stranger.

We're back at the bar and I should've smelled a rat when Paul buys the round... and he doesn't seem at all disappointed. I'm broke. No money in my shoe, certainly none in my pocket. Then his sweaty bearded friend shows up, starts talking in his other ear, Brazil talk. Paul flicks his eyes my direction, shrugs Birdman off. Birdman retreats to the other end of the bar, knocks back a shot of something, keeps watching us. You see, what I don't know is that Paul tells him I have the dough, the winnings, and that I, the mean gringo, don't want to cut Birdman in... so Paul is scamming us both.

Birdman. I don't know this asshole's real name, as we were never properly introduced. Next thing I know, he's back, babbling and shoving me, trying to get his cut, I guess. I don't like being shoved, man, especially when I'm on the second plateau. So I shove him back. When he rebounds, the bastard is coming at me with a knife, level with my gut or my liver, what we call a palm grip in HTH training... and I turn just enough so that the knife rips through my shirt, bounces off my rib. Lucky. The Sicilians call that a half-tack balzo. Get sober in a hurry? You betcha. Now we're on the floor, crouched and circling, and you'd think people would be rushing to get the hell out of there, but no, I guess a fight is nuthin' new for these cariocas. Now Birdman comes at me with his knife raised in his right hand, so I fence him with my left forearm, stop the blade's descent while counter-fencing with a right fist to his gut, and then the old swivel, a fast arm around this throat and a fast jab with my knee into his spine and he's flying across the room like an exploding frog. I'm thinking that's the end of him, but no way Jose. He bounces off his ass, picks himself up, smashes a bottle to replace his knife, and there he is, panting, red eyes and foaming mouth coming for me again.

Where's Paul? The cops? Somebody, don't know who, hits me from behind with a piece of furniture. Fortunately it shears offa my back. But it hurts, and I know I'm in tough, that Birdman has friends and accomplices and I got nobody. If it was just Birdman, I can take care of business, but it isn't. I manage to clip him on a knee with a commando kick, then head for the door, knocking over tables and women. They're coming after me, I know it, and I really don't know where the hell to run to. It's not like hey cabbie get me outta here or hey Kilroy I'll take this alley and vanish.

Hear a hiss, see the guy they call the Angolan beckoning from the shadows of a doorway. Jesus, so there are angels in hell after all. He starts running, an easy trot, gesturing for me to follow. Haven't been doing much running lately but that doesn't matter, I'm running. Somebody takes a shot at me too. Hear the bullet throb as it passes like a dead bird falling. Bloody hell. My old man gave me a Colt for a reason, so why in the hell don't I carry it? Ahead, I hear the easy splat of the Angolan's feet on the stones. We're running through a maze towards the glow of the municipal centre. I'm hurting like hell, got a stitch in my side or maybe a knife wound and my shoulders feel like I'm packing a 200 pound cross.

O Centro. This is where we part company. He waves adios and I see him pulling away fast across the floodlit plaza, and then there's no one but me and a dog who's sniffing the arches of the arcade.

CHAPTER TWENTY:

ALFREDO RECEIVES A MESSAGE FROM GERMANY

"WHERE'VE YOU BEEN?" says Alfredo. *"Wir dachten du warsct tot."*

"Thought I was kaput, did we?" I say. "I had business to take care of."

"Ja? What sort of business?"

"Female business, Fredo," I say. "Anything wrong with that?"

"You're unreliable."

"Oh? Is this a clock job? Do we have a contract?"

"Eddie went to your hotel, and you weren't there."

"I'm here now."

He wants to get rid of me, can feel it. No problem. I want to get rid of him too.

He says, "There seems to be a problem with the radio."

"Yeah? What's the matter—it speaks too much English?"

He just shakes his head. What can you do with this Canadian juvenile etcetera. Well, there's nothing wrong with the radio. He just doesn't know how to use it properly. The sensitivity, the fine tuning. It eludes him.

The radio cabinet is open and the table has been pulled out. There's another table nearby with a typewriter. Alfredo has been trying to get himself organized. I sit down, put on the headphones. "Who are we listening for?" I say.

"Hamburg," says Alfredo. "The Association has an important message for the network."

He's still continuing the pretence that this is "culture", not spying... and we're all artists, I guess. Doesn't take long to get Hamburg. The usual gobbley-goo-guck code. I know for a fact the German Embassy has a machine that encodes and decodes all their diplomatic messages, the same thing they use on their submarines and warships. Be a lot easier than this, but I guess they wouldn't want one of these ciphers falling into the wrong hands. I mean, would the Abwehr entrust one of them to a clown like Alfredo? No. Pity, though. If I could get my mitts on one I could make a few serious bucks.

I write it out, pass the message to Fredo, who leaves the room. I take the pencil, shade the top page on the pad, get an impression of the message. Hmm. I wonder if Mac or someone else could read this. Might work on it myself, just to pass the time. I tear the page, fold it, slip it into my hip pocket. Time for a snooze.

A while later when I'm in the bathroom cleaning my teeth, I open the venting window a crack, see Alfredo talking to Ida on the patio below. They're too far away and speaking too low for me to pick up any of what it's about but whatever it is, it's pretty intense. As usual, Ida is dressed in black, like she's either heading for a convent or leaving a convent, something I've yet to figure out. She keeps turning away from him, eyes downcast. She's listening, but she doesn't want to. Alfredo is almost spitting in her ear. He backs off, waits for an answer, and he either doesn't get one or doesn't like the one he gets, as he moves in more forcefully. Can almost make it out. German. Know one thing—they're not flirting.

Watch him leave by the door in the wall, head down Amazon Av, keeping to the side with the small stream, like he's trying to lose the hounds or something. He's wearing a Panama hat, first time I've seen that. Guess he thinks it's a disguise. Same old routine, though—he'll go down the hill to the *mercado*, pick up a taxi, head back to Ipanema or wherever.

Got an abrasion on my side where Birdman tried to run me through. Not bad, no stitches needed, just clean it up with a little disinfectant. Shoulder hurts, but what can I do? Got a sore ankle too, might be sprained, so I bandage it up for support. Start to laugh just thinking about it all. Sure, I got taken, but it won't happen twice. Live and learn, learn and live, it's all the same. It's that sonofabitch Paul I want to see. I'm not going to look real hard but if I see him, watch out.

Find Spengler, unlock the pages, let the Colt drop from its cradle, put it below the pillow on my bed. From now on, I'm packin'.

Strange thing happens just before sunset. Ida makes me something to eat. Fried balls of shrimp, black eyed peas and onions. What they call *acaraje*. Hell, whatever Fredo said to her, well, he should just keep on saying it. "It's fresh," she says. "But I purchased too much shrimp, so eat it."

Beats popcorn. Tastes great. "I never would've left if I'd known you could cook like this, Ida," I say.

"It won't happen every day," she says.

"Of course not," I say. "But thanks anyway."

"Did the voodoo man catch you?" she says. "I notice you limp."

"Twisted my ankle is all."

"How."

"Some real bad pavement in Rio, Ida."

"Aren't you homesick?"

"Not yet."

We get on with eating, then, just when I think I'll pump her about Alfredo, she says, "You should go home."

There you go—the good old Ida, the real Ida, she who talks like a bitch, looks like a nun. Guess that's what Alfredo was telling her to tell me in the patio earlier. Go home. But know what? I'm dead wrong about this. Hang around my room, do a little reading, a little thinking... about women, mostly. Wish Lucy would show up, find me with Eddie's help. I'd break my rule about her. She's not too young. Of course Uma would be better, wherever she is. I sweat when I think about her. Then I remember Bobby, how handy she was, such an incredible piece of plumbing, a perfect fit. But Uma... I fall asleep dreaming of Uma and when I wake some time in the wee hours there's a big moon on the *morro* and the room is lit like a photo negative, all shadow and shape, so I don't notice right away that someone's standing in the doorway watching me. I don't move, just let my eyes close, wait. Ida. Can hear her breathing, then a slight whisper as she moves back, closes the door softly, disappears. What was that about? I lie awake listening, and you know it's like I'm on the ship again, hearing the mysterious knocks travelling through the pipes as we sail through the night.

Next morning I find her on the patio having a coffee and a smoke. I say, "I dreamed about you last night, Ida."

She doesn't look at me, just says, "Yes... without my permission."

That's funny, isn't it? But with Ida, chances are she means it. I say, "A person can't help who he meets in a dream... surely you have had unexpected encounters."

She says, "No. Dreaming is a bourgeois disease."

I laugh, say, "Ida, Ida, you sound like a bloody Marxist!"

"What would you know about Marx, child?"

"I read him... some. Not the big book, but some."

"In *Deutsch*?"

"Ja, in *Deutsch*. 'The only fix for mental pain is physical pain.'"

"Marx said that?"

I nod, she ponders. Then she gets up, goes into the house. Make me breakfast? Seems not. Take a walk up the street past some empty lots, get a better view of the morning. Lots of the usual mist down on Guanabara Bay and Sugarloaf. Windows flashing in the sunlight and back on Corcovado the hundred foot statue of Christ rises above it all. Must get up there some day, check it out. Must hit the beach, take a swim like any normal visitor to Rio... but my visit isn't exactly normal. Must be bored if I'm thinking like this, though.

Spend the day doing push-ups and squats in the back yard. Hell, I'm so bored I actually do some grooming and pruning with some tools I find in the small garden shed. Disturb a large gray spider, strange looking customer they call The Wanderer, ugly bite apparently, you end up suffocating to death. Disturb a snake too, a six footer, no idea what it is, a Lancehead or a common garden snoozer. There you go—I had no idea this garden could be so dangerous. That's Brazil—looks great but just watch out. Behind the smile is death.

Need something to read, but what? Right now a Mexican Bible would do, some *Senhor* Prolific. Read some of my Oswald Spengler, the undamaged pages. Not exactly H.G. Wells. Puts me to sleep.

Once again I wake up, two, three o'clock in the morning, big full moon. And there's Ida, black as a shadow, standing looking down at me, a gun in her hand. A Walther PPK, a snug little German jobbie. Can see all this cause the moonlight is strong and suddenly I'm very alert. Sure, I've got my Colt below the pillow, but the lady's got the drop on me.

"Ida," I say. "What's the matter?"

She's as cold and silent as a statue below the sea.

"Ida," I say. "Jesus Christ."

I'm looking for tears but I don't see any. She speaks slowly and deliberately. "Alfredo received a message from Germany... the message says a Russian NKVD agent came to Rio on an American ship. This NKVD agent is pretending to be German. You came here on an American ocean liner, yes? Yes, so you did. Alfredo believes you are this Russian agent."

I'm at a loss. Maybe I'm a sorta, kinda double agent but I'm sure as hell not Russian.

"So Alfredo ordered you to shoot me?"

"Yes."

"You?"

"Yes."

"The yellow bastard... *die gelbe Bastard.*"

"They'll kill my mother."

"Bastard... you believe I'm NKVD?"

"I don't know what I believe."

"You know I'm not, Ida. You said it yourself: I lack ideology."

I sit up. Now I'm more mad than scared. She lowers her gun. "You must go home."

"Yeah? Not before I settle up with Fredo."

"You must hit me."

What's she talking about? I don't want to hit her.

"They'll kill my mother if I let you go. Hit me. Make it look good."

"Is Eddie in on this? Is he?"

"I don't know. Perhaps."

I stand up, say, "Look, I'll just split. You can say I left in the morning, didn't come back."

She stares at me, then spits in my face. Garlic.

"Thanks," I say.

But that's not the end of it, she hauls off with the Walther, whacks me across the face, hard enough to ignite stars. I react like I've been bitten, lash out, connect with a fist that sideswipes her jaw. She staggers but doesn't go down. We're both panting. Garlic, goddamn.

"*Gut*," she says. "Now you must assault me."

"Enough, Ida," I say. "Don't be stupid."

She's flushed with derision and her housecoat has come undone.

"What? Am I so undesirable that a strong young man cannot rape his victim?"

She slaps me again, pretty hard.

"Bitch," I say.

She drops the gun, rips her housecoat so nothing is left to modesty. Good body, but I suspected this. Once again I've let my guard down, as she comes at me fast, grabs my hair, bites my neck close to the shoulder. We crash to the floor, thrash like alligators. Christ, man, this woman is strong, and I'm thinking she's had some HTH training. Yet I feel she isn't trying to injure me, is holding back... and you know, I'm right for once. I get hard and we meld, easy as ballerinas. If this is rape, what is love? Completely abandoned, no script, no conductor. Violence never has rhythm does it? This has rhythm, but believe me, it's violent.

Once, twice... I dunno. The moon passes.

I never see her again. I leave just before dawn, kit bag over my shoulder, Oswald tucked above my ass. Think I've got the hang of this sex thing, but as for the rest, I don't know.

Chapter Twenty-One

THORSEN GOES TO THE MOVIES

SUDDENLY I'M A REAL POPULAR MAN. Go to the Embassy to deposit my passport for safekeeping, find there's a couple of messages for me, one from Mac, the other from my old shipboard acquaintance, Colonel Powell. He's staying at the Gloria, which is in the embassy district, so not far away. Message was left a couple of days ago. Hotel stationary. It's succinct: "Let's talk."

Decide to walk there on the off-chance he's around. What a joint— big, white, modern, very classy. Big grounds, big trees. Not really downtown, but you can walk it in 15 minutes. Lots of gardens, grand old houses, Sugarloaf always in sight. Not that I can relax and enjoy it, as I keep glancing behind to see if anyone is on my tail. Even passing cars spook me, and the ice cream seller with the skinny moustache and shades on the last corner looks like a fascist assassin.

Go into the lobby which has the old hacienda stucco arches and carved wooden furniture that a lot of famous asses have sat on, not that I see anyone famous on my way to the desk. They have someone page the Colonel, and what do you know, he's out in the patio garden having a coffee and a smoke. He really looks the part, linen suit and Panama. He's chatting with a woman, a middle-aged Latina who splits when I arrive.

We shake hands, sit down.

"Mr. Thorsen," he says. "You look older. I knew there was more to you than meets the eye."

A patrolling waiter rolls up with coffee. Tastes good, real good with a Lucky Strike.

"Oh?" I say. "Guess you read about the jaguar."

"I did," he says. "And I also read Directive 49."

I'm surprised... but then, maybe I'm not. "Archie McDonald," I say. "He said he knew you."

There's a nice garden pool with a rock waterfall nearby. Hanging vines, flowers, little birds. Very pleasant.

"Actually I've never met him," says the Colonel. "He approached someone at our embassy with a microfilm he wanted to sell, and we bought it."

What the hell is this, I'm thinking. What kind of a two-bit operator is McDonald anyway?

"Mac said it came from me?"

"No, he didn't say how he got it, just that it belonged to Stefan Z. So, I thought about it, and I thought of you, kid."

I'm trying to remember if I told him about my assignment to deliver the chess piece.

"Colonel, are you American Military Intel?" I say.

He has the amused look of a skilled card player. "I'm just a canary... like you."

"Oh yeah? What's a canary? Archie McDonald said he was a big canary, now it turns out he's just a two-bit hustler making money from other people's distress."

The Colonel nods, "Yeah, he's rogue. More like a criminal than a patriot, but a patriot when he needs to be... I guess. I dunno... what's a Canadian patriot? A fur trader who pays his taxes?"

This deserves a couple of chuckles.

"So you think Directive 49 is genuine?" I say.

"Let's put it like this: if it isn't, it's still good enough to cause a lot of trouble."

"My involvement is pure chance."

"Is it? Look, you might as well tell me the whole story... after all, we're both on the same side."

I decide he's right because, after Mac's little stunt, who am I going trust? So I tell him how the Z's gave me the chess piece and an address, and how I thought it was some heirloom or something like a diamond cache and they didn't want to run customs. I wasn't sure. But they paid me a small fee and I did it, no sweat. Then I recounted the trip to Petropolis and the grisly discovery.

"But you didn't discover their bodies, correct?" says the Colonel.

"No. The police had the house staked, so after I talked to the neighbours, they picked me up. They asked me to I.D. the bodies and I did."

"Were they in the condition as stated in the papers?"

"Yeah... right through the middle."

"A hemicorporectomy... my God, whatever for?"

"Don't know, Colonel. Cops seemed at a loss too. Later, when I found out what was in the chess piece, I wondered if the killer was looking for it in their stomachs or something. It's just too strange. I know Zion felt he was being persecuted by the Nazis."

"Yes, by Hitler himself."

Then I tell him about the strange encounter with Kallingram at the party. The idea that the Magician could be a Major in the SS stuns him.

"He was in uniform?"

"Yeah."

"Did he recognize you?"

"Must've. We shook hands."

"So is he a suspect?"

"Got no idea, Colonel. He saws people in two, so he should be."

The Colonel reflects, then shakes his head, says, "Too obvious."

"Not if he's a double agent --"

"Double, how...?"

This is where I get creative, because I've left out the whole business of me being a radio operator for the Abwehr. "Russian NKVD."

"NKVD... but that's an agency for internal Soviet security. What gives you this idea?"

"A radio intercept... says Mac. Don't know where he got it from. A Russian NKVD agent pretending to be a German was supposedly on the SS Southern Cross when we came down from New York. Who's your guess?"

He's thinking this through.

"The head of the NKVD is a man called Nikolai Yezhov, a vicious gent they call the Poisoned Dwarf, and he was replaced recently—late August, actually—by a man called Beria. Now Yezhov has disappeared. Some say Stalin put him in an insane asylum, others say he had him shot or strangled. Yezhov was accused of sodomy, probably a frame up because he knows where all Stalin's victims are buried... but it might be true, as sodomy is a popular form of birth control with some of these folk. You know, things are nuts these days in Russia. Not much intel getting out, but what bits and pieces we do get, nobody wants to believe, because there's a lot of sympathy for the grand Soviet experiment. We do have reliable information that Stalin issued a Directive ordering a roundup of all perceived enemy minorities living in Russia, in particular Poles and Germans. Reports suggest they are being murdered in high numbers... I mean, thousands. Use whatever words you like: cull, purge, extermination, liquidation. Doesn't matter if they're commie converts with Russian citizenship, illegals or workers with permits. They're getting arrested and murdered. I've seen a copy of this Directive... actual orders that come from it. You know what they call these mass executions? 'Weddings'. Privileged officers and party members get to watch, have a few drinks, maybe join in. There's also a rumour around that Stalin has ordered Beria to go after Germans in other countries. This is one reason Germany and Russia will eventually have it out. Hitler won't allow these liquidations to continue, and he'll respond in kind."

"Hitler knows about this?"

"If I know, he knows. He'll respond... and he'll add a few others to his list of undesirables. So, considering the way things are, I suppose it's not impossible for the NKVD to have a double agent posing as a German, or who really is a German, and who might even be a Major in the Gestapo. He'd be a communist... but then, who knows? There're so many goddam double agents out there these days you don't know who you're dealing with. How did McDonald come by this information? Was it passed on by Ottawa, or London? Or a local informant?"

"I don't know, Colonel Powell. But I do have this...."

Reach into my pocket, pull out the tracing I made of the last Abwehr message, more or less my death sentence. Put it on the table, turn it towards the Colonel, who eyeballs it eagerly.

"Copy of the radio message," I say. "It's in code."

"Can you read it?"

"Afraid not."

He picks it up, scrutinizes it. "How'd you get this, Thorsen?"

"I'd rather not say. Maybe you have someone who can decipher it...."

"So I can keep this?"

"Why not? No use to me. It might confirm what Mac said."

I'm taking a gamble here, although I think the odds are in my favour. Alfredo issued my death sentence after reading it. He was making a mistake but so what. Career move or personal revenge, it provided a perfect excuse.

The Colonel slips the tracing into his inside pocket, says, "Crazy world, isn't it?"

"Sure is."

"Otherwise, how are you enjoying Rio?"

"Like the girls."

"Good for you. Dating the Barasso kid?"

"Sort of."

"Little beauty. I met them on the ship, had dinner with them."

"You know he's an Integralist?"

"Yeah, sure. Might be a pretence, you know. He's like Vargas, plays both sides."

"I like *Senhora* Barasso. She's had an interesting life. You know, when I asked her about Kallingram, she claimed she never saw him at the party."

"You don't say."

"But he was there. There was another guy, an Italian officer. Said he was here to promote the airline Alitalia."

"Really? Remember his name?"

"Not at the moment. He's a writer too. Mrs. Barasso says he's big time."

"Huh. Who could that be?"

Waiter swings past with refills. He pours with the flourish of a bullfighter. Trained from the cradle, I guess.

"Say, this is a real nice hotel," I say.

"Isn't it? I usually stay here," says the Colonel.

"Been in the Copacabana Palace?"

"Sure. It's show business. The Gloria is my kind of bunkhouse. The lady I was talking to when you arrived—that's *Senhora* Santana, the head housekeeper. She knows everything that's going on here. We get along just great."

"Important people, important intel, sure."

"Sometimes. More often than not, the mice can tell you more. You'd be surprised at the gossip in a place like this."

There are some very nice looking babes walking by.

"Fashion show," says the Colonel. "So much perfume in the corridors this morning a man needs a gas mask."

"These are models?" I say hopefully.

"Everyone's a model in Rio. You sell what you've got."

This remark makes me think of my own situation. Just how much cash do I really have, and where can I get some more? Maybe I should be paying Alfredo aka Vanderzalm aka van Rottingen a surprise visit.

"Colonel, what you were telling me about Stalin, the NKVD, all the murdering that's going on... what's the cause of this? I mean why?"

The Colonel sighs, says, "The death of religion? Ideologies based on scientific reasoning? Humanity disappears in the haste to build utopia.

Stalin's name means 'steel', you know. Besides its proletarian appeal, there's an inhuman sense to it. Cultural diversity has no appeal for an ideologue in a hurry."

"Isn't it just Darwin? Your neighbour is your next meal?"

"Racial scrubbing isn't harvesting, boy."

"It is if you think your neighbour is a disease."

"Well, is any of this really new? We're always killing in the name of religion."

"Are the Japs killing Chinese in the name of Zen?"

"Now that's a damn good question. The answer is, I don't know. Europe distracts us, and we've taken our eye off the East...."

We talk on like this for awhile, big picture stuff. But this is all just passing scenery for old men, y'know? Politics, power hustlers, bullshit. When guys are trying to kill you over it, sure, it deserves your attention. But beautiful women are more of a priority for a young fellow. Honeytraps? Fine. I'll take my chances.

After we finish talking and agree to meet again soon, I just up and follow the scent like a bee. The show is in the Santos-Dumont Room but of course I don't have a ticket. Hang around, get a few fleeting smiles from the passing pedigrees, but that's it, no Uma.

You know the old saying, revenge is best served cold? Fine, if you've got amnesia. I head for Ipanema. Don't expect to surprise Alfredo snoozing in his apartment, but at least I can start drawing a bead on him. Quiet in the street, quiet in the building. Hot, muggy hot. My feet sound unusually loud on the tiles, on the stairs, on the landing. Still have my key from the week I spent as a guest of mein host, first time in Rio. Ear to the door, key to the hole... ease myself in. Place is empty and it looks like he was never here, except he's left his smell. German TARR aftershave, sweet and boozy, like he enjoys getting hammered from licking his own face.

There's a local newspaper, open and folded at the classifieds. Car ads, movie ads... nuthin' that catches my eye, except I wouldn't mind seeing *Balas ou Cedalus* (Bullets or Ballots) with Edward G. Robinson and Joan Blondell or the new Garfield flick.

Where the hell could he be? Got a new place, a hotel room, bunk on a visiting submarine... where? If I spoke Portuguese beyond asking for beer and smokes, I could try the landlady, but chances are he left without a forwarding address. Cruise past the Cafe Azul, have a coffee, pass an hour, just watching, then stroll along Viera Avenue as far as Arpoador, where I hop a bus travelling along Copacabana. Yes, the thought occurs to me to get off near the Copa Palace, see if I can spot Uma but... right now there's only one bitch I can stalk at a time, so I ride on to *O Centro*. Get off at *Praca Floriano*. Passed through it before but never took in the action. Older buildings... muncipal hall, law courts, national theatre... an old palace, an old nunnery, bars... bars and a few movie theatres. Lots of people. Hustlers among the statues and trees, benches, bus stops and the steps that lead to darkness. What do you want? A watch? Candy? Shoe shine? A monkey, a lizard... a woman, a boy? *Qual e o su desejo, senhor*?

Find a bench, a spot where I can see 360 if necessary. Kid comes by with a couple of voodoo dolls, one in each hand. Dark, looks like an Amazon Indian, who knows, he's talking gibberish and being a pest. Wave him away, but he's very insistent. He puts the face of one doll into the crotch of the other, points at me, then at himself. Goddamn. What some people gotta do to make a buck. Give him a couple of *reais* just to get rid of him. I end up with a doll I don't want, an ugly little painted skull on a stick, and I'm still looking at it when the kid disappears.

Some sort of disturbance going on northwest end of the plaza. Construction site. Probably a union thing, Comintern thing. Motorcycle cops come roaring up... and yes, a truck load of marines. But the public is just ambling by, some even doing samba steps, don't give a damn. Just another noisy day in downtown Rio.

See a running man crossing the plaza, naked from the waist up. He's a ways away and almost out of sight when I realize it's the Angolan, the beer guzzling athlete with an Olympic dream. This makes me think of Paul, the guy from Guyana who cost me a packet and almost got me killed. At this stage I still haven't figured out for sure how he scammed me, and I'm thinking yeah, he would know a good place to hole up and stay low. So I'm dreaming, like the voodoo doll has me stupified, so that I almost miss Alfredo.

The prick is standing outside a small movie house, *Cine Teatro Bristol*, which is no more than fifty yards from where I'm sitting. Yeah, I got Oswald below my shirt, tucked above my ass but I'm not gonna shoot him down in the street, take out a knee, unless maybe a riot starts at the construction site. Put on my shades, duck through the traffic, all the while locked onto him like I've got him in a sniper scope. What do you know... Fredo's wearing shades too and he's still wearing them when he slips into the theatre like a lizard finding a crack in the wall. Movie is called Satan Met A Lady, starring a bunch of nobodies. Subtitled in Portuguese. Just as well it's matinee prices, find your own seat.

Can't be more than ten people scattered around the slope, heads like soccer balls, most of them wearing shades like Alfredo. I know it looks like a silly movie but what the hell. Several young boys moving up and down the aisles, hustling. Takes me a while to figure what's going on. Bent. The Bristol calls itself a movie house but in reality it's a whorehouse for the love that dare not speak its name. Someplaces, anyway.

Alfredo is sitting a couple of rows from the back. I watch as he's approached by one, then two kids, but it's no deal. The third is different. The Indian kid who sold me the voodoo doll, no less. Doesn't seem to be any talking, negotiating. Kid disappears below the seats, Alfredo stiffens, arches, throws his head back, eyes closed, glasses gleaming in the screen light. I move softly and quietly along the back row, take the seat behind. Remove my belt. Sonofabitch. Fredo, a lonely guy craving human affection? Normally you'd say get a dog or a cat, not a toy boy. I wait 'til he blows and his eyeballs are back in their sockets, then I garotte him with my belt. He struggles, but really what chance does he have? Got the barrel of my Colt against the side of his head.

"*Wie ware es dass?*" I hiss. "Get a new after-shave, mister!"

He gurgles, flails weakly. The kid is frozen.

Keep the belt tight, give him a good whack, so he slides low in his seat, lights out. Let him dream of the steep red roofs of old Germany, eh. Slip the gun back into my pocket, then relieve him of his wallet. Yessiree, fat with those 3rd Reich US dollars.

Figured the kid would've split, but no, he's holding out his hand. So I give him twenty or thirty *reais*, change I have in my pocket. What the heck—he's good voodoo. This makes him so happy he's kissing the money as he swaggers out of there. Check Fredo's neck pulse, just to make sure his hibernation is going as planned, then head for the lobby where I restore my belt and shades before stepping outside and rejoining the samba.

You might think I got some dinosaur morality going on here. Maybe I do. It's 1938, remember. This guy ordered a woman to kill me, put a bullet in my head while I was sleeping. He made his cowardly decision based on desire, not evidence. So you know, it's either him or me, simple. You think his superiors in Hamburg and Berlin would approve of his actions? The movies he watches? Don't think so, not that I give a damn. As my old Major used to say, don't call 911, call Colt.

CHAPTER TWENTY-TWO:

HOTEL VENEZUELA

I HAVE TO GET CLEAN. Head for the beach, the nearest one, which happens to be Flamengo. There's a park, lots of trees. Buy trunks and a towel from a kiosk on the street. Busy, but nothing like Copa. The water is calm, so it's a bit polluted, and I guess you could call the swim a failure. I'm used to lakes. Still, now I feel initiated, so it serves a purpose. Dry myself off, dig into the sand, recover Alfredo's wallet, which I'd wrapped in a sock. Deluxe. Nice soft black leather, embossed with the Nazi eagle and swastika, like it's military issue for officers. Manufacturer is called Hugo Boss AG, Metzingen, Deutschland. Seems a tad unwise for someone who's supposed to be a Abwehr spy pretending to be Dutch. Expect he won't be reporting the robbery to the Rio police, so I don't need to ditch it just yet. Sweet haul, close to a grand.

Need to get some *reais*, because dollars draw attention on the street, in the bank. Don't imagine Alfredo will be reporting his loss, although you never know. His I.D. is completely bogus even if he has a local job with an address.

Wile away an hour or two lying back, Panama over my face. Military plane flies over, circles the bay. A Junkers 87 dive bomber, the one with the siren that's supposed to scare the shit out of you. Yeah, the Nazis love Wagner and President Vargas and the Brazilian military love German equipment, so you can see which way they're leaning. The Yankee needs to start investing in this country, kissing a few asses, cause the only thing between Brazil and outright fascism is the samba. These guys are loose, about as organized as a horse without a saddle or as Mac says, a fart without a toilet.

I'd stashed Oswald in a small tree in the park, so when I get it back and tucked below my shirt, I hop the first bus going through the tunnel to Copa. I'd paid the desk clerk at the Cabral a few shekels to mind my kit bag, just in case. What do you know—people have been looking for me. There was a *carioca* with a woman built like a brick shithouse—that would be Eddie and his girl. Then there was the beautiful young *senhorita* who speaks with a high class accent—that would be Lucy. In fact, it is, as she's left me a note. Then there were the two men—could be cops, could be *bicheiros*, meaning, a couple of gangsters who don't have my best interests at heart.

"When they say, is the gringo still in Rio, I say no, he catch the clipper for Miami," says the clerk.

What a brick.

"This is what your friend with the *rainha da beleza* suggest I say if strangers ask."

Eddie and his beauty queen girlfriend, eh. Could be he's still on my side. I pull out an *azul*, a 20 *reais* note.

"I need two things, amigo," I say. "Some *reais* for dollars, and a room near *O Centro*."

"Hotel Venezuela, Lapa," says the clerk. "Sometime I work there. How much dollars?"

"Hundred, maybe two. Need a better rate than the bank."

"Joseph at the Venezuela. He can guide you, *senhor*."

He's a little guy, indeterminate age... forties, fifties, face that's been burned through the vineyard. Have a feeling he's in with Eddie, part of the Barasso network. Think I can trust him—after all, got my bag and its contents back intact.

Give him the 20, say, "Thanks, amigo."

He nods, says, "See you in Venezuela."

Backtrack to the Lapa district, check into the Hotel Venezuela, once again under a phony name: Mat Sundin. Building is colonial with an interior courtyard like the Cabral. Not a dump, just old and traditional. Iron and stucco and terra-cotta. The flowers hang from baskets and the birds sing.

Next morning I'm still in bed when Eddie shows up, humping the door that I'd stacked a chair against just in case some wise guy came lookin' during the night. Don't recall falling asleep, so this visit really catches me by surprise, even though the sun is up and there're a couple of lizards running up and down the wall. I roll out of bed, gun in hand. Eddie squints back at me through the small opening.

"Take it easy," he says. "It's me, Eddie."

"What do you want?" I say.

"The boss wants to see you... and I don't mean Alfredo."

"Barasso?"

"Yes yes... we have a job for you."

I let him in, but wait to see if he is alone before stashing Oswald.

"Nice gun," says Eddie. "Where you get it, *mano*?"

"My girlfriend," I say.

He gives me the slow know-it's-bullshit nod. "I've been looking for you all places... how do you say it? The smell has hit the fan?"

I pull on some zoot strides and a fun shirt, say, "Tell me about it. Fredo tried to have me killed. Where is the asshole?"

Eddie has this smooth cynical way. "The *veado* has been arrested for an unnatural act at the movies," he says. "They have detained him in the Black Cathedral. His German friends will bail him out... maybe, maybe not. We have no capital punishment in Brazil, yet sometimes unlucky people get executed. Will Alfredo be unlucky?"

"You speak with him?"

"No, *senhor*... why? We walk alone."

"Guessed that. What about Ida?"

He gives me a long, testing look, then says, "Some *bastardo* hit her, can you imagine?"

"She say who?"

"No. I think Alfredo."

"Sure... why not... when she didn't shoot me, she disobeyed his orders, so he thumped her. Where is she now?"

"She left two days ago. Paulo."

"Too bad. I was getting to like her."

"I have the radio."

"Good show. What now?"

"I can be Alfredo."

Have to laugh at his audacity. Eddie knows sweet fugg all about short wave... but then, what did Alfredo know? Some code keys, that's about it. "Eddie Alfredo...," I say, measuring the words. "Works for me, amigo."

Eddie laughs, slaps me on the back, says, "There is an old saying, 'When a horse wanders without a rider, there must be a rider who wanders.'"

I keep laughing because, uh, at heart I'm a compliant guy. It's all the same, but tell me, what's funny about anything? I'll tell you what's funny:

the headline in the newspaper I see when we go for coffee and some breakast in a nearby bistro Eddie says is a favorite hangout for journalists and lawyers. I mean, the headline hits me in the face like a revolving door: *SENHOR PROLIFiC PRESO*! (which in our lingo is *Mr. Prolific Arrested*). Man, I recognize that sorry mug right away: the jowls, the hook mouth clenched piss tight, scruffy eyebrows, receding hairline and angry eyes, yeah, that face, that's Archie McDonald.

"So they get the *Senhor*," says Eddie. "An American hiding in Santa Teresa."

"An American?" I say, thinking, well they got that wrong.

"So it say... *pra caramba*, they'll bring back the death penalty for this... the President is one very pissed-off hombre. You see the slander with him and Carmen Miranda? Aye yi yi."

"It say if he was working with anyone else?"

"No... but everyone knows it is an American plot."

"How so?"

"The gringo will do anything to bring shame on Vargas because he likes the fascists."

"I don't believe that. These Mexican Bibles are just an easy way to make some dough."

"*E mesmo*? Really?"

"They're popular everywhere."

"Really? You have them in Canada?"

"Well no, don't think so. The market isn't big enough."

"The Americans pretend they come from Mexico. It is their way to bring shame on the Latin people."

"No, Eddie. The reason they're called Mexican Bibles is because the machine they use to print 'em is set up to print bibles."

"Really? How you know this?"

"Hey, I'm an educated guy. The one with Vargas is just a copy of one they got in the States with the gangster Al Capone."

"Al Capone... *e mesmo*?"

"Yeah, the Vargas Bible is just a heist. Don't you think it's funny?"

He's got a very serious expression, like a priest who drinks during confession. "I swear on my mother's grave I keep my eyes closed when I read it."

We laugh. That's Eddie—just when you think he has a Judas in his hand, he throws down an ace. Hey, breakfast is good. That's the great thing about Brazil—food is cheap and you get lots if you want lots.

I say, "Alfredo make the newspaper?"

Eddie's licking his chops, drumming a dessert cigarette. I reach over, flame him with my lighter. "Unnatural sex is not reported. Officially it doesn't exist, unless it is political."

"What about natural? What about rape?"

"Rape, sure... especially if it is political."

Now I get down to it. "You think Alfredo will talk, Eddie? Tell them about us?"

"So what? He's a liar. There is no radio. I have the radio in a secret place."

"You remove the antenna?"

He tries to shrug this off, says, "Antenna, what antenna? Is just a clothes-line."

"Like hell, Eddie... a clothes-line that's 20 feet off the ground, goes through the window sash into the room? Has a Y-fork contact?"

"Eh, people have radios."

"Eddie, an expert will know. We gotta take it down."

"Alfredo won't talk. His culture work has nothing to do with what he do in the movie house."

"Yeah sure... but he might cut a deal. Like, 'I'll tell you something if you drop the paedo charge.'"

"Eh, don't worry. *Senhor* Barasso will take care of it."

"He will? Enlighten me, brother, cause I just don't understand."

"You will see. We will have fun, amigo, we will have fun!"

I like his confidence. Of course Eddie doesn't know about my connection to Mac, and I got no idea what Mac might do or say to save his neck. One thing is clear: I'm no longer on holiday.

We pay up, head for Barasso's estate. Cut through Botafogo, head along Botanico west of the big lagoon, music on the radio, window open, hand on the roof. Everytime we pass a motorcycle cop straddling his hog in some dirt pull-off, my hand hits a little harder to the beat, and I look in the rear view, think about Cyclops and his buddy, probably working over Mac right now in some damn dungeon in the Black Cathedral. Ah the hell—life goes on. Hercules salutes as we drive through the gates. Nice touch. Pull out my comb, give my hair a sweep as the house comes into view.

"I got your note," I say. "So here I am."

Lucy is dressed in a cheeky little outfit. Tennis, I guess.

"You're too late," she says. "I found another partner."

There he is, a lanky young bloke in white court gear. Slick, but soft. Bet he's never worked a day in his life unless you call being an escort work. Some might call him handsome but to me he's just 20 years removed from being a rodent in his mother's nest. Could be the teeth, could be the eyes... could be the black fur he calls hair.

"Thorsen, this is Fernando."

He nods, says, "*Senhor.*"

I have two smiles—one for my friends, one for my enemies, and I swear to God my smile predicts who will be who. They look the same but feel quite different. It's in the jaw, in the teeth, primal like T-Rex.

We don't shake. After all, he has a racquet in one paw, and the other hooks onto her waist, travelling by way of her ass. She giggles.

Eddie clears his throat, says, "Lucy, is *Senhora* Barasso in her studio?"

Lucy says, "I don't know, Eduardo. Ring the bell."

Eddie beckons and I follow him into the house, go to the big kitchen where the room ringers are. The bells have been replaced by buzzers. Button for each room, upstairs and downstairs, so you can summon or be be summoned. Eddie buzzes the studio—five short ones, like he's doing Morse. Five for "Eddie" I'm guessing. There's a short buzz in return.

"Let's go," says Eddie.

We head down the hall.

"Thought you said *Senhor* Barasso needed me," I say.

"He'll be here later," says Eddie. "The *Senhora* also requires you."

She's wasting her time, I think. I got dough now, so I don't need to be taking my clothes off, renting out my body for art.

She's leaning on her stick today. Must be a full moon.

She's apologetic, says, "Mr. Thorsen... how good of you... you've caught me at my worst, I'm afraid. I've been standing in front of the easel so long the past two days my back is acting up. Please, have a seat."

As I drop into the sofa, Eddie murmurs in my ear, "I'll wait for you, o.k.?"

"Thank you, Eddie," says *Senhora* Barasso. "*O chefe vai esta de volta em breve.*"

He nods respectfully, slides on out of there.

"My husband will be back shortly," she says. "In the meantime, have you thought about my offer?"

"Not really," I say. "Things have been a bit hectic."

"Yes, we've had a devil of a time tracking you down... young men do have a knack for finding trouble. Cigarette?"

These are no mere fags. Gold cigarette box, the nails so nicely tailored you might eat them or stir your coffee with one. Sweet smell, just like a tobacconist's shop. I whip out my Zippo, but for once it doesn't fire. Out of gas, I guess. She smiles, reaches for her Ronson which never fails, natch.

"Turkish?" I say, exhaling.

"Perhaps," she says dismissively. "The true addict is beyond pedigrees. But you're too young to be an addict. I smoke these because they remind me of Paris... of my youth."

"I think I smoke because everybody else smokes."

"Ah yes... cigarettes are an easy entre... classless, in a way. They break the usual boundaries. Now, sir, what I need from you is very simple. Do you see that mannequin over there? I want to photograph you wearing that outfit."

The mannequin is dolled up in a safari suit, very chic, top dollar threads.

"I guess I could permit that," I say. "But, uh, will it fit?"

She has a husky laugh. "Oh I think we have your measurements, Mr. Thorsen. I have spies, y'know."

Right now all she wants to do is a test photo, so she can set it up for real tomorrow. I dunno. I've never liked any of my photos, always look like a hick or a psycho, sometimes both.

"Shouldn't you be using a Brazilian? Someone who looks like he lives here?"

"No. These days, everyone wants that aryan look."

"Is that me? The guy with the aryan look?"

She just smiles, gets me to stand beside the mannequin. Then she opens the long curtains about a foot, so the light can jump in. Still hasn't said how much I'm going to get for this and I don't like to ask because, um, asking money for art seems like prostitution. Crazy? She'll probably make a bundle from the advertisement she says it's supposed to be. So I'm standing there, stiff as a fence post and she's telling me to move my face this way and that, don't smile, look dangerous.

"German camera?" I say.

Black, pop-out bellows lens, bit like a Kodak.

"Yes," she says. "It's an Agfa Isolette. New model, shoots two formats, big and less big."

"Looks fancy. Germans make good gear."

"Hold still now, please... that's it, think of your mother."

Think of my mother? I don't know if I should laugh or cry. I'm happy to sit down again. Posing is for ballerinas, I figure.

I nod towards the big easel, say, "What's below the shroud?"

"The reason my back is punishing me."

"Can I have a look?"

"I'm not sure... we wouldn't want you to turn into a pillar of salt, would we?"

197

"I'm interested, really --"

She pulls the dust cloth away and holy christ, what a painting, what a nude, what a body... and the decapitated head, sitting close to the severed neck as the green serpent coils around what's left of it admiring his evil work. I know her. I know that face, and I know that body because I held it once, however briefly. Now I know what art is: no, when you mean yes... yes, when you mean no.

The *Senhora* sighs, says, "Decadent, *claro*. If I showed this in Berlin, I would be sent to a concentration camp."

"She's not really that beautiful, is she?" I say thickly, my tongue gone stiff.

"Perhaps I exaggerated her charms... but then, perhaps I underestimated them."

"Did she, did she pose for you? I mean, was this done for real?"

"Well I didn't paint her from memory, darling. If you behave yourself, I'll give her to you."

Well, I don't know what to say to that. Like, what am I going to do with an eight foot painting? Right now I'm just a homeless wanderer with an erection. The *Senhora* throws the cloth back over the painting, thank God, and I get to sit down again, suck on a smoke.

"How come she's in two pieces?" I say.

"You don't like that? Oh, you think I've been influenced by the fate of your Jewish friends, perhaps. How can I explain it? It's like breaking a statue, making a picture of the parts. It's a modern thing, a conceit, possibly. I'm sorry if I spoiled her for you."

Out of my depth here. My knowledge of modern art isn't great. If I didn't know the model, maybe I wouldn't give a flying fork.

"Wasn't thinking Jack the Ripper, honestly," I say. "It's a great picture."

"Thank you. Then you won't mind if I cut you up?"

Afterwards we go to the terrace, have coffee. Can hear the plunk and ping of the tennis game somewhere out there in the garden, happy laughs, shrieks and babble. Can see over the tree tops down the slope, glimpses of Leblon and Ipanema, all hazy in the midday heat. Cooler here.

"I appreciate that you didn't take advantage of Lucinda," says *Senhora* Barasso. "She really has a bad crush on you."

"She's a beautiful girl."

"Yes, a young beautiful girl."

"Is this guy Fernando her boyfriend?"

"Boyfriend, friend, something. Fernando is from an old carioca society family. His father is a judge."

"Does Fernando work?"

"He doesn't have to. Perhaps he's studying to be a lawyer, who knows. It's not polite to pry."

"He looks really Brazilian."

"Meaning?"

"Well, Brazil is very interracial, isn't it?"

"Just the underclass. Officially."

"Hmm. Such a strange place. Everyone's white where I come from."

"Are there servants?"

"Some rich folks have them. Nobody I know."

"Everyone has servants here. Even the servants."

"How can they afford it?"

"Most can't, so the servants steal. In fact, it's part of the servant culture."

"Do your servants steal?"

"Of course. Nothing personal, just food, loose money... stuff. You just cost it in."

"Why have servants at all?"

"Oh you're simply not allowed to do that. They just move in, squat, insist on their right to be servants. No no, one simply can't live without servants in Brazil. It's part of the social compact. Unspoken, unwritten, part of the weather."

"Seems crazy... like, I dunno."

"Racism? You see, here is the question: does the maid use the back stairs because she is a maid, or because she is black? Brazil is a slave culture. A lot of poverty, a lot of resentment. Communism could easily take hold here."

"Figures. Get the feeling the leaders want to be fascist but how can it work? Brazil is just too, too --"

"Messy? I think the Italian example suits us Brazilians better than the German. For the German, everything has to be a straight line. They lose patience with circles or anything that meanders. The Italian mind can reconcile opposites better, I think. Germans scheme, Italians dream. For example, the thinking behind the so-called 'New Man' and Futurism. Violence is reconciled with Art... well, so they say."

The sound of her voice is soothing, smooth like a radio in the night... but what she's saying is a bit too heady for me. I need something simpler.

"Are the people behind Vargas?" I say.

"GG? It's crazy, but I believe they are... most of them. They believe in him... like children, perhaps. There's a saying you hear everywhere. '*O Presidente nos lembra sempre*'—it means, 'the President always remembers us'. They write it on the walls, especially in Sao Paulo."

"Anyone can write stuff on a wall."

"Mmm... keep-saying-it-and-people-believe-it sort of thing?"

"Sure. Ah, what exactly is Integralism?"

"Don't ask me, sir. I'm just the wife. I can't cook and I can't do politics."

It's like a cough, someone or something in the distance, bottom of the garden. Hiss and a thud, swack, and the big mounted flower urn with the red jasmine vine cracks, a chunk of it falling onto the tiles beside us. Swack. The *Senhora* utters a mild exclamation. Eddie, who's just coming out the door, ducks instinctively.

"*Em nome e Deus!*" he yelps.

My mind is working real slow, cause I'm dozy from being stroked by Leonora Barasso and life in the high zone. I'm thinking tennis and Braz coffee when I should be thinking assassin. The second and third shots are like firecrackers, popping together—two shooters, I think as I pull Mrs. B to the ground. The bullets chip the stone cladding, frag in different directions. Piece catches Mrs. B in the ass or maybe a bit higher and she curses, moans, curses. Eddie's crouching like a knuckle-dragger looking for a mate, sniffing the air, hoping for direction.

Real urgent, I say, "Eddie, get a rifle!"

He nods, scuttles back into the house, keeping low. I have Oswald, my Colt 911, so I'm going after the bastards. The bullets keep coming in intervals. No automatics, no semis, I figure.

This is crazy. Mrs. B, *Senhora* B, *Dona* B, what does she want to talk about?

"What sort of girlfriends do you have back in Canada? Students?"

I'm on top of her like a blanket, head up, squinting through the gaps, trying to see the where the hell the shooting is coming from.

"Yeah. Mostly waitresses, though."

"I was a waitress briefly... hard to believe, I suppose. Am I dying?"

I take a look. Piece of marble or something has plowed a furrow on her shoulder.

"No. Messy but not fatal."

"My bloody teeth have fallen out. Damn. I hope to God Lucinda is alright. Manuelo is going to be angry... so very angry."

"I really apologize for this, Mrs... uh, Leonora, honestly I never meant to bring my troubles to your front door."

She starts laughing, then fades into a moan. "Oh God... you think this is about you?"

Can hear Lucy and Fernando still playing tennis, unaware of what's going on, their noise is more important than any other noise, tennis balls, bullets, what's the difference. Pop, crack, pop, whack.

The shooting stops. "I need a cigarette," says Mrs. B.

I roll off her as Eddie reappears packing a couple of rifles, tosses me one, the good old M 1 I shot the jaguar with.

I say, "Get in the house, stay with the *Senhora*, Eddie."

She gets her dentures back in, says, "Lucy, Thorsen, Lucy—"

Drop down into the garden, head for the wall using the bushes and trees for cover. Swing past the court, find Fernando trying to grope Lucy at the net. She's pushing him off as he gets more aggressive. She's laughing, like this is old news. When she spots me, she calls out, "Really, Thorsen... a gun?"

Fernando desists, gives me the evil eye.

"Look, kids, someone's been taking rifle shots at the house. Your mother's been hit, Lucy... just shrapnel, nuthin' to be alarmed about."

Etcetera. Lucy translates this for Fernando, who starts looking around suspiciously, like he's next on the menu. Hustle them back to the house, then go looking for the shooter or shooters but of course whoever it was is long gone Johnson. Hard to say if the shots came from inside or outside the wall. As I'm looking around for some casings, I come across an empty animal cage, fairly big like the sort of thing a circus might have, wheels and towbar. Empty. Some dried dung, and a pissy smell. Some outbuildings here too, probably used by the gardeners. Stand and listen, but nobody seems to be around. Line-of-sight to the terrace? There is, but not great. Two hundred yards or more anyway, and you'd have be a damn good shot to nail someone at this distance.

You think this is about you, she said.

If it was a couple of Abwehr agents looking to finish what Alfredo started, surely they would try to catch me in a room or in an alley... but if it was some voodoo *favelados* they might not be so professionally discreet. I'm standing there like a bandit, my Colt stuck in my waistband, the butt of the M 1 on my hip, when an avocado bounces off the side of my head. This wakes me up, goddamn. First think I've been shot, then when I see the avocado bouncing on the ground, think who the hell threw it? But they're lying all over the place below the tree, so they're dropping in the heat like pensioners.

Like they say, sometimes it takes a whack on the side of the head to get smart and I get smart right then. I'm looking at that empty cage, realize I didn't shoot some hungry wild cat who wandered into the party that evening uninvited, but maybe just maybe I shot Barasso's pet.

CHAPTER TWENTY-THREE:

GUN FOR HIRE
(HUNTING IN THE TIJUCA)

BARASSO'S PROPOSITION is a little more simple—no photos, no posing, he wants to do some hunting. Where? Right next door where his pet used to roam, take care of business... only now he's got no panther to let loose when some jive ass voodoo doll or commie commando tries to shoot his family and his guests.

The Tijuca Forest. It's mountain jungle, separates the South Zone from the North Zone, at one time clear cut by the coffee growers and then replanted when the *cariocas* realized their water supply was going to zilch. Some places it looks like a friendly park, rare birds, lagoons, exotic trees and even that mountain with the big statue of Christ, although you wouldn't want to be spending the night in there without a weapon. For a start, it's full of reptiles like snakes and caimans and a lot of homeless people sleep in the urban edges, live like animals, are involved in all the usual forms of crime. Then there's a *favela* called Machado, which is a shanty town for the tree planters, although most of them don't do much tree planting anymore, so it's become an outlaw enclave and whitey doesn't go in there without some special entre. Reminds me of the wild west. Anything goes, life is cheap. Big on music, though. Samba. Well all the *favelas*, all the poor districts are big on samba. They just drum on anything that comes to hand—bottles, tin cans, gourds, bones, pots, pans, hands, your ass, my ass, anything and everything. They even drum on the trees, especially those dry dead ones that are like the chimneys the dinosaurs left behind.

Some of these guys, the voodoo guys, or what they call candombles, like to go into the forest, do some drumming, get back to Africa, rendezvous with the old gods even if sometimes they dress them up as Christians. The forest has the vibe, and it can be private. If you want to go out of your mind drinking kerosene blues and doing dope, private is good. The government doesn't really care for this slave religion stuff, sometimes sends an army platoon into the favelas or into the forest to restore a bit of Christian order, and then of course sometimes the big shots send in their own boys because sometimes official justice works a little too slow. So there's quite a bit of direct-action justice which is viewed as something of a sport. Slavery was done away with in Brazil 50 years ago, about the same time they got rid of their emperor, although the guys who got rid of him weren't really interested in getting rid of slavery. Politics, man. Vested interest shit. Brazil is like Mississippi. Godfathers and boogie, and the only law is the Ten Commandments, and who really believes that stuff anymore? Even Vargas, the President, skips church, although he's letting the Catholics teach their kids again. So you got your bullies and you got your patsies, and when some of them are white, some of them black, it's just easier to pass judgement. Like targets at the range. It's the shades in between that mess it all up.

Anyway, we're going hunting. I'm wondering what Manuelo B's real feelings are about the death of his cat... if it was his cat. Of course I got him out of a bind at the big party, as I can't imagine the cat was released on purpose to feed on the guests. He doesn't say anything, expresses no nostalgia, although if he did, this would be an admission of guilt as it seems the jaguar killed several people recently. These deaths went unreported because they were homeless vagrants and riff-raff *favelados*, and the government controls the press... actually, the Rio Police Chief, Filento Muller, controls the press, and I understand Barasso is his good buddy.

Integralism. Sigma. Greek. Means "I hiss". Guess fascists are good at hissing.

Barasso has assembled a hunting party, bunch of Brats dressed halfway between commando and cowboy. Some of them are buddies, some are part of his security force, like me. Eddie said he had a cool job for me and he does. Pays good enough and the future... well, who knows? The man has properties north and south, he's big business, and he needs some *schnelle Schutztruppe*, some security that can move around when needed. Fact is, I'm probably more qualified than he realizes.

It's just after dawn, and the mist is on the sierra, the way it is most mornings in Rio. He draws me aside for a little confidential. "I want you to teach Fernando how to shoot," he says.

He has me on a retainer and I'm supposed to say no?

"Eddie could teach him," I say. "I don't speak Portuguese."

Fernando is lurking nearby, wearing a safari vest, way too big for him, the sort of thing that has cartridge loops for bird hunting.

"Bullets speak the same tongue everywhere," says Barasso. "Eddie is many things, but a good shot? You, Mr. Thorsen, you are a good shot."

Fernando has an expectant look, even though he doesn't know what we're talking about. The idea of helping this weasel makes me gag but what the hell, all men have a right to protect themselves. I guess.

We ride into the Tijuca on these fine long-legged ponies Barasso keeps in a stable back of the house. I know he's a member of the Jockey Club but never expected him to know sweet something about horses but it turns out some of his family are gauchos from Rio Grande do Sul, and he even has a hacienda with a few thousand acres down in Santa Catarina, which is Kraut country in Brazil. First I thought he was just a guy with a coffee plantation. Or two. Then I thought he was a politician, an *Integralista*, a shit-kicker, a warlord, a patron of the arts, a family man with a talented wife and a beautiful daughter, and then I find out he's a flippin' cowboy to boot, could ride in a circus.

Hunting. Pigs, I guess. Understand they got some wild ones in the gullies of the sierra.

Suddenly it's hot and sticky, the sort of heat that bubbles your skin, makes the trees and rocks float. You'd never believe it's nearly Christmas, or Natal as they call it hereabouts. Hard to adjust to, like the toilets flushing against the clock.

Very interesting forest, very interesting animals, like this big long-snout pig raccoon they call a guati. Gold hand monkeys that look like Chinese philosophers. Birds—you wouldn't believe the birds, some so weird they haven't got names. Rivers, waterfalls, lagoons, rock stacks and cliffs crazier than Arizona. They got trails, sure, and they've even got a road going through a lot of it called da Vista Chinesa, which was built by a bunch of coolies back in the days when this was an empire.

Some great views but so far we haven't shot a thing. We're taking a break, smokes, the view. Can see most of Rio, the beaches, the ocean. Can see all the way to Africa, looks like. Down below on the China Road can see a guy running, coming at a steady clip like a marathon runner. One of the party is scoping him with a pair of binoculars, says something to Barasso, who takes a look. Barasso passes the nocs to me.

It's the Angolan.

Barasso says, "What do you see, *Senhor*?"

"A distance runner... pretty good one too."

Barasso takes back the nocs, has another look. "Yes, he runs, but why does he run?" he says.

"Maybe he wants to go to Tokyo."

Barasso repeats this to his buddies, and they laugh. Olympic Games, shit.

"It's a long way to Tokyo, *senhor*," he says. "I will tell you what he is: he is an *aviao*."

"*Aviao*? A plane?"

"Yes, a plane. A 'plane' is what we call a drug courier. He flies, entende?"

I nod, say, "So he's making a delivery?"

"Yes, money or drugs. They have an operation in the forest."

Barasso beckons to Fernando, who slouches our way. Barasso points to the runner, says, "Shoot him."

Fernando looks, says, "Mata-lo?"

"Yes, Fernando, shoot him. He is the criminal we are hunting."

The Angolan must be three hundred yards away, a problematic target for even an army sniper with an appropriate rifle, and alls Fernando has is a shotgun. Barasso goes to his horse, pulls a rifle from the sheath holster. A German Mauser 98K. Never fired one myself but know it's good for a thousand yards in the right hands. Trench warfare special, millions were made. Took out a lot of good Canadians back when.

"Use this," says Barasso, handing him the rifle. The other honchos have amused expressions. One even spits... maybe he has to clear his mouth. Older guy.

Barasso looks at me, jerks his head. Guess I have to help the kid. Get him to lie down at the drop-off, use a bump as a rest for the rifle. Bolt action, naturally... and he doesn't know how to chamber the shell, naturally.

I help him with that, and pray he doesn't get lucky. Barasso's yapping at him, don't know what, but could be something like, shoot the bastard and if you miss, don't come around sniffing my daughter no more. Almost feel sorry for him.

He misses, and the kick just about rips his shoulder off. I warned him about the recoil but of course, as I told Barasso, we don't speak the same language. He yelps, rolls around like a kid practicing epilepsy. Barasso and the others think it's funny. Guess he was deliberately pulling the kid's chain, setting him up for the humiliation. Don't think the Angolan noticed, as he keeps running, same pace, flickering through the trees and shadows, nice rhythm. What's a shot in the forest? The echo of an axe?

The others want to take a shot but Barasso wants me. I'm thinking security is one thing, and murder another. Is the bastard trying to box me? It's one of those situations where it's not wise to say fuck you and turn your back to the host.

I say to Barasso, "I'm not familiar with the Mauser."

Barasso says, "One hundred dollars if you hit the plane."

I say, "And if I miss?"

Barasso smiles, just like his coffee crop has come in bigger than expected. The older guy who likes to spit spits again.

Move around, find a rock, get a bead on the Angolan. He's wearing a red undershirt and his bare arms and shoulders are flashing with sweat. Looks like he's running barefoot although it's too far away to say for sure. He was the night he saved me from the rumble at the cockfight.

I'm not worried about the kick, as I've had plenty of experience with the Enfield which kicks like a mule. I fire once, rechamber, fire again, real fast. The Angolan staggers, weaves over the road in a crouch, keeps going. The older guy exclaims thickly, "You hit him, *senhor!*"

The others murmur in agreement. I don't think I hit him. I didn't want to.

By now the Angolan has left the road, is in the forest. Can still see him easily enough, as the trees are thin, scrawny stuff, although there are a lot of shadows... and it's into one of these shadows that he disappears like Houdini. Barasso barks "Mount up!" and pretty soon we're heading down a trail in pursuit. The road is empty, although I can hear a truck coming, labouring like it's in low gear. Takes awhile but one of the dogs flushes the Angolan out of a shallow gully where he's concealed himself in a puddle of dry leaves. I hit him alright, winged him on the arm, a nasty slicer hot enough to cauterize the flesh, glue the blood. Hope it didn't chip the bone. Don't know if he recognizes me or not, as the boys are working him over like cops on riot patrol. Drag him to his feet, punch him, bark nasty words. Says nothing back, no pleading, just glares as the dogs jump around like he's dinner. Mulatto, one of these guys who looks older than he is. Quite black, sorta handsome.

The old guy with the pencil moustache and leathery dog-face moves in, takes over, spits, frisks the Angolan, then yanks down his pants, revealing a hard skinny ass. Looking for money, looking for dope, looking for a feel, I dunno, but he doesn't get any. Now it comes to me... guy's name is Iambic. We were introduced before we saddled up and y'know, I think he was at the party that night. They got a lot of weird names like this in Brazil, ancient stuff, like Mediterranean pagan. You think names like Hercules or Jupiter are found only in a circus or an encylopaedia? They got lots of guys called Hercules, even if they're just broken-assed accountants or grim fishermen from Bahia Norte. Anyway, this asshole Iambic cocks his pistol, jams it against the Angolan's head, starts shouting death threats.

"Fer fuck's sake," I say. "He's just a runner!"

Iambic's eyes flick back at me. Yeah, he speaks English as well as Death.

"This?" he sneers. "This? This is a gangster!"

"Then turn him over to the police."

Iambic spits, hisses, "I am the police, Bobo."

He whacks the Angolan with his pistol, well-placed behind the right ear, quite professional. The Angolan collapses to his knees, stunned.

Guess I should've seen this coming. Turns out Iambic is a graduate of the old Rio Grande do Sul gaucho militia, back in the days when the States ran their own armies, before Vargas cut their tails, gave all the new guns to the Feds, established the Estado Novo. Grievances? Sure. No wonder the Integralistas have lots of support, tried to stage a coup against O Presidente last year, had him under siege in the old palace, him and his daughter like Bonnie and Clyde swapping shots with the insurgents... and what did the army do? It just waited around long enough to make Vargas sweat, show him just how important the military is to any dictator trying to be a Mussolini in Brazil. Especially when you're only five foot two. Yep. The political situation hereabouts is quite loose, quite fluid these days. Eddie told me all this. Don't know whether Eddie's bitter or proud because, let's face it, this kind of scene provides lots of opportunities.

As the boys rope the Angolan, get ready to drag him out to the road, Barasso takes me aside for a friendly murmur. "Thorsen," he says. "Don't you understand? We're completely legitimate. Iambic Fontana reports directly to my friend Filente Muller, who is the Chief of all Police. Our operations are sanctioned by the highest authority, contracted, you might say. Look I don't need to explain my actions to anyone but with respect to you being a foreigner—an intelligent one too—I give you these facts because clearly you don't understand the situation here in Brazil. Am I being clear?"

Bit of menace here. Just a bit behind the cultured smile.

"Yessir," I say, just like the old days on the parade ground.

"*Excelente*," he says, patting my shoulder. "Good shot by the way. One hundred dollars when we return to base."

Iambic is leading the Angolan, rope half-hitched on the horn of his saddle, and of course the poor bugger keeps falling down, is being dragged like a log by the time we reach the road. Here's Eddie in the truck, which I stupidly thought was for transporting game, maybe some birds, some pigs or a wild cat. The Angolan is thrown in the back like a cheap coffin, the tailgate locked, and we move to the next rendezvous further on up the road. Obviously this is all part of the plan, which a mere hired gunslinger like me isn't privy to.

What we're looking for is the camp, the location of this particular gang of desperados and their dope warehouse and whatever it is they're running. Eddie drives the truck further up the Estrada to a prearranged spot. We head into the forest, do a few sweeps. Obviously Barasso has some intel, plus dogs, plus—and I just notice this—a yellow biplane doing lazy eights over the forest. He didn't need all this. I could've told him, just follow the water.

The camp is hidden away in the bush not far from a big pool in the stream that cascades down the *morro*. Trip wire on the main path, tied to a couple of gas cans hanging in the trees, act like warning bells. But our guys are savvy to this sort of defence, disengage it, no sweat. Camp's like something you'd see in Africa, a few stick huts and some chickens wandering around, reminds me that Rio was settled by white Portuguese who pushed out the Tupi, the local Indian tribe. Lot of Tupi got wiped out, although they were always fighting among themselves and were cannibals. The other day I wandered through the National Museum, which isn't far from my room at the Venezuela, just something to do, and I learned quite a few things about this place, the early days, the cannibalism and the Kraut adventurer they took prisoner, and how lucky he was to escape being eaten. That's what this camp looks like—a place where you could get eaten. There's even a big boiler pot bubbling away over a fire pit.

Lots of candomble idols around, wood and plaster figures, the sort you see in the religious shops around town. Some look Christian, some African, some hard voodoo. All sizes, shapes. Must be how they make their money or maybe it's just a front.

Seems very quiet, except for a radio that's playing, some samba, some talk. Sounds like *Hora do Brasil* or Brazil Hour, which Radio Tupi broadcasts every afternoon. Don't understand a word but later learn that it's the Minister of Propaganda Marcondes Filho, a Vargas stooge. Very ironic. These idiots are all napping like a lot of *cariocas* do this time of day, so we hit 'em completely by surprise. Ten, maybe a dozen, some of them maybe narced out.

I dunno. Guess one or two escape into the forest. They're young, my age or younger. No white boys here. The illiterate homeless, the young *favelado* trying some free enterprise on the dark side of town. There is some shooting, cause these dudes have weapons. Couple of pistols, a rifle, not much. Plenty of machetes but machetes are useless against the sort of artillery we have. Pretty soon they're on their knees, hands in the air and the boys are roping the shacks, pulling them apart with their horses. Normally in this sort of operation you'd torch them but here, in this heat, in this forest, fire is not advisable. The whole thing is a shit scene, a blight, yet somehow I feel bad. Sure, maybe they're criminals, and sure, the place is a squalid dump, yet the destruction and the humiliation seems wrong. But this is nuthin' compared to what happens next.

I'm doing a sweep around the pool, which is a very nice mountain grotto by the way, and there're a couple of happy guys in there taking a bath. The noise of the stream, the small waterfall, is so loud they don't hear anything but their own goof talk. Fernando's with me and I'm about to flush them out when he ups and blasts them with his shotgun, the stupid bastard. It's murder, plain and simple, yet he acts like it's part of the plan. Shoots them, one at a time, quite deliberately, easy, first guy in the face, second guy in the back of the head. What a mess, guys didn't have a chance, and my first instinct is to whack Fernando, put a bullet through his head. A natural born homicidal lunatic on a mission to prove that he's a natural born son of the ruling class... I guess.

He spits. Honest to god, that's what he does. Spits.

Barasso shows up, says, "What happened here?"

Fernando says, "*Eles tantaram fugir.*"

Barasso says, "Tried to escape?"

He looks at me.

"He shot them," I say. "They had their hands up."

Barasso spews something at Fernando who gives a sulky shrug.

"We'll deal with this later," says Barasso. "Let's go—we have prisoners to move."

Yeah, we got prisoners, a sorry-assed bunch alright, two or three wounded, lucky to be alive. Of course now I'm wondering just exactly what is going to happen to them. Got their hands tied behind their backs, ready for the Ilha das Cobras or the firing squad or slave duty in the Mata Grosso. Take a look at the wreckage. Iambic is busy looking for cocaine and maryjane, pharmaceuticals, money, whatever. Couple of the others are still playing cowboy with the huts, what's left of them. It's a fever, this smashing, this wrecking. Much easier than making something, but just as satisfying, evidently. A box comes tumbling out of somewhere, breaks open. Everyone's busy, so I check it out, and what do you know, it's full of jewelry, money, and—get this—passports. Must be a dozen, various countries.

I signal Barasso, and he comes over, takes a look.

"They have been robbing tourists," he says. "Secure this box and bring it along."

Do a quick flick through the passports, and holy christ, what's this? Two Austrians: Stefan and Lotte Z. Can't believe it, yet the believing is in my hand. No time to think about it, though, so I slip them into my hip pocket, secure the box and tie it to my horse.

Barasso sends me and Fernando ahead to meet up with Eddie and the truck. Fernando's not bad on a horse, and he takes the lead. I don't mind. I'm thinking of shooting the bastard anyway, be real easy... but y'know, it isn't the Canadian way, is it? Still, I'm thinking about it. Oswald's in my waist band, ready to go. Death is nothing special in the forest. Bodies come and go like vegetation. Fernando would just be some bad fertilizer or food for the ants, as they got lots of ants in the Tijuca. Here today, gone tomorrow. Year from now you wouldn't even recognize his bones. There he is, right in front of me, bobbing up and down in his saddle... be real easy.

Eddie's smoking a cigarette and watching the biplane that's doing some fancy circles.

"You find them?" he says. "Any trouble?"

"A little," I say. "Fernando had to execute a couple of guys."

Eddie, *claro*, thinks this is a joke.

"Eh... *bom trabalho, bonito*," he says to Fernando. "You'll get two hundred bucks from the Sehnor."

Fernando ignores this, says something pompous, like, we have the prisoners, and Eddie says o.k. ride back and tell them I'll bring the truck up. He points to the biplane, meaning he knows the spot, will get as close as he can on the Estrada. Fernando nods, rides off, and I'm just about to tell Eddie what happened when there's a hiss and a thump, and Fernando's horse rears up and dumps him, then bolts off. Eddie responds faster than me, as I'm thinking, couldn't have happened to a nicer guy and all that, so I just amble over, hoping for the worst. Well, it's the best, if the best can be the worst. Asshole has an arrow right through his neck, and his carotid artery is spurting like an uncapped oil well. Eddie starts dragging him to the truck, trying to get some cover, and I'm ducking around trees trying to see who we're dealing with. Hear someone or something scrambling away, and you know, I have no interest in following. I fire a shot, just for appearances.

Well Fernando's dead. Blood's still pumping but barely. Not much of a river, and he's a lousy stiff.

"He had it coming," I say.

Eddie's taking it a bit more seriously now. I tell him how Fernando gunned down the two men in the pool. "It was murder, Eddie," I say. "And I guess someone saw it and took justice."

Eddie nods, looks into the distance. Rio is sitting pretty down there, just like a postcard.

"What now?" he says.

"Just leave him," I say. "Collect him on the way back."

"No," he says. "The boss will be angry if we leave Fernando."

So we throw him in the back of the truck with the Angolan. The Angolan's sitting there, says nothing. Eddie closes up, secures the pins.

"You ride with me?" he says.

"No, I'll ride through the forest, see if I can flush Robin Hood."

Takes him a minute to get the truck fired up. Meanwhile I undo the latch on the rear door, signal the Angolan. His eyes say he understands. But no nod, no smile.

I mount up, salute Eddie, head into the bush. Have a rifle and a semi-auto pistol but I won't be seeing anyone, good or bad, I'm certain of it. Just want to find a private spot, take a look at those passports. Could be that the Z's killer was carrying their passports, got robbed, so one of the others might be his. Just an idea. Find a spot where I'm not likely to be bushwhacked or disturbed, tie the horse to a branch, open up the box. Can hear the truck in the distance going through the gears, working the incline. Angolan's probably bailed by now. I smile. See a shadow ripple over the trees, look up, see the yellow biplane banking nearby, realize the pilot has cut the engine. Does a loop around my position. I wave, and the engine kicks in again, and the plane drops away towards the city and disappears. What was that all about, I wonder. Spooks me, so I get the hell out of there, get back to the encampment.

The others have already moved out with the prisoners. Notice an idol that's still intact and I'm thinking hey, might be a good trophy, then notice there's a wad of bills beside it. Excellent. Double scoop, how did these clowns miss it?

"Don't touch that!"

Look back and there's Barasso, sitting on his horse, mean as a conquistador.

"Money," I say.

"Don't touch it," Barasso says. "*Derocho.*"

"*Derocho* what."

"A payment for the business we have conducted here. Come, let's go."

This is crazy stuff, not for me to question. You come and trash the joint, kill a couple of guys, then pay some idol for the privilege? Never figured Barasso to be superstitious, wanna stay friendly with the dolls.

We ride on, catch up to the others heading for the rendezvous spot. It's like a slave caravan, these guys with their tall horses and rifles leading a dozen of these poor suckers in a rope chain. Iambic's got a bullwhip, and he's not snapping at bugs. It's very hot now, and lizards are darting here and there over the rocks, or coming and going up and down tree trunks. Barasso's in the lead. Seems obvious now this is nuthin' new for him.

Eddie's waiting at the switchback near the stone idol with the bullet pocks and graffiti. Maybe some sort of Tupi Indian thing. He waits until I pull up before giving the boss the bad news.

"We got a problem," says Eddie.

Barasso immediately looks around, realizes Fernando is missing.

"*Explicar, amigo.*"

Eddie is very uncomfortable, is making noises, not sense. I step in.

"Fernando is dead," I say. "We were talking with Eddie when someone took him out with a bow and arrow, ripped his carotid. Nothing we could do."

Barasso is grim. "I heard a shot," he says. "Was that you?"

"Yeah," I say. "I gave chase but no deal."

"You see them?"

"No. Heard him take off, that's all."

Barasso curses softly, "The kid is dead? What the hell am I going to tell his father?"

Well, I'm thinking, you could tell him his son murdered two men in cold blood, and just got what was coming. Much sooner than later, of course.

"We tried, boss," says Eddie.

"He was marked," I say. "From the moment he pulled the trigger... someone else was there, saw it, followed us, got revenge."

Barasso thinks about this, keeps shaking his head. Meanwhile the prisoners are being loaded into the back of the truck.

"Where is he? You didn't leave him on the Estrada, no?"

He's agitated, never seen him like this.

"No boss, he's in the back of the truck," says Eddie.

But of course he's not in the back of truck, and neither is the Angolan. Poor old Eduardo is mortified. Barasso is in a black rage, although he just grinds his teeth, keeps it locked.

We find Fernando on the road not far from where he died. The Angolan probably threw the body out when he bailed. This certainly dampens the festive mood of the squad, job well-done, mission accomplished and all that. The arrow is still stuck through the neck like a turn-screw and Fernando's death face is no peaceful repose. Mouth twisted, eyes rolled in reverse. Enough to make a man spit, eh, and that's exactly what Iambic does. He looks, steps back, spits, then goes to the shoulder of the road and relieves himself.

CHAPTER TWENTY-FOUR:

PASSPORTS OF THE DEAD

LOOKING THROUGH A PAIR of 7 by 50 binoculars at Mars, quite low and red in the sky. A flash, a thin streak of brilliant light heading towards earth... and so the nightmare begins.

The Martian visits me in my room at the Hotel Venezuela, stands at the end of the bed, looks me over. He's like a human being, although pretty ugly by any definition. Maybe he's an old man or even a woman, because the mystery of his flesh can be like nothing we know. Yet he— it—is familiar. Face like a collapsed bladder, back twisted like his ass got stuck between the beats last time he danced. Looks like a cripple, talks like a cripple, but amazingly, not a cripple. In conversation, he prefers E.S.P.—ask him a question, answer it yourself kind of thing. Maybe you do all the talking because you're afraid.

"Has the invasion begun? Soon? So you're part of the advance intelligence network. You use radio? What frequency? Do you use encryption? Need decoders or is your language beyond human comprehension... maybe you use English, like now. Tell me, do you have sympaticos here? Sure... at the highest levels. Do you eat meat? Human meat? Just wondering. A German came here three hundred years ago, nearly got eaten. Hans Staden. People here thought he was from another planet, just like you... sir, madame. No, this is not a threat. Are you allowed to kill? Is death part of your mandate?

"Why am I using an alias? I think you know why. I think you know all names are aliases... I mean, what name do you go by here on Earth?

I'm sure it has nothing to do with the name you use on Mars. Tell me, are you travelling with a passport? Legit... or is it phony?"

He wants my worry stone. Why the hell, I don't know, but he wants it and he climbs into the bed to make sure he gets it. Start kicking, desperate to keep him away from me but can't wake up, defend myself. My feet are awake... legs... but I'm asleep from the waist up, like I've been cut in two. Wake up with a jolt, like I've just come out of a swoon falling backwards into a grave. Sweating, and just for a moment or two I don't know where I am or who I am. A stroke? Too young, surely. Breathe deep, amigo. Breathe.

Sit up, dress, leave the room, the hotel, take a walk to pull myself together. Street's empty, cars parked like dead bugs in the shadows. The night is balmy, quarter moon behind the cluster palms and when I reach the beach, see a black woman tossing white flowers into the surf, feeding the ocean god. Common sight in Rio but until tonight I've never understood why. When Mars shows his face, all the gods get crazy.

These passports... what's going to happen with them? Am I going to let Barasso keep them? What I do is look through them, see if there's another one or two I should hold back. Rest of the booty I don't care about, although there's a nice Breitling wrist watch, looks pretty new, has all sorts of gizmos, special military gear maybe.

Here's one: American, red jacket, gold lettering. Karl Heinz Boettner, New Jersey, born 1901, Köln, Germany. Five foot eight, grey eyes, no wife. Tattoo on the left wrist. Picture is like a mug shot, fish face and fish pout, looks dead except for the fanatic's eyes... and boy do they look familiar. Boettner, Boettner... profession, ship's purser. Boettner, of course, the sonofabitch purser on the SS Southern Cross!

The other stuff, the wallets, the rings, necklaces, cuff-links, bracelets, foreign currency, all the highway man stuff I don't care about. But Boettner... I slip his passport into my pocket, then leave the stable. Can hear one of the horses shitting. Good omen.

Deliver the box to Barasso in his study, which is more neutral than I expect. No trophy heads, suits of armour, just a few framed family photos and a couple of his wife's paintings. He's talking to Eddie, and they both smile when I come in.

"Ah... *o que esta na caixa do diablo*?" he says.

Eddie translates: "What's in the devil's box, man?"

I set the box on the desk and the man immediately dumps the contents.

"You take anything?" he says.

"No way," I say. "I don't wear necklaces."

Yeah, they chuckle, the boss and his capo. Barasso flicks through the loot, picks up a passport, studies it.

"This lady was on the ship," he says. "Recognize her?"

I lean in for a close-up. Late middle-aged dowager.

"No," I say. "Must have been in 1st Class."

Barasso grunts, tosses the passport aside. He picks up the Breitling, nods appreciatively, then tosses it to me. "You can get all the whores in Rio with this, Thorsen," he says. "Are we square?"

I don't care one way or the other. Guess it's the same as cash. "Sure," I say, slipping it onto my left wrist. "Thanks."

Eddie sidles over for a look.

"You're a dude, *manoluco*," he says.

"I know," I say. "I got the aryan look."

Again, they laugh. Me too.

"Eddie?" says Barasso. "Something you like?"

Eddie passes his hands over the booty like a dowser looking for holy water, settles for a handsome wallet and a gold ring.

"You getting married, Eddie?" says Barasso slyly.

"No, *Senhor*," says Eddie. "I just like gold."

"Very good," says Barasso. "Now, gentlemen, I think we can turn the rest of this over to the proper authorities."

What he means by "proper authorities" I really don't know. The longer I'm in Rio the more confused I become about who or what authority is. Everybody, high or low, seems to be working outside the law, at least some of the time. Even the cops. Nearly 40 million people in Brazil and teach just can't control the class. It's like this watch. Yesterday, it was on someone else's wrist, today it's mine, tomorrow, who knows?

Take a walk through the garden, down near the sheds where the cage is. That's where they put the prisoners, eight or nine of them. Maybe there were more but now it's eight or nine and they're in the cage and it's feeding time. Keep my distance, watch from the bushes. It's a degrading scene really but I guess that's what we do with animals, even if they stand on two hooves instead of four. The big sleepy black guy, Hercules the gatekeeper, is throwing corn cobs into the cage just like he's feeding the pigs. Yeah, some guys fight over them, but a couple more just sit listlessly slumped against the bars, not hungry I guess. Do they give a shit that the fascists are winning in Catalonia, are about to take Barcelona? Do I?

"Niteroi A.C. from the north shore become Rio State soccer champions," says Eddie, scowling. "They beat up on Fonseca A.C. Once again. How come? Is everything in this town fixed?"

We're driving to the Hotel Gloria, where he thinks I'm meeting a chick. Of course I'm forever hopeful but I'm looking for the Colonel, need some advice. Don't know how to read these passports, just what's going on here. Killer X is out there, could be Boettner, could be the Magician, could be somebody we don't know.

"You seen Lucy?" I say. "She know about Fernando yet?"

Eddie shrugs, says, "Haven't seen her. She's in Paulo for a concert."

"Playing or listening?"

"I don't know. Maybe the boss wants her out of the way. Fuck Fernando anyway. Cuzao... Punteta. He was crazy jealous about you."

"You don't say."

"Lucy use him, man. Hey, why all the women like you? What is your secret?"

I'm white, I think. And I look like a Nazi and these days Nazis are chic. That's what Leonora Barasso says and who's me to say she's wrong. Not saying it's cool. In fact it's like walking around with a hard-on and everyone's lookin'.

Pass a barracks and there's a bunch of recruits doing the goose-step samba.

"Look at that bullshit," I say. "Toys."

"You don't like it, *amigo*?" says Eddie. "Women love it. Eh, they know these guys have big *cajones*."

"Yeah? Makes you impotent."

"*Impotente*? You're crazy, man."

I make a fist, say, "Crushes the testes, the prostate gland, the rectum. Bad news."

"You mean, like homo?"

"I mean it's a stupid way to train a soldier."

"Indians and niggers, man, who cares?"

He doesn't really believe this, is just punching words. We pull into the Gloria, park facing Sugarloaf.

"Wait for me, Eddie. Maybe she's not here."

She's not, 'she' being Colonel Powell. I ask if he's booked to come back. Desk clerk speaks to a dark haired woman in the inner office, who comes out, looks me over.

"Is there a message?" she says.

Quite a sexy accent for someone pushing forty. I remember her from last time: hotel housekeeper, *Senhora* Santana.

"Is he coming back soon?"

"In a week, perhaps. He has business in San Salvador."

Looking for airfields, I guess... er, 'plantations'.

"I'll check in a week," I say.

"Your name, *Senhor*?" she says.

"Mr. Chess," I say. "We're old friends."

Her eyes are rolling over me like paint stripper. I'd blush if I was telling the truth.

IT'S A WORKER'S BAR, don't recall the name... maybe Lotus or something like that... they all look the same, smell the same, bare and basic like cellars even if you just walk in at street level. Painted arches and pillars, sometimes two-tone, plaster all grimy from smoke and tropical sweat, and the tables are like something the seven dwarves knocked together from hurricane lumber. Beers and smokes always cheap and there's always something going on, even when you think there isn't. Kids trying to sell you dolls, old men peddling lottery tickets, whores lookin' for a fast load. This one, this place, it's not far from where I kip, and come to think of it, it's not far from the bar where the cockfighter tried to stick a knife in my guts, so there's no reason to be surprised when the Angolan strolls in, takes a table with his back to the wall, more less out of sight in the cloudy light.

Don't know if he sees me or not. Next guy does, though.

"*Amigo...*!

It's Paul, dressed like a stud, all smiles and big ideas as usual.

"You owe me some money, I think," I say.

"Of course, of course," he says. "Can I get you another beer? Sure, let's have a beer. I have a proposition."

As hustlers go, Paul is like a flippin' vacuum cleaner, always ready to suck up anything in his path. Yet I can't stay mad at him, as there's something sympatico here. Not a fag thing, no—more like a lost brother or someone you bonded with in jail.

We have one, we have two, then he gets down to it.

"You want to make some easy money?" he says. "It requires a little bit of risk."

"Oh you mean like some crazy cocksugger with a knife telling me goodnight Irene?"

He chuckles, says, "You handled yourself very well, manny. Tell me, you ever been a commando?"

"I was in the Boy Scouts, Paul," I say. "Does that count?"

He nods, gives me the we're-all-cool-here look, we-don't-have-to-reveal-all-our-cards look.

"The Boy Scouts, of course, of course. Every boy in Canada must do service in the Scouts. I was in the local troop myself for a brief time... I got court-martialed and that was that."

"Still, I expect you know how to use a knife."

"I can sharpen a pencil, yes."

"Ever rob a bank?"

"Why rob a bank when you can rob a tourist? Much easier."

"You specialize in tourists?"

"As a matter of fact, yes."

"Glad we got that out of the way, amigo. And your proposition is?"

His proposition is that I join him and a couple of his friends and rob a party of tourists on a sight-seeing trip through the Tijuca Forest. Wow. Glance over at the Angolan but he's barely visible, seems lost in his own thoughts. Opportunity is just the face of fate.

"You know the Tijuca?" says Paul.

"A little," I say. "You don't need me for this."

"You been up Corcovado?"

"Not yet."

"Tourists love Corcovado, love the Redentor... but there is a new thing to love."

"Yeah? What's that?"

"The bungalow that Charles Darwin lived in. You know Darwin? Of course you do. But I bet you didn't know he lived Rio for a while in the Tijuca... at the bottom of Corcovado."

"No shit."

"It's true. The bungalow no longer exists but this doesn't matter. We can work around that. You get the picture, see the movie?"

I sure do. Lure a pack of foreign dummies into the forest, rob them, leave them to get out best they can. No cops, no soldiers, no gaucho hit squad, no pursuit.

"Why do you need me?"

"You're smart, know how to handle yourself."

He's selling me guff here, and he knows I know it.

"Well," he says, "the professionals I usually recruit have left town."

"Sure," I say. "Know what I think? You've been talking to the Angolan."

This pushes the smoke through his nostrils. He wheezes like a broken gasket, tries to laugh it off. Notice he glances the Angolan's direction, savvy to the fact that his accomplice is in the building.

"Ah ha *amigo*, as I say, you're smart, very smart, a true operator."

"Know what, Paul? If I was you, I'd be thinking how can I trust a guy like me? Know what I'm saying?"

"Of course. But we know we can trust you... Mat, isn't it?"

"These days, yeah."

"Well Mat you've proven you can be trusted."

"Even if I'm working for the enemy?"

Paul just blows this aside with a wave, says, "You're a soldier of fortune, *amigo*. I know—I'm one too."

True enough, yet I have to wonder why he takes such risks.

I say, "Why don't you get a regular job?"

"You must have a *cartiera* to get a job and I don't have one, sir. Do you?"

"What's a *cartiera*?"

"A small book with your certified birth date and a police clearance that says you don't have a criminal record. Government bullshit, man. Anyway, who wants to fucking work? I've done that, and I don't like it. I don't do clocks. For slaves, amigo."

"You should join a political party. They have dough."

"I don't like politics... politicians, police, priests, government dudes... all these titled *bastardos* are corrupt, they all want *um cafezinho* with their whiskey, beat their donkeys when they go home at night. Integrity is moolah and how you get moolah is of little consequence."

"Right. So you're not a Christian."

"I'm voodoo, man. I move with the beat."

"Thought so."

"My father was a minister, yet this didn't stop him from getting drunk now and then. He had a favorite saying: 'There is as much charity helping a man downhill as there is in helping him uphill.'"

"Groucho Marx, right?"

"Maybe... maybe a poet from the olden days... maybe my daddy. In a way he was a poet who wasted his life as a minister instead. When he was drunk, he was very poetic. What about you—you have a daddy?"

"Mostly, no. But technically, yeah."

Paul is puzzled. "You're illegitimate?" he says. "No shame, man."

"No no I'm as legitimate as any kid found on the steps of a church. What I need is a passport."

"A passport? Two days ago, no problem... I had a number of passports but unfortunately... look, if we do this job, there will be passports."

"Sure... tourists have passports."

"Exactly. So, what do you say? You want to get rich, get some I.D., some integrity?"

I'm looking at him, taking my time.

He says, "What's the matter? Don't you trust me? I trust you."

I say, "You familiar with the *Integralistas*, Paul?"

"Sure. They be a gang. Fancy name, but a gang anyway."

"What about vigilante squad?"

"Hey, *amigo*, why talk about this shit? Told you I don't mess with politics. So, you in?"

"I saw some passports... they were in a box, along with some other stolen stuff. Two of them belong to a couple of friends of mine who were murdered in Petropolis."

"The couple who got butchered? I read about that."

"We wouldn't be talking about the same passports, would we, Paul? The ones I saw, the ones you had...."

"Hey what you say, man—I kill people for their passports?"

"No, amigo. You rob people, so maybe you or one of your associates robbed the person who murdered these friends of mine."

He looks at me like a gun: maybe it will, even if he won't. "I'll ask my 'associates,'" he says, slipping back into his Caribbean accent. "I help you, you help me is how she works, yes?"

I nod.

"So," he says. "You in?"

I spin the ashtray, which is just an old saucer the cat has spurned. Figure it's his cause there's a gray and white Tom napping on the bar, one paw hanging free. I spin it, just like the game spin the bottle. If the butt points at me, I'm in.

Well hit me daddy eight to the bar... what's this? I'm seeing but not believing. There's a black panther on the floor, just like the one I shot, maybe is the one and the same after a trip to the taxidermist and back. Leonora Barasso is moving the lights around, trying to get the right effect.

"Just me and the cat?" I say.

She stops, smiles. "So pleased you could come, Thorsen," she says.

"Did I have a choice?"

"Don't be a silly boy. You're not a hostage."

Notice she's perspiring, and the circles around her eyes are almost black, like they're leaking mud. Malaria, I believe... either she told me or Lucy did. Half of Brazil has malaria, all levels of society. They blame the Amazon, people and bugs migrating south.

Go behind the screen, put on the costume she wants me to wear. German uniform, desert khaki. Looks like new Waffen SS gear to me, but modified. Instead of lightning bolts on the collar, the Integralist Sigma symbol, the capital 'E' that looks like it's been punched in the spine. Cotton. Trousers with in-built cloth belt. Nice jacket. Feels good, smells like victory. Now I'm getting it... a fashion ad, sure. But it's got a double agenda—behind the product, it's a recruitment drive.

"Makeup?" I say, stepping out.

She circles, looks me over. "You didn't shave this morning... good boy. Just the hint of the beast."

I'm a beast alright. Slept on the floor again last night cause I just don't trust beds. Easy target.

"Like your uniform?"

"Yes. Not exactly frogskin... more like desert rattlesnake."

"Camouflage is a form of cubism, did you know?"

Cubism? Sure I know. Keep on smiling, Sergeant.

"Want me to wear the cap?"

"Yes please... and the goggles... just let them dangle around your neck."

The radio or maybe a player pops on. Little bit of crackle as Artie Shaw and his band do the shuffle with Begin the Beguine. Turn around and here's this woman coming towards me wearing a carnival mask and a cocktail dress with her platinum hair all piled up in a nest of braids, old style, like Marie Antoinette. A wig but I'm not thinking that right now as she moves right in and we dance a few steps in half-time. Think I know who it is, although maybe I'm just hoping I know who it is.

She says nothing, cold and beautiful, and me, I just go with the flow. Leonora B. herds us into to position with the cat, sets up the scene, takes a few shots with the Agfa Isolette. Can feel the heat, and it ain't just the lights.

We try a number of positions, attitudes.

"Perhaps we should try a more casual look," purrs Leonora B. "No belt, open jacket... that's it, more relaxed... as if you're just getting dressed... or undressed. See what I mean?"

"Then maybe I should just have the undershirt...." Peel off my shirt, so it's just my undershirt and a bit of flesh below the natty combat tunic. Then we try a shot or two with no tunic. We face the camera, we face one another, we hold hands, we hold hips. Yeah, think I could get into being a model.

"Brilliant. Show a little skin, yes indeed."

Even a hick like me can see some of it's a bit silly. Holding a rifle in one hand and her waist with my other, and a boot on the neck of the cat might be o.k. for selling cigars or a corny Hollywood comedy but not the Integralist Party. Admit I liked the one where she gets down and embraces the panther and I'm lying tight against her. That'd be good for perfume. I don't want to get up but she gives me the elbow.

We finish up and I light up a cigarette, look her over, murmur, "*Uma... die schone Uma.*"

"*Schwein,*" she says, low and private.

The beautiful one calls me a pig? Before, I was just a boy, and calling me names hurt; now I'm a man and I like it.

She disappears somewhere in the back of the studio, behind the stacks of canvases, must have a nest there or something.

"There's a costume ball at the Copacabana Palace," says Leonora B. "Every Christmas, as a warm up for the Carnival. The magazine wants a pictorial that fits the season."

I'm thinking about Uma, wondering if she's coming back. This is when I notice the doll lying beside the panther, a small male figure in a tan uniform, with breeches and jack boots... face is familiar, the heavy black eyebrows, big forehead... but assume he's generic, just a soldier doll, and wonder if Uma was holding him or what. Why didn't I notice? Guess I was too busy making faces for the camera and feeling the heat of a masked woman.

Chapter Twenty-Six:

CASA DARWIN

PAUL IS PASSING HIMSELF OFF as a tour guide, has somehow managed to get himself a government ticket saying he's *um guia touristico* and is right there on the dock to meet the chumps who think they're on their way to see the great Charles Darwin's *casa de campo*, the cottage he stayed in briefly back when the dinosaurs still roamed the earth, er, 1833. They wanted me to be the guide cause Paul knows sweet Dick about Darwin but no way Jose was I putting myself in that position. The info Paul gave me about those stolen passports didn't warrant that sort of risk. He says they were stolen from a German guy, and I deduce that German guy was Boettner but don't know for sure. The German guy was mugged in Copacabana, says Paul. He didn't do it but one of his "associates" did and this associate is "out of town", meaning he's probably in jail or dead. Or, of course, Paul is full of shit.

The shit he tells these tourists about Darwin must be something, although I'm not around to hear it. Me and this other guy will be staked out in the forest, waiting for the chumps to come walking by. A very simple plan really—some impersonation, some fraud, some highway brigandage. Oh there's a shack, an abandoned Ranger station that the jungle is using as an arboretum and is now a favorite hangout for the monkeys. Who's to say it isn't the very place that Darwin used as a base for his surveys? Not me. Hey, I'm just a passenger.

Supposed to go like this: after the party of gringos take a ride up the mountain on the electric railway, check out the statue of the Redeemer or Redentor as folks around there call it, enjoy the magnificent views and all, Paul will lead them along a trail through the forest to Darwin's shack... or the Monkey House as I call it. There we'll bushwhack 'em, relieve them of their valuables, then vamoose.

Takes about 20 minutes for the train to get up there. Distance is about two and a half miles and it's rising over two thousand feet. I'm sure it's a nice ride and a nice view but you know, all the time I've been in Rio, I never had the pleasure. Watch Paul arrive at the station on the bus with the chumps, then go and kill some time in the square. The neighbourhood is called Cosme Velho and these days it's making a killing off the sightseeing business, especially since they finished building the statue of the Redeemer, which everyone in Brazil wants to see. With this other guy, a young favelado associate of Paul's called Rigo, although his nick name is Rotten Rodrigo. Needless to say I don't trust him, despite the smile and the tooth necklace. He's got the bones of a predator around his oily neck, man. And you don't pack a snub-nose 38 below your happy shirt and have a machete stashed along the trail if you're a heads up guy. We're watching some Christmas buffoonery or Carnival rehearsal in the square. Couple of guys dressed as Roman Centurions herding a near naked Christ who's packing a huge cross.

"*Carnaval*," says Rigo. "*Natal*."

Natal? Christmas? Doesn't look like Christmas to me the way those Centurions are laying on the whip. The guy, the Christ, the sucker with the cross, is staggering, falling down, and his cries are drawing a crowd, just as those whips are drawing blood. Some people throw coins, others flowers. Very confusing. I know there can be money in suffering, but if this is an act, these actors should be in Hollywood.

Rigo is scanning a lottery form. "Eh, should I bet on the *Jacare* or the *Macaco*?"

He points at the animals: the caiman and the monkey. Numbers 15 and 17.

"Why not the snake?" I say. "Or the camel?"

"Because in my dream, the caiman eat the lamb, *senhor*."

"Then I'd bet on the caiman."

He shouldn't smile—his teeth are pretty bad. The story I heard about him is he went to a dentist recently but the dentist wanted too much money, so RR shot him in the knee. Tough. Watch him head inside the tobacconist's to place his bet. The Animal Lottery. *Jogo do Bicho*. Supposed to be illegal but like a lot of stuff around here it's only illegal if the cops at the local precinct aren't getting their fair share of the winning numbers.

Meanwhile Christ has been whipped clear across the square, seems to be heading for the station to meet the train coming back down. Like I say, there's money in suffering. When Rigo returns, I tap my watch, indicate we should be on our way. Kill our drinks, head for the jungle. The trail is wide and legitimate for the first part, then we veer off. We did a dry run, couple of days ago, when it was raining and we were walking through clouds.

"So where you learn English, Rigo?" I say.

"The docks. Sometimes I unload ships."

Figures. Anyway, we're doing a fast clip through the forest, close to the Monkey Shack... it's maybe a half mile from the station, remote enough that no cries for help will be heard. Ah what a cruel, heartless universe it is, eh. Anything can happen in the Tijuca. Lots of dangerous animals, reptiles, spiders, pretty birds. I mean, they got Boas and Bushmasters... and if you're near a stream, watch out for the Fer de Lance.

RR tosses his cigarette, reaches into a tree, recovers his machete, and you know, I'm half-hoping there's a Boa in there just waiting to take care of him, pull a few teeth maybe. He spins the blade in his hand, then chops a tropi like he's decapitating someone, whoosh, a six inch stem cut clean in two. Satisfied, he hooks the machete onto his belt, and we continue on.

"So what kind of booty you like?" I say. "Any preferences?"

He trots like an Indian, small steps, keeps the engine warm 'case he needs to accelerate.

"*Dinheiro*," he says.

"Sure... money's always good. I like jewelry."

"Yeah, gold, silver... *bom*."

"What about passports? Any money in passports?"

Doesn't answer right away, then says, "Passports be for specialists."

"Yeah?" I say. "Tough sell?"

He just grunts, like the subject bores him. I drop it. When we get to the Monkey House, the Angolan is already there, waiting for us, feeding the monkeys. Tossing seeds at them, don't know what. He nods as we pull in. RR says something to him in Portuguese but as usual the Angolan is pretty quiet. Maybe he's a dummy, I dunno. But what I'm wondering is, is he still my friend when it comes to the crunch.

Some comedian has put a crude sign on the shack: Casa Darwin. Just an old board someone with a paint brush got creative with. Maybe one of the monkeys. Somewhere in the far distance there's a rumble that fades in and out, maybe thunder, maybe engines. We hunker down and wait, listen to the birds and beasts, watch the shadow patterns in the clearing. We're in a triangle, the distance of strangers. No talking. Yeah, we wait.

Maybe twenty minutes before we hear them coming, buzzing like bees behind the Caribbean melody of their guide, 'Paulo', a cute bit of suck for the occasion. We fade back into the trees, pull bandanas over our faces in the old outlaw tradition. Mine's red. We got hats too. Mine's a Panama. Weapons? You know what RR's got. The Angolan doesn't need anything other than the mule he has not far away. He's the courier. Me, I got Oswald, full clip, another in my pocket.

"This is where the great Sir Charles lived with his Rio mistress," Paulo is saying. "She was a local woman of Tupi Indian and Portuguese heritage. Her mother was a Countess, although it is often said that all Portuguese women in Rio are countesses."

Blah blah. They're loving it, even if the journey has left some of the older folks a little worse for wear.

He has a monkey on his shoulder. Nice touch.

"These monkeys are a wonderful curiosity to the few lucky people who see them... what do you think they look like?"

That's right, Chinese philosophers. Suckers.

"These monkeys are Confucius monkeys," says Paulo. "The Chinese road builders brought a couple of them to Rio... and now we have a colony."

"Look like Capuchins to me," says a voice. "I've never heard of a Confucius monkey."

"Ah ha come to Rio and you will learn many things," says Paulo.

"This is Darwin's cottage?" says a woman. "Who says?"

"The sign says, *senhora*," says Paulo.

This gets a few laughs.

"What do you think about Darwin's 'survival of the fittest' notion?" asks a fat American who looks like the Kaiser.

This when we step out of the jungle, weapons displayed.

The Newspapers:

O Globo: Three men disguised as Christmas Carnival players robbed a party of 20 foreign tourists in the Tijuca yesterday morning. The incident occurred not far from the Cosme Velho electric railway which takes visitors up and down Corcovado mountain. The party had just returned from a visit to the statue of the Redeemer and were travelling along a forest trail when they were ambushed and robbed by three men.

The men were described as Indians and were armed with a variety of weapons, including swords, spears, and whips. One had a pistol. They escaped with cash, jewelry, clothing, cameras, passports, wallets, personal medication, sun glasses and other items.

Witnesses describe the trio as experienced Carnivalistas who abandoned their costumes near the station, including the Cross of Calvary. They were last seen travelling on the train to the top of Corcovado where they mysteriously disappeared. Police say that while the witness reports are conflicting, they are confident they will find the perpetrators and bring them to justice. Last year, the municipal police apprehension record for the capture of violent crime offenders was 1:48, although this figure is disputed.

"This sort of brigandage brings shame on the city of Rio de Janeiro," said the mayor Gonzales Bigamisto.

Three people died. One person had a heart attack, one person was shot, one person escaped but was later found dead from a snake bite wound. Numerous members of the party were injured when a herd of *javelinas* happened on the scene and attacked. The guide contractor who is named as 'Paulo Cortazar' disappeared during the robbery. There is no record in the Rio de Janeiro municipal Tour Guide licensing authority of anyone by that name.

O Lapa Voz: Three, possibly four, armed robbers ambushed a group of tourists in the Tijuca Reservation yesterday sometime around noon. The tourists are from the American liner the SS Southern Cross, which docked in the morning en route from New York to Buenos Aires. Most of the tourists are said to be American and European, with a few South Americans. Among the group was a Mr. Pat O'Brien, a retired New York detective, who described the robbery as 'an unprofessional heist' which was probably "the work of a local political group who need cash to fund their revolutionary activities."

Chief of Police Filente Muller said that a number of communist cells are operating in Brazil. "While they receive money from Moscow and the International, armed robbery is their easiest way to raise funds while at the same time dressing their crime as political necessity. For example, this Tijuca attack can be rationalized as an attack on American imperialism or the Estado Novo."

When asked if the police received a message from a communist group or any leftist organization claiming credit for the attack, Chief Muller said the police had received several calls and messages claiming responsibility. He declined to name any group specifically.

The majority of the tourists have been treated in hospital and have returned to their ship. The SS Southern Cross will sail on the evening tide for Buenos Aires, and is scheduled to be back in Rio in five days as it returns to New York. It is hoped that the few remaining injured can rejoin the ship then.

O Mundo: Our reporter has new information on the Tijuca tourist robbery. Confidential sources say it was an inside job, planned by an unnamed European criminal who arrived in Rio de Janeiro on the SS Southern Cross, and was with the group when it was robbed. He is thought to be German and has come to Brazil to establish an elite terrorist group dedicated to the overthrow of the Vargas government.

The same sources say the criminal is pretending to be a German military intelligence agent. Echelons of the government have been rife with rumours for weeks about a German plot to occupy key Brazilian islands and launch a revolution from the South, possibly in the province of Santa Catarina which is predominantly German speaking.

There was an *Integralista* uprising on May 11 in the South that was widely supported by the German settlers.

It is not known if the suspect has rejoined the ship or remains in our city.

Foreign Minister Oswaldo Aranha has dismissed these allegations. "They are worthy of a romance novel, put about by provocateurs to damage our friendly relations with Berlin," he said. "Rio is full of paranoia these days. People should forget about this rubbish and go to work with confidence about the future. 1939 will be a good year for Brazil."

"*Feliz Natal*," he concluded. "*E um feliz ano novo.*"

(Happy Christmas... and a Happy New Year)

They're like a herd of frightened sheep spooked by a mad dog, cluster together whimpering and crying after Rigo whacks a dowager on her fat shoulders with the flat of his machete blade and she stumbles forward, then drops, lights out. Christ. Rotten Rigo, no kidding. He makes a move as if he's going to give her another whack on the neck, maybe decapitate her, so I have to step in, pull him off, wave my gun. He turns on me like a mad dog, like I interrupted a sacred act.

Paulo starts babbling. "Peace, brothers!" he shouts. "Have mercy on this poor woman, a well-meaning visitor to our buh, buh beautiful city!"

Did they rehearse this? Sounds like a play.

"What do they want?" says somebody. "Are they hungry?"

"We don't want your fucking Coca Cola!" shouts Rigo, waving his weapons. "Wallets, purses, bags... jewels, watches, have them ready or you will die!"

They're panicking... if they turn and run, the heist will be a failure.

A sharp looking woman steps out, says to Paul, "Negotiate with them for God's sake."

Son of gun... it's Bobby! Why didn't I notice her before? Bobby, almost forgotten, except in moments of horny nostalgia. She has her hair tied in a pony tail, just like the first time I saw her... guess the sun hat threw me. She's looking around defiantly, then our eyes lock. Got a kerchief tied around my face from the nose down and my Panama is tipped forward so's alls that's showing is my eyes and I swear to God she recognizes me. She looks at my gun, then back at my eyes, and know what? She smiles. Honest to God, she smiles. Women. I'll never understand them. Never.

Paul, er, Paulo says, "*Caros... vamos faze-los implorar.*"

"What's he saying?" says someone shrilly. "Have they killed Gertie?"

Seems the Kaiser knows the lingo, cause he says to Paulo, "Hey sonofabitch no begging... Americans don't beg, ya hear?"

Well that gets him a whack on the knees. Rotten is as Rotten as Rotten can be. Down goes the Kaiser, rolls and roars like a stuck pig.

The Angolan rolls up with a sack, and our victims start dumping their valuables into it. He's wearing a burlap bag over his head, holes punched so he can see. Rotten Rigo is hissing and screaming, acting the real nasty asshole, and quite frankly he's testing my patience. All the money... rings... watches... passports... into the bag.

"We' taking hostage!" Rigo barks. "You—*vem com agente, Punheta!*"

He gestures at Paulo with his pistol, and he and his monkey scuttle over our way. All part of the plan.

"I'm takin' a hostage for myself," I say, thinking of Bobby.

"One is enough," says Rigo, like he's the boss of me.

The monkeys in the Casa Darwin are agitated, start bailing for the surrounding trees when a herd of wild pigs bursts out of the jungle. Peccaries, or javelinas as they call them some places. Skunk pigs as I call 'em, vicious brutes that can swarm a man and leave him looking like a fish skeleton in a matter of minutes. The smell, Jesus Murphy. Must be two dozen of them and they just attack. Ugly. People run or fall where they stand and it's everyone for himself. The pigs are acting out of fear, because something is out there that's spooked them. A plane? What?

The Angolan's already on his way with the loot. He knows the animal trails, has a burro to help him with the load. Rigo and Paul have split too and I'm vacillating. Shoot a pig, shoot another, look around for Bobby. Some of the smart people, some of the younger ones, are climbing trees to safety. Shoot a pig, shoot another. What a fiasco, the screams, men, women and monkeys and crazy crazy leaping pigs. The best laid plans... we had a plan. I suspected there was a second plan, the one in which I was the patsy, but I'm thinking all plans are broken now and it's everyone for himself. There's the Kaiser trying to crawl to safety in the Casa, his belly draggin' in the dirt, looks like a pig himself, so I guess he's safe. Then I see Bobby running away with a pig in pursuit, except, you see, the pigs aren't really pursuing, they're crazy with fear, completely confused and lashing out.

Head after Bobby, catch up to her by a stream which hasn't got much water in it, more like a gulch than anything. She's hanging onto a root and the pig is long gone.

"Dance?" I say.

"I knew it was you," she says, panting. "But I never, never figured you for a crook, Thorsen."

"I'm worse than that, baby," I say. "No time for talk. Let's go."

She's hesitant, thinks she has an obligation to the others. Probably does, but what's she really capable of doing? Better to get help. She takes my hand, and I pull her onto the bank.

She sniffs me, says, "Well you smell better than those horrible pigs."

A roar comes up from nowhere, very quick, like a low, slow flying bomber that's coming from the dark side of Corcovado. It's an airship or Luftschiff as the Germans call it. Christ, it's huge, like the Hindenburg, except it can't be the Hindenburg as she went down in flames, couple of years ago. No swastikas on the tail fins, no markings, no company, no country. What is it? American? Italian? Brazilian military? The sun is glinting on the windows of the gondola like semaphore. Four engine pods that I can see... maybe five, if that's one at the back. Man, what a magnificent machine, like something from another world.

"Watch out!" screams Bobby.

So busy ogling the airship that I miss seeing the archer drawing his bow back, taking dead aim at us, his eyes slits of focused hate. It's Paul, the fuggin' Judas.

He hasn't forgotten about Plan B, has he? The payback Plan where his good buddy yours truly dies for the raid on his camp HQ and takes the rap for the Darwin scam. All suspected, all expected, cause I knew going in these guys weren't stupid. Greedy, yes, although I never figured them to be that ideological.

I dive, knocking Bobby aside as the arrow thunks into the ground, close enough to piss me off completely. He's on higher ground, and we're ducks, whatever way you slice it. But he's pissed me off and I have Oswald in my hand, and I'm blasting hit me daddy eight to the bar. His own words are in my head like a radio: 'There's as much charity in helping a man downhill as there is in helping him uphill'. Bam bam bam... I'm on my belly, home on the range, two hands clasped on the grip, triggering bam bam bam. He gets one more arrow off, Paul the Hood, guess he's had training or he's a natural born son of a jungle juju. I think I got him. I certainly meant to. And if I didn't, I'll get 'im next time.

The airship fades with the gunshot reverbs, memory or dream, take your pick. Paul, he went down, naturally or unnaturally, and when I get up there and check, there's nuthin' but a dead monkey, a victim of fate. Damn, he does look like a philosopher, the white face, big forehead, big eyes, long whiskers, wide mouth and no moustache. Serene. Bullet through the heart. I'm not in the business of shooting monkeys or pigs for that matter, but shit happens. Paul? Long gone Johnson.

"Was that Paulo who was trying to kill us?" says Bobby.

"Kill me," I say. "And yes."

"But why? Aren't you crooks together?"

"Looks that way, doesn't it? Fact is, I'm working for the police."

"What police?"

"A special contract unit. I was just along for the ride."

"But you let it happen—"

"You don't understand."

"No I don't."

"It's part of the dirty politics in Brazil, Bobby. I'd love to fill you in but I can't."

"When I first met you, I thought you were just a boy."

"I am."

"Oh, is that so? A boy who knows how to use guns like a man!"

"I thought you knew that from the start, doll."

Gives me an unhappy look, then says, "Head Office is going to be really angry about this. How did this happen? How did this fellow Paulo get hired? Sure had me fooled."

"He was an imposter. Fake credentials. Probably substituted himself for someone legit."

"But, but where's the real person?"

We're navigating through a lot of rough bush. Can hear the Corcovado train, the whine and the rumble. Not far, but not close.

"No idea," I say. 'Never knew him to begin with."

"This place is corrupt!" she exclaims. "Bet they paid him off!"

Or worse, I think. Instead, I say, "Artie's Begin the Beguine is number one in Rio."

She sniffs, says, "Fading in New York."

We come to a nice spot, a grove with some sun and a view of Guanabara Bay. We take a breather.

"You got a new woman yet?" she says. "A samba queen?"

"Been too busy," I say. "Like you wouldn't believe."

"Busy men like chippies."

"No chippies in Rio, doll. Just Countesses."

I slip my arm around her waist, feel her hard, familiar ass, get stiff and undeniable.

"We don't have time for this," she murmurs. "I should report back to the ship."

"Sure," I say. "Report."

We find a friendly surface, lie down, take off some clothes, let the sun eat us. You can do this in Rio around Christmas. We do some other stuff but I don't want to think about it too closely. Details can be dangerous.

Sure, we did some more catching up as we tried to find our way out of the Tijuca. When I asked if she'd found my replacement yet she was coy. But when I asked her about Boettner, the ship's purser, she says he was arrested.

"They say he was a German spy."

"Who arrested him?"

"The police, last time we were in Rio."

"So he's in jail here?"

"Don't ask me... you're the cop... aren't you?"

CHAPTER TWENTY-SEVEN

SAFARI MAN GOES TO THE JOCKEY CLUB

WE'RE AT THE JOCKEY CLUB which is where all the big shots in Rio like to hang out, and I mean big. It's a treat from the boss. Me and Eddie, so I guess I'm a capo now or near enough.

"Excellent, excellent," says Barasso when I finish my report. "The newspapers have risen to the bait. These communists who attack our tourists must be rooted out, put to the sword. The American press will go crazy, and Washington will start to understand just what's going on in South America."

He laughs, reaches over the low drinks table, slaps me on the shoulder. Yeah, I'm the man.

"How unfortunate the pigs are hungry these days, eh?"

Oh yeah, very unfortunate. That's why we're laughing. I'm looking around this club room thinking South America's going pretty good if this is any indication. Driven past the place a few times, as it's on the south edge of the Botanical Gardens near the swamp or lake as locals prefer to call it. The big racetrack, the clubhouse that looks like one of those shiver sepulchres you see in a ritzy graveyard. Members call it 'the Lodge' which makes me think most of these fat cats are Masons.

Gets noticeably quiet in the room and I look over my shoulder to see what's going on. There's a little white guy in a suit shadowed by a big black sonofabitch, kind of mean and dangerous, obviously a bodyguard. Black guy's packin' heat cause I can see the bulge over his heart. Barasso stops talking, looks up expectantly. Eddie leans towards my ear, says softly, "Vargas."

Vargas is wearing soft sunglasses, the sort you get from Switzerland if you have the dough, probably give you the fourth dimension and an X-ray of the soul. The man looks harmless, though. Easy demeanor. Nods at various plutocrats as he passes by, just like Julius Caesar passing through the lobby of the Roman Senate. Imperial without trying.

He stops just behind me, says to Barasso, "Manuelo."

Barasso sets aside his cigar, says, "*Presidente.*"

"The *Senhora*?"

"Leonora is well. *Senhora* Vargas?"

Vargas sighs, says, "The *Senhora*... you know. I just saw Iambic as I was coming in. I believe he's looking for you."

Barasso nods. Don't know if the three of them have got something going or if *O Presidente* is just passing along the fact. Can feel the bodyguard's eyes on my neck.

"How goes the battle, Getulio?" says Barasso. "Keeping the opposition at bay?"

"Eh, it depends on who you mean, Manuelo," says Vargas. "Some of them have resorted to *ogo*... yes, witchcraft."

"There are always some among us who deploy false religion," says Barasso.

"True. I hear the candomble outlaws are making a fortune selling Vargas dolls."

Barasso laughs softly. Eddie sorta follows.

"Getulio, you are nothing if the street sellers aren't hawking your juju...."

"*Claro*... yet it isn't the humble street seller that gives me insomnia, Manuelo. There are dolls, and there are... dolls."

Barasso has restored his cigar to his mouth. Think he's biting on it to keep from laughing.

Vargas says, "Anyway, my regards to Leonora. *Senhores*...." We half-rise from our seats like puppets, but he's already on his way to the dining room where he has a private booth.

Barasso looks at me, says, "Now you can tell your grandchildren you met the President of Brazil, Thorsen."

Well we weren't introduced, but I guess close is close enough. If he'd seen my face, maybe he would've had me shot.

I say, "Is his wife ill?"

Barasso grunts, says, "He has a mistress and his wife is sometimes 'under the weather'. Just the way of the world."

"What's this doll he's talking about?"

Eddie laughs. Barasso sorta laughs. Don't get an answer because these guys think I like to play dumb.

Iambic Fontana finds us just when the second round arrives. Can't lie, don't like the sonofabitch. His dreams are not my dreams. How do I know? Instinct. Feel it in my gut, right from the start. Any man who calls you "Bobo" should be on your list... and don't lie, we all keep a list.

He's got a magazine in his hand, drops it on the table.

"The eagle has landed," he says.

Rio Life, a glossy for the villa class. Barasso flicks through it until he finds what he knows is there, studies it, nods slow and easy like a rocking horse warming up. He passes it to me. Eddie leans in for a look.

"Leonora is a good photographer," says Iambic F. "An artist."

Well it's me and Uma, what else? And there's that doll in her hand, a plaything. The reclining shot with me at the back, looking at her, too blind and horny to see she's looking at the doll, Vargas, no question. Vargas, under the spell of the Nazi Cleopatra. It's good.

"Beautiful woman," says Eddie. "How do you do it, man?"

"I just do what I'm told," I say.

"You had her, didn't you?" says Eddie. "He did, didn't he, boss?"

Barasso chuckles, snaps his fingers, and Eddie grabs the mag, passes it back.

Barasso dismisses us, so he and Fontana can plot.

We go to the lobby where there's some sort of ceremony going on with a racehorse. "Who's this?" I say to Eddie. "Seabiscuit?"

"No no, the best horse in Brazil, Vendetta," says Eddie. "Three time winner of the Jockey Club Stakes. Belongs to some *pessoa* I don't know."

Big, powerfully built black mare. The jockey is perched in the saddle... a small doll about two feet high. Shit, looks like Mussolini, although maybe not. Sure isn't Joe Stalin. The bridle is being held by a statuesque model wearing a red sash. It's Uma. Takes me a minute to figure out what's going on. But when I see Leonora Barasso and her daughter nearby I realize Leonora's in charge of the show, or is at least its designer. Lots of people checking it out. Some guy in a green suit who looks like he's been drinking too much olive oil is telling everybody what a great horse this is, too bad the jockey couldn't be here because of an unfortunate injury. Hell, who needs a jockey when you've got a fascist doll and a hot German bitch for a groom?

"Why no jockey?" says Eddie through the side of his mouth. "He was told to get lost or take a bullet in the knee. Not needed. Nice show, eh?"

Sure is. Of course I'm checking out Uma, savouring the memory of our modelling work together. The horse might be well put together, but believe me, Uma's better. She sees me, knows I'm watching, knows I'm running surveys.

Lucy hustles over, grabs my arm, kisses my cheek, cries, "Thorsen! Where've you been?"

People are looking. "Been doing stuff for your dad," I say.

She's holding on tight, and I suppose that's o.k. cause she's looking pretty good. She and Uma are the best lookin' dolls in the room... excluding the horse, of course. And the jockey.

Leonora B. comes over. Still limping a bit but otherwise o.k. Smoking her fag through a long-stemmed holder, wearing a masculine sports jacket, waistcoat, cocktail dress. Bohemian look you'd call it.

"Thorsen, dear," she says in that husky upper Brit accent of hers. "What luck—I want you to stand beside Uma so I can take a picture of my new stars together."

"Leave him alone, mama," says Lucy. "Thorsen's shy."

"It's true," I say. "People make me nervous."

"Tosh," says Leonora B., starts to lead me away. Lucy hangs on, tries to keep me back.

Eddie whispers in my ear, "How you do it, man?"

People are milling about, checking out the horse, checking out the model. Uma's sash reads '*Senhorita Berlim*' which is 'Miss Berlin' for you and me. Lucy doesn't let go of me until I'm positioned beside Uma, and only then because her mother pushes her out of the way. A bit of a buzz in the crowd. Guess some of them recognize us from our photo in Rio Life.

"Hi Uma," I say, slipping my arm around her waist. "Hear about the death threats?"

"*Was*?" she says. "*Todesdrohungen*?"

"Somebody doesn't like our photo in the magazine. Seen it?"

She's still smiling for the crowd, although it's an expression more than a smile. It's like 'maybe' or 'maybe not'.

Leonora takes a couple of photos with a small camera, and there's a news guy there with a flash camera.

"Kiss," says Leonora.

I hesitate, but Uma just pivots into me like a coffin lid, sealing my fate forever. She kisses me, full and hard. Flash. We kiss again and the crowd murmurs its approval. Even the horse whinnies. I'm thinking, this is very unwise considering what I've been up to recently. I don't need my face in the newspaper.

Can see Lucy isn't pleased about this. If she had a gun, not sure who she'd shoot first: Uma or her own mother.

Barasso shows up, says, "Eddie, I need you to drive me to the office. Thorsen can take care of my wife and daughter."

He talks briefly with Mrs. B, who then kisses him on the cheek.

237

I get to drive the Bugatti.

"I'll sit up front with Thorsen," says Lucy.

"No you won't, dear," says Leonora B. firmly. "You and Uma in the back."

This doesn't sit well with Lucy, but she's too well bred to be ignorant about it. Hey, as should be: Princesses in the back.

We drive to the Copacabana Palace, which isn't that far away. Notice there's a nice stack of Rio Life magazines in the lobby. Leonora pauses, inspects a copy briefly, smiles.

"Take my arm, Thorsen," she says. "Girls, walk behind."

This is how it's done, is it? Feel like Legs Diamond, man. Pretty good for a hick from Kelowna, British Columbia. Rio? What's Rio? An apple? Folks back home haven't got a clue about life in the alternative universe. Heads turn, natch. We get settled out on the terrace. The usual fantastic view of the sparkling sea, the beach. Some guys playing soccer. Someone flying a kite. Couple of people on horses riding through the surf. Swimmers, sun bathers, kids messing around. Some boats, not many.

"The last time you were here, you nearly got arrested," says Leonora B.

"Won't happen again," I say. "I'm with you."

Once again I'm pretty fast, light her, Uma and myself... but when Lucy reaches for a cigarette, her mother slaps her hand.

"Don't get started," she says to Lucy. "I had a dream last night. I gave birth to a cigarette, only this cigarette grew hands and tried to strangle me."

"Oh mother," says Lucy. "Another one of your funny dreams."

"Do you dream, Thorsen?" says Leonora B.

"Sure," I say. "I dream about Martians."

"Are they hostile?"

"Yes."

The drinks arrive, then the menus. While we're taking a look, a couple stops at the table, congratulates Leonora. Guy's got long hair, sunken eyes, big forehead and teeth like a barracuda. Supposed to be a crime novelist, goes by the name of Jeff Lisbon or Lisboa. Mean anything? Not to me. His woman is called Coco, skinny and sunburnt all to hell. Dyed hair, black eyebrows. Lots of gold clanging on her bones.

"And these are your models," says Coco. "How lovely."

"Where's the little hombre?" says Jeff. "He's the one I like."

Lucy rolls her eyes, Uma looks serenely at the sea... or Berlin, somewhere over the horizon.

"Darling, was the little fellow really meant to be our President?" says Coco. "We're dying to know."

"Draw your own conclusions," says Leonora. "The doll is just a prop."

238

Coco looks at Uma, then me, says, "Well I do like your props."

We could be cuts of meat, I guess.

"Have you heard about the new expedition to find Colonel Fawcett?" says Jeff. "Has Manuelo been asked to contribute?"

"Another search party?" says Leonora. "Surely not."

Fawcett's the guy who disappeared in the Amazon looking for the ancient city he called 'Z'. You might think of it as El Dorado. I was a kid in school when Fawcett went missing. 1925 or 26.

"There's something in there," says Jeff mysteriously. "Our jungle has secrets."

"Communists, most likely," says Leonora.

Oh they laugh. It's a crazy world. Anything could be going on in the old Amazon. They slide on. Others take their place... must be a dozen who pay their respects, pass on their compliments. Leonora plays 'em all, we just eat our grub, drink our drinks. This is the life. *A doce vida*... the sweet life.

"You see kids?" says Leonora. "People are crazy about you."

"What about these threats?" says Uma.

Feel like kicking her leg. Would've, except Lucy has hers jammed against mine.

"What threats?" says Leonora.

Uma looks at me, says, "Schön here says threats... ja?"

"I was just kidding, Uma," I say.

"Did you hear something?" says Leonora. "Somebody say something to you?"

Shake my head. I'm keeping my trap shut. Maybe I was reading too much into Vargas' remarks. Maybe.

"The doll is proving controversial," says Leonora. "Well, that's art."

"You worried me, Thorsen," says Uma. "See? I eat nothing."

"Sorry," I say. "Just teasing, is all."

"You must eat, Uma," says Leonora. "Otherwise you'll lose your figure."

A silence drifts over us. A kind of uneasiness or more maybe that something's going on we don't know about. Too much attention isn't a good thing.

"I want to see a movie," says Lucy. "There's a zombie movie showing."

"Zombies?" says Leonora. "Why? Why do you want to?"

"It's called '*White Zombie*'. Supposed to really good. How about it, Thorsen?"

I shrug, say, "Whatever the boss says."

Leonora mulls it over, looks at Uma, says, "You want to see a zombie film, Uma?"

Now her leg is jammed against mine, so I'm pinned.

"Whatever the boss says," says Uma slyly.

"Where is it showing, Lucy?" says Leonora.

"Just around the corner," says Lucy.

"How will you get home?"

"Taxi."

Leonora slides her car keys across the table. "No," she says. "Thorsen can drive you and Uma. I'm tired. I'll take a taxi."

There's never any bill when you're with these people. She just initials an invoice at the waiters' station on the way out, and when we reach the lobby, she slips me a hundred, whispers, "Lucy never carries any money." Fine. I'll carry it. The doorman hustles her a cab and after hugs and kisses she's on her way. We retreat via the passages to the side door where the *Senhora* likes to park the Bugatti.

As we walk, Lucy says, "Thorsen, what happened to Fernando?"

I say, "Accident, Lucy."

"What sort of accident?"

"Fell off his horse."

"But he was a good rider."

"Maybe so. I didn't see it."

"Did he hit his head? Nobody will tell me."

"Something like that."

"He wasn't shot, was he?"

Jeepers creepers, this gal isn't as young as she looks.

"Who'd shoot him?"

"My dad... maybe."

"Lucy, get a grip. Your old man wouldn't do that."

"Wouldn't he? *Senhor* Manuelo is capable of anything."

"Not that, Lucy. He didn't."

"Poor Fernando."

Yeah, poor Fernando, the boy killer from Leblon or whatever rathole in Rio his folks call home. I could tell her exactly what went down but for what percentage, eh. Besides, Uma is here.

Turns out the movie isn't just around the corner but in old town, and isn't in a regular theatre but some workers hall. Some students are running it for the union a.k.a the Comintern, cause the dudes at the door have red kerchiefs around their necks and Joe Stalin caps and call us 'comrade' whenever they point to the box for our 'donation'. Christ, are we dressed for this? From the Jockey Club to the Copa Palace to the Simon Bolivar Hall? We should just get back in the Bugatti and drive clear all the way south to Montevideo. Be lucky if we get out of here with our clothes intact. The seating is rough, bunch of wooden chairs rowed up and facing a low stage. The projector is in the middle. Just what the hell interest these comrades have in a zombie flick is beyond me. Bunch of people there, mostly men, some women, and none of them are from the Jockey Club. Some guy gets on the stage, gives a speech. Looks like an intellectual. What I mean by this is he smokes a pipe and has a hot looking woman, a real South American cha cha cha chick, ass that swings, lips that bleed. Just one, mind. I got two.

"What's he saying?" I whisper to Lucy.

"He's saying the Indians in the Amazon are being killed by the government... he's saying that our comrades need our help."

Hmm. The usual thing. Some big corporation probably wants the land... mining, timber, pharmaceuticals, whatever. When he finishes up, there's some applause, and wouldn't you know it, we're clapping too. Ah yes... the clenched fist salute. The audience rises, and there's a forest of clenched fists. Thank god we're sitting at the back. Anyway, I'm hoping cha cha cha might get up and say something but instead some student takes the stage and preps us for the movie. Yes, it's a gringo film about zombies, yet it exposes the cruelty of the corporate lie, just as we see it in Brazil, comrades. It might be set in Haiti but the situation is the same as many of our workers find themselves in, slaving as zombies on our plantations and in our sugar mills. The worker as zombie, the death in life as imposed upon us by the privileged classes. O yeah, clap clap. Let's see it.

The cigarette smoke is so thick it makes the projector beam look like a searchlight. Anyway, it's good to be in the dark. It's not long before I realize I've seen the movie before. Bela Lugosi as the evil voodoo guy and the white chick who becomes a zombie and who quite frankly isn't as attractive as either of the women I'm sitting between. After while Lucy whispers in my ear, "I'll be back," disappears someplace. I take the opportunity to slide my arm around Uma's waist, feel her up a bit, nibble an ear.

"*Zombie-Frau,*" I whisper.

"*Schwein,*" she murmurs.

Groping her is great, can't tell you how great. She goes slack, slumps in my arms, allows all sorts of liberties. Her mouth is better than any movie. Do believe we'd be doing it if we were on the floor.

However, even whales have to come up for air. She lights a cigarette, seems shaky. I adjust my chair because, close as we are, we're drifting apart. After a while Lucy still hasn't returned. Uma says, "Let's get some fresh air."

Surprise surprise... Lucy's sitting on the front steps with the skinny kid who introduced the movie. Dark hair, glasses, long face, narrow face, some fuzz shadow, holds his smoke with his thumb and forefinger the way guys do with butts and rollies. Student.

"Thought you liked zombies," I say to Lucy. "Thought you'd been kidnapped."

Lucy laughs, says to her friend, "This is Thorsen... he's my bodyguard."

He doesn't understand, so she repeats it in Portuguese. Guy looks at me, nods, but obviously he's more interested in Uma.

"Rhino is studying Russian literature," says Lucy. "*Nao e voce?*"

Aren't you, Rhino... Rhino, short for Reinaldo. He nods, sorta lazy.

"We should be going," I say. "I promised your mother."

Lucy groans, makes a face, says, "Don't be square! There's a party."

You know, Lucy's going through a change or maybe I just didn't see anything but the girl before, didn't see she had her own ideas. Her parents would never have let her come here if they'd known the politics.

"I have instructions from the boss," I say. "Let's go."

Lucy looks at me, then Uma. Uma says, "I need to change my clothes."

Lucy says, "Will you drive me if mama says o.k.?"

Sure kid. Whatever the boss says. Not sure about Leonora but if Manuelo's around, he'll say no. Lucy tells Rhino what's up and he makes a show, sort of pleads. Then it changes to insults.

"Rhino, I said maybe later," says Lucy.

"*Seu merda, entao se mover ao longo,*" says Rhino petulantly.

When we're driving back to Leblon, I say to Lucy, "What did your boyfriend say to you?"

"Doesn't matter," says Lucy. "He's not my boyfriend. Just a student I know."

"Come on, what'd he say?"

"If you really want to know, he said 'shit, then move along.'"

"Lovely."

Uma laughs.

"Just a local saying," says Lucy. "'The horse shits, then moves along.'"

"Who's the horse?" I say.

"Me, I guess. I don't know... us maybe."

"Us maybe... well maybe I should turn around, go back, slap this Rhino some. He a communist?"

"I don't know. Socialist maybe."

"Don't be stupid, Lucy. That was a nest of commies you took us to."

"I didn't know! Rhino said the film society was showing this swell movie with zombies, so I thought o.k."

"Rhino his real name?"

"Reinaldo."

"Figured that. Who's the Professor with the tart?"

"Don't know. Never saw him before. You won't mention this to my parents, will you, Thorsen? Please, I'll do anything...."

Uma laughs. Of course when we get back to the villa, the Senhor and the Senhora will have none of it, especially after I whisper the facts to the mother. Her, rather than him. If Manuelo got a full description he'll probably send me and Eddie off to shoot 'em up, burn the hall down or something. Well maybe not that drastic. Manuelo might go fearless full throttle sometimes but as I'd come to appreciate, he never does anything without a plan. Lucy and Leonora want us to stick around but Miss Berlin and I say we're tired, so we get a cab to take us out of there down to Flamengo. It's the next day or the day after I find out someone nicked the red Bugatti insignia badge, pried it off the radiator grill. Well, that's commies for you, but of course we blame it on a bellhop at the Copa Palace. Commies would've smashed the headlights.

Big ghost moon up there throwing its silver blanket over the palms and mountains around the bay. Find a nice spot on the sand, watch a couple of black women throw white flowers in the surf. Uma thinks they've just put someone's ashes in the sea.

"Feeding the sea god," I say.

"Superstition?" says Uma. "Ja, they are very superstitious in this country."

We're talking in German. Seems easier with her.

"So Uma, whatever happened to Herr Kallingram?"

"He had a job opportunity in Sao Paulo."

"You didn't go with him?"

"No... look, he was just a means of getting to Brazil."

"You weren't in love?"

She hisses dismissively.

"Not even when you were drunk?"

"I admit booze goes to my head quickly."

I pull my worry stone from my pocket: "Remember this?"

She takes it, rolls it between her fingers.

"That's when I knew," I say.

"Knew what," she says. "I am a rock collector?"

"That's when I knew," I say.

She closes her hand in mine, the rock between our palms. That's pleasure.

"Silly little rock," she says. "Ugly, actually."

"Mysterious and smooth," I say. "Just like a beautiful woman."

"Oh? And who is this beautiful woman?"

"The woman of my dreams, of course."

"That's why you keep her in your pocket...."

"Yeah... nice and close."

She laughs, lifts my hand, kisses the stone. An ambulance passes by quickly, heading towards O Centro, then a bus. But it's quiet really, most of the sounds distant, like yesterday or tomorrow, fading or coming.

We lie back, look at the stars, the trails of mist.

"Why Brazil, Uma?"

"Why Brazil, Thorsen?"

"I asked you first. Are you really Miss Berlin?"

"Are you really Thorsen?"

"What... you think I got another name?"

"*Schatz*, the only Canadian staying at the Hotel Venezuela is called Mat Sundin."

This almost makes me sit up, my voice go weird.

"Are you a spy or something?"

She giggles. "Leonora told me you were staying there. Her husband is one of the owners, I think."

"Why didn't you leave a message? I've been looking for you every day since we left the ship."

"Such a liar. Been months."

"It's true. I saw Kallingram at a party given by the Barassos, looked for you."

"I was there. I saw you romancing Lucy."

"You were there?"

"And you shot the wild jaguar. Everyone was so impressed."

"But why didn't I see you?"

"Because you weren't really looking. You were busy with Lucy."

"I saw Kallingram. He was dressed as a Nazi officer."

"Oh that... yes, sure. Just a joke."

"A joke?"

"He's a magician. He likes playing tricks."

"So he's not really a Nazi pretending to be a magician...."

"I don't know what his politics are. He might be anything. He's actually Hungarian although maybe not. He's all show business."

"Sounds like a dangerous hustler to me. How'd you meet him?"

"At a party... government big shot party in Berlin. The agency sent me and a couple of other girls to be hostesses."

"Hostess...."

"Yes. They often hire pretty girls to dress up the function. Why, you think I'm a prostitute?"

"I didn't say that. Guess I'm just not big city."

"You think I'm big city?"

"Well, you're not a cowgirl, Uma."

"Ah, if only you knew. I went to a *Reichbrauteschule*."

"Reich Bride School—what the hell is that?"

"Academies for girls to be trained in the Nazi idea of what a good housewife should be. You've never heard of them? Your relatives never mentioned them?"

"My mother doesn't keep up contact, so...."

"Well, we were just glorified milkmaids, groomed to look like we just came off a farm. It's Hitler's way of providing suitable wives for his Nazi friends, especially the *Schutzstaffel*. You've heard of the SS?"

"Yeah, I've heard of it. Elite unit, isn't it? Outside the control of the German Army."

"Yes, the Nazis have their own army. See? I could've married a Captain, had a nice house."

Few blocks away a bell is tolling... Hail Mary, Hail Mary.

"How'd you miss out?"

"Someone saw my photograph in the *National Socialist-Frauen Warte* magazine, which liked Bride School girls. So, I became a model." *So I became a model, and I allowed a magician to saw me in two on an ocean liner going south.* "That trick you guys did... did Kallingram ever make a mistake, cut you?"

"Everybody asks that."

"If I looked, would I see a scar?"

Run my hand across her tight, smooth stomach. Nothing. But of course you never see the cuts that matter.

EVER GET THE FEELING something's going to happen, even when everything appears cool and copacetic? Sure. Only idiots dream on, even if it's 80 degrees in the shade and all the people on the street are smiling and snapping their fingers. There are too many shadows out there, even if some of the danger lizards are in jail or out of town. Figure I better cruise by the embassy, check my mail. Yep—one from Aunt Renie, one from my mother. All my mother can talk about is Hitler, how she would love to visit old Deutchland, which is one helluva turnaround from her position a few years ago when the old country was the shithole of the world filled with miserable losers... and Aunt Renie just tells me what I already know, that is, Klaus Gerwing got arrested and no one knows where he's being held. Well, there's one thing: my father has gone overseas, hush hush. Renie thinks he's back in the Service.

And there's a message: it says 'your passport is ready, please speak to the Attache'. Unsigned, doesn't say who the Attache is. I don't need a passport, so this is either a mistake or something else. Go to the desk, show the note to one of the secretaries. She's English alright, like one of those grass hockey players who chop your ankles when you don't surrender the ball. Stern. Doesn't have the Rio spirit.

"Mr. Thorsen?" she says in the firm voice of the supremely organized.

"Yes," I say. "Is this meant for me? My passport is good for another three years."

"If you could just have a seat in the Reading Room, someone will speak to you shortly."

Nobody in there, so I pick up a local newspaper. Holy... what's this? I'm getting so native I can sorta read the papers, get a sense of what they're saying.

O Globo. The body parts found on the empty lot on Laguna Y Street, a few blocks from the beach... identified as Hans Ulrich Boettner, a citizen of the United States...

"It was in three parts... the lower torso, the upper torso... the head...

"It is believed that Boettner was a German national with US Citizenship who was recently arrested on suspicion of spying. Filente Muller's office issued a statement saying Boettner had been released 'for lack of evidence' more than a week ago but refused further comment... dah diddy dah... brief mention of the invasion conspiracy... Jack the Ripper... the Petropolis murders... fear in the streets etc. Big melodramatic headline: O ESTRIPADOR GOLPEIA OUTRA VEZ... the Ripper Strikes Again."

Young fellow, maybe thirty, shirt and tie, no jacket, brown hair buzzed clear of his ears. No nicotine on the fingers, looks fit.

"Mr. Thorsen?"

"Yes?"

"Some identification? Passport?"

"Er, my passport is deposited here for safekeeping."

He has it, and he's checking the picture. "Right you are," he says. "Can't be too careful."

"Is there something wrong?"

"London is wondering what happened to you. We work with Ottawa, as I'm sure you know. We're wondering what happened to the network."

"Shouldn't we be talking in your office?"

"Better to be semi-public. We have Brazilian employees, and to be honest, we're never quite sure who might be tattling to their intel."

Faint smile, then he adds, "Not everyone reads Rio Life, but let's assume they do. You're almost famous."

"That was a mistake. I'd no idea what it was about."

"Hmm. Beautiful woman. Wish I could make a mistake like that."

"One day you will."

"If I do, bang goes the pension. Now, as I was saying, the network?"

"Tits up. The Abwehr man got arrested for an unrelated matter."

"Alfredo?"

"Yeah."

"Serious?"

"Paedophilia."

"So the network is no longer transmitting?"

"Don't know. I'm not."

"Hmm. So you're unemployed."

"Not exactly... I got other things going."

"You mean your career as 'Safari Man.'"

Not quite sure how much I should be telling this guy. My private business and my business for King and country have become blurred.

"Can you tell me what's happened to Archie McDonald," I ask.

"Ah McDonald, the pornographer. Ottawa has asked us to help if we can, but hands are tied and all that. Officially he's just a criminal who disappeared, is hiding in Brazil beyond extradition. We don't know if the local authorities know of his surveillance work or not. The 'Senhor Prolific' charge might be a duck blind, we just don't know. We made the usual sort of inquiries on behalf of a British Empire subject, and all they would tell us is he's being held in prison, which one they wouldn't say."

"I heard the Black Cathedral."

"Quite possibly. It won't be the Municipal jail. Could be Cobra Island or even one of those prison ships the military run."

"So Ottawa has sent no one to replace him?"

"Not that I know of. McDonald was ad hoc. He was here, he could be useful, he was put on retainer. We do this sort of thing all the time... which is why we're wondering about you. We realize you're, ah, unofficial, a contract player."

"A canary."

"Yes, indeed. A canary. Can we still count on you?"

Hand him the newspaper, point to the Boettner murder article. "Boettner was the purser on the SS Southern Cross," I say. "Was he involved in spying or not?"

"The Brazilians thought so."

"The reason I ask is because of the similarity between his murder and the murder of the Austrian couple in Petropolis a while back."

"Hmm, yes. No arrests."

"They were on the Southern Cross when I came down to Rio."

He's nodding, like he's wondering if he should tell me something.

"You think they're connected?" he says.

"Obviously. Even the newspaper thinks so."

"What are you suggesting?"

"Well, was Boettner murdered in prison or was he released, then murdered? Why was he cut up like the Zs? Why no arrest? I wonder about these things."

"Worried you might be on the list?"

"Most nights no, some nights yes."

Yeah, I'm feeling something. Maybe it's love, or maybe it's the sense that the odds are running out. Maybe it's something Paul said before he tried to kill me, put an arrow through my neck, a thing he said back in the Lotus bar when we were talking about the Ripper job on the Zs.

"Were any of their organs removed?" he said. "The voodoo fellows like human vitals, like heart, liver, testicles... strong mojo, brother. Beware of the priests."

Wasn't so sure about this then, now I don't know. V priests look like clowns but even clowns can kill if they think it will get them a laugh.

"These murders are made to look religious," I say. "But obviously they're political."

"Could be," my man says. "We think there are others that've been kept quiet."

"Ripper killings?"

"All foreign nationals. Look, I'll get to the point: we have intel about a plot to assassinate President Vargas. We don't know if it's left wing or right wing, or even when it's supposed to happen... our source says soon. Have you heard anything?"

"No."

"If you do hear something, however minor, would you let me know?"

"What's your name?"

"Sorry... Charles Eton. Just call me Eton."

No handshake, just a reciprocal nod.

Start receiving letters from strange women, c/o **Rio Life**, which are passed on via Leonora B. One addresses me as 'Dear Safari Man' your woman is very pretty, yet she cares more for her doll... there is unmistakable loneliness in your eyes, *Senhor*. I have the cure for your condition. Meet me at the *Campo de Santana*, near the monument, 4 pm. My vitals are 36-22-36. I shall wear red shoes & red blouse. Love, Samba Girl.

Another: 'I know you are wicked, and you kill the lovely animals but I think I can help you stop.' Signed 'Diana' with lipstick kiss imprint. Phone number. Old town, apparently.

And then this one, maybe a joke, maybe not: 'We have the doll but not the one you think. It is you, Safari Man. We squeeze your eyes, you go blind; we squeeze your throat, you choke; we squeeze your balls, you die.' Signed 'Loricha, the Priestess'.

This is tempting: a photo of a nice looking girl, the sort you see in the big shops downtown, mixed blood but quite light skinned, just dark enough to be exotic and look like she really belongs here. 'My name is

Astrud, and I am looking for some modelling work. Even though I have no experience I believe I have the nice face and figure necessary. I speak English and I fast learn. Hope to hear from you soon. *Minha gratidao com antecedencia...* my gratitude in advance.'

Leonora translates these for me and we chuckle together. But this one takes her fancy.

"If I were a young man, I might look her up," she says.

"Is there an address?" I say.

"Yes there is. It's in Lapa."

"The girls in Lapa romantic?"

"All the girls in Rio are romantic... and most of them need money."

All this attention is going to my head, so I'm getting stupid. Bobby's still in town, although leaving tomorrow when the Southern Cross comes back from Buenos Aires. Staying at the Gloria, doing liaison work for the company with those passengers who were hospitalized after the robbery in the Tijuca. Slipped over to her room for a romantic soiree once, then bailed on the second date because, well, Uma is now my woman. Bobby was annoyed and all, but I have principles. She doesn't know about Uma but she's quite demanding, treats me like a gas pump. Come on stud, fill me up. This is new for me. Maybe she's a nymphomaniac, if there really is such a thing. Anyway, I burned her off, and our last conversation was anything but pleasant.

Women. They know you're getting it and giving it, so they want a piece. It's telepathic, invisible love rays. The further you fall, the faster.

So now I'm feeling pretty good, no uneasiness. Seeing Uma. She's like a tuning fork—one bang and we die for hours. What's wrong with me? She doesn't look like my mother, yet maybe it's an Oedipus thing someway. She's 23, 24, and she's got secrets. She's running away, but when she's in my arms I feel she's arrived. I have.

Tell you, 1938/9 is a good time to be some sort of fascist, even if you're only five foot two, like Vargas. But when some folks think he isn't fascist enough and ask me to shoot him, I'm thinking maybe it's time to split, catch the Clipper North or South, put myself anywhere but Rio. Here's how it goes down. One day Barasso calls me in, says his pal Iambic Fontana wants to talk to me about a lucrative deal that requires my special talents. I'm a radio man but ever since I shot that jaguar, these guys see me as a shooter. So now I'm an assassin? Anyway, I drop by his office.

"Look, *Senhor*, I have a client," says Iambic F. "A member of our association."

"*Integralista*?" I say.

He doesn't bother with this, just sweeps on: "I know you're good with a gun... eh, as a foreigner, you have no visibility with the police. We need to send a message."

"Send a message?"

"Yes. You get a message, you send one back."

"What sort of message?"

"Like, when someone tries to shoot you, naturally you shoot back."

"Who shot who?"

"Someone shot at *Senhora* Barasso, yes?"

"Yeah... but who?"

"We know who, and in good time we'll deal with it... you will deal with it, if we agree."

Iambic Fontana's office isn't far from the Munroe Palace, the building on Rio Branco Avenue where the Brazilian Senate sits to take care of business, and in fact I can actually see it from one of the windows. Pretty fancy, not modern, has that classical look, lots of pillars and domes, and big wide steps. It sits by itself, so it isn't munched between other buildings the way a bank is or government buildings downtown. If you told me Alice in Wonderland lives there, I'd say sure.

"We're going to stage an attack on the palace."

I nod towards the window, say, "That building over there?"

"The Senate? No. One day maybe, but not this week. The pigs can continue to sleep in peace."

"You say 'stage'—is this for real?"

"Real enough, *Senhor*. Real enough to send a message."

"So this isn't a solo assignment."

"No no, this isn't an assassination, this is a coup. Well it isn't precisely... it will resemble a *coup d'etat*. We will shoot the place up, then depart. No police, no military. They will be busy in other locations."

"If you don't mind me asking, *Senhor* Fontana, who is the client?"

Fontana never smiles, not around me anyway.

"Not your concern," he says.

"What if I—if we—get caught?"

"You won't get caught."

"You mean, no guards? No shooting back?"

"The guards will be resting."

"Guaranteed?"

"Guaranteed, *senhor*."

"How do you know you can trust me?"

Iambic gives me the death stare.

"If my good friend *Senhor* Barasso says you can be trusted, then I

251

know you can be trusted. You want us to look after your girlfriend, yes Safari Man?"

He's shifts his chair so he's looking at a couple of big birds grazing in the park. Well, that's what I'm seeing. Big ones, like a couple of vultures looking for tree frogs.

"When is this to happen?" I say.

"Day after tomorrow."

"Rehearsal?"

"Eh, you will be briefed."

"Money?"

"Speak to your boss. It's Carnival season and we give bonuses in Carnival season to those who dance the best. You dance?"

"I do."

"*Excelente.*"

He stands up and as I leave, he says "*Boa caca*" which means "good hunting". Sure thing, Iambic. As I leave the building I get that old uneasy feeling again. This is another stitch job, has to be. Target has to be Vargas, the very plot Charles Eton at the Embassy was talking about. A scare job? How do I know this? How do I know I'm not being groomed like the guy who shot the Archduke Franz Ferdinand? I don't. Still, I more or less trust Manuelo Barasso, mostly because of his wife Leonora who has been nuthin' but good for me. We'll see. There's tomorrow between now and then.

Chapter Twenty-Nine:

SAMBA GIRL

I HAVE HER ADDRESS, she who wants to be a model, has the face and the figure. The direction takes me past the Catete Palace near Flamengo Park. Vargas lives here. Always good to do your own research. Just a three storey box, nothing fancy, except for the five big bronze eagles on the roof, real enough they could fly. Lots of wall, lots of windows to shoot at. Just do a drive by, a Capone machine gun sweep, keep going. And as I'm thinking this as I walk past, it seems obvious that the client must be Vargas himself.

Get myself to Lapa, find the address is just a few streets from my room at the Venezuela. Could be handy. Old building, apartments. Neocolonial they call it, the old Mediterranean look, wooden shutters for the windows, iron bars where necessary. Typical chipped yellow. Sit on a low wall and watch for awhile. Kids playing hop on the sidewalk, guy juggling a soccer ball on his foot as he passes by, couple of drunks sharing a bottle, women with shopping bags, music from an open window, a tucan perched on a roof... no dolls, no babes, no Samba Girl, no Models. So I stretch out, newspaper over my face, sorta doze while keeping an eye on the doorway across the street.

Then, in the sleepy hour, when everything's hot and quiet, she comes out. She's got it, alright, walks like a star, swings her ass in slow rumba time. Red shoes. Seems familiar, like I've seen her before, but then I have her photograph in my head. I follow, keeping to this side of the street, wondering if I should just go ahead and recruit her. But I hang fire—

discipline is essential. I follow. I follow until she hops a bus near the old church (Our Lady of *Lapa do Desterro*). Thought about hopping it myself but then the jig would be up, wouldn't it?

Get a taxi to take me to the *Campo de Santana*. Could've walked, I guess, but my white legs can't take the pavement in this 3 o'clock heat. The Campo is the Ground Zero of Rio, a park these days, a swamp back when Brazil was a colony of Portugal. Bit of demolition going on around the railway station, so it's noisy. The ducks and peacocks don't seem to mind as they wander casually through the wooded parts. I find some shade near the monument and wait.

Sure enough, a few minutes before the appointed hour, here comes she who calls herself 'Samba Girl'—red shoes, red blouse. Goes right up to the monument, looks around, sits on a ledge, lights a cigarette. I stroll by.

"Samba Girl?"

She smiles. Yeah... definitely 36-22-36.

"Diana?"

Raises her eyebrows.

"How about Astrud?"

Smile changes, wiggles her shoulders, pouts. I repeat 'Astrud's' address.

"You live here? Look, baby, I saw you leave this address."

"You follow me?"

I hold up her photo, say, "What man wouldn't follow a woman like this?"

She laughs, offers me a smoke. Sit down beside her, take a light from hers.

"So," I say. "Who are you? Astrud?"

"Which girl you like, Safari Man?"

"Well I don't like Loricha the Priestess."

"Who is Loricha?"

"You didn't send that one?"

Shakes her pretty head.

"So why pretend to be different girls?"

"Men like different types."

"True, sure. So, you interested in being a model?"

"If you like."

I look into her eyes, trying to figure her game. Not brown, the usual Latin color. Black, like precious stones.

"Want to go someplace?" I say. "Discuss this?"

She stands up, says, "My place?"

In the back seat of the taxi, the motion bumps us together, makes me go electric. I'm all hard in places I didn't know could get hard.

"How do you know English?" I say.

"Convent school. Surprised, *Senhor*?"

"Yeah... thought Latin was compulsory."

"It is. Some students do French as well. I do English."

"So you didn't become a nun?"

"Disappointed?"

"Would I be here if it was Teresa the Nun?"

"You tell me, Safari Man."

They say orgasm leads to early male blindness. Guess I'm close, one or the other.

When we get there and I'm paying the cabbie off, a skinny mestizo guy with a guitar wanders up playing a nice soft samba rhythm, and I swear to god she just starts moving to it as we go through the portico and up the stairs to her apartment... or what I assume is her apartment. I'm following like a zombie, hypnotized by the female pendulum. Uma? Sorry, doll, I'm just flesh, a man who appreciates art. The musician is hanging around outside, playing the same theme, like he's waiting for the orchestra. Now I know how Errol Flynn does it... Fatty Arbuckle... dames come running when you get your picture in the paper or up on the silver screen. Easy, the grapes just fall.

Pay no attention to the apartment, the color, the furniture, what's on the walls, if more than one person lives here. All is shape, the blur of desire. Nervous giggle as she discards her bag and I quickly back her against the table. We kiss, and her hands dissolve my shirt right off my back. My first mistake is I close my eyes in the thrall, as a flicker of recognition comes, I know this bitch from somewhere. Then her gasp, *Voce poderia ter me dado mais tempo!* followed by the thump on the back of my head that drops me into the stars like a dead spaceman.

You could've given me more time. Sure, doll, you and your buddies the Martians are all heart. I was condemned from the minute I decided to check you out, left all my principles and common sense and even Oswald at home. The Martians a.k.a Marxists cause that's what these dicks are, a gang run by the 'Professor' and his bitch honey-trap cha cha cha lady... knew I'd seen her before (would it have made any dif?)... supported by you-guessed-it Paul the Archer and Rotten Rodrigo and they've got me lashed to a table in some dump no place I know. I'm on my back, ankles tied to the table legs at one end, my hands to the legs at the other. Bad situation. First they gave me the hammer, now it will be the sickle.

Guess we're in some *favelado* where screams are just birds being shot for dinner. My head hurts like hell... never blacked out in my life before except maybe the time I put my hand through a church window, ripped my wrist all to hell... so there's a distant bell ringing in long, slow gongs that surge as static in my ears. What do these guys want? Are they really that pissed at me for the raid on their Tijuca operation? Do they think I'm a lynch-pin for something really important? Guess they do. Guess they hate just like anyone else. Guess they know what side they're on.

Rotten is sawing up some wood for the stove. Maybe they're going to cook and eat me. The sound is grating, although it's not just that... there's a samba school practicing in the neighbourhood, the clatter of the drumming just adding to the headache. I'm regaining consciousness but somebody wants to help me along, throws some water on my face.

Asshole Paul.

"I thought we were pals," I say, best I can.

"Pals, perhaps... comrades, no," he says.

"Gotta smoke?" Takes his, sticks in my mouth. "Where's my watch?"

"Your watch? My watch, *Senhor.*"

Well, is it? Possibly he stole it first. Looks good on his wrist, though. Adds class, makes him look legit, almost untouchable.

"You've been a naughty boy," he says. "Trying to screw the Professor's lady."

"Set-up, man. Bullshit."

"This is bad, Safari Man. A person with integrity would not behave like this."

Normally I love his sense of humour. Now the Professor comes in from another room where he's been listening. He's not Brazilian, although he's Latino, has the Spanish inflection. Argentinian or Mexican maybe.

"Speak to me about Ida.

"Ida... what Ida?

"Your housekeeper on Amazon Avenue."

"What's she got to do with anything?"

Of course I realize immediately that she's connected. All the signs were there, and things are starting to make sense. Some things.

"Ida is a comrade of ours. She was keeping an eye on your activities for us."

"Hey, I was just hired to do a job. I didn't know what Alfredo was up to."

"Si si, you would say this, of course. Still working for the Abwehr, *Senhor*? Or have you turned?"

"Man, I was just a sucker. I was told it was a cultural association."

"No no, you lie. You're a natural born fascist pig."

What can I say? Obviously he has his mind made up.

"I ask you again, fascist pig, what happened to Comrade Ida?"

"You tell me."

"Don't lie. You beat her."

"It wasn't like that, *Senhor*. I don't beat women."

Samba Girl hisses, but stays in the background.

"So what happened to her?" says the Professor. "I ask you nicely."

"Maybe Alfredo did something...."

"This is your position? Alfredo made her disappear? He perhaps killed her?"

"I hope not. I liked Ida."

He's looking at me skeptically, like a turkey that just isn't fat enough.

"This is your position?"

I feel giddy, start to babble. You know, like when you're scared and the words come out as a joke. "Want you to know I like Joe Stalin... he's decisive, knows how to act for the people... a humanitarian. I like those purges, those executions... oh they're good."

"What're you talking about? Purges? Stalin isn't a murderer."

"What about all the German migrants he's been shooting? The Poles? The Jews?"

"Is this the brainwash the fascists fill your head with?"

He turns to Samba Girl, says, "You hear the propaganda the fascists spread around? This is Trotsky. Comrades who doubt the justice of his liquidation warrant are like children. The damage to the revolution caused by his apostasy has been terrible. The fascists now use his lies to invent more lies. It breaks my heart. These French swine and their Fourth International... it breaks my heart."

"The Fourth International?" says Samba Girl.

"The Trotskyites... those counter-revolutionary scum. As if the Comintern doesn't have enough problems with the fascists."

His eyes are closed, like he has a headache worse than mine. Being a Stalinist in Rio must be tough. It's getting dark, although darkness reveals personality just as much as daylight.

"Let me sit up," I say. "I can't speak properly like this."

"You're a mercenary, aren't you? You kill for money."

"No."

"You killed Ida."

"Doesn't she live in Sao Paulo? You check with her mother?"

"Where is Alfredo?"

"In jail, far as I know."

"Who pays you—Berlin?"

"*Senhor* Barasso."

"Not the *Senhora*, Safari Man?"

"Yes, the family. I work for both the *Senhor* and *Senhora*."

"Then you're a mercenary, si?"

"No, *senhor*."

"You shoot people, are paid to shoot people, so I think this makes you a mercenary."

"I helped the Angolan to escape—"

"So you did... a political act for future sympathy. By the way, he just won the Rio-Petropolis Marathon, did you know?"

"That's good. I've met two decent people in Rio and he's one of them."

"Only two? I suppose you think my woman is a *puta*."

A whore? Not exactly. A bitch maybe.

"Can I ask, sir, why people call you 'The Professor'?"

He snaps his fingers, and Samba Girl fetches him a drink. He kicks it back and his face goes sour. He motions to Rotten, who slouches over, saw in hand. Oh Christ... can they really be this sick? Rotten drops the blade onto my stomach, the raw teeth immediately piercing the skin.

"You killed those people in Petropolis," I say, my voice thick.

"Did we?" says the Professor. He turns to the others, makes a mock appeal: "Did we?"

"Not me," says Paul. "Did you, Rodrigo?"

Samba Girl moves in, shoves her tight angry face close to mine: "Tell me what happened to my sister!"

Rotten moves the saw... lightly, I guess, but goddamn it hurts. Clench my teeth, moan. Ida is her sister?

"Ask Alfredo for god's sake!" I say.

Rotten rags the saw a full stroke, opens me up a half inch anyway. Almost painless, gradually real bad. The way I'm stretched makes the wound open like a bitter mouth, bleed like crazy. I scream raw and hard. The Professor waves Rotten away, says, "Did Alfredo kill her?"

"Don't know, don't know," I moan.

He looks at Samba Girl, shrugs, says, "*No sabe....*"

"He knows... somebody knows!" says Samba Girl.

"I swear," I say. "Alfredo ordered her to shoot me and she didn't, so I cleared off... you should be talkin' to Alfredo, I'm sayin'!"

She's staring at me as I writhe, then swoon. Don't look so pretty now, neither of us.

"I want to be alone with him," she says calmly.

The Professor rubs his hand across his jaw, massages the stubble, thinks it over. Nods to Paul and Rotten, heads for the door. "Comrades, let's go for a beer."

Hear them leaving, like gravediggers taking a break, but bound to return to finish the job. Samba Girl brings a damp rag, mops up some of the blood, but I'm bleeding bad. Can see it now... sisters... sisters of touch. Harsh words, soft hands.

"The truth," she says.

"Untie me," I say. "The stretch is making it worse."

"Pain is good for truth," she says.

The words are soft, but the eyes are like night.

Tell her what happened, best I can, minus the rough edges.

"You were lovers?" she says.

"Yes."

"Were you in love?"

"No."

"Close?"

"In the end, yes."

She nods, says, "The last time I see her she was beaten here and here... she say the Nazi do it. I begged her not to go back."

"Why did she?"

Shakes her head slowly. Ida: stuff to collect, I guess... or maybe she figured she could fake Alfredo out, stay in the cell. That was the idea, what the rough stuff was about. And I'm thinking, some cell Alfredo set up, a communist, a fascist, a chump and him the only bonafide Nazi. Is this just Brazil or is this the way it is everywhere?

"I didn't know she was missing," I say. "You know Eddie? Did you ask him?"

"Too risky," she says.

"Let me go," I say. "Ida let me go. She could've shot me in my sleep but she didn't. I owe her."

"Easy to say, Safari Man."

"Are you really a communist?"

"I am a woman who loves her sister."

In the end, she lets me go. Don't know if the Professor and the boys have this in mind or whether she's pragmatic or plain soft-hearted. Anyway, she loosens up the ropes, tosses my shirt at me.

"You can escape," she says. "Be quick."

The samba drumming is everywhere now, the whole *favela* going at it, seems like. Nobody gives a shit about me staggering down the morro looking for a ride to the clinic and twenty stitches.

CHAPTER THIRTY:

WANTED FOR MURDER

THINGS DON'T GET ANY BETTER right away. My story is that some guy came at me with a knife in one of those bars in Old Town that gringos like me shouldn't be in. So I have to pull out of the Iambic Fontana faux coup, which pisses him off royally, and not because he loves me or anything, and he suggests to Barasso I wounded myself deliberately to get out of the assignment. A cut like this? Twenty something stitches, a needle in my arm, a needle in my ass? Doc at the clinic said I'd be lucky if it didn't infect, go to septicemia. I'm good for nuthin' right now. I'm a chastened man. Made a dumb mistake, which nearly cost me my life, and of course I feel guilty because of Uma. And then the news that Ida is missing, maybe murdered, is depressing. Sure, I'd like to get Rotten Rodrigo, put him in a wheelchair for life, maybe the Professor too, but revenge isn't the first order of business. I have to get better, and I have to figure out just what the hell I'm doing with my life.

Nope, things don't get better right away. Days pass, sometimes comatose, sometimes restless. When Eddie finds me and takes me see Barasso, there's more bad news: Judge Goa has issued a warrant for my arrest on the charge that I murdered his son Fernando, which is absolutely crazy.

"He's got a couple of policemen looking for you," says Barasso. "Some *bastardo* has poisoned his mind."

"They were here yesterday," says Eddie. "You can't go back to your hotel."

"They know I'm at the Venezuela?" I say. "One of them got a weird eye?"

"Yeah... bad hombre. They call him Horus."

"Oh him," I say. "Been on my ass before."

"We'll get you out of town," says Barasso. "You can go to my ranch in Santa Catarina. I want you there anyway, as there's a project underway that needs your special talents."

"Radio?" I say.

"Yes. But we're putting together a small security force and as the recruits will be, shall we say, a little rough, they'll need some refinement of the basic skills. You have military training, correct? No need to pretend, Thorsen. It's obvious."

I nod, shuffle a little. Maybe the sore gut.

"You'll like the ranch," says Eddie. "Beautiful."

"We have some German associates there already training," says Barasso. "So your knowledge of German will be damn useful for us."

Krauts... that's interesting. Locals or straight from the old country, I wonder. Brazilian military uses them sometimes.

"How do I get there?" I say.

"Leonora has some ideas. We'll discuss it tonight."

"What about my stuff at the Hotel?"

"Anything important?"

"Couple of things, yeah."

"Eddie will work it out. Eduardo?"

"Sure, boss. On it."

I leave with Eddie, convince him I should ride along. Leave the police band radio on just in case. Pump him about this security force Barasso and associates are forming. Seems there's trouble brewing at some operation up north, one of his plantations or mines, not sure what. Eddie doesn't seem to know exactly or he's blowing smoke. Sounds serious to me if they're preparing a paramilitary unit.

"Are you part of this, Eddie?" I say.

"Not now," he says. "Boss needs me here."

We're driving along the seafront. Going to miss Rio.

"I know who killed Fernando," I say.

"Yeah?"

"Pretty sure."

"Got a name? Address?"

"Yep."

"Give him up, *mano*. Take the pressure off."

"Yeah yeah... I'm thinking about it. What's the best way to do it, etcetera."

261

"Give the name to the judge."

"No no, something else going on there. He wants me. Don't know why exactly. Like the boss says, someone poisoned his mind. What do you think of Iambic Fontana?"

We're going into the tunnel between Copa and Bota.

"Dangerous," says Eddie. "Secret police."

"He doesn't like me."

"He doesn't like no person. You think he...?"

"He wants me to shoot Vargas."

The tires are clipping the expansion joints in the road surface, like they're in time with the intervals of the tunnel lights. Clip, flash... clip, flash. Normally I like it, part of the local magic, but now it seems sinister, part of the trap I seem to be in.

"That's serious shit, Thorsen," says Eddie. "And he thinks you wound yourself to get out of it... and so maybe he talks to Judge Goa."

"Yeah. So I'm thinking."

"Boss is right—you gotta get out of town."

"Fontana tried to tell me it was just a scare job for a client."

"Eh, *um falso telegramma*... we call it a fake telegram."

"Yeah. o.k. You get a message, send one back... empty."

"Yeah, they mess with you, you mess back."

"He inferred that Vargas was behind the shooting that day when the Senhora got wounded. What do you think—bullshit or not?"

"Eh, maybe... is possible. When we visit the Jockey Club, remember his bodyguard, the big guy?"

"The African?"

"Yeah."

"The African likes sending telegrams. It's a dirty business. You don't get to be number one without depositing a few bodies in the sewer, *senhor*."

We break out of the tunnel in a beautiful flash. Wish I liked the beach. Wish I liked being lazy. Wish I wasn't wanted for murder.

"Remember the first day I got here, Eddie?" I say.

"Yeah... you and the radio."

"I said to myself, which of these two guys do I trust?"

"Yeah?"

"It was easy then. Now it ain't so easy."

"This is why it's necessary to get out of town...."

Man running along the sidewalk above the beach. The Angolan. Eddie's head swivels. "Forget him," I say. Eddie adjusts the rear-view, watches him recede. "He just won the Rio Marathon," I say.

"Never heard of it," says Eddie.

We get to Lapa, do a drive by of the hotel, scope it out, then park a few doors down. As the heat climbs, bunch of men outside a grocery store start drumming and dancing. We assume the hotel is being watched. Eddie could get my kit bag and stuff easy enough but it's my gun and some money that's stashed in a secret place that's problematic.

"I go in, talk to our man on the desk," says Eddie. "If the coast is clear, we'll unlock the service door around the corner. I'll come to the front door, light a cigarette, then you move, *compreender*?"

Yeah, *estou entendendo*... I understand, I get it. Watch him cross the street, flirt with a young woman at the entrance, do a little dance step with her, a feint and a retreat, before going in. Rio's really heating up for the 'Carnaval', chaos in the air everywhere. These people ever work? Rio's the only place you can rob someone in the morning, get robbed yourself at noon, and in the evening still feel like dancing. No capital punishment. They just let Death choose his own victims.

Five minutes later Eddie comes back with my kit bag. "Your luggage, *senhor*," he says, climbing into the car.

"What happened to the plan?" I say.

"Desk clerk has your stuff ready," says Eddie. "Jube."

"Yeah I know Jube," I say. "But I gotta get my gun."

"Is not in the bag?"

"No. Any cops around?"

"Jube say no. I didn't see any."

Alright, the hell with it, I'm going in the front door. Eddie thinks I'm crazy but crazy is as crazy is. Wait for a bus to pass, then duck across the street. The chick at the door is relaxing provocatively against the wall. Hooker, I'm thinking.

"Cigarette?" she says. I'm thinking fast now. Pull my Luckys from my shirt pocket, get her fixed. She inhales quickly, then lets it go with a satisfied sigh.

"Carmen Miranda," I say.

She laughs. "Americano?"

"Close enough," I say.

"You got a room, Americano?"

"Sure... wanna see it?"

Love For Sale. Cole Porter. Sure, I wanna dance too. Not that I dig hookers but they can be used in other ways. Go up the stairs to the desk. Jube is surprised to see me.

"I got my bag," I say. "But is the room open?"

He's looking at the girl.

"Yes... there's a telegram for you."

"For me?"

"Is in your room."

Who would be sending me a telegram?

"Lottery ticket?"

He pushes the Animal Lottery sheet forward, points at the dog. Funny guy. Cousin of the desk clerk at the Cabral, who sometimes covers for him here. Has telegraph eyes, just wide enough to send parallel messages.

"The juju favours the dog, eh," I say. "I'll keep it in mind, Jube."

'Carmen' is a tough looking chick, actually. You could kick her fenders and she wouldn't break. If Cyclops and his pals are around, she just might come in handy. We head for the room I used to call my own, used it for a month or more. Actually wrote a couple of letters there to send back home. Never sent them, though. Every time I started to tell the truth, I knew I was in deep shit. What can I really tell my aunt or my mother? 'Every night a woman comes and knocks on my door. Sometimes it's the same one, sometimes another. I send her away. Prostitutes, although they don't look it, seem honest and friendly, pure as Sunday School teachers. Carmen here isn't one of them, though. She's new, although she looks a bit old. She smiles through hard eyes and old paint. But at a distance, she does look like Carmen Miranda.

Tell her to wait in the room while I take care of business down the hall. There's an alcove with a small door going out to the mezz balcony that runs around the inside courtyard and there's a small decorative shrine here, sort of typical of catholic Brazil. I'd stashed about $300 in the statuette of the Virgin Mary, some US green, some Brazilian blue, and Oswald in the crucifixion cross above the door. Figured I might be away for a couple of days, so... anyway, get the dough o.k. without breaking the Virgin, then use a chair to get the cross. There's a window and you can see into the street below and who's sitting in a cafe but Cyclops, a.k.a Horus, a.k.a Lieutenant Jorge Horace Repo, and he's polishing his glass eye with a napkin. I'm mesmerized. Not every day you see a cop cleaning one of his balls. Sway a bit as I unhook the cross, distance vertigo, the cross, the street, near, far... get the gun o.k. and I'm just rehanging the cross when Cyclops looks up. Can he see me? One eye psychic?

Thinking I'll just head straight down and out, don't need a human shield, but change my mind as I pass my old room, think, what the hell. Mistake. Carmen's waiting for me with a German shepherd and a pair of handcuffs.

"Safari Man," she says. "You find thyself arrested."

I'm too pissed at myself to marvel at her exotic English.

"Who are you, a bounty hunter or something?"

"Your hands, *por favor.*"

She tosses the handcuffs over, says, "Put them on, please."

"Or what?" I say. "Your dog gonna eat me?"

Now I know what Jube was going on about with the Animal Lottery. Can see by the depression on the bed that the dog has been making itself at home. Booby trap, honey trap, and a cop across the street. Crude.

"On!" she says sharply. I toss them back and this is all it takes for the dog to go nuts. Growls, barks, breaks free and lunges at me, fangs bare and we crash to the bed as it tries to rip me apart. Tragedy, as I end up shooting it. What choice? Busted stitches and the Black Cathedral? Either she or me, brother. Had my gun in my pocket, managed to get it free, and blast her, one shot to the head. The savage roar of the beast dies to a sad moan. I'm too wired to give a shit, yet once again I find myself shooting an animal. Shot a cat, shot a pig, shot a monkey, shot a dog. Good work, Thorsen. You know, I came here for work and maybe some fun... and what happens? I find myself just a couple of bullets away from being a fully fledged hoodlum.

But I'm not done yet. Carmen's coming at me with one of her shoes, using the heel as a spike to maybe mulch one of my eyes. She swings it like a hammer, and it shears off the side of my head, goddamn bitch her mouth stretched wide and ugly, goddamn my ear. Heave the dog off but Carmen's on me, teeth sinking into my gun wrist like a necklace of nails. Goddamn. Whack her on the side of head, whack, break free as she goes cold. Goddamn. What's wrong with some of these *carioca* women? Straight from the bodyshop or something... and I thought they were all convent girls.

Just straightening myself out when who strolls through the door with a Walther PK in his mitt but Cyclops. Got his glass eye back in, yet he still looks like he's just come from the asylum.

I hand him my Colt.

"You kill her?" he says.

"Just the dog," I say.

He nods, sorta smiles. "*O cachorro*—the dog. How unfortunate. Much loved by our department. The German Ambassador gave her to us as a goodwill gesture, the hand of friendship from Berlin to Rio. Blondie was well trained. Fully trained, *senhor.* Berlin police, Gestapo rules. Usually affectionate... but if she thinks you're a Jew or someone naughty, well watch out. Gestapo rules. Well well, she's dead, yet now we have you, so her death is not in vain."

"You know, I didn't kill Judge Goa's son."

He shrugs, obviously doesn't care one way or the other. Guilt and innocence are meaningless—power is all that matters.

"Sundin," he says. "Is this a gringo name?"

"Scandinavian," I say.

"And before you have this name, you are *Senhor Prolific*...."

"No, Lieutenant. Prolific was captured."

"Was he? Mmm... maybe there is more than one Prolific. I think it would be best if you try to escape."

Escape? Sonofabitch is gonna shoot me. Carmen moans, shifts a little. Her skirt is ripped, has shifted close to her crotch.

"You fulfill her?" says Cyclops in his childish monotone. "Yes, you must try to escape."

Eddie's coming in just behind him. Must've been listening in the hall. Hits him on the back of the head with the plaster statue of the Virgin. Cyclops stumbles forward, fires a shot into the floor as he collapses like a midnight wave on the beach. Nod to Eddie, jam my foot on Cyclops' shooter hand, break a few fingers I hope, kick the Walther away. Collect my Colt, then drag the dog off the bed and dump it close to Cyclops. Eddie's looking at Carmen.

"What happened?" he says.

Got one knee on Cyclops' head and I'm squeezing myself a glass eye. Pops out, toss to it Eddie, who juggles it and curses like it's real.

"You can have that or his gun," I say. "Let's go."

"It's fake," says Eddie.

"Take the Walther... it's a nice piece."

But Eddie doesn't want either. Cop gun be too hot, and a cop's eye means he'll be with you forever. I ain't superstitious. I take the eye... and then, what the hell, the Walther. After all, I am leaving town.

No sign of Jube as we pass the desk. Want to tell him there're three telegrams in the room now but I guess he knows when to get lost. Street's really jumpin', people blowing whistles and singing, banging drums and dancing, and we just blend in, dance along in the flow.

Couple of motorcycle cops in baggy riding britches sitting on their Italian bikes near the Embassy, watching the traffic, watching the pedestrians, watching for us maybe... although who knows, their presence isn't unusual. Fortunately they're looking the other way when we come around the corner, slip into a empty slot behind a Packard sedan that's big enough to hide a teenage elephant. We have the radio on listening to the police chatter. So far nuthin' about me, us, or them.

A horse and cart go past, clip clop, clip clop and I use the slow travelling shadow to slip into the Embassy. You know what they say about Rio: people live simultaneously in different centuries. Hoping Eton is here, otherwise I'm going to have to write a letter... something I hate to do.

"He's in the garden, having a cup of tea," says the imperial secretary.

For some reason I think her name must be Beryl. It'll do. Follow her directions, down the hall past the 'lavatory', the door that says Staff. Take the opportunity to scoot in, have a piss. Just washing my hands and the glass eye in the sink when Eton bungles his way in.

He's on crutches. "I can't dance," he says. "I try and this is what happens."

I pull up my tropical shirt, show him my wound. "I can't either."

Whistles, stutters, "I say --"

Fill him in quickly. My version, natch, minus lots of stuff. Basically I have to get out of Rio, so he and his handlers won't be hearing from me for a while. I'll leave my official passport with the Embassy for now.

"Germans, you say? Paramilitary unit? What's it all for?" he says.

"I don't know... Directive 49 maybe."

"You mean the infamous chess piece."

"Yeah... maybe, maybe not. Probably just corporate security... mining, rubber... something for something in the wild places of Brazil."

"You'll let us know, won't you?"

"If I can get near a radio... message to Traben on the usual frequency?"

"Alrighty... hear anything on Vargas?"

Sure. I let him have the gospel according to St. Thorsen.

"You know Iambic Fontana?"

"Secret Police?"

"Yessir. He's got a contract out."

"You must be joking... on Vargas?"

"Could be *um falso telegramma*."

"A false telegram... oh you mean a phony job, like the Reichstag fire?"

"Exactly. But it could be for real."

"Fontana... we've had some bad reports about him. You know how and when?"

"He's using a local commie cell run by a guy called The Professor."

Eton nods. "We know about The Professor. He's a Mexican."

"Fontana is using a cop to run the operation."

"Got a name?"

"Alls I got is 'Horus'—mean anything?"

"Yes it does: Lieutenant Jorge Horace Repo, known as Horus to his victims. He's a torturer. City cop, but really part of the Secret Police."

"He's the guy. Got a glass eye."

"You know him?"

"Tried to arrest me when I was first in Rio."

"You were lucky to escape, if I may say so. His glass eye is a voodoo eye."

I can feel it in my pocket. Smooth, appealing, completely at my mercy.

"What does that mean?" I say. "Voodoo eye?"

"*Mal-olhado... mal ojo* in Spanish. The bad eye... the eye of doom, the eye that curses, the eye that sees the spirits. If you believe any of this rubbish. The thing is, Horus believes it and acts on his belief, so if you run afoul of Horus, be prepared for the worst. A bad, bad customer. He tortured one of our agents to death --"

"Not Mac?"

"No. McDonald escaped."

"Mac broke out of jail? How... when?"

"Recently, don't know how, or where he is. Buenos Aires if he's smart, Miami if he's smarter than smart."

Allow myself a chuckle. Good old Mac. Please God let me escape too. But first things first.

"The Professor has a shooter called Rotten Rodrigo," I say. "Know him?"

Eton shakes his head. "I'd remember that name."

"Remember it," I say. "He's a killer."

Eton sighs. "This pretty city is full of pretty killers."

"He's not pretty."

"So how are they supposed to be doing this?"

"Drive by."

"The Palace? That's rum... didn't work the last time. Must be a phony show."

Look in the mirror, comb my hair with my fingers. Jesus I look older. Must be the sun burn and the graveyard shadow. Make a move to leave, but Eton blocks my exit with a crutch. "Hold on, Safari Man," he says. "Full report. What can you tell me about your employer?"

"Barasso? He's an avocado."

"Sorry, I'm not following you."

"Black on the outside, green on the inside. He's a nationalist."

This amuses Eton. "First time I've heard an Integralist described like that."

"Live and learn. I gotta go, Eton."

"Hold on, old boy—you have an address for The Mexican?"

I give him the one Samba Girl used for her honeytrap. Might work.

"You'll pass that on, make new friends?" I say.

"Right away, should think. We're always interested in doing favors for certain Brazilian diplomats."

Eton nods towards the stall. "Flush the toilet."

"Uh?"

"Make it real. You wouldn't want Beryl thinking we're in here for immoral purposes."

Oh no, that would never do, would it? I flush the toilet.

"Anyone else we should know about?"

Wasn't thinking of shopping Paul, but hey, might as well clear the ledger. "Paulo Cunningham. He's in with The Professor."

"Brazilian?"

"Paulo is from Guyana. Easy to identify. These days he wears a Breitling."

"How did you come by all this, er, intimate information?"

"Don't ask, Eton. Gotta work some ugly places in order to make a living, let's say."

"Really?"

"Well I got big ears and big eyes."

"Yes, quite. We hear you're big all over... just a joke, Thorsen."

"That's o.k. I can take a joke."

Outside I find Eddie playing soccer with two kids on the sidewalk, just a little back and forth with the ball as they pass by. The cops have split. Apologize for making him wait. Writing those postcards took longer than I expected blah blah.

MOST RATIONAL PEOPLE would say I should just get out of town quietly and quickly, quit messing around in political intrigues that really don't concern me. Fact is, I'm angry, really pissed. When someone ties me to a table, threatens to cut me in two like Jesus (the Socialist) feeding the multitude or like what happened to a couple of nice people I knew, this shitty behaviour can't be ignored. Don't know if The Professor and Rotten Rod had anything to do with the deaths of the Zs—and my hunch is they didn't—yet messin' around with saws is bad. They can be communists if they want, they can be fascists or crazy voodoo if they want, but anyone who tries what they tried on me can expect retribution. I appreciate that Samba Girl might think I had something to do with the disappearance of her sister, and I appreciate that she believed in the end that it was nuthin' to do with me, or at least believed me enough to let me slip away. I can appreciate all this, I can. I'm grateful... but only to a point. Her associates were prepared to go all the way. They would've killed me. It's a sport dressed as politics, which makes it easier for them to sleep at night. Contrary to popular belief, some animals kill for fun.

Same with Fontana. There's no doubt in my mind that he was looking for a patsy. I don't know whether he wants Vargas dead or not, but either way dollars to donuts I would've been caught and thrown in jail or I would've been shot between the eyes or in the back of the head, coming or going, no difference. He was stitching me up, brother. But listen, we Canadians can do a bit of stitching ourselves.

We drive to Central Station, use a payphone. Eddie does the Portuguese.

"Lieutenant Repo, *por favor...* who? Doesn't matter who is me... tell him I got information concerning...."

We're doing the old handkerchief over the mouthpiece routine. It works, muffles the voice enough so even your own priest wouldn't recognize you. Old Cyclops, though, his voice is as thin as a windup phonograph with a burnt needle.

"This is who?" he says.

"I have the eye," says Eddie. "Pay attention, *porco*."

There's a shrill, unprofessional cry at the other end. "Sundin, I kill you!"

'Clops actually says 'Soodeen' not because he speaks like a kid but because he's Brazilian and they sound like soft chocolate.

"Pay attention, this is not Sundin. I have the eye and if you want it back, *porco*, listen carefully."

"Where ees Sundin?"

"Forget about Sundin. I have the *alho*. Shall we say one thousand *reais*?"

Cyclops is crackling like a worn out record: "Just one thousand?"

"Communists are not greedy, *Senhor* Horus. We'll call later, arrange the time and place."

"Your name, comrade."

"My name? Unimportant. Our name? *O Punto Fechado, porco*—the Clenched Fist, pig!"

Eddie holds the phone up just long enough to let the noise of the station get through. Then he hangs up, laughs at his performance, then sobers.

"No more, amigo," he says. "This is a dangerous game."

"Sure," I say, real loose and frisky. "So what, we're dangerous. Beer?"

We drive to Ipanema, go to the Azul where it all started months ago. We order snacks, beer. Yeah... how to survive in Brazil, Police State. I'm all wound up, tense and excited, one hand clamped on a cold grenade, the other in a warm pocket, squeezing the bad eye.

The next day or the next, looking at the newspapers:

Brazil continues to default on its foreign debt... hmm, c'est la vie. Guess Vargas needs the dough to pay all these new pensions his buddies are getting. The Integralist Party is still outlawed... there will be trouble. Foreign languages are outlawed in schools... so what? The national illiteracy rate is 70 percent or worse. Plans to spray the worst affected malarial areas of the Amazon are put on hold due to lack of money... remind me not to go to the Amazon. Some unions are o.k., some are not... guess it depends if they're commie or not. Strikes are outlawed. The new minimum wage policy is seen to be a sham. Vendetta wins at the Buenos Aires Hippodrome, is proclaimed the best race horse in South America. The fatalities at the Sao Paulo Grand Prix two years ago when the French racing maven Helle Nice's Alfa spins out of control and spectators are cut down 'like reeds to a scythe' is ruled 'an act of God' and Nice is declared free of all liability... hmm, Brazilians love her, name their children in her honour.

What's this? Some guy called Milton Rodrigo wins the Jogo do Bicho... the Animal Lottery... will he pay tax on the half mil? Guess not. The Animal Lottery is illegal, run by racketeers. Even the Estado Novo is rumoured to be an investor.

Have a bad feeling this 'Milton Rodrigo' is none other than Rotten Rodrigo. Probably bet a chunk of his Casa Darwin heist share, got lucky... or maybe even laundered some booty through the zoo. Sonofabitch. Fortune smiles on psychopaths and killers in 1939. This is gonna be one strange year, I'm thinking.

For the hell of it, I take a look at the astrology column written by *Senhora* Santander:

The chart most Brazilians use is the rectified chart from the declaration of indecency in 1822 with Pisces rising and the Sun in Virgo. Now people are quoting the anthem, the words that say Brazil has woken up. A Sun in Virgo in the 7th House explains why we point out the flaws in others, not in ourselves. Pisces rising gives the masses an idealistic desire and as it's a mutable sign, it symbolizes the collective. It is the collective thinking that generated the confusion about what person or group started all of this, as Pisces puts confusion in space as Neptune transits through the first House. So this conjunction shows why many people cannot understand the reason behind the protests and coming chaos.

Have lots of time to think as I'm waiting to exit. Been sleeping in the guest casa at the Barasso estate. To pass the time I clean my gun, then make myself a couple of new passports, using photos that *Senhora* Barasso supplies, and the two best fits from the ones in my collection. My hair is shorter—Lucy and one of her friends, a student called Clarice, had some fun with a pair of dog shears....

IT'S A MILITARY TRUCK, just like the ones I've seen the police units using downtown and around and about, somewhere between gray and green with a canvas canopy over the deck and a cab that seats three. Eddie's driving, and I'm sitting in the middle, between him and Barasso. Don't ask me where Barasso got the truck. He seems to be able to get anything he wants. We're wearing combat uniforms, the very same camouflage style that I wore for the Safari Man ad, although Barasso is the one with the Colonel's cap. Pistols? Yeah, I got my trusty old Colt 911 in my holster and there's a shitload of rifles and ammo in the back, sleeping in crates. American M1s. Now I know what Barasso was doing in the USA besides picking up his daughter from school. And he's got my old radio in the back and he's got me in the cab, so I guess I was part of the package right from the start.

It's late, and the streets are empty and dark, even a major route like the Avenida Rio Branco. As we pass the Munroe Palace heading North I look for Iambic Fontana's office on the right. It's there, a bland box as faceless as the secret police who work there. Light on, top floor, which could be the third or fourth... and sure, it could be Fontana's. Working late? Janitor? Barasso is looking at the light too, hisses, signals Eddie, who slows the truck to a crawl. We're all bent forward and looking, although I got no idea what this is about. Barasso jerks his head and Eddie wheels a left into a side street that cuts through the park grounds that dress up the Palace which has some lights on even though the Senators will all be home in bed. Eddie turns the truck around, then parks facing Fontana's office. DOPS is the short handle for his outfit, a secret police department that Vargas created not so long ago to answer to the National Security Tribunal, a rough justice court for political opponents and agitators of all description and size.

Sit there a minute or two, as if we're waiting for someone. A convertible glides past on Branco, young couple heading south. Quiet, although you can hear some carnival drumming, bits and pieces far away.

"Think you can put a shot in that window, Thorsen?" says Barasso. "Clean?"

What's this? I thought Iambic Fontana was his buddy. But hell, the subtleties of Brazilian politics aren't for me to question.

I nod, say, "Be a pleasure."

"Good," says Barasso, chewing hard on his cigarillo. "Let's send a telegram."

We get out and I use Eddie's shoulder for a steady aim. Using the same M1 rifle I shot the jaguar with, the one with the Sigma symbol branded on the stock. Can't be anymore than two hundred feet. Pop off two rounds, shatter the window. The light stays on. A shadow flutters across the space like someone diving for cover. Smell the gas vapor from the M 1. Yep—my pleasure.

We drive off, nice and steady, no panic, legitimate as a squad of marines doing street patrol, continue street hopping, reversing south as if we're retracing back to Barasso's place. But no, we head for Campo Grande and the district known as Santa Cruz. It's a ways, 35 slow miles. Open space, some farming, believe it or not, by Japanese migrants. Eddie and his girl drove me through here once but if I can't remember in daylight, I certainly can't recognize by starlight. Guess we're heading to the airfield. Barasso said we'd be flying.

"We've been waiting for a favorable wind," says Barasso. "The best is no wind at all, claro... a light south-easterly will do."

"You fly before, Thorsen?" says Eddie.

"Me? No," I say. "You?"

"I'm staying behind," says Eddie.

"What'll we be doing in Santa Catarina when we get there?" I say.

Barasso laughs, dry and husky: "Weathering the weather and the criminal actions of men," he says. "You were born for it, *meu amigo*."

"*Tropa de Elite*," says Eddie. "You lucky dog... wish I was going."

Elite Squad... *Schutztruppe*... Protection Force... a mercenary outfit, maybe legal, maybe not. Whatever it is, money's good.

Truck's growling along. German Opel Blitz six cylinder, not fast, but seems o.k. for hauling. Bumpy, of course, and heavy in the hands. We leave the asphalt, travel a dirt secondary. Flashes of housing, mangroves and stretch palms. Lights flicker. Pretty flat. Believe this is where the Hindenburg airship used to dock.

Checkpoint at the gates. Eddie gears down, rides the clutch, glides to a stop. The sentry is waiting for us. Skinny, like he's got rickets, face so emaciated and pocked he looks like he's just been dug up. Indian, or Indian and something. He looks into the cab, views us very suspiciously. Barasso flashes some I.D. The sentry looks back at the guard shelter and an officer steps out. Army Airforce. Young, more or less white, moustache, cigarette, unbuttoned holster and a nonchalant walk.

Looks at Barasso's I.D., hands it back, says, "*Boa noite*, Coronel."

Barasso glances at his watch, says, "Morning, I think, Lieutenant."

"Hmm... manifest?"

Eddie hands him a piece of paper. The lieutenant doesn't even look at it, just puts it on the hood, scribbles a signature, hands it back.

"You hear about the emergency?" he says. "See any roadblocks?"

"We saw nothing," says Barasso.

"Somebody shot up the Catete Palace. The President wasn't there, thank God."

"The Catete Palace? Who?"

"The rumour is some communist zealots. Well, if you saw no roadblocks, I expect they must've been captured."

"The Catete... you sure?"

"Yes, definitely the Catete. We heard it on the radio."

"Dangerous times, Lieutenant. Thank you."

The Lieutenant salutes lazily, steps back, signals the sentry to open the gate. Easy. The fix is in.

Certain generals in the Brazilian military are either outright Integralists or are sympathetic to the movement. They long for a military dictatorship, view Vargas as a self-serving populist who is playing up to Roosevelt and the Americans. There are coalitions of the like-minded within the military and the Catholic Church and the corporations that form and dissolve like clouds, so you're never really sure who has control or who has the upper hand in Brazil on any given day.

Remember that Irish politician, Edmund Burke? Used to yawn when his name came up in class, yet I remember a couple of things he said: "Good order is the foundation of all things" and "a nation is not governed that is perpetually to be conquered". Burke was wise when talking about revolution but I don't suppose anyone here has read him or gives a damn. Brazil is too hot to be reasonable.

We're driving between rows of service huts towards a large hangar. Well it's big, the biggest thing like this I've ever seen, must be a couple of hundred feet, floor to roof, and as we pull in there's a sleek Zeppelin floating a few feet above the ground testing its engines. It's big, just like the one I saw that day in the Tijuca circling Corcovado.

"Son of a gun," I say. "Are we flying in that?"

"Afraid, *senhor*?" says Eddie, chuckling.

"I thought the Hindenburg was kaput," I say. "I know it's kaput."

"Magnificent, eh, Thorsen?" says Barasso. "Behold the LZ 131E... not the Hindenburg but like it. The LZ 131E is a 2/3rds scale... the 131 is designed for military recon and mapping with decent cargo lift. You're in for a memorable experience, *meu amigo*."

Leased, I'm guessing. But just how the *Integralistas* got their mitts on it is beyond me... obviously some collusion between the military and the Party. Another contract job, something dirty, something devious, something without a face. Even I know the Brazilian military is largely equipped by the Germans and the Italians. Colonel Powell told me, and I got eyes. German planes, Italian planes... German trucks, Italian trucks... German marching, Italian marching. It dates back to before the Great War. Advisors, equipment, bonhomie. Still, kinda interesting that Barasso went and got himself a shipment of American M 1 automatic rifles. Makes you wonder how he did it. Sure, he's got the dough to buy them legal or illegal... yet is it possible the Yankees let him have them with their blessing? This year, 1939, anything's possible.

There's the moon sliding along the morro giving the Zeppelin a lead silver look, muted between gray and black. Gunmetal. No markings. No swastika on the tail, no face to the beast. Aircraft look like idiots compared with this beauty. As I get out of the truck, my feet feel like they're sprung. I never ever thought the privilege would be mine.

Some gophers are on hand to transfer the guns and ammunition crates to the airship. An unmarked van arrives with some prisoners. Seems they're being shipped to a penal camp in the Matto Grosso. Four of them, chained together in pairs. Civilian clothing, like they've just been dragged off the street. Curious sight, and as they're herded towards the ship by a couple of the crew packing MP 40 sub-machine guns I'm wondering what's so special about them that they get a midnight ride on a Led Zeppelin. Little guy in a suit follows, and I think he's packin' heat below his jacket.

I say to Eddie, "What's this?"

He shrugs. An officer comes briskly towards us, young, blond, German and if I'm not mistaken, wearing a Waffen SS uniform. The airship is venting spurts of ballast water, which distracts me. The German goes to Barasso, who standing a few feet away. A brief salute, regular, not Nazi.

"Colonel Barasso? I'm Lieutenant Voss, *SS-Obersturmführer* liaison officer for this mission."

Barasso nods, says, "Voss."

I'm looking at Voss now, the gears moving the sprockets in my brain. The combat uniform can't disguise that soft Brunswick voice—it's Kurt Ulrich Voss, the guy I shared a cabin with on the SS Southern Cross. He isn't as surprised as I am when we're introduced.

"Ja, Thorsen? I believe we've met."

Quick handshake. "Lieutenant Voss," I say. "Didn't you used to be a monk once upon a time?"

Barasso laughs. Bastard must've known all along.

"Mackenzie King," says Voss.

"Hardly," I say. "Thorsen."

"Ja ja, Thorsen," says Voss. "A tourist who reads Spengler."

When we're done laughing, Barasso says, "Lieutenant Thorsen is in charge of our detail."

Lieutenant? Not wearing any tags as per the irregular nature of our squad, and although I knew I was gonna be bossing some recruits around, I didn't think of myself as 'lieutenant', a N.C.O. straight from the academy. Once again Fortune smiles on the man with the aryan look.

"How many men, Colonel?" says Voss.

"Ten," says Barasso. "All have some experience... perhaps criminal."

Voss nods sympathetically, "Anyone can be a criminal accidentally. Redemption is all we ask."

"Exactly," says Barasso. "When do we leave?"

"As soon as your men board."

Voss nods to me, salutes Barasso, turns and heads for the ship. Eddie tosses me the M 1.

"The boss wants you to have this," he says.

Barasso nods, then gestures for us to follow him into the passenger terminal, which is just a more ritzy hut with better furniture. I had nothing to do with the recruitment, and these hard looking men are complete strangers to me... except for one. In a night full of surprises, why should the appearance of Archie McDonald be unusual? I'm still dumbed by the reappearance of Kurt Voss, so to see old Mac lined up as a member of the proposed *Tropa de Elite* isn't so much a surprise as it is funny. I'd heard he's escaped. Charles Eton, the guy at the Embassy, had told me that... but for Mac to show up here is bizarre. Makes me wonder if he was given an offer he couldn't refuse. Maybe all these animals are from the Black Cathedral. I'll be asking him, although not right now. He's looking into space, mouth twitching, chewing his stumps, pretending he doesn't recognize me.

None of them have weapons, just light kit bags with personal possessions. Tough? Maybe. Crazy? Sure.

I turn to Eddie and say, "Eddie, it's been great. Hope to see you again. Look after the girls."

Eddie grins, says, "Lucky dog."

Barasso catches my eye, nods. I turn to the squad, bark, "Let's go! *Vamos!*"

No formation marching here, just an 'at ease' dissemble. The men crowd out of the terminal, follow me and Barasso fifty yards or so over the concrete runway to the airship. Downsize? This baby's big enough. Must be a hundred and twenty in diameter, five, six hundred long. Squads of Brazilian airforce men are working the spider ropes, ready to pull the ship clear of the boarding area. Tail fin is touching the ground by its landing wheel and the ship is facing into a light south-easterly. Boarding is by gangway, single file. One of the crew, a rotund German officer, is acting as gatekeeper, counting us off on his clipboard. I pause, allow the recruits to go ahead, then follow. Excited? You bet.

Didn't notice this time but the crew was dumping sandbags as we boarded in order to keep equilibrium. Not a simple op. You think it's an aircraft but really it's a ship and is crewed like a ship. In the bridge they got a wheel just like a ship and a guy steering that, and an elevator man working the levers to ascend and descend. It floats along, but just in the air rather than on water. In some ways it's like a flying submarine, and just as dangerous. In a sub, water pressure can implode the hull; in an airship, the gas cells can explode the hull.

Well I'm not thinking about any of this... not thinking about the fiery end of the Hindenburg in New Jersey a couple of years ago, or any of those other gas bags that met with tragedy, and there are plenty of them. Hydrogen gas. Imagine. Duraluminum skeleton. Imagine. Diesel fuel. Imagine. And in our case crates of ammo and grenades and god knows what else. Captain is a German called Weisbaden from someplace near Lake Constance in Bavaria where old man Count Zep was from. Churchill would call Weisbaden a 'Hun' because he took part in two of the last zeppelin bombing raids over England in 1918, although I'd call him an 'experienced Hun', and if he could survive flying these airships for two decades what have we got to worry about, etcetera.

A thing of beauty, though. Liftoff as smooth as smooth can be and you can barely hear those four big diesel engines. Guess all that rubber and gas just sucks up the sound. One thing, though, when you're walking along one of those long gangways between bow and stern, you hear a melodic humming. Like a radio wave oscillation, I guess, although a bit sinister the way an opera by Wagner can be. The airframe is supported by a series of wire circles that look like bicycle wheels—and the spokes vibrate just like a chain of wind harps. If you think the sound of a big ocean liner is full of mystery, try a Zeppelin at 600 feet heading down the coast of Brazil on a starlit night.

I get a tour, courtesy of the 3rd Officer, an Italian bloke called Gaspari—George Gaspari. Late twenties, thin, doesn't look Italian, although what does a generic Italian look like? Toto the comedian? Maybe. No skinny moustache, no opera belly. Says he's from Milan, studied aeronautics at the *Politecnico di Milano* (Milan Polytechnic). We talk in German and he's fluent, certainly more poetic than me. He could be leading me on a tour of a cathedral.

"The skeleton is an amazing piece of geometry," Gaspari says. "We have a cruciform brace at the tail fin which is locked at the hub by the main axial corridor than runs the length of the ship. All strength is in the tail section... in the cross."

"Fuel tanks?" I ask. "In the engine pods?"

"No, the fuel and water tanks are in the stub keel which runs along the bottom just as the keel does in a ship," he says. "Ah, this is the radio room... it's just behind the Control Car where the Captain guides the ship."

Stick my head in, take a quick look. Oh yeah—primo German gear. Telefunken. Same as they use in their submarines. Same thing with the bridge: a quick look, see the helmsman and the elevator man and the 1st Officer. No sign of the Captain. Guess he's in the lounge with Barasso.

"You want to see the cargo bay?" says Gaspari. "We need to go aft."

"How fast are we moving?"

"Depends on the headwind. With luck we'll cruise at 90 or 100 kilometers per... say, 60 miles per hour... should reach Eden before noon. We'll be turning west, going inland north of Florianopolis."

We head past the lounge and the passenger sleeping quarters. Our squad of irregulars was told to turn in right away, get some shut-eye. Once the lights of Rio fade there's not much to see anyway and Barasso has ordered no drinking. Except for himself, of course. A little schnapps and a cigar with the Captain is part of the form. His tab, his game, his rules.

Gaspari says to me, "You're not German, are you?"

"Canadian," I say.

"Really? I have an older brother in Toronto."

"Never been there. Big country. I'm from the west."

"Interesting. What is your platoon? Not Brazilian military."

"Sigma... special security for business interests... plantations, mining, that sort of thing."

"Just so, just so. Colonel Barasso is one of the wealthiest men in Brazil, I gather."

"Oh yeah, he's a corporation or two."

"I'm curious... what will you be doing in Catarina?"

"Training for a couple of weeks. After that I don't know."

"Interesting. I ask because we—the crew—have been told to get ready for a long flight to the Amazon."

"You mean, up river? Or just to Recife."

"Up river. Not sure what for. Perhaps surveying, mapping, that sort of thing."

"You think our squad is involved?"

"I don't know... this is why I'm asking. There is a platoon of German soldiers already at Eden."

"Mmm... Waffen SS... jungle unit or something new. I met one of them."

"Lieutenant Voss? He's o.k."

There's a small cargo bay before the crew's quarters which aren't far from the cruciform and the tail section. There's a hatch in the floor and pulley system for raising and lowering. This is where they're holding the four prisoners. Christ, thought there was something familiar about them—Paul and the Prof, Rotten and Rhino, chained together in pairs, slouched against the wall, dozing. Actually Rotten and Rhino are lying on their sides, curled up like kids. Only Paul looks up when we come in and his eyes are so dead, don't know if he recognizes me or not.

The little guy who's their shepherd looks like secret police for sure: mean eyes, thin fuzz stash, knuckle duster ring, and a broom handle Mauser C 96 machine pistol slung over his shoulder. Suit, no tie. Street legal.

He's happy to see us. "Amigos, am I hungry. The steward said he'd bring me a drumstick and some cassava... guess he forget about me... I'm dying, been with these pigs since we captured them."

I say, "You wanna take a break? I'll watch these guys for 20 minutes."

"You need my gun?"

I pat my holster. "Don't think so, *senhor.*"

"Twenty minutes? All I need is a little something... a *misto*, something."

"Officer Gaspari can get you fixed up."

Gaspari moves closer to my ear. "If you have to shoot someone, don't miss, otherwise we'll all perish."

Right. The gas bags. Bullets can bring the ship down. "Understood," I say.

Gaspari nods, says, "*Bis spater.*"

See you later. An officer and a gentleman. He leads the spook out of the bay, leaves me with my former 'associates'. Could shoot them, just drop them through the hole, sweet payback for what they did to me. But hey, isn't this payback enough? Shackled and on their way to some hellhole penal facility in the Big Swamp?

Paul's pretending to sleep, but I know he's watching me. I light a cigarette, crouch down, stick it in his mouth, then light one for myself. We just smoke for a while, listen to the hum of the ship. It's soothing.

"Somebody shopped us," says Paul bitterly.

"Bad break," I say. "Of course you were taking too many risks, in my opinion."

"Don't know why I trusted you."

"You didn't trust me. You used me... and you tried to kill me."

"If I need to kill you, I kill you, *senhor.*"

"Likewise. What happened to my watch, uh?"

The Professor's face is swollen on the left side, like he took a boot to the jaw or a rifle butt. He's rocking softly where he squats and moans. "Fascist scum," he says thickly.

"You talkin' to me?" I say. "Better be nice."

Rotten has woken, sits up.

"How's the millionaire?" I say to him. "Life any better?"

He spits. No cigarette for him. "You guys really shoot up the Catete Palace?" I say.

"Somebody shopped us," says Paul.

"Who arrested you?" I say. "The one-eyed cop?"

"One day he will die," says Paul.

I pull the glass eye from my pocket, hold it up. "Know what this is? Some heavy voodoo."

"What is that?" says Paul.

"That's his mojo eye," I say. "*Mal-ohado.*"

"So you can make a joke," says Paul.

He's not sure, though. I shrug, flip the eye before returning it to my pocket.

"How you get it?" says Paul.

I smile big. "Safari Man always gets his trophy, *amigo.*"

"You shopped us, you bastard," says Paul.

"Not my game," I say, face as straight as a passport photo. "Too bad. Hear they're sending you into the Grosso."

Rhino starts to dry retch. He's been looking nervous.

"What's wrong with him?" I say.

"Doesn't like flying," says Paul. "His first time."

Doesn't feel like flying to me. Ship is so steady we could be on the ground.

"I need to piss," says the Professor.

"So piss," I say.

Raises his right hand, shakes his chains.

"I need to stand like a man," says the Professor. "Does this fascist ship have a toilet?"

Know the crew quarters are nearby, but I can't be leaving the others while I shepherd him in search of a pisser.

"You'll have to hold it a while longer," I say. "Be less of an individualist, comrade."

"No *entiendo....*"

"Don't understand? A bright guy like you? A guy who likes sawing people in two?"

He's glowering, unshaven swollen face and all. Actually he's looking more like Pancho Villa every minute.

"Know what I think? You murdered that Jewish couple in Petropolis."

He says nothing.

"Might as well 'fess up. You're going to be shot anyway."

He hisses. "Why fly me to the moon if the plan is to shoot me? Be serious, *senhor.*"

"I might shoot you myself, you prick."

"Go ahead, shoot. Then we all die."

"Oh I think I can be precise, comrade professor."

He shifts, looks at the others. "You see? Another bourgeois reactionary."

"Yeah, sure Prof. I think you like the idea of killing on an industrial scale like Stalin. The Cheka, the NKVD... they been at it since 1918."

"What would you know about what goes on in Russia? You're just a kid. You can't even see the horizon."

Well he's right, of course. Still, I remember something of that history lesson Colonel Powell gave me at the Hotel Gloria one sunny morning not so long ago.

"Maybe I'm just pulling your chain, Prof...."

In the middle of the floor is a trap hatch, surrounded by a low safety rail. Above this is an I-beam with a pulley system for doing vertical lifts and drops. The trap has a safety lock, **verschluss** painted below the handle, which I release, then start turning the geared wheel that rolls back the hatch. Immediately there's a low roar from the air rushing over the hull. It's dark below, although you can see the sea well enough to get a blast of vertigo. Unholster my pistol, look at the Prof, jerk my head towards the open hatch.

"*Aufstehen*!" I bark.

Oh he's not sure, is he? Is that fear I see in Comrade Professor's slug eyes?

"Come on, get up... haul ass... you want to relieve yourself, don't you?"

Paul's chained to him of course and he just rises, pulls the Prof with him, says, "I need to if you don't."

"North side," I say. "Unless you want a mouthful."

The other pair, Rhino and Rotten, are now alert and watching. Guess this is fun. Maybe not as fun as tying a guy to a table and drawing a saw over his belly but pretty good for the moment. They stagger over to the railing, chains clinking. I move behind them, hover.

"What do you think?" I say. "Think you could survive the drop, swim for shore?"

Paul's already unbuttoning himself. The Prof has his head swivelled, trying to see my intention.

"Don't swim?" I say. "Or don't swim very well chained to another guy who can't...."

I circle around, face them. Paul's already letting his piss flow in the wind.

"Must've been drinking beer when you got arrested," I say. "Come on, Comrade Prof, start pumpin'!"

His dick must be shrivelled with fear cause he has real trouble getting going. Or maybe he doesn't like an audience. Paul gets impatient, tries to pull him away, but the Prof snarls, holds onto the rail with his free hand. Man, he's welded. Can't piss, can't move... can't think... guess you could call this the dialectic of the possibly impossible.

I circle behind him, put the pistol to his head. "This is how they do it in Moscow, isn't it?" I say. "Bullet behind the ear, and you just collapse into the hole. Hey, one executioner could shoot a hundred a day real easy. Get a sore wrist maybe... but like Joe Stalin says, one is a tragedy, a million a statistic."

Did I just make that up? Where am I getting all this moral superiority from? Books? Dreams? The savage heart? I go on: "A bad dream, isn't it?

An uncontrollable fall into chaos. Look at it, asshole. That's where you're headed!"

Poke the barrel behind his ear hard enough that he yelps, then pisses wildly, some of the spray missing the hole. Paul curses.

"Ah... Hark the Herald Angels sing!" I crow, giving him another jab.

Now I'm looking at Rotten. He's squatting there, either scowling or in pain. No tooth bone necklace now. Red scar on his neck, so maybe whoever arrested him took a trophy. Meanwhile Rhino's curled up again, eyes closed, like he's playing dead. Go over, prod him with my boot.

"Hey zombie boy, need to piss?" I say.

Rhino continues his pretence. It's true—he doesn't understand movies without sub-titles.

Rotten says, "I smell you, gringo. I know you be a gringo spy from the start."

His nostrils flare like a mare in heat. Oh, so he's got machismo? I kick him hard enough to break a rib or a kidney but not hard enough so's he can't crawl and fall through the hole if necessary. Lift my shirt, show him my scar, which has healed o.k. but still looks ugly. But he's blind with pain, moanin' hymns or whatever these urban monkeys moan.

"You're damn lucky I don't have the key for your shackle you sonofabitch or you'd be through that fuggin' hole right now!" I snarl.

"I 'ave the key, *senhor*," says a voice.

It's the DOPS guy, and he's got his Mauser horizontal and pointing this way, finger on the trigger. He's still chewing and licking the fingers of his left hand.

"Hey," I say. "You're back."

"There es a problem?"

"I tell him to piss and he won't piss."

DOPS looks over the rail and through the hatch.

"Looks *perfeito* to me."

Paul and the Prof have retreated, are hanging around the north corner. DOPS moves quickly, unlocks Rhino from Rotten. Rhino slithers as far away as he can get. DOPS drags Rotten over to the railing, then hooks the overhead pulley chain to his shackle. Jesus Christ—I started this game but I had no intention of taking it this far. DOPS is as crazy as a clown at a picnic—feed him and be amazed. Big crank wheel on the bulkhead... you know, it's like DOPS trained as crew for this ship, or maybe it's just the natural skill of a police sadist. Where I would take one step, this guy takes two... and there's nothing personal in it for him. It's just a career.

As he gets yanked off the floor Rotten claws futilely at the air like a naughty cat and next thing he's hanging over the hole... then he's in the hole, then it looks like he's going through the hole... screaming. This isn't what I was expecting to see on my first flight aboard LZ 131E.

A German crewman appears, doing his rounds, I guess, or maybe he heard the screams. Coveralls like a mechanic, so maybe he's from one of the engine cars.

"*Was ist das*?" he says.

"Toilet training," I say.

He goes to the rail for a closer look, guffaws. "Works... but please, you must close the hatch... we're cruising too fast, so it's dangerous to have it open."

I make a circular motion to DOPS, who nods, winds Rotten clear of the hole, drops him on the floor where he lies still, passed out. The crewman closes the hatch, locks it. I give him a cigarette.

"Sorry about that," I say. "They demanded to piss."

"What'd they do?" he says. "Rob a bank?"

"Who knows," I say. "Political."

"Terrorists," says DOPS, joining us.

Guess he deserves a cigarette too. I light him.

"Commies?" says the crewman. "They're a fucking problem everywhere. Back home, if it wasn't for Hitler, we'd be paying taxes to Moscow."

I nod sympathetically. "Say, you hear anything about a flight to the Amazon?"

"Ja... there's talk. You boys going?"

"Not me," says DOPS. "Quick visit with my brother in Florianopolis, then back to Rio for me."

"You're not taking the prisoners to the Grosso?" I say.

"Not me," he says. "Far as I know, they're Ducks."

"Ducks? What do you mean, ducks?"

"Live targets... Lieutenant, isn't it?"

I nod.

"Well Lieutenant, you got yourself some Ducks."

The crewman laughs. "Ja—the only way to train for a mission! Duck hunting! Ja ja!"

Bloody hell... talk about expediency. Talk about using your teabag twice.

The crewman stubs his cigarette, says, "No smoking on the ship, you know. Hide your butts."

Well that was careless of me. Lucky this Fritz is so bent. Me and DOPS quickly snub our fags. I put mine in a pocket and DOPS eats his. The motion is so casual I almost miss it.

"And there's a toilet down there...."

He points towards the tail, then steps back, throws up his right hand: "Heil Hitler!"

"Ja, Hitler, sure, hmm...."

We watch him leave, and then, as there isn't much more for me to do around here, I say goodnight to DOPS and head for my cabin to get some shuteye.

I get five hours, and then Barasso is knocking on the door. Sun's up and the views are magnificent from the lounge where we're having some breakfast, some talk, and I get the dots filled in. The squad is there, guys sitting at various tables, eating ham and eggs, drinking fresh juice and primo coffee, probably the best grub some of them have had in years. Man, this almost like being on holiday... except for the air pocket we hit as the ship turns away from the sea, makes the plates and cutlery levitate for a moment, throws a couple of guys off their chairs. Some shouts, then laughs and curses. We're beside the railing and the vista windows which are pitched about 45 degrees to match the hull, so you've got views of what's going on down below as well as out there towards the blue horizon. We're heading southwest up a valley beyond a coastal town called Itajai, which is a ways north of Florianopolis, the capital of Santa Catarina state. Can see the curdled water of the river, the town spread out, the traffic moving, everything glittering in the morning sunlight. And the mountains, which are higher than we are. Flying? Nervous? Sometimes you can see too much, sometimes not enough.

I'm sipping my coffee. Flat, no sugar.

"Like it?" says Barasso, cutting into another sausage.

Real teeth, no falsies.

"Best I've ever had," I say.

"Brazilian, *claro*. Probably my 38 Highland crop."

"Coffee is your main business, right?"

"Used to be... the Barasso family has always been about coffee. But now it's maybe 30 percent. We're a corporation now, and corporations have many interests."

"Have you got a mine in the Amazon?"

"Might have. I have a rubber plantation and forest leases... some accumulations I don't even know about. I let my managers take care of these things."

"And a ranch here in Catarina?"

"Five thousand acres. We're nearly there."

"I hear there will be German instructors...."

286

"Yes, you met one last night. You can't beat German military know-how."

"The Abwehr aren't so great...."

Barasso sticks a thumb nail between his teeth, tries to pick a piece of food fibre.

"Eh, you mean the radio network? We never wanted that to be successful. This is our country. Cooperation of that nature is more diplomacy than real... is like a mistress, *amigo*. Fun, exciting, secret... maybe sincere at the time... but never lasts."

I get it: court, get engaged, get laid... but never show up at the altar.

"Is Alfredo still alive, y'think?"

Barasso heaves his shoulders, makes his face a fist. He doesn't know or he knows and doesn't care. "Tell me, Thorsen," he says. "You knew you were engaging in espionage. Be honest."

"No no... not at first, *senhor*. I really thought it was a modern way to link up the German communities with the mother country. It was only later when they started using codes that I figured it wasn't legit. Ask Eddie. He knows."

Barasso stares at me, then nods, says, "Yes, Eddie knows. Eddie knows you are a man who knows which way the shit flows. And my wife is a good judge of character—she likes you. If Leonora say o.k., then o.k. you be."

"She's been very nice to me, sir. Very nice."

"Safari Man... a brilliant piece of work. If she was in London or Paris, she'd be famous."

"She's famous to me."

"Yes, yes... everyone in Rio know her, and anyone who counts in Sao Paulo."

"Do you deal in art, sir?"

"Eh... if art is an accident waiting to happen, well *claro*."

He chuckles at his witticism. Actually, I think I've heard his wife say that.

"You mean like a bullet through a window at night?" I say.

"Exactly," he says. "Action accidentally."

We both laugh and I feel I'm getting tight with the boss. Well, Eddie's not here, so I guess I'll have to do.

"I don't get it... we shoot up Fontana's office, somebody else shoots up Vargas. Big coincidence."

"Is it?"

So I think but Barasso is amused. He signals the waiter, holds up a thumb and forefinger, one inch gap: "Cognac."

"Two, sir?"

Barasso nods, then turns back to me, says, "We say... we say the melons will find their place with the movement of the cart."

Folk wisdom, eh. But already I'm seeing how the melons roll into place—we shot up Fontana as a favour so's there'd be distance between him and the Vargas attack. 'These communist assholes tried to kill me too, Presidente... or, 'No one will believe the attack is genuine unless the secret police are also attacked' etcetera. Machiavelli 101.

"So what's going to happen to the commies who got nabbed?" I say.

"We'll think of something," says Barasso.

Ship is a bit lower now, like we're descending gradually.

"What's that town? Looks European in a rustic kinda way."

"Blumenau. German settlement... started with just seventeen people nearly a hundred years ago. Can you imagine? Now look at it—all those little Germans!"

Germans. No kidding. There's a swastika flag flying on an important looking building, could be city hall. Big and proud, like it's in Bavaria or Thuringa or some other German satellite community.

"We have a new theatre opening soon... we have cinemas, radio... libraries... this is a sophisticated place, *senhor*."

"I see that. I see the Nazi flag."

Barasso frowns, looks down. "*Sommerfest*," he says. "A festival. They like to celebrate the old country."

"That's a really big flag," I say. "I mean, is that legal?"

"Only if I say so."

Assume he's joking. "When I was coming down to Rio, there was a man on the ship who said Hitler had a plan to take over South America. I thought this was crazy talk, of course. But when I see that flag, I wonder."

"Don't concern yourself, Thorsen—it will never happen. Integralism is the way forward. If Brazil is to have a New Man, it will be an Integral Man... not a National Socialist Man."

I'm still wondering what the difference is. Well, racial purity—that's out the window.

The airship is doing a circle, putting itself on display for the people in the streets. Seems to be a parade going on, couple of marching bands and an open top Mercedes leading the marchers. Blonde woman standing in the front passenger well.

"See her?" says Barasso. "Beauty queen... for the summer festival. That street is called *Rua XV de Novembro*—Fifteenth of November Street. Some fine women in Blumenau, Thorsen... too bad our stay will be brief."

Too bad indeed. Blumenau looks like a town I could get to like. The cognacs arrive. Not used to this at breakfast but what the hell... bottoms up.

"Salut," says Barasso. Raise my shot, nod, then kick it back. Sieg Heil and all that.

"So it's the Amazon, is it?" I say, licking my chops.

Barasso's black eyes unfocus as he nods slowly.

"What's the op?"

"In good time, Thorsen... be patient."

A yellow biplane comes into view, flying parallel with us as we continue along the valley southwest. Some of the boys get up to take a look. If I'm not mistaken it's one of those hot Fiats that the Italian Air Legion has been using in Spain. Got a dropped air-intake like a shark's mouth and natty streamlined wheel fairings. No markings.

"Nice," I say. "Isn't she?"

Barasso smiles, says, "She is."

I'm thinking that duster is awful similar to the one that flew with us that day in the Tijuca when we trashed the voodoo camp and Eduardo got killed. Keep the thought to myself, though. Like all powerful men Barasso likes his mysteries and today he's told me plenty, so there's no need to push it. Plane waggles its wings, then does a half-roll and disappears.

About an hour later we arrive in Eden, or so it looks to me. A wide flat-bottomed valley of forests and meadows and beautiful sub-tropical light. And there's the landing strip with the yellow biplane parked beside some sheds and a bunch of men waiting. The ship descends slowly, valving gas and dumping ballast water, engines throttled back. When we're within a hundred feet or so three crewmen rappel to the ground through the underside cargo well, take charge of the squad detailed with the docking. One of them looks like Gaspari, and he's certainly giving orders, what ropes to grab and how to guide the bow towards the mooring tower. Piece a cake, despite the soft drizzle that's passing through.

When we disembark, once again my boots feel like they've got springs. Might be the hydrogen or the intoxicating smell of the vegetation... like hops one second, wine the next. Eden... rainbows in the meadows, forests, mountains, yeah.

Beautiful flight. Despite what everyone has been saying since the Hindenburg disaster, airships are the future.

LATE FEBRUARY IS LATE AUGUST south of Capricorn, where we are, and can be quite hot, especially if you're climbing a three thousand foot mountain that looks like a wall with a cross on the top. Actually the mountain's like a bowler hat, more like a ridge with big cliffs and forests running up the shoulders. Anyway this is our conditioning exercise, climbing this mountain with rifles and rucksacks loaded with 40 lbs of rock using a trail that's not much better than a dry stream bed full of loose stones and gravel and in the later stages is a 45 degree incline over exposed bedrock... and god help if you complain because these Nazi bastards have no mercy. Old Mac's definitely not cut out for this. He's too old. Tough, sure, but forty something tough isn't twenty something tough. Powerful hands, lousy back. Bit too much weight although he's lost a bit during his two months in the Black Cathedral, the old barracks prison back in Rio.

He says, "Thorsen, you got no idea. People disappear in that place and nobody knows where or how. Chances are the shepherds torture them to death or the inmates eat 'em, cause they feed you nuthin' in that joint unless you got someway to pay for it. I was lucky. I drew some pussy pictures and everybody wanted one... good for a cigarette, bowl of rat stew... massage, whatever a guy wants when it's just guys, eh... but that bastard Horus damn near was the death of me. Horrible man... not human. He likes torturing... a confession means sweet fuck all to him... he firmly believed I was Prolific, so that was that... better than thinking I was a spy, maybe. 'You are a criminal *barata*,' he says. '*Um pornografo...*

foreign parasite' and so on. Cockroach isn't so bad... pornographer... I can take it... but the Hot Tube, brother, you never ever wanna experience that. A Black Cathedral speciality... I'd heard whispers, sure, but it seemed so perverted it had to be bullshit. You ever hear of the Judas Cradle? Sure you have. A spike up the ass. The Iron Maiden? A spike for every fuckin' organ that matters. But this guy Horus, this one-eyed prick... 'Thy hour has come' he says and by christ he meant it."

"What'd he do to you, Mac?"

Mac shows me the raw circle on his gut. Six inch diameter.

"The Hot Tube, kid," he says. "Piece of pipe that's closed at one end, and they put a rat in it. I'm tied to a chair... and they heat the pipe."

"I get it, man, I get it."

"I felt the rat, kid... I felt it nip... but they were just playing with me. See how tough I was. I just clenched my jaw and stared right back at that one-eyed bastard, never flinched, kid, never flinched. He had that pipe in tight and one of his sappers was heating it up with a blow-torch. You never wanna meet that bastard."

"I met him...."

Flip the false eye, catch it, hold it up.

Mac starts to laugh: "That's his eye? How in the hell you get that?"

I just play cool and mysterious, say, "How do you spring a trap on a rat?"

"Gas? I'd use gas. How'd you do it?"

"I'll tell you sometime. Right now we gotta get you back on your feet."

"It's my knee, kid. Something's wrong."

Torn MCL or something, I figure. "Look," I say. "Why don't you just get yourself back to camp best you can? We'll talk later."

"Thought I could do this but I can't," he says. "Guess I'm going back to jail."

"We'll talk later."

Voss shows up. We talk Kraut. "*Was ist los*?" he says.

"*Sein Knei*," I say. "He needs a doctor."

"His knee? What's wrong with his knee?" Voss says. "Is he faking it?"

"I doubt it," I say.

Voss looks Mac over, then states the obvious: "He's too old. Why was he selected?"

Mac is sitting there on the side of the trail like a bad schoolboy, kind of evasive and sulky. Of course he doesn't understand a word.

"Find a stick and get yourself back to camp, soldier," I say sharply. Probably pisses Mac off no end to find himself in this position. He could

291

be faking it. For me to be his boss is bad enough but to find himself physically humbled in this situation is even worse. Voss has that old cynical half-smile as he watches Mac hobble off into the trees, and then we move along briskly to catch up with the others.

"American?" says Voss.

"Must be," I say. "We'll put him in the kitchen. He can peel potatoes."

"Americans are soft," says Voss. "No racial discipline."

"Not tribal, you mean...."

"Ja. Soft."

"A soldier, no... a monk, maybe."

Voss gets the jab, smiles, says, "You believed I was a monk, didn't you?"

"At first... then I wondered a bit, maybe."

"Why?"

"You guys looked too hard to be religious."

"You think I look hard?"

"Maybe not you... the others. That guy Schmel."

"Sergeant Schmel? Ja, farm boy. Horse kicked his face, perhaps."

Yeah... or a half-track ran over it, I'm thinking.

"He's ugly," I say. "He married?"

"No, just the SS for him. He was in Spain."

"Fought in Spain? Figures. How about you?"

"No, I only joined up a year ago. I have a cousin who's a Major. He got me interested. The Waffen SS is new, elite... more exciting, with more opportunity than the *Wehrmacht*. My cousin made it easy for me."

The others are moving ahead pretty good, although there's still a long way to go. Remember doing some of these rugged terrain marches back home in Rattler Canyon. Dehydration and vertigo were always on hand. Some guys are short-distance tough, but when it takes five hours to reach the snow-line, well, they ain't so tough. You gotta have a long game. And long games are hard for young guys.

We stop to catch our breath. "Listen," I say. "How come you guys travel as monks?"

"On an American ocean liner? You think a German military unit on active service would be welcome?"

"Obviously not... but still, the disguise must have a purpose."

"Such as?"

"Well maybe it was a dry run for a hijacking."

He doesn't laugh, just takes a moment, then says, "What would we do with an ocean liner?"

"You tell me," I say. "If there was another big war, an ocean liner might be very useful."

"How?"

"Moving troops, maybe...."

"Good idea. Where would these troops move?"

"Anywhere they'd be needed. South America maybe."

"South America? That's crazy!"

"Is it? You're here, aren't you?"

Voss is looking at me closely, shakes his head slowly. "All that time we shared a cabin and I never knew you could speak German. Why is that?"

"It's not something I do on a daily basis, Lieutenant. Just me and my mother... and that not so much anymore."

"Hmm. And how did you become a mercenary?"

"Is that what I am? Well, by accident."

"Come come, Thorsen, you don't become a 'Lieutenant' by accident—"

"In Brazil? Sure you can. You can be anything in Brazil. The *Unidade Sigma* squad is irregular. If you can shoot and punch your weight, you're in."

"I understand you know something about radio. True?"

"Yeah, true enough. Maybe a bit more than I know about women."

"Hmm. Canadian Army?"

"Boy Scouts. We learn everything."

"How about that? I was a Scout too. I hiked in the Thuringian Forest. Beautiful. But so is this...."

He's right. The forest is very nice, with lots of Brazilian pine... they call it Araucaria moist pine, with some of them well over a hundred feet high and three or four feet thick, with all the branches and foliage whorling at the top like a mushroom. The leaves are like arrow heads and damn sharp, bit like what we call monkey puzzle. Right now they're heavy with cones and are pollinating, playing hell with anyone who has an allergy. Nice to look at, nice to smell, but can be deadly for some. Those powder blue jays like the seeds. Some people eat them too. Good with a beer or a chug of wine.

Birds... plenty of birds. The parrots are as green as the Brazilian flag and if they didn't have a red mask around the eyes and beak you'd never notice them sitting in the green flush. The monkeys are Howlers, look like little gorillas and sound like them. You just want to shoot the bastards sometimes if you're trying to get some shut-eye, but of course they're harmless. We see them foraging in the pines and brush now and then. You know, Darwin must've had a great time when he was in Brazil, and that naturalist whose statue is in Blumenau, Fritz Muller. One of the boys fired a bullet at Muller one night pissed and stupid, spent the night in jail and would've been fined except for Barasso.

Barasso is with us for about half, riding his horse, and then it's too steep, so, after a few words of encouragement, he heads for home. There's nine of us, and three of them. Voss, Schmel, and a private with worried eyes. One of these long-boned guys who looks older than he is, and you can't get a laugh out of him because Lutherans don't laugh. Zero. That's his name, and it fits. Our guys are something else. Couple of clowns who can't shut up, everything's a joke, taunting is the only form of address. And we have a psychopath or two, absolutely essential, I suppose.

One of them is a guy called Francisco Gomez, an Americanized Mexican we call Frank. The file on him says he worked in a gold mine in Minas Gerais which is the state next door and has lots of mines and black folk, so the mulatto aspect made it easy for him to fit in, I guess. He was a miner in New Mexico and before that a conscript in the Mexican Army, so he knows how to pull a trigger. I mention this guy because when we made the top after four hours of slogging and cursing, he got himself lost. The plan was to camp overnight, so he went off in search of some firewood and didn't come back. Lot of bedrock up there, bare shelves of granite with magnificent views in all directions, with a glimpse of Blumenau, about thirty miles away. Somewhere between 2,500 and 3,000 feet maybe and pretty cool up there, with a hint of alpine, so a fire is more than a singalong ornament or a wild animal guard. And the boys do plenty of singing when it gets dark because as Voss says, it might help Gomez find his way back... unless, of course, he's done a bunk.

We do a quick search, fire a couple of shots in the air... but nothing. Don't even find the cross which although you can see it plainly from different spots on the way up, seems to be an optical illusion. Might be a dead tree or a streak of white marble or something else, but there's no actual cross up there when you arrive and see what's what.

The men dump the rocks from their packs, build them into a cairn. This will puzzle some hiker someday.

These Germans certainly like singing, like all soldiers who do a lot of marching. They like the corny folk stuff, and Sergeant Schmel is like a bloody jukebox, with a heavy voice that you could hear in Rio, if not Berlin. "*Ich liebe es, eine Wanderung entlang der Bergspitzen gehen...*" (I love to go a wandering along the mountain tops) and this regimental beauty "*Wie ist die Welt so grof und voller Sonnenschein/ Das allerschonste Stuck davon ist doch die Heimat mein*" which roughly translated is "The world's so great and wide... and full of bright sunshine/ but the most beautiful part of all is still that home of mine...." Ridiculous shit, enough to make me reach for my pistol.

But sleeping under the stars beside the slow hiss and crackle of a fire is great. Reminds me of home.

In the morning the yellow biplane comes over, drops a message. Old style. Hand written, bundled in a small sandbag. Voss can't read it but with the help of one of the Brazilian Sigmas I can. Portuguese. Seems Frank is lying on a ledge someway down the face of the cliff. Message is signed X... presumably the mysterious aviatrix who, rumour has it, is Barasso's mistress. Haven't seen herself myself as yet, so who knows. The plane circles, then does a series of runs and swoops at the location. Man, it's a bad spot, and we're thinking how the hell did someone who's supposed to an experienced miner get himself in this predicament? It's right below where you'd expect the cross to be... if there was a cross.

Fortunately we have about 300 feet of rope with us. Don't know how injured he is, as he's lying still so as not to drop any further. He knows we're there, waves, and when we shake the rope out and get it down to him, he's able to get the loop over his head and under his arms. Another wave, and we start hauling, all of us in a tug-o-war chain, and pretty soon we have him back. The plane does a low pass almost like a strafing run, waggles its wings, then flies away into the valley in a series of graceful swoops, just like an eagle searching for prey.

Gomez is banged up but not hopeless, doesn't seem to have any broken bones. When he gets to his feet, he crosses himself.

"I passed out," he says.

Seems reasonable. It was a helluva climb, even for a young guy in reasonable shape.

"Glad to hear it," I say, "because, um, you got no wings, soldier."

He wants to show us something. He scouts around, then points to some footprints on the bare rock surface which go to the edge of the cliff.

"See?" he says. "See? The footprints of Jesus."

The footprints are near perfect impressions, like someone walked over the bedrock when it was still soft.

"I followed them, and then I stood where Jesus stood, and passed out," says Gomez.

Me and Voss exchange a look. Gomez is catholic but is he crazy catholic? Seems to be.

"You should be more careful, soldier," says Voss.

I jerk my head, say, "O.k. Frank, go get yourself some coffee and something to eat."

Gomez crosses himself again, heads back to the camp with the others. Beautiful morning. Below us, the pine forest looks like a green ocean, full of birds and wraiths of mist. I kneel down, trace one of the footprints with my finger.

"Dang weird," I say. "This is very hard rock."

"Supernatural, eh?" Voss says.

Shake my head slowly, say, "I'm not saying Jesus made them."

"My guess is they're prehistoric," Voss says.

"You mean some caveman hunter?"

"Must be."

"But why can you see a cross when you look up from below? That's mighty strange."

"Brocken Spectre. I have seen such a thing back home."

"Nothing illusory about these footprints."

"Aryan."

I laugh, say, "Aryan? Here, in South America?"

"Why not?" says Voss. "Have you heard of the *Horbiger Welteislehre*? The World Ice Theory?"

"No."

"Some day I will tell you about it. It explains everything, how the universe was formed, our world, the origin of the aryan race, the diaspora... ja, this footprint could be aryan."

Don't suppose the Nazi mind is any different from any other mind when it figures it has everything all worked out. Who knows? Anything's possible. We can fly... not long ago we couldn't. But I don't know about these footprints. Don't think I'd do a Frank and follow them into space.

Chapter Thirty-Four

LITTLE GERMANY (GERMANIA)

BARASSO'S RANCH HOUSE is a cross between a hacienda and a log cabin, big and pretty comfortable, much better than the bunkhouse where the rest of us have to kip. Anyway, he wants the radio in the house, so there's a room for that and I get it set up pretty swift. Power is from a windmill and some batteries, very basic but good enough.

One of the first things I pick up is an Argentine station, Radio Belgrano, broadcasting a radio play about Catherine the Great, starring some actress with a shrill voice called Eva Duarte. Well, sounds shrill to me. Might be the reception, might be the Spanish. Catherine's the woman who plotted against her husband and when he was strangled following a coup, she became Empress of Russia for nearly thirty-five years. Really a German, as her father was a German prince, another flippin' Lutheran like Hitler. She said all kinds of wise things but the one that sticks in my head is, "The more a man knows, the more he forgives." Don't know if this play uses this line or not. Don't hang around long enough to find out. Air's full of stations, Argentine, Uruguay... Chile... Sao Paulo and places I don't know.

Run a few tests, talk to the airship.

"Station Sigma-one-Eden requesting Zeppelin-one-three-one. Radio check, over."

"*Hallo*, Sigma-one-Eden, this is Z131, send, over."

"Sounding loud and clear, Z131."

"Likewise, Sigma-one-Eden. Today is the Führer's birthday, over."

"Present will be dispatched, over.

"Beer, please. I will make sure he receives it, over.

"Sure thing, Z131. Over and out."

What a joker. Guess the Fritz is bored hanging around waiting for something to happen. The rest of us are busy, the usual drills, target practice, fitness exercises, a few tactical lessons from the Waffen, nothing I'm sure most of these irregulars don't already know. You want to slit somebody's throat? You do it like this. You want to blend with the jungle? Like this, soldier. How about target spotting and clock codes? Vector like this, Scutzen. The mystery to me is why the emphasis on military tactics if Sigma is just a security detail for a rubber plantation or a remote mine in the jungle. Far as I know, none of the Indians have any tactics beyond a blow dart and a spear. Barasso has yet to lay it on me, reveal the plan. Still, something's about to happen. A fuel truck passed through yesterday, primed the airship. Diesel. And we're picking up some supplies in Blumenau later.

I'm taking Mac with me and Frank Gomez. Easier this way—we all speak English.

Last night I had a private pow wow with Mac when everyone was distracted by the beer someone had brought in for "Hitler's birthday" which was a joke I guess because it's not this month. Seems everytime the Waffen boys wanna have a drink, they say it's for "Hitler's birthday".

I give Mac one of the mystery passports. American. Joe Blow. The picture looks a bit like Mac, especially after a little touch up. His plan is to head south, get into Uruguay, make Montevideo... and then Buenos Aires. Should be easy.

"If I had some grease," he says, "be easier."

"You just gonna walk across the border?"

"Don't have wings."

"Need a visa?"

"Not if I have some grease. If I go to Chui, I can probably go in at night, no sweat. You just cross the street. Maybe I could rent me a driver, get to Montevideo. It's an hour."

The Embassy there will fix him up.

"So you need money...."

"Yeah, be nice to have a little extra... well, I got nuthin."

"Guess I can help."

He smiles. "Never know, might be able to get a boat in Porto Alegre. I gotta get out of here. You understand, right?"

"Completely."

Mac looks really old and fubar. Think that rat must've ate something important, then covered up the crime. The cigarettes are killing him. Coughs like a lawn mower, all flash, no spark. He wouldn't be joining the mission anyway, and who knows if they'd let him walk. He's been real quiet about the nature of his contract. The other day we used the Ducks for some live ammunition practice. First the Waffen suckered them by using blanks, so the Ducks figured it was just a training game, like hide and seek for soldiers and civilians. But then, during a pursuit in the forest the boys got the thumbs up to fire real bullets, so rounds were splintering off trees and chipping rocks like Hopalong Cassidy. Nobody got killed, nobody got seriously hurt, although they were scared shitless, screaming like babies when the roundup was over. Was there any real value in this? Maybe. But I'm wondering... I mean, I'm just along for the ride, but now I'm wondering if this is a ride I really want to be on.

Ducks out in the garden today, hoeing the vegetables, supervised by Vasca who says he's from Portugal and is really a stone mason but would rather be a farmer, especially if he has labourers to do the grunt work. They're not shackled but have the iron ring on the ankle, which kills any big ideas. Vasco seems to be in charge of the house, although there is a foreman for the ranch and a few guachos to look after the cattle. Right now they're away in the hills, following the cattle in their fall grazing, so we never see them unless one or two ride in for supplies. The life is nomadic, as they just follow the herd. I could do it. In fact, I have done it for a summer on the Big E ranch above Merritt, which is a half-day drive from home sweet home in the Okanagan. In a way, this part of Brazil is similar, same sort of temperatures, plateaus, mountains and valleys, and I believe there's some semi-desert to the northwest. It's the same, but not the same. We got orchards, vineyards, farms, ranches... wops, krauts and rattlesnakes, but no Nazis.

Except for Klaus Gerwing and my mother. And Gerwing's in jail and my mother thinks National Socialism is a social club like the Daughters of Votan and Hitler is a sexy guy.

It's strange, I'm thinking, that the more distance I put between me and them, the closer I seem to be.

Anyway, me and Mac and Gomez drive into Blumenau, and while they're taking care of business—which requires a few stops in different places—I wander around a bit, find this street which looks like it could be a German village with all these timber framed buildings, pop into this tavern called Das Jager Haus where they serve the real deal, big jugs of locally brewed pilsner. Not busy, and while there's some Portuese in the air, I'm picking up more German conversation than anything else. There's a guy sitting by himself near the door, a tubby little bastard in lederhosen, the whole outfit, leather shorts and braces, boots and knee-high socks and a Tyrolean hat with a feather, and he's watching me as he sips his lager and smokes a cigarette. Well, guys do that in bars, and sometimes they even send you a beer if you're young and look like you're switched for their kinda action. When I stare back, his eyes flick away. Then, when he finishes his cigarette, he starts to laugh... and I mean laugh. Rolls into it real easy, slow at first and then crazy loud like he's sharing a joke with a phantom. Nobody pays him much attention, although it seems to me others are laughing a bit more, and glasses are being raised and clinked. It's pissing me off, actually, cause I'm wondering if the laugh is on me. Then, out of the blue, the guy stops and lights up another cigarette. It's like he's mad, and I've walked into an asylum. And the other folks are either mad too or they have a different idea of normal. Laugh, laugh, laugh. Goddamn. Feel like smashing the guy's face in.

When the barmaid delivers me seconds, I say, "What's wrong with him?"

She chuckles, says, "*Die Lacher.*"

Die Lacher: The Laugher.

"He mad?"

"No no... he gets paid to be happy. People drink more, understand?"

You ever hear of that? Getting paid to laugh? My introduction to 'The Laugher'. The only woman drinking in the place, a middle-aged biddy who's so brown she looks like she's got leprosy, is laughing her head off too, and I'll be damned if they don't raise the temperature in the place, get everybody laughing and drinking like it's the end of the world and tomorrow we die. Briefly the place is crazy packed and real delirious and these two factotums are sitting at different tables doing call and response like a couple of mating hyenas. The Laughers. Bar should be called that, although for these folks there's nothing unusual about it. The way it's explained to me is that's part of the atmosphere of 'back home'— meaning Germany—and goes with the beer. The fact that the guy looks like Hitler doesn't occur to any of them because, well, the Hitler look is quite common around here. Moustache, hair shaved behind the ears, pursed lips, tight shoulders, hint of a hunch... eyes that photograph. A cop, judge and butcher all rolled into one. Virtually no blacks to be seen, like they know better, but plenty of the 'New Man' types. Even the quarter skins—the Portuguese Indians—have picked up on it, like it's not only patriotic but sexy. The Latin Hitler. Go figure.

Barmaid takes a break, sits down at the next table, lights up a smoke, says, "New in our country?"

"Ja," I say. "Beautiful place."

She's pulling a thread of tobacco from between her lips.

"Army?"

"Yeah... maneuvers."

"What part of Germany you from?"

"Hamburg."

"My dad's from Munich. He's always talking about it."

"You born there?"

"No. I was born here... Florianopolis. Blum's o.k. but Florian's better."

"More action?"

"More everything."

"I like the beer."

"Sure, it's good, I guess. Any Fritz can make a beer."

She's sizing me up. Older bird, thirties, tits like udders. Thinner once upon a time I guess.

"You play cards?" she says.

"Poker? Sure."

"You should meet my sister... she was the Sommerfest Queen last year."

"I believe you. I thought maybe you were."

She snorts, says, "Me? I had my chance ten years ago. I was engaged and my boyfriend was so jealous he said he'd kill me if I put myself on display. It was a rotten thing, soldier. There was money in it cause they send you around the State as a rep... Florian, Porto Alegre... maybe even Paulo or Rio."

"Ever been to Chui?"

"Where's that? Oh, the border dump. No, never, but I know it's a dump. I worked in Porto Alegre for a couple of years. You might like it."

I sigh, say, "Little chance. I just go where they send me."

"We get the odd German guy passing through. They're always doing things with our boys. What do you do?"

"Me? Oh, march around... you know."

She's grinning. "Your secret's safe with me, soldier. Ever shoot anyone?"

"Intentionally or unintentionally?"

"I mean, have you ever been to war?"

"Soon... maybe."

Her eyes get big: "Not Peru," she says. "Don't tell me those bastards are provoking us again."

"Why, what'd they do?"

"They insult our football team. And they steal our land and our resources."

"Peru?"

"And Bolivia."

"Bolivia? I thought their beef was with Paraguay."

"They all want what we got, mister. I hope you're here to set them straight."

She seems quite wound up about this, banging the table a bit, fidgety in her chair. You see, it's not so sleepy and out of it around this place as you might think. Who was it told me about the Chaco War? Colonel Powell? Eddie maybe. When he was in the Brazilian army, he was stationed next door in the Grosso for a while. The Paras and the Bolis went at it hard and heavy for three or four years and I think they only officially quit shooting a year ago. The Gran Chaco, just south of Amazonia... west, northwest of where I'm sitting right now. Extension of the Mato Grosso, so lots of swamp, lots of forest, some wet, some dry... who would want it? No gold, not much of anything. But now they smell oil, so they start fighting over it. Everybody was involved: Peru, Ecuador, Chile, Brazil but it was Paraguay and Bolivia who drew their swords and when they'd finished this installment there was close to a 100,000 dead. The rivers were full of gunboats, flyingboats, armed launches... attacking forts and settlements... and there were some pretty big army battles, using all these latest European and American weapons... Vickers, Krupp, Maxim... Curtis, Potez... I mean, they had planes and tanks, machine guns and field artillery... both sides used foreign officers, like Spanish, German, Italian... mercenaries from all over. Who knew? Back home, I never heard of the Chaco War yet this war had it all, mountain fighting, desert fighting... river, jungle... just about the whole school yard. Guess the war in Spain was more sexy, more 'white', more in the news, so the Chaco War just got lost in the tropical drumbeat. Of course people south of the Equator are blaming the gringo, say it was—or is—really a war between Standard Oil and Royal Dutch Oil. Standard backed the Bolis, Royal Dutch the Paras. Waste of time? No oil found so far. But you never know, one day somebody might find something. The future is like that— it's full of stuff you don't know about or need right now.

No matter why you fight, you're always practicing for the Big One.

Talk too that Bolivia wanted to get itself a corridor to the Atlantic. Fat chance. Forget Paraguay—Brazil and Argentina would never countenance that.

I smile at the barmaid, say, "Actually *fraulein* I'm here to learn the samba."

She says, "Are you now? Well you should meet my sister, she's the dancer."

"The Beauty Queen?"

"Her name is Gisella. How long are you around for?"

"Might be back in town on Saturday."

"What's your name?"

"Mat."

"Drop by, Mat. First drink's free. Bring a friend. Could be a poker game going too."

While me and the barmaid are talking, I notice The Laugher is watching us, and when she gets back behind the bar, he starts laughing again. Extra hard and dirty. Coincidence? Damn bloody ignorant, I say. Heat up a couple of coins with my cigarette, drop them on his table as I head for the door. Hey, tip the clown, I say.

Everybody's riding horses around here—horses and mules. Oh they have cars and trucks and the odd motorcycle, but they like horses and mules for packing whatever needs packing. Economics, I guess. Rural economics. So there's quite a bit of horseshit in the streets, and clouds of blue-bottle flies. Otherwise it's nice as nice, like endless summer. A few Pedros hanging around a fountain, guachos by the look of them. Couple have bull whips, are snapping at the flies like they've got a competition going. Their *companheiros* whoop and laugh, start tossing coins as targets. Idle bullshit, eh. This is a very strange town, like a dream because it's all mixed up, like Germany on one side of the street, Mexico on the other... and they call it Brazil. An open top Mercedes cruises past, two men in the front, two women in the back, like they've just come from the castle. The Pedros take notice.

"Cocksucker Guaranis from Paraguay," says a voice behind me.

It's Frank Gomez.

"Indians?"

"Yeah. Borders mean nuthin' to them. They just follow the cattle."

He should talk, I think.

He goes on: "I worked in a mine with some of them. Mean, vicious, totally without morals."

"Don't you have a bit Indian in you?"

"Sure, but not like them. I'm Yaqui, from the Mexican altiplano. These Guaranis be one fuckin' step from cannibals."

"Where's McDonald?"

"Sleeping in the truck. Can't take the heat... he's saying. Lazy jerkoff. Had to do all the lifting myself. 'I got a bad back and bum knee' he's saying. He'll be heading down the road."

"He say that?"

"No... but if he can't cut 'er, they'll send his ass down the road. You know that... Lieutenant."

Look at him, shake my head, say, "You're pretty tough, Gomez."

"Sure. I've cracked a few rocks."

"Next you'll be telling me you can fly...."

That pushes him back. He says he fainted and fell down that cliff up there on the mountain but I have a feeling it just wasn't that simple. Some of these Indians can be quite mystical, especially the Mexican ones.

Truck's parked below a shady mango tree that's leaning over a fence from somebody's yard. Flip back the canvas and there's Mac stretched out between the freight. Grab his boot, give it a twist, and next thing you know he's sitting up with a .38 in his hand, his face melting with rage. Wonder where he got that? We got Lugers and Walthers but I don't remember any snub-nose nailers coming down from Rio.

"Don't creep up on me," says Mac. "I can be dangerous."

We're laughing, sort of. "Where'd you get that?" I say. "Thought you had no money."

"We got paid, didn't we?" says Gomez.

Now Mac is looking guilty. "Yeah," he says to me. "We made a delivery for Vasca."

He slides off the tail gate, moans as he shakes his bones.

"What sort of a delivery?" I say.

"Meat. He sells to a local butcher."

"*Senhor* Barasso know about this?"

Mac shrugs, and Gomez looks way into the distance. Guess the 'gardener' has a little free-enterprise going.

"Who's the gun dealer in town?"

"Indian guy in the street. He came right up to me, asked if there was anything I needed. Didn't have time for a woman but a pistol's always useful. So I got me a pistol."

"Guarani," says Gomez.

Well, what's it to me? If Mac needs a gun to go travelling, that's his business. Better this way than nicking one from the Sigma armory.

Drive back is nice. Road winds through farms (*fazendas*), orchards, tracts of forest, sometimes follows the river which is muddy from the recent rains. I could live here. Find a sweet little *senhorita*, get some land, a vineyard maybe, some rifles and what the hell. But... am I ready for that?

A Gazeta Florianopolis. Reprinted from *O Globo*. MYSTERY AMAZON EXPLOSION

Reports about the extent and destruction caused by the mysterious explosion that occurred recently in a remote region of Amazonia are now reaching authorities. Several mining prospectors claim to have witnessed a large meteor or possibly a comet lighting up the sky above the jungle in the Rio Curaca basin (Latitude 5) close to our border with Peru. Corroborating reports come from catholic missionaries working in the area and members of the recent search party looking for Colonel Fawcett who disappeared while on his quest to find the lost city of "Z". All witnesses describe the sun becoming "blood-red" in the minutes preceding the explosion of "a large fireball or bolide" followed by a flash that caused temporary blindness lasting hours or days for anyone looking in the direction of the impact.

Dr. Fonseca, Director of the Astronomy Department at the Federal University of Rio Janeiro, said that the solar discoloration could have been caused by dust in the line-of-sight. "Possibly this dust could be from the tail of a comet," he said.

When asked about the reports of a fine white dust falling on a large area of the jungle before the explosion, Dr. Fonseca said this was unlikely and if true, was probably "post-impact ash".

Several witnesses saw a glowing residual trail in the sky.

A local pilot, Johnny Urco, reports seeing a tract of forest more than twenty miles (32 kilometers) (90,000 hectares) long which has been destroyed. Urco states that the shattered jungle is elongated rather than circular, as occurred at the 1908 Tunguska explosion in Siberia. Experts attribute Tunguska to an air blast caused by an object entering away from the vertical (the most likely entry angle for all cosmic projectiles is 45 degrees).

Fired and de-populated: the forest burned for several months, and it's believed that one or two indigenous tribes were wiped out. The mission at Poca has been treating a number of survivors for burns and blindness. Some are believed to be suffering from amnesia, although this is unconfirmed.

The Ministry of the Interior says it will send an investigation team to the area "soon".

The disappearance of the Air Inca flight from Lima to Manaus two years ago in this region of the Amazon remains a mystery. There were sixteen people on board and as yet neither the government of Peru nor Brazil has conducted an official search. An unnamed official in Rio de Janeiro said, "It's an impossible place, it's over a million square kilometers, and we're supposed to do what? Send in the Marines?"

O Voive de Sao Paulo (The Voice of Sao Paulo): SPACE ROCKET FROM THE STARS?

Our reporter in the Amazon delivers the latest facts about the mysterious explosion that turned night into day and left witnesses with no sense of time. Local hunters and miners in the Zube Valley claim that the photo-electric residue from the explosion left the region in sustained daylight for 48 hours. "Darkness only returned properly after a week," says a prospector who calls himself 'Mysterioso', the name he used as a professional wrestler in a previous career in Bahia Norte.

"It was like the Land of the Midnight Sun... it was always daylight and the air was full of dust and the smell of burning oil or burning something, because the forest was fried... dead fish, dead animals floating... I even saw people or corpses that looked like people... when they been cooked like that, who can say what it might be. I hadn't crossed myself in forty years, *senhor*. My dog and my mule bolted and I haven't seen them since." Many people say they heard a loud whistling sound in the minutes before impact. Scientists say that while such electrophonics often accompany large celestial objects, this one was unusual. Instruments at the government meteorological station at Izaga registered what they call a "symmetrical acoustic."

Consuelo Mateus, a technician, said, "This is puzzling because usually such noise would be random, not symmetrical." When our reporter asked what this meant, she said, "It could mean intelligence." When asked if this meant the object was a spaceship from the cosmos, *Senhorita* Mateus said, "Not necessarily, as the perceived symmetry could result from an equipment problem at the station."

CHAPTER THIRTY-FIVE:

VON SCHELLENBERG DEMANDS A DUAL

THERE'S A CAR PARKED in front of the house that looks familiar, and it should be—it's the Mercedes touring convertible I noticed in Blumenau earlier. Interesting. Barasso has visitors.

Can hear shots, so I wander down to the target range, which is in a gravel pit near the airstrip. It's Zero, the 'worried man'. Sub-machine gun. Watch him go through the moves, like stand and shoot, kneel and shoot, run, fall to the ground and shoot. He's got a good imagination. He's sees the enemy, not a dummy stuffed with sand. Accurate too with single shots and short bursts. Impressive acrobatics. He's putting on a performance, like a ballet, although he doesn't know he's being watched. Waffen SS. They say they're elite and I guess they are. Fanatics? Maybe. Damn serious for sure.

Walk over to the airstrip, check out the yellow biplane. Beautiful machine. As I thought, it's a Fiat CR 32. Some aluminum, some fabric, and the lower wings are shorter than the upper. Don't know what the engine is but it's a beast for such a compact little plane. Looks about 20 feet prop to tail and the upper wings might span 27. Black propeller. Surfaces are corrugated to improve the airflow. Forward cockpit is just behind the wings, about midway, and there's a foot stirrup, so I hop up, take a look.

The usual dials, pedals, stick... nice leather seat... and a small teddy bear fastened to the dash beside the altimeter.

A voice behind me says something in Brazilian, then repeats it in English. "Curiosity killed the cat."

I step down. It's a woman. Older but not real old. Thin, brunette, dark Azorean eyes, wearing slacks. Could this be the mystery pilot?

"I'm thinking it'd be a pity to shoot one of these beauties down," I say. I let my hand brush the fuselage as if it's a horse.

"Unless it was trying to shoot you," she says.

She moves past me, steps on the stirrup, takes a quick look in the cockpit.

"I didn't touch anything," I say. "Just having a look."

"I heard shots," she says. "Was that you?"

"Not me. I don't waste my ammo."

"So I've noticed."

"How so?"

"I've been watching you, Lieutenant."

Give her my best smile. "Of course... I've seen you up there flying around... but I didn't know it was you. I thought maybe it was some Italian ace."

"How do you know I'm not?"

Shrug, say, "Is that your teddy?"

"Teddy? Oh, my *ursinho*."

"What do you call him? Mr. Lucky?"

"His name is... private."

"What about your name, *senhorita*? That private too?"

She sort of smiles, then walks away. She says, without stopping or turning, "I'll be in the garden tonight."

Later I find out from Gaspari the Zep officer all about her... or enough for now. Daniele D'Anza or Dani to her fans. Family Italian-Brazilian from Sao Paulo. Went to school in Europe, became a dancer doing cabaret and other shows until she got into the sports car scene and from then on her thrill was speed. She had a rich boyfriend who was into flying and connected into the Italian aircraft industry and the next thing you know she's flying, doing airshows in various countries, races like the Marseille to Damascus and getting her name in the papers and doing some modelling at art shows. Now she's apparently trying to help Fiat sell some of its planes in South America and this CR-32 biplane fighter is one of them. They say Fiat's making some of the best military aircraft these days, as the wars in Spain and Manchuria have proved, so there's dough to be made and I guess a woman with a hot plane is a good sell. I'd buy one... if I was buying.

How far Barasso fits into Dani's life, I still don't know.

That evening I'm in the radio room doing some listening to whatever noise is going on when Barasso comes in with this blond guy who's wearing a smart looking double-breasted suit. Even though it's a light tropical material, he's perspiring. Aryan? I'll say. Those blue eyes and Viking bones gleam with Master Race superiority. Still, not everyone who looks like a prick turns out to be a prick, so I smile nice and friendly when we're introduced.

"This is Major von Schellenberg," says Barasso. "Major... Lieutenant Thorsen."

Von Schellenberg nods... slightly.

"The Major has just flown down from Rio," says Barasso. "He'll be joining us on the mission. He's brought some new mapping equipment with him which we'll be testing."

"Radio?" I say.

"Radar," says von Schellenberg. "The latest in weapons technology. It can be used for targeting, and for mapping."

This sounds interesting. I assume the gear will be installed on the Zeppelin.

"German gear, Major?" I say.

He nods, says, "Yes. We had it ferried in by flying boat."

"Italian?"

He's testy. "The Reich has its own aircraft, Lieutenant. Our Dornier 24 has a range of 2,700 kilometers. No one has a better one."

I nod as humbly as I can. He's got a tic, left eye, cheek. Guess it travels when he's feeling tight.

He says, "I've heard of you, Thorsen."

He must mean that damn Safari Man Ad.

Barasso says, "He's a good shot too."

"Yes? Good with guns, good with women?"

Me and Barasso chuckle. Just being polite, you understand.

"I saw that magazine piece," he says. "Your wife's work, Colonel Barasso?"

"Yes it was," says Barasso.

"The girl is one of her models?" says von Schellenberg.

"German," says Barasso. "Right, Thorsen?"

"From Berlin," I say.

Von Schellenberg dabs his brow and cheeks with a hanky. He's about forty years old, still in shape. *Schutzstaffel* for sure.

Clicks his heels (sort of), bows (sort of), says politely (sort of), "I look forward to seeing you shoot, Lieutenant."

Barasso nods, then escorts his guest from the room. That was weird, I think. Nazi, sure, and maybe one of those old time Junker class aristocrats. When he says 'lieutenant' he says it the British way, 'left-tenant'.

Can hear the Zeppelin running its engines in the distance, routine warm-ups to keep them sweet. Crew does this every twelve hours. Faint wafts of fuel and unfamiliar vegetation. It's warm, and there's a bit of after-light in the garden. Never been to California, yet this must be what it's like—easy sub-tropical.

Barasso and his guests must be eating dinner or having pre-dinner cocktails, and I can't imagine Dani not being part of that or why I'm even here. She's old enough to be my mother... well, if my mother was thirteen when she had me. Curiosity killed the cat. No kidding. I'm bored, no question... and Uma... well Uma's in Rio and Rio might as well be Canada for a mercenary who has no clue what tomorrow might bring.

Voss appears, and he's got The Worried Man with him. Both are in uniform. Me, sort of. Got the boots and pants but I'm wearing that striped tropi shirt I bought, second day in Brazil. Well, the replacement I bought to go to Barasso's party.

"Lieutenant Thorsen," says Voss awkwardly. "I've been asked to give you this...."

Got a cigarette in my right so I take the note with my left. It's in German.

"Lieutenant Thorsen... sir, you have injured my name and reputation by your unlawful involvement with my wife Uma von Schellenberg... therefore I must seek redress for this egregious affront. For this matter to be settled, I call on you to meet me at dawn at the Pouco Corcovado forest path. Please confirm with my second, *SS-Obersturmführer* Voss if this is satisfactory and declare your choice of weapon. Signed, Erich von Schellenberg, *SS-Sturmbannführer*."

I look at Voss who's acting pretty stiff. His sidekick Zero doesn't look so worried, is enjoying the joke.

"What is this?" I say.

"A duel," says Voss.

"You're crazy," I say. "This is a joke, isn't it?"

"He believes you had an affair with his wife."

"She never told me she was married!"

"Was she the one on the ship? The Magician's assistant?"

"That's right... von Schellenberg should be talking to the Magician, not me."

"Ah yes... the one who called himself Kallingram. The Major has already dealt with him."

310

"What do you mean 'dealt with him'?"

"A duel," says Zero. "The Major killed him... so we've been told, anyway."

This is incredible, has to be a joke. But as I try to think back, I can't remember if Uma said she'd been married or not. She went to that Bride's School, didn't she say? Maybe I didn't get the whole story. But then a cock in love is like that—all head, no ears.

"This is 1939," I say. "You don't have duels to settle disputes anymore."

Voss nods perfunctorily, says, "The Herr Kallingram situation is more complicated. He was actually a Russian spy."

I'd heard this accusation before.

"Is that what he was?" I say. "Well, too bad."

Voss hesitates, then says, "I don't know you well, Thorsen, but you seem like a decent fellow. If you were a member of the SS, Major von Schellenberg couldn't do this even if his honor was offended. He's a *Sturmbannführer* and you're a *Leutnant*, so he would be violating the protocol of rank. But you see, you're an irregular, so...."

"Voss, I don't sword fight... never lifted a sword in my life."

"Be pistols," says Zero.

Smug bastard. He might look like an unhappy monk worn away by the weight of God's work but in fact he's just another sadist in a uniform.

"Perhaps if you apologize," says Voss. "It's not easy to save face, I know."

"Apologize for what? I was a dupe!"

While I stew, they shuffle around in the eighteenth century. Duels. Women. Honor, bullshit.

"Barasso know about this?" I say.

"No idea," says Voss.

"You can always run," says Zero.

"Why don't you shut your fuggin' mouth, soldier?" I say.

"Perhaps the *Leutnant* would like to try," sneers Zero. "I am at your service."

What is this guy? A sergeant? A *Hauptscarführer* or "*Spiess*" as they call them? I drop my cigarette, stub it with my toe, then just snap him, a fast jab between the eye and the ear and he goes down with bells.

Voss jumps between us, although Zero isn't getting up in a hurry. He's been decked.

Voss draws his pistol, says, "Friend, you could be court-martialled for this!"

Me, I'm panting with rage. "Don't be stupid, Voss, I'm not part of your outfit!"

"Maybe so, maybe not. The SS is in charge of this mission."

"Is it? Not what I heard."

"Calm down, Thorsen... I'm sympathetic to your position... really, I am. Let's work this out like reasonable men."

I point at Zero, who's trying to stand up.

"You," I say. "Not so acrobatic now, eh, asshole?"

He's trying to unholster his Luger but Voss draws down on him. "*Speiss*," he barks. "*Aufhoren!*"

I'm jabbing, almost spitting. "You... Zero, pieca shit, you want a dawn patrol? You and me, dawn, tomorrow, let's settle it."

Oh he wants me, wants me bad, but Voss has the rank... and it seems that in matters of Kraut honor, so does von Schellenberg.

"This business is between you and the Major," says Voss. "What shall I tell him? To expect an apology?"

Think about it, then say, "We could talk, air it out."

Voss sighs. "Impossible... the Major will want it in writing and to be blunt, he won't go for it."

I'm thinking there must be more to this than Uma.

"Lieutenant Voss... Kurt," I say. "Tell me something: is Major von Schellenberg really *Schutzstaffel*?"

Voss holsters his pistol, runs his hand through his hair like he's trying to lose the sweat. "Ja, the Major is SS."

"He wouldn't be Abwehr as well?"

"Intelligence? I am unable to say."

"Meaning? Don't know or won't say --"

"The Major is a stranger to me. Before today."

"But you'd heard of him?"

"Ja. We knew he was coming."

My lips are dry, so I fish a cigarette, light up. Offer one to Voss who shakes his head, waits. Take a couple of drags, then say, "O.k. Dawn." Voss seems relieved. "Weapons?"

"Pistols, I guess."

"One shot? Clip?"

"Whatever. I'll use mine, he can use his... just as long as it isn't a Mauser."

"Second?"

"Dunno. I'll find somebody."

"Gut."

Voss holds out his hand but I just laugh. Voss smiles, nods like he knows it's all absurd, ridiculous nonsense.

"Tomorrow then," he says, drawing his heels together, raising his hand in a half-assed SS salute... which is just like the old Indian hand greeting. Ridiculous.

He leaves, with Zero slinking after him. Take out the Major's note, read it again. Christ, what have I got myself into? Hear the radio in the house, some dance music. Voices, laughter. Obviously Dani has something better going.

Find Mac behind the bunkhouse playing horseshoes with a couple of the boys. They've got a light rigged up which is swarming with bugs, and I tell you, my head feels like that. Swarming. I've been called out for fights before, but nothing like this, winner keeps all.

Take Mac to a quiet spot below the water tank, fill him in.

"You're right," he says. "This smells."

"Gotta be a setup," I say.

"The woman is an excuse... although it's enough for bullets to fly. God knows, I should know. She say she was married?"

"That's just it, I can't remember."

"You'd remember. Would it have made any difference?"

I thought of Bobby and what she said. Married but not really. Uma could be the same. Women who travel alone are always single.

"What am I gonna do, Mac?"

"Talk to the *Senhor*, yet?"

"Barasso? No. Think I should?"

Mac ponders, then says, "Come with me, kid."

"You think?"

"Yeah... I mean, you really give a rat's ass about any of this?"

I'm thinking, I'm thinking. "I like Brazil... some of the people, but it's too hot."

"Then it's settled? Sure it is. Cooler in Buenos Aires."

"Daresay, but I gotta think about this. I'll let you know."

"Better be soon, because I'm just about done peelin' potatoes."

"Tonight?"

"Yeah. Just take the truck and we'll be long gone Johnson this time tomorrow."

I'm thinking, I'm thinking. "Was gonna ask you to be my Second."

Mac gives a husky laugh. "Who do you think you are, kid? The Count of Monte Cristo?"

"If we steal the truck, they'll send the plane after us."

"The crop duster? No problem."

"Mac, it's an Italian fighter plane and it's got a couple of Breda 12.7mm machine guns that'd rip us to shit if they caught us on an open road. Think again, amigo."

"Plane is armed? I thought it was just a toy."

313

"No toy, Mac... it's one of the best there is. We'd have to dump the truck by daylight and get along some other way. No, it won't do. Let me talk to Barasso first."

Now Mac surprises me. "You do that, kid, and sure, he'll smooth it over and then all them Krauts will think you're yellow. Either you cut bait and run now, or you gotta face him."

He's right. How can I get out of this, save face, retain authority, and continue along as if nothing had happened? Cat's out of the bag and my pay check and rep is going with it. Unless I take care of business.

"He's a fuggin' Major!" I say bitterly. "A hot shit duellist!"

"Maybe he is, maybe he isn't. I hear you're pretty good... Safari Man."

"If it was rifles, no sweat."

Mac's a wily bugger, no question. He's already on Plan B.

"We agree it's a setup, right?" he says. "Then let's have a setup of our own...."

I don't get much sleep, even with Plan B in my head. Death is like insomnia—the eyes stay open even when they're closed.

Chapter Thirty-Six:

MODERN ART

FEEL COLD EVEN THOUGH it's a nice morning, the birds coming up full throttle with the dawn light and all's right with the world. It's not fear. Heart beats nice and steady, can feel it in my ears. We're here first, me and Mac, although we know the others are on the move. We know Zero has moved into the forest at first light armed with a MP-40 sub machine gun, the same weapon I saw him practicing with yesterday. We figured there'd be a bushwhacker, so we're ready for that. Old Shatterhand... hey, the SS aren't the only people to read a novel by Karl May.

Following the phony protocol of the old time duel, the Seconds are supposed to meet, lay the ground rules, maybe negotiate a last minute settlement while the adversaries hang back. But it's just hunting, with some rules to make it seem civilized. Doesn't matter if it's face off at ten or twenty paces or hide and seek in the forest, it's hunting.

Here they come, von Schellenberg and Voss, marching down the path from the wine press.

"You shared a cabin with Voss on the ship?" says Mac, low.

"Yes. Seemed o.k."

"And you think it was a coincidence?"

"At the time, yeah. Now I don't know what the hell to think."

"I think somebody in Canada was talkin' to somebody in Hamburg."

The two Germans are close enough now so's we can hear their huffing. Sound like a pair of donkeys in a briar patch.

"If I don't come out of this, take my dough," I say. "In my room,

315

there's a book, The Decline of the West, by Oswald Spengler. Look inside."

"Just follow the plan and you'll be o.k., kid."

Draw a deep breath, look up at the mountain. Some morning mist, some steam as the sun begins to roar the way it does down here in Brazil. And there's that phantom cross, the damndest thing, as real as the smoldering cigarette in my hand.

Von Schellenberg is wearing camouflage fatigues, green, black and brown, like a northern pond frog. No cap. Square shoulders, tight waist. Hair so white he might be albino, although I don't see any red demons in those photomatic eyes. He's fit, he's mean, he's fascist... and he's certainly killed more people than I have. Will he settle for an incapacitating wound? I'm not counting on it. As Mac says, this is a political execution dressed up as a love quarrel.

Voss approaches Mac, says, "Pistols?"

Mac says, "Just so long as they be even."

Voss turns, looks at von Schellenberg, who unholsters his Luger, dangles it carelessly on his finger.

Mac says, "7.6 millimeter, isn't it?"

Von Schellenberg says, "This one is a 9... that a problem?"

After the Treaty of Versailles, Germany was restricted to 7 mm pistols. But since Hitler took over, said fuck you France, I guess they're back to 9.

I hold up my Colt. Voss insists on taking a look.

"A 1911," says Voss to von Schellenberg, who just shrugs.

"This is an eleven millimeter."

"*Amerikaner*," says von Schellenberg dismissively.

The arrogant prick can play loose and carefree, but the Colt has a fifty foot range advantage over the Luger. One less bullet in the clip but it's got heavier ammo and can cut daisies at a 190 feet.

Voss hands the Colt to Mac, who passes it back to me.

Voss says, "Gentlemen, can this point of honor be resolved by another means?"

Von Schellenberg's jaw is clenched. He just stares hard and heavy.

"Uma's a Jew... did you know?" I say.

Why did I say that? Just came into my head. But it gets the tic going in his face. "How about you, Major? *Sie Jude*?" I say.

Voss is smiling thinly. Not every day a commanding officer gets shit thrown in his face. Uma told me there was no bigger insult going in Germany these days, especially in the Nazi Party. Hitler's Racial Purity Laws were spreading a lot of paranoia around and not a lot of proof was needed to bring a good man down.

I say to Voss, "I don't duel with subhumans. Prove to me that Major von Schellenberg isn't a subhuman."

Von Schellenberg snarls, "He's a coward! So, I shoot you now, coward!"

He's reaching for his pistol and Voss is making restraining motions.

"I take it no rapprochement is possible, gentlemen?"

"No reasoning with *ein untermenschen*," I say.

Von Schellenberg raises his arms to shoulder level, then stretches left and right, flexing his fingers like a diver. Perfect cross, perfect target.

"You see?" I say to Mac. "He submits."

Mac nods, keeps his hand close to his 38 which is in his pocket.

Voss says, "Whatever do you mean, *Leutnant*?"

"Homo code, Voss. The Major is signalling submission."

This does it. Von Schel goes nuts, draws his Luger and I'm running for cover. He lets off two, three rounds by the time I'm in the trees. Very foolish, cause now he's got five bullets instead of eight.

I'm standing in an arcade somewhere just as the sun goes down and the shadows are reaching. Finishing up an orange I bought from a vendor not far from the *pousada*. Don't recognize her at first. Thinking, what a great looking woman. She's looking at me, a smiling stranger, just arrived in front of one of the arches.

"You're hiding," she says. "Still think you're being followed?"

"What've you done to your hair?" I say.

"Don't you like it?"

What's not to like? She's like a new woman every time I see her. But feels the same, the narrow waist, the firm ass... and the teeth that can do more than nibble. I kiss her neck, her ear, or maybe she's kissing mine. Can feel the full length of her body against me in a perfect match. You know the way you try on some new clothes and the fit is right on? Hardly ever happens but when it does you never want to take them off.

"How much time we got?" I say.

She's got a job at a casino in Copa for a company selling a line of whiskies and cigars. Puts on the sash, Miss Berlin, smiles, lets the men check out the goods. Two, three hours, make a few shekels. The other evening she was a hostess at gathering of German businessmen in Rio sponsered by the German Embassy.

"Enough," she says. "I start at 10."

Have a couple of drinks in the lobby, don't say much, just watch the people. Not busy and this really isn't a bar, just a hit and run counter beside the check-in desk. Not really a regular hotel either, even though it's got a cage elevator. You can get a room for a night or an hour, whatever you think you need. Hookers use it, and people like us, lovers without a home. Feels illegal, but I guess sex is like that when strangers become friends. Don't say anything in the elevator and don't say much in the room. We start out quietly, then get a bit rough.

Afterwards she says, "You needed a woman."

"Hmm," I say, keep looking at the ceiling without really seeing it.

She starts to dress. Christ, what a body.

Sees me watching, stops, says, "What?"

"Just thinking," I say.

"And what are you thinking, *Liebling*?" she says.

"About jealousy."

She looks pleased. "You? You jealous of... who?"

"Just thinking... if you had someone else, Uma. Another guy, a husband someplace maybe."

She shimmies so's her skirt drops over her hips. She jacks a leg on the chair, rolls on a stocking. "What might you do?" she says.

"Kill him," I say.

Reach over, run my hand inside her thigh, feel the heat. She sways a bit, her eyes close.

"What part of me do you like best?" she says.

"All," I say.

"If I was cut in two," she says. "Top or bottom... tell the truth."

"I'd kill him," I say.

"I love your saw, baby... only your saw."

Guess we have time for seconds. And guess she looks a bit messy when she leaves for work.

But he cheats. Watch him reload his clip, kneeling behind a tree. Hundred feet away, could probably wing him. I'm thinking, is he really Uma's husband? Would he pursue her all this way or was he coming anyway? All night I racked my brains trying to remember anything she might've said, like I married this officer, a bit older than me, but he turned out to be cruel... so when he went to Spain to fight the Bolsheviks, do some intel work, like maybe watching the Straits of Gibraltar, trying out new radar imaging equipment... maybe this, maybe that... maybe anything... I took my opportunity to clear out and fat chance he would ever find me in Brazil, darling.

Did she say this?

But I can't remember anything she said about a man. Von Schellenberg has to be a liar... unless... unless Uma is his Bride School trophy.

A single shot makes both of us look north. Some birds get noisy, fly off. Von Schellenberg listens, then moves through the brush in that direction. Ground is dry and gravelly, so it's not easy to be quiet as I follow. The thing is, does he know I'm following? Who fired the shot? His bushwhacker? We figured he'd use dirty tricks but knowing doesn't mean ready. Ready, absolutely. I'm following... but am I being led?

Some fallen trees, ripped from the slope in the last storm. Paw my way through them, lose sight of von Schellenberg. Also watching for Zero, because I know they'll try and draw me into a crossfire.

When you're in the thrall of a romance, you're never realistic. If you see too much of each other, sooner or later you get bored. Sex is like basic training -- once you get into shape, what else is there to do? You can get married or you can split. While I didn't want to see it that way, my problems with Judge Goa and the other stuff in Rio allowed me to separate from Uma without making a decision.

Truthfully, I always felt I was sucking someone else's candy.

Hear a shot, followed by an explosion, big enough to throw sod and rock a couple of hundred feet, so I'm on my belly and covering my head with my hands. Can feel the shock wave in my ears, like everything's got real small and under water for twenty seconds or so. Look up, and there's a hand stuck on a tree, the palm impaled on a branch spike.

Take a look, see von Schellenberg tottering through the trees in my direction. Yeah, it's his hand, and yeah, he's done for. Watch him collapse, then hear a whistle. It's Gomez. He waves, trots down the slope with his rifle at the ready.

"What the hell happened?" I say.

I'm spitting dirt.

He holds up his rifle proudly. "Just one shot, Lieutenant."

"One shot?"

"The guy was nailed by a booby trap mortar shell. Saw him setting up the trip wire... didn't know it was boobied, figured it was an alarm. It was rigged up in the small arroyo. He has a camo shawl on and when he stands up it slip and I see he has a machine gun."

"Who? Zero?"

"*Si...* Zero... so I popped him and the bullet must've passed through and hit the trigger."

Or maybe he fell on the wire. I nod slowly, as their dirty plan is revealed. "So they were setting it up to look like an accident, like I was whacked by a piece of forgotten ordnance while taking a morning stroll in the forest."

"*Si, senhor.*"

Gomez has a crazy smile and I guess I'm feeling a bit crazy too with the way things have turned out. Nothing left of Lieutenant Zero except bug food on the trees and rocks, and Major von Schellenberg is only slightly better. Sure, most of his body is intact but he's one grossly mutilated cadaver. No eyes, like the flash took them straight to infinity. And the blast ripped off most of his hair... and his left hand.

"This gent ain't from the Heidelberg school of duelling," I say.

Pretty brave talk, because the sight is making my stomach lurch. Hear a shout. It's Voss and Mac.

"It's done," I say as they arrive.

Voss looks at von Schellenberg's body, then at Gomez.

"One bullet," says Gomez.

Voss is incredulous. "You ambushed the Major?"

"No way," I say. "He and Zero were fixing to ambush me."

Voss looks around. Guess he sees the blood and guts, the modern art.

"Where is *Leutnant* Zero, please?"

Wave my hand, say, "Here and there, Voss. He was too close to the blast."

"Mortar shell?" says Mac.

"Yeah," says Gomez. "They had a trip wire set up. Guess Zero fell on it."

"I heard a shot," says Mac.

"Yeah," says Gomez. "Zero had a sub-machine gun, so... one shot."

Voss is dubious. "I heard two. One, then later, another which is followed by an explosion."

"Zero fired a shot to lure me into the trap."

Voss is shaking his head. "Ja? I cannot believe that Major von Schellenberg would cheat in such a manner. There has to be an investigation."

"What for?" I say.

"Berlin will demand it," says Voss.

"He was an assassin," I say. "You know it."

"He was an angry husband."

"Believe what you want, Voss. I got a witness."

Voss looks at Gomez, who's poking at von Schellenberg's body with his boot.

"Alright," he says. "I'll believe what is necessary."

They wrapped von Schellenberg's body in a tarp, strapped it onto the bomb carriage of the Fiat biplane, which then flew the short distance to the coast where the body was dropped into the Atlantic. Dani then flew to Ascuncion, where she demoed the CR 32 for the Paraguayan Airforce who liked it so much they ordered five or six. She was a big hit. That's what I heard, anyway.

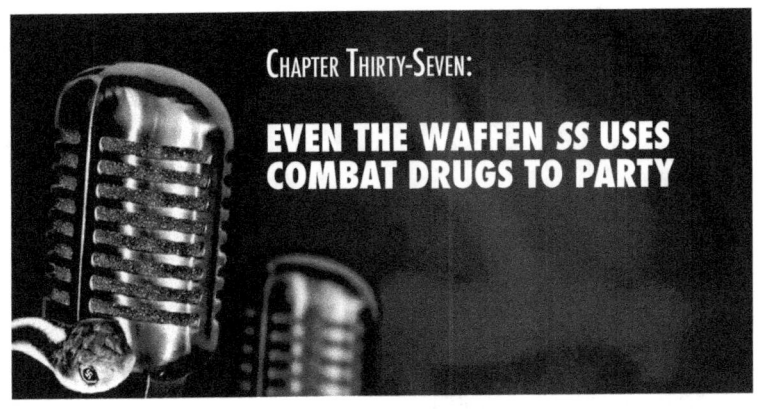

Chapter Thirty-Seven:

EVEN THE WAFFEN *SS* USES COMBAT DRUGS TO PARTY

MARCH 15, THE DAY HITLER invaded Czechoslovakia and took over Prague, I was in Blumenau getting supplies... or shall I say supervising the acquisition which had already been ordered, which means I was in the pub having a couple of Schornstein pilsners, you know, the place with The Laugher and the barmaid who looks like a mature Heidi, a bit punched out but still punchable. So some local Krauts come in and announce that Hitler has just given a speech in Prague and that old Bohemia is now a protectorate of the Third Reich. Well this gets the beer flowing and pretty soon it's standing room only, although this doesn't matter as people are taking their steins outside as the party just keeps getting bigger and bigger. People doing polka steps and firing guns in the air. Radios with Hitler shouting across other radios with samba music. Real crazy and getting crazier.

I'm standing outside rubbing some aloe vera on my face to chill the sun and a guy on crutches stops and shakes his head. "Look at the fools," he says. "They come here for a new life and now all they can do is carry on like they never left the old country. It's insulting."

"Crazy," I say.

"Hitler, Man of the Year," sneers the cripple. "How many good Germans gave their lives in the Great War?"

Shrug my shoulders... don't know, of course.

"Four million dead," he says. "More than eight million wounded. I'm one of the eight."

"You fought the War?" I say.

"I fought it. Lost my leg in 1918. Got a wooden one but I don't like it. People think I'm drunk when I'm not, so I chucked it in the closet."

"German?"

"I was. I'm a Brazilian citizen now. How about you?"

"Not yet."

"You're not German, are you... I hear a bit of an accent. American?"

"No... listen, you think there's going to be another world war?"

"Ja ja. It's what Corporal Hitler wants. He won't stop."

"But he's getting all he wants without firing a shot...."

Skinny guy. Dark eyes, ragged eyebrows, fleshy face like a withered potato. Stick him in a field and the birds stay airborne, I'm thinking.

"Got a cigarette, soldier?" he says.

I fish him a Lucky, say, "What makes you think I'm a soldier?"

"You're at Eden, right? We know it's one of them secret military bases."

"Not so secret, huh."

"Unmarked Zeppelins aren't used for spraying crops, *mein herr*. Don't worry, we won't tell Vargas."

We chuckle, part of the conspiracy.

I say, "So you're bilingual, then?"

"Of course I am—I speak drunk, I speak sober!"

Pretty good. Guess this means I'm buying him a beer. We go inside, push our way to the bar. As we're waiting for Heidi to pull a couple, I spot The Laugher sitting in his corner watching us. He crooks a finger, beckons to The Scarecrow (his real name is Heinz but for me, he's The Scarecrow) who hobbles over and hears what the man has to say. The Laugher is wearing his usual rig, the lederhosen and boots. Got gold crinkly hair, slicked back like marmalade. Hooded prick-face eyes, never happy even when he's laughing for a living. Scarecrow sits down and waves me over. Not really in the mood, but what the hell, it's happy hour. Mac and Frank should be here any minute anyway.

Give Scarecrow his beer, remain standing.

"What's your name, soldier?" says Scarecrow. "Sit down."

"Mat," I say.

"Sit down, Mat. Save your legs. This is Jose."

"Jose?"

The Laugher expels two jets of smoke from his gills, says, "Jose Mengele. I was Josef but now I'm Jose."

"Been here long, Jose?"

"Long enough to be Jose," says Scarecrow. "Mat here is doing things at Eden."

"Chasing rainbows?" says The Laugher.

Knew he was a joker but it's the sarcasm that makes me want to haul off and drop him.

"I don't chase anything," I say.

"Want a cigar, Jose?" says Scarecrow.

"Does Winston Churchill?" says The Laugher. "Who's buying?"

"Bar is giving away free ones to celebrate the Führer's latest triumph," says Scarecrow.

"Well let's celebrate!" exclaims The Laugher. "*Sieg heil!*"

A pretty girl is moving around handing them out. Some of the men try to cop a feel but she's pretty good with her elbows. Blonde, thin, maybe seven or eight on the Richter Scale. Smiles nice.

"Gisella!" shouts Scarecrow. "Over here!"

Gisella spins and comes our way.

"Heinz," she says, "who let you in?"

"My friend Mat," says Scarecrow. "Mat, this is the *Sommerfest Queen*. She wants my wooden leg but I won't let her have it."

"You know what you can do with your dummy leg," she says. "So what brings you to Blumeneau, Mat?"

"Chasing rainbows," says The Laugher.

"Cigars," I say.

She has a fistful. Cigarillos, or gauchos as some folks call them. Scarecrow tries to grab a couple but she slaps his paw, says, "One each, gentlemen!" But she gives me two.

"Thanks, *fraulein*," I say. "Does the Sommerfest Queen have any matches?"

"I might," she says. "You'll have to search me."

This gets a rise out of the other two. Free beer will do it every time.

"And how about some fresh pilsners?" says The Laugher. "All this excitement is making me thirsty."

"Aren't you working, Jose?"

His lips roll back and his teeth flash as if he's gonna let go one of his horse laughs. "On my tab, Highness."

"On my tab," mutters Gisella. "I'm not a waitress, Jose. You'll have to get your own."

I follow her through the mob to the bar, where she gives me a box of matches. Nice hands.

"You play an instrument?" I say. "The harp maybe?"

Don't know if she heard me or not, it's so damn loud.

Heidi, the barmaid, shouts, "My sister—remember I told you about her?"

Smile, nod.

"Can I have another round for my new friends?"

Well this is all fine and dandy, I'm the man with the big bucks, ready for a party—and not because Adolf Hitler continues to enlarge his real estate, restore the self-respect of Germans everywhere, even here, a couple of degrees south of Capricorn. Any man who survives an assassination plot dressed up as a duel deserves a few drinks. Still have the smell of TNT in my nostrils, no matter how many cigarettes I smoke. I want to get loaded.

Get six steins, a double round.

The Laugher lets out a modest guffaw, raises his mug: "Heil Hitler!"

"Heil Hitler? Fuck Hitler!" says Scarecrow.

"Credit due where credit's due," says The Laugher. "Right, Mr. Mat?"

I just drink my beer, let them figure it out.

"I was in Munich in 1923, time of the putsch," says Scarecrow. "I know all about Herr Hitler and his tactics."

"I thought you were already in Brazil in 23," says The Laugher. "That's my memory."

"No, Jose, I came here in 1924, so I was in the old country when Hitler started out. He was a socialist."

"Bolshie... Hitler's no Bolshie. If it wasn't for him, the Commies would have Berlin... and the way things are headed, they'll have Brazil."

"Not a chance."

"So you think, Heinz. I hear that commie bastard Prestes escaped."

"Who says? You're making it up, Jose."

"Prestes escaped. Right, Mr. Mat?"

I don't even know who this Prestes is.

"Who says, Jose, who says?"

"His wife is German. People talk."

Scarecrow scoffs, says, "Vargas has him locked up good, and his wife has been deported back to Germany and you know what that means, don't you? The Nazis have her in a concentration camp. Hey, Prestes isn't so bad. You know what the situation's like for workers, some parts of Brazil. It's the shits."

"Indians... breeds... blacks... what do you expect, Heinz? Fortunately we don't have many in our enclave. Right, Mr. Mat?"

I just grunt.

"I'll tell you what's what," says Scarecrow. "Hitler is a warlord. What was the DAP? The German Workers Party? The *Kampbund*? A bunch of angry ex-soldiers, and Hitler was the angriest one of them all. Thugs, Jose. Armed thugs—this is how Hitler got power, how the Nazis got power."

"They had to be armed to stand up to the Bolshies, Heinz," says The Laugher. "You know that. The Bolshies had weapons and money from Moscow. World domination, that's their game. Stalin is a godless criminal."

"Perhaps, perhaps. Hitler is, for sure."

"Man of the Year, my friend."

Scarecrow snorts. He's so agitated his stein is wobbling while his free hand is rubbing the stump of his missing leg. The Laugher's eyelids are almost closed. He's like one of those political cartoons in the newspaper—his head is twice the size of his body and releasing bubbles.

"Admit it, my friend... it feels good to be German again."

"I'm Brazilian," says Scarecrow. "I voted for Vargas."

The Laugher doesn't smile, just shows his teeth. They click as he wheezes, kinda laughs. "You didn't vote for Vargas, Heinz. You don't even speak Portuguese."

"I speak enough. I speak German because it's the language of culture, if you want to know. Ask Mat—he speaks pretty good German."

I'm looking around for Gisella. There's no better cure for a bad case of death than a woman.

"Have you been to the old country?" says The Laugher.

"Me? No," I say.

"Is Roosevelt a Jew?" says The Laugher. "Some say he is."

"Was Christ a Jew?" I say. "Some say he was a Roman agent provocateur."

"See?" says Scarecrow. "I told you Mat was cultured!"

I light up my cigar. The others follow suit.

"Mmm... he slithers well," says The Laugher.

He's not looking at me, says this like he's Shakespeare thinking or talking to himself. "An American chasing rainbows," he murmurs.

"Hey, I'm not an American," I say.

His head revolves my direction like a slow gun on a slow battleship.

"*Englander? Nein*," says The Laugher.

"Jose, don't be so nosey," says Scarecrow. "Mat here is a gentleman and a man of culture. He's bought us beer, so enough of the propaganda!"

I'm giving The Laugher the hard eye, the *mau-olhado*, and he knows it. He starts laughing, that stupid ugly jackass hawing he calls work. Just a short outburst. Maybe he's rattled.

"No offence intended, my young friend," he says. "I thank you for the beer, indeed I do. It's just these reports of American spies...."

"He's crazy," Scarecrow says to me. "It's the National Socialist disease."

"Crazy? Me?" says The Laugher indignantly. "I know about Operation Rainbow, ja. This makes me crazy?"

325

"Illuminate us, Master-Komiker," says Scarecrow. "Even though he's never been in the army—as I have—Jose here thinks he knows a thing or two."

I'm listening. These days the word 'spy' always gets my attention.

"Oh I do, Heinz, I do... I know about the Amerikaner plot."

"Operation Crossbow is it?"

"Rainbow... it's called Operation Rainbow, Bobo."

"What is it, Jose? What is this Rainbow?"

"Like I say, it's a plot."

"Against Vargas?"

"Against Brazil. First, our airfields. Then the whole country. Operation Rainbow."

"You're being ridiculous, Jose. When have the Americans invaded a country?"

"Canada for a start... Mexico, Cuba... the Philippines... Panama. I could go on."

"Raids, Jose. They were raids. Let's have more beer. Your turn."

The Scarecrow thinks The Laugher is full of shit but I'm thinking otherwise. Don't know where he gets his intel from, but when I think of Colonel Powell and his 'survey' work in the northern states of Bahia and Parana... and from what I've heard both him and Mac say, well hey, The Laugher might be right. Airfields. The Germans have their plan, and I'd be surprised if the Americans didn't have theirs.

At this point I notice a couple of the Waffen SS boys at the bar clinking glasses. Sergeant Schmel and a corporal who's name I don't remember. They're in civies, look like they've had a few on their way to the coliseum. Schmel's a heavy man, built like he pulled ploughs alongside the oxen in his youth, big shoulders, thick waist, pillars for legs, no neck and a head that sorta hangs because he always has to duck for doorways and low ceilings. Shaven like a natural born criminal, although it seems to be a style the German military favor. Easier to fit those square helmets on, I guess. Knows his stuff, though. These Waffen SS are no slouches. First to the top of the mountain as I recall.

Somebody puts on a record. I recognize the tune: Rumba Azul. Uma told me it was a big hit in Berlin, despite the Nazi phobia about jungle music. Next thing you know, Gisella is dancing with the Corporal, who seems to know what he's doing. Not a bad looking guy, cut more like an officer than a grunt. Hugo Boss suit, no tie. My age, slim, moves like a pro. Wonder if he has the tattoo... all these core SS guys have the blood tattoo on the inside of the left arm, the letter or letters of their blood type. Voss showed me his, real fancy gothic script, like a religious order would have. Also has a small cross on his chest, something these jungle SS guys got in Paulo to set them apart from the other brigades. Cross with a serpent. Some of our squad have been talking about getting a tattoo, a Sigma symbol or something, but me, I don't like being branded. I have my reasons.

They dance. I drink, smoke. The Laugher starts laughing. Scarecrow puts his hands over his ears. I take my beer, move to the bar, nod to Schmel who actually grins back. Guess he's pissed. Wish I was. Sometimes you're too slack wired to feel it, the signal just passes right on through on its way to hell.

Schmel motions me closer. His eyes are dancing.

"Soldier, what really happened to the Major?" he says. "Give me the dope."

"Stepped on a mine or something," I say.

"Ja, but who put it there? Don't bullshit me. I saw stuff like this in Spain."

"You were in Spain?"

"I was. Lots of accidents in Spain and I don't mean the kind that God created. Come on, what really happened to the Major?"

"Ask Voss."

Schmel's big face stretches in disgust. "He's a *Leutnant*. He keeps his secrets in the clubroom."

I shrug, say, "I'm a Lieutenant too."

Schmel gives me a skeptical look, says, "Irregular."

"What—you think we don't know what we're doing?"

"Mercenaries. Maybe you do, maybe you don't. Sigma isn't a real army unit."

"Neither is the SS, from what I hear."

"Oh, you think we're cowboys?"

"No... just maybe a bit... irregular."

His eyes are still dancing. He's doing schnapps sidecars with his beer. Drunk or sober, he could flatten me with one swat. Wags a meaty finger, says, "I remember you from the ship, Thorsen. I said to myself, that fellow is a soldier of fortune."

I shrug. What is fortune but an accident by another name?

He continues: "You had suspicions about me, am I right?"

"Not at all. I thought you were a friar... you know, a deacon or something."

He guffaws, says, "Me? A deacon? Ja, why not? I could be the 'Deacon of Destruction', ja?"

"Or the 'Deacon of Death' maybe...."

"Deacon of Death... perhaps a bit dramatic... perhaps not. I had a reputation in Spain, you know... hand to hand...."

Of course I don't doubt it. Who would want to meet this beast on the battlefield? His eyes have settled down and the smile is gone. Another guy who can't get drunk.

"What happened with the Major, soldier?" he says.

He's trying to bully me, fuck's sake. How can I work him? He's no yo yo on a string.

"Who was he?" I say. "You ever see him before?"

Obviously not.

"Where did he come from?"

"Munich... I don't know for sure. Himmler sent him."

"As your commanding officer?"

The Corporal comes back, holding onto Gisella. Was watching them with the corner of my eye. Didn't like it, don't like it.

"Hey Edler," says Schmel. "You knew Major von Schellenberg at Headquarters, didn't you?"

"No, Sergeant," he says. "I was with Amt 1 before coming here."

"Eh, *Allgemeine-SS*," says Schmel. "Berlin pretty boys."

Edler is a strange fellow. Big forehead, long face. Full lips like a woman, but crooked like a boxer, so his mouth sits twisted. Kinda negro, but not likely of course.

"This is the fellow who shot the Major?" he says.

"I didn't shoot anybody," I say.

"You're the Canadian, aren't you?" he says. "Everyone knows what a great shot you are. We heard it was a duel. Congratulations."

"Thanks," I say. "Nice suit."

"Men wear uniforms," says Schmel.

"Where's yours, Sergeant?" I say.

He juts his jaw towards me. "You trying to be funny, Thorsen?"

Gisella steps between us, says to me, "Oi... don't you want to dance? You promised."

Slip my arm around her waist, move into the festive mob. She's still hot from her turn with Edler. Heidi turns up the radio. Another rumba. Guess Gisella is the house rent-a-dance.

"We don't want any fights," she says. "It's bad for business."

'We weren't gonna do any fighting," I say.

"I've seen so many stupid German men," she says. "They drink their Steinlagers, eat their sausage, behave like pigs. Believe me, I've seen it more times than I care to remember."

"Aren't you German?"

"My parents. I was born here."

"In Blumenau?"

"Little Germany? No. Sao Paulo. Can't you tell?"

"Uh, what's so special about Paulo?"

She jams her body against mine. "Paulistas dance differently. More tango than samba."

I don't know what the hell we're dancing, there's such a crush on the small space there is between the bar and the tables. We're just bumping around a bit in one spot. Could be love.

"So how do you like being the *Sommerfest* Queen?"

"*Sommerfest* Slave is more like it."

"Er, so you're working right now?"

"*Claro... bom para os negocios.*"

"Meaning?"

"I'm good for business... don't you think?"

"Sure."

"Sometimes the customers need heating up... sometimes cooling down."

"So you're like a nurse in high heels?"

"You're funny... are you a Nazi?"

"Do I look like a Nazi?"

"You've got blue eyes."

"Yours are brown."

"Brown? They're black!"

"Oh so they are. Black diamonds."

"Black diamonds? You mean like coal? Oi oi... you insult the Queen?"

"No no, I mean like precious stones."

She's laughing. Yes, I'm talking nonsense. Somebody said we talk in order to conceal our thoughts, not illuminate them. When a man's talking to a woman, this seems to be the case.

See Mac and Gomez have arrived, and are talking to Schmel at the bar. Edler is leaning lazily against the counter, not part of the conversation. He's watching us. Then, what's this? Girl comes in, a real looker, Brazilian, the way you see 'em in Rio. Maybe mestizo, maybe not. Couple of guys with her, blades in white linen suits. Moustaches, glossy eyes like young serpents. Crowd opens up for them.

"Who's this?" I say.

"*Sommerfest* Queen," says Gisella. "Her name is Minolta."

"Aren't you the Queen?"

She bites her lip, scowls. "I'm the German Association's Queen. She's the Merchant's pick. Excuse me --"

She struts off, disappears in the back, leaves me stuck like a statue. Meanwhile Minolta has a crowd of admirers, like autograph seekers around a movie star. Slinky inky black hair down to her ass, smile as wide as the Amazon. She looks at me, looks at Edler... travelling eyes checking the bees. Her bodyguards have beers, are flirting with Heidi. Don't see any money on the deck.

Scarecrow's tugging at my pants.

Turn around. "Nice piece of ham, eh," he says, jerking his head towards Minolta.

"What's the score, Heinz?"

"Dangerous."

"Who's the real Queen?"

Scarecrow shrugs, says, "Gisella, of course."

"Seems to me a real Queen has bodyguards."

I sit down. The Laugher looks like he's on the verge of singing, if you know what I mean.

Scarecrow pulls in close, says, "German people around here want their own queen, understand? They want a white girl."

"Minolta looks pretty white to me..."

"You blind, soldier? You got cataracts? She's Indian."

"Nice lookin' Indian, ask me."

"Stay clear, son. Gangsters. Two boyfriends dead already."

"Yeah? What is she, a black widow spider or something?"

Scarecrow shakes his empty stein, "Just a friendly warning, Mat. Thanks for the beer."

Mac and Gomez wander over.

"Wanna play some poker?" says Mac. "Some guys are looking for a game."

"Boring," I say.

"Sure, I get it, you'd rather dance with the ladies," says Mac. "Mind if we do? Me and Frank are feeling lucky."

"House got a game?" says Scarecrow. "I wouldn't mind playing."

"You got the money, honey, you can play," says Mac. "How about it, Thorsen? A few extra hours in town sound good?"

I owe Frank, I know that. Mac too, probably.

"Yeah, o.k.," I say. "It's the Führer's birthday, isn't it?"

"Near enough," says Mac. "Game's in the back patio if you change your mind."

Gomez is grinning like an alligator, gives me a friendly nod as he follows Mac back to the bar. Mac talks to Schmel, Gomez says something to Heidi, then Gomez clues the two guys in the white linen suits. Gomez speaks Brazilian Portuguese. Heidi leads them all out back. The Laugher starts laughing.

I motion to Scarecrow, and he leans over to hear what I say: "Tell that clown Jose I'll pay him to shut up!"

"How much?"

"Two hundred."

"Dollars?"

I pull out some reais, count out two hundred. The butt of my Colt is poking from below my shirt. Maybe Scarecrow sees it. He scoops up the money, shouts in The Laugher's ear, "We're in the game, Jose!"

What can you do but laugh? I would but right now I don't have any laughs in me. See a yellow biplane flying low above the sea, let go its bundle, which torpedoes into the waves. Look away, see a tree covered in blood.

Edler's talking to Minolta, or trying to. Bit of sign language going on. Eventually they come over.

"Do you speak English, *senhor*?" says Minolta.

"Sit down, please," I say, kicking the chairs out. "No *sprechen Deutsch*?"

She grins, says, "*Claro*... heil Hitler!"

Well this is a good start. Even Edler gets the joke. After the introductions, Edler says in rough English, "Minolta is, ah, how is it said, is sensitive."

Bet she is, I think.

"I tell fortunes," she says.

"Oh you're a gypsy," I say. "You can read the future."

"Yes, my grandmother was Guarani, she have the gift," she says. "Interested?"

Sounds more interesting than a game of poker.

I say, "You speak Guarani?"

"Yes," she says. "It isn't so popular today, as everyone wants to be white. But even you know some Guarani, *senhor*."

She's looking into my eyes.

"I do?"

"Yes. The word 'jaguar' is a Guarani word. It has special meaning for you, perhaps?"

Godamn, this is either a fluke or she's been reading Rio Life.

"Yeah, I like jaguars," I say. "They're like women. If you don't feed them, they just swat you aside."

Another smile and a toss of the cascading hair. Long enough to make a rope ladder or a noose.

Edler says, "You're educated, *fraulein*."

She says, "I could be a nun, *sim*? I went to a convent school in Sao Paulo. Ever been there?"

Edler shakes his head.

She says to me, "You? No? *Ay caramba*, how did you arrive here without going to Paulo?"

I say, "We fly. We're modern men."

"Shame. Sao Paulo is a so interesting city... a pirate city, much crazier than Rio."

"Pirate? It's not on the sea...."

"Close enough... you could walk it. The *guaruja* drive takes a tiny hour. It was the centre of the slave trade. *Bandeirantes*... Yes. Imagine, in a past life I might be a slave."

"And the mistress of a plantation owner."

She's turning a lock of her hair between her fingers. Dagger nails.

"Maybe I am."

"So who are those two guys? Bodyguards?"

"Bodyguards... *sim*. My brothers."

"Are you really the *Sommerfest* Queen? Gisella says she is the Queen."

"Eh, Minolta is the Queen. Gisella is so thin she 'ave no reflection in the mirror. Look, I got no quarrel with Gisella. Some guys like her."

She looks at Edler, says, "You?"

This guy is smooth. Know what he says? "If we were in Berlin, I'd be in love with Gisella."

"What have you got in your pocket?" says Minolta.

"Why?" says Edler. "Am I a thief?"

"Anything... a coin, matches," says Minolta.

He stretches to get his hand in his pant pocket, brings out a bullet. Looks like a 9 millimeter.

"This do?" he says, dropping it on the table.

Minolta's long fingers rake it in like a crab. As she fondles it, she gazes steadily at Edler. "You are in love with a girl," she says. "Something unfortunate happens to her... she is violated by someone with power... he can be the boss of you or her... an officer who is corrupt and deserves to die... before you can avenge this girl's humiliation, her attacker is sent to another place. You carry this bullet until you find him."

Edler doesn't laugh. Instead he says, "Perhaps the bullet is for me."

"You humiliate women, *senhor*?"

"If I do, the bullet is for me."

"You love your mother?"

"I don't need to answer that."

"Your mother gave you the bullet. Am I right?"

Now Edler laughs. Harsh and bitter... you know, like cheap whiskey. He says to me in German, he says, "*In Berlin konnete sei ein Gestapo sein.*" Which is to say, he thinks she's as devious as the secret police.

I say, "She got the file on you, man. 'fess up."

Edler says nothing, just puts the bullet back in his pocket. He smiles, says something to himself, too low to catch.

Minolta says to me, "Your turn. Give it to me, first thing in your pocket."

"Pocket's empty," I say.

"No cheat... give it to me!"

I roll the glass eye across the table. She just stares at it.

"What's this?" she says.

"A kid's marble, isn't it?" says Edler.

"Too hot to handle, eh," I say to Minolta.

"Could be a glass eye," says Edler. "Where'd you get it, Thorsen?"

"She's afraid of it," I say. "Isn't that right, Minolta?"

"I'm not afraid," she says, staring transfixed like it's a rat about to leap. "I know what this thing is."

"It's nice and warm," I say. "Like my pocket."

"Take it," says Edler. "His turn, gypsy."

"What is it?" she says to me, confused. "For a moment I thought it was...."

She reaches out, draws it into her hand. Then she faints. The eye comes rolling back at me, so I scoop it up, put it back in my pocket. Dames... always good for a little bit of acting, I think. Edler is more gallant. He slaps her face (gently) and when this doesn't work, lays her out on the floor. This gets people's attention. Heidi rushes over with a glass of water and splashes some on Minolta's face. Then all of a sudden as if nothing had happened she sits up and smiles.

Heidi whispers in my ear: "Epileptic."

Minolta gets up, says, "Soon I will marry. I want to have some fun."

Try a couple of hands just to be sociable but as usual I'm just subsidizing the pot. Mac wins the first hand with a pair of eights, King high, and one of the Brazilians wins the next with three sixes. The hell with it. I fold, wander into the yard to stretch my legs.

Edler's standing near the hedge, smoking. For some reason I join him.

He nods, says, "Tired of games?"

He's got that right. Never been any damn good at poker anyway.

"Just a bit wound up," I say. "Stress."

"Not surprised," he says. "I've never fought a duel."

He takes a small tube from his pocket, empties a lozenge into his palm, offers it to me. About the size of a dime. "Try one of these," he says.

I hesitate. He pops it himself, then draws another one.

"What is it?" I say.

"A 535," he says. "Better than Benzedrine."

I'd tried a Benny or two. Nothing special but maybe one would work now. He tips his hand and the pill falls into mine. I pop it, wash it down with some beer.

"German?" I say.

"Yeah. Experimental combat drug. You'll like it."

Experimental...! Christ, what is this? Heroin?

He reads my mind: "It's three milligrams of cocaine, methedrine, morphine... mixed 5-3-5. Troops in the *Wehrmacht* use Pervitin, which is just methedrine. This is supposed to be an improvement."

"What say you?"

"I like it."

"You hooked?"

He rattles the tube. "Ask me when these run out."

"So you boys aren't carrying it in your medical locker?"

"I daresay we have some Pervitin. I got this at the KZ. I volunteered, you might say."

"You like jazz?"

"Yes, I like jazz. You might say jazz is my downfall."

"How so?"

His mouth pulls to one side as he smiles. His lips seem to swell. I wonder if he's homo.

"They say I'm charming. At least, that's what my commanding officer said when I was demoted and sent here as a punishment. He said, Edler, you need to get out of Berlin. You can use your charm to kill a few monkeys in the jungle. I thought it was a figure of speech... never expected to be put on a flying boat and sent to Brazil."

"You didn't come with the others?"

The thought amuses him.

"The Knights of the Holy Cross? I heard about that charade. No, I wouldn't be good as a monk."

"You were a Lieutenant?"

"Automatically. My cousin talked me into it. He's a Captain in the Waffen SS. And I might as well tell you, my father is a Generalmajor in the *Wehrmacht*."

"That's rich...."

"Not really. There are dozens at that rank. He was a cop with the Berlin police, then the National Socialists gave the detectives some sweet offers. How about you? Got a father?"

"Sure. Never see him. He and my mother separated early on."

He nods, says, "The same for me. I never saw him until a couple of years ago. We went to a nightclub together and he introduced me to an UFA actress. Well, we hit it off, and pretty soon we were in love... at least, I was. Then I discovered she'd been my father's mistress. I was so depressed I requested a transfer, and do you know where they sent me? Ravensbruck."

"What's that?"

"A KZ... concentration camp for women and children. I can tell you, Thorsen, the opportunities were continuous."

"Sounds like a gas."

"It was corrupting. I felt like shit. The cruelty of it all... Himmler, ja? His idea. Our great Waffen SS leader. Gypsies, Jews, intellectuals, foreign subversives... tender creatures from near and far. It was my education in sex as loneliness and survival. I started drinking, let myself become degenerate. One weekend in Berlin I went AWOL. Of course they found me. So now I'm here... Corporal Edler at your service."

Quite the confession, and I'm wondering why.

"What do you think of Brazil, Edler?"

"Warm and lonely."

"You miss Germany?"

"Not really. I just don't believe in anything much."

"Why don't you just quit?"

"No one quits the SS."

"No?"

"You only leave in a box, Thorsen. Brazil is my box."

Gloomy fellow. I recognize he's different, and it's not just the long hair. Or using a combat drug off-duty. Maybe it's the Berlin personality. Different than other Krauts, more fatalistic. Uma's like that. Fate is the Hunter.

"Do you have to be a Party member to join the SS?"

"It's expected."

"But you're not—"

"I don't have a tattoo either."

"One thing I don't understand about German fascism is the Jew thing. I don't get it."

"Anti-Semitism? You don't understand it? It's simple. Christ was the

335

first reformation. Luther the second... Hitler, the third. It's a pattern of revolts against Judaism. National Socialism is at war with Bolshevism, which is 'World Judaism', the most dehumanizing force in the modern world other than 'Americanism'...."

"Americanism? What the hell is that?"

"Yankee democracy. They're fanatics. Say, which one do you want?"

"One what?"

"Which Queen. Shall we flip a coin?"

I'm thinking this is pretty crass, yet Edler's manner is pragmatic, like this is the solution to a chore.

"You can have 'em both," I say. "Although I know for a fact that Minolta likes you."

"Minolta? *Eine untermenschen*?" he chuckles.

"Subhuman? No way. Not Jewish, and very pretty. My feeling is she's off-limits."

"Off-limits? No woman is off-limits. If they were, there would be no reason to live."

"If you feel that way, why are you in the army?"

"I told you. I was hoodwinked by my cousin, then by my father. It's a form of suicide, ja?"

Shrug, say, "Can be, I suppose. Only if you have no confidence."

"Confidence... what is that? It takes confidence to ride a bicycle or drive a car. It takes confidence to speak to a pretty girl. But what kind of confidence does it take to be a killer?"

He rattles his tube of 535.

I say, "You can have a successful career without killing anyone."

"Yes, that's so. But in the military, killing is the measurement of success."

"Soldiers fight. Killing is a matter of fate."

"Very good, Thorsen. I suppose that's what happened to Major von Schellenberg. And by the way, whatever happened to *Leutnant* Zero?"

"Zero? He gave his body to art."

Damn, listen to me. Careless talk. That 535 must be working.

"You mean he was vaporized?"

"Fuck around with bombs, you get bombed."

His eyes are wandering all over my face like I'm a movie screen. He's fascinated. Again, I wonder if he only pretends with women, and men are his real targets. He's searching. He might not know it, but he's searching. Cursing breaks out in the patio. Hear Mac chuckle. Guess he won again. Here come the women, smiling like they're sisters, not rivals. Somehow I end up with Minolta in the pergola at the bottom of the garden and we roll around a bit and giggle and all that, but I'm not into it. Might be the 535... might be the whiff of garlic on her lips... might be the fact that she keeps trying to get the glass eye out of my pocket, keeps finding my gun... or it might be her two brothers who are cursing frequently in the near distance, losing big time.

Edler and Gisella take off someplace. Pity—we could've swapped.

ROADBLOCK UP AHEAD, soldiers' eyes glistening like ghost cattle in the headlights. Gomez is driving, and Mac's stretched out in the back, loaded, pockets stuffed with money, happy as a pig dreaming under a blood moon. We pull up. Indians, khaki uniforms. Rifles, old stuff, could be Mausers. One guy with a motorcycle.

I say to Gomez, "Brazilian Army?"

Gomez says, "PM... state police."

They're using a truck to block the road. An officer hops out of the cab, short guy, strolls over as a couple of grunts check out our unit. Gomez has the window open, says, "*Boa noite, Capitao.*"

His voice is slurred. He's a bit pissed, and certainly tired. Officer has a double wiper moustache, and is smoking a guacho. Some gold teeth. His eyes look Japazilian, but what do I know? Probably thinks I'm a Kraut. Twists his head to get a better look at me.

"*Destino?*"

"Eden *rancho,*" says Gomez.

He nods slowly, says, "Eden, *sim... a Corporocao Sigma.*"

The Sigma Corporation. He knows something. Looks at me, says in English, "You, *Senhor*? You work at Eden?"

"Foreman," I say.

"Hmm... a cowboy from Texas, perhaps," he says. "You have a fast draw, *senhor*?"

Gomez laughs before I do. I just avoid those Hari Kari eyes.

"You 'ave identification, I'm sure," he continues.

Gomez looks at me, worried. I don't give a shit. I got 535 in my blood.

"Eh, let's not waste time," says the officer. "Some criminals have escaped. You see anyone suspicious as you travel this suspicious road?"

"No, *Capitao*," says Gomez.

"The man in the back... who is he?"

"A cowboy," I say. "He's drunk... *bebado*."

"Uh. How far is Eden?"

"Another ten kilometers... right, Frank?"

Gomez nods, says, "About that, yeah."

The officer looks at Gomez, says, "Have you been drinking? Yes... good, good."

He slaps the hood, says, "We will follow you!"

That's odd, but hell, this is a very odd country. They move their vehicle aside so's we can pass, and then they fall in behind. Road follows the river in places, others it cuts through fields and forest. Cattle often wander across the road unexpectedly, so the corners can be an adventure, especially at night.

I say, "State police, eh. Rough looking bunch."

Gomez grunts, says, "Vigilantes, maybe. PMs use volunteers... a lotta poor people."

"They got a prison around here?"

"Who knows? Maybe a prison farm. I don't like this...."

"Hold the road. Don't sweat it."

I'm thinking about Minolta, relieved I got away. Not my cup of tea. Great looking babe but just too weird. And the vampire garlic....

I say, "You win or lose in that game, Frank?"

"Came out ahead... enough for a bottle of hootch maybe. Mac made a lotta dough."

"He cheat?"

"Nah, he was just extra lucky."

"Who lost the most?"

"The two brothers." He adds, "Soon be your family, Lieutenant, si?"

I brush aside his joke, say, "You think these boys are here to collect? The officer look familiar at all?"

"Mr. Moto? No."

"Japanese, you figure?"

"Yeah. He's not Indian. They got Japs in Brazil. Paulo is full of them."

"Aren't they just slaves for the farmers? The planters? The factory owners?"

"Yeah, mostly... some get rich. I worked in the mine with a couple.

You can always tell—they got the seagull eyes."

He must be talking about the eye-brows.

I say, "What about Indians—what kind of eyes they got?"

"Depends... South America is different from North, and the coast is different from inland. Me, I got eagle eyes."

Guess this is why he likes to fly off cliffs and sit in trees. I know this is how he picked off Zero. He just climbed a tree and waited.

The motorcyclist accelerates past us, takes the lead, so now our truck is boxed between him and theirs. He's standing on the boot rests like a stuntman. Breeches must be tight.

"They must think we're important," I say.

"Don't like it, Lieutenant. Maybe I'm pissed but I ain't dumb."

"You got your weapon?"

"Nope."

"Nuthin' behind the seat?"

Right now is when the cyclist loses control of his machine. It's one of those downhill curves that just keeps coming, so that you think it must be a circle. Not far from Eden. You could walk it in fifteen. Don't know if an animal spooked him or what, but we see him start to slide. Too fast into the curve, maybe because we're pushing him, pedal to the metal. I mean, we're sliding too, but the difference is we got four wheels instead of two and Gomez is a good truck driver drunk or sober. The dust just obscures the final crash, when the rider hits the dirt, goes airborne and we clunk over the motorcycle, rag it for a few yards until we stop.

This wakes up Mac.

Mr. Moto and his squad arrive, quickly check on the rider who's back there in the ditch someplace. Wait for the dust to clear. It's dark, but I can see them carry the guy to their truck. Dead, they're saying... or near enough for the Judge.

"You're under arrest," says Mr. Moto to Gomez. "You're drunk."

"Hey wait a minute," I say. "Your guy lost control all on his lonesome."

"You ran the officer off the road," says Mr. Moto. "I saw it."

"How? You were behind us," I say.

"He swerved," says Gomez. "There was a steer."

Moto's head pivots, sweeps the darkness. "I see no cow," he says.

"You guys boxed us in," I say. "You're the cause of it, ask me."

"You're under arrest too," says Mr. Moto.

Right now I'm hoping Schmel and Edler come along, help us out. But I have no idea what their furlough allows... twelve hours, twenty-four... what exactly. Then I see Mac edging around the hood of our truck. I know he's got his 38... and I've got Oswald.

340

"Who'd you say you were?" I say. "Let's see some I.D., huh."

Stalling, of course. If Mac can ease in a little closer, we can take Mr. Moto hostage.

Moto ignores this, says, "Who is the commanding officer at Eden? I want to speak to him. You will get in your truck and drive there. We will follow."

This seems reasonable. If we get back to Eden, there won't be any arrests. Of course I don't tell him Colonel Barasso is in Paraguay trying to sell airplanes. Well, he might be back already, but why say anything?

"You," he says to Gomez. "You will ride with us."

"No way," I say. "This man is under my authority."

"Oh?" says Mr. Moto. "Well, we can always shoot the both of you right here."

Strangers making threats make me very, very tense. I'm just moving my hand towards my Colt when he says, "You have a medical facility at Eden? A first-aid man?"

I'm looking past him at Mac, who's edging closer.

"Yeah, we got a first-aid guy," I say. "We got medicine."

Moto nods, says, "You will take us to Eden. Pray that my officer doesn't die before we get there." He turns to Gomez, "You'll come with us."

"You arresting him?" I say.

Moto scowls, says, "We'll see... *vamos!*"

I figure if we get to Eden, there's no way Moto and his paramilitary goons will be calling the shots. So I signal Mac with my eyes to hang back. Gomez also understands, exaggerates his incapacity. He lurches to their truck, clambers in the back with three of their PMs and the injured rider. It's not far. Mile, maybe two. Mac rides in the cab.

"State militia, eh," he says.

"What's their problem? Motorbike try to cut you off?"

Amazing. He slept through all this. He's old.

"You think these guys are legit?" I say.

"They got uniforms, don't they? State police are kinda vigilante. Vargas put the squeeze on them couple of years ago, brought them under federal control... after the Paulista revolt, I think. When I woke up, I figured they were after me, guys trying to get their money back."

"No, they say they're looking for some escaped criminals. The guy lost control of his bike... was riding like his ass was on fire."

"How's that?"

"Like an Italian, standing in the stirrups."

"That's the way they teach 'em. Fascist parade shit. Goes with the goosestep."

Never occurs to me that maybe the guy was positioning himself to jump. We drone on, shaking the belly fat on the bumpy road. You know the way these trucks are—screech transmissions, low-geared for hauling, lungs like heavy smokers, so you're lucky if you can hit fifty, tops. The big wooden gates come into view. They're open. Wonder if there's anyone in the gatehouse.

Mac says, "What's the plan?"

"When we get to the yard, I'll lay on the horn, hope some of the Germans get angry."

Well, there's no guard on the gate. That's what happens when the big cat leaves for a few days on business. The out-buildings around the yard are stone, laid out the old European way, even if they're just for pigs and machinery. The bunkhouses are wooden, a hundred yards further on near the airstrip. Figure I'll just keep going until we get there, because that's where the medic is anyway. Lights are on in the old hacienda on the hillside near the winery, but they would be.

But Mr. Moto and his boys just pull up and park in the yard. We back up. This could be even better.

I jump out of the cab, go over to him, say, "I'll send my man to find the medic."

Mac's behind me.

Mr. Moto stretches. He's a stocky fellow, so his boots make him look shorter than he really is.

He says, "Where's your commanding officer?"

"He's away on business," I say.

"Colonel Barasso, correct?" says Mr. Moto. "Pity. I've heard much about him. How many men are here?"

"Couldn't say."

"No? Are you the foreman or not?"

"Some have the weekend off... some are way out on the range with the cattle."

"The cattle... really? What about foreign advisors? Germans, I hear."

"Guess some of the boys are German. You know what they say about Santa Catarina... 'Little Germany', eh."

Moto flashes his teeth, politely amused. "This is a big property... it was once a monastery, I believe. There's a mountain with a cross—is this true? This is what I've heard. Very big place, big as the *Serra Geral Catarinense*. You know, these men... these criminals we're looking for, they could be hiding here."

Could they? I shrug, say, "Sure... but not likely."

"Perhaps not. It's so dark, who can say?"

He doesn't seem terribly concerned about his injured man.

"Who are these criminals?" I say. "What's their crime?"

"A danger to civilization, *senhor*," says Mr. Moto. "These are very maladjusted individuals."

This could cover anything, although I think we're talking about political crimes here.

I say, "You think it's going to rain?"

Moto looks surprised, says, "Why? What have you heard?"

"I've heard it's the best wine harvest in years."

"Eh, the one good thing about a dry summer. So, are you an *Integralista, senhor*?"

"I'm just a gringo who wants to go to bed, Captain. Do you want our medic or not?"

"Well naturally... that's why we're here, correct? Please, find him. We will wait here."

I nod towards Gomez, who's shuffling around between a couple of Indians. Not exactly their prisoner. Detained is the word.

I say, "Frank, go down to the bunkhouse, see if you can find the medic."

"Sure, boss," says Frank. "Take the truck?"

Moto raises his hand. "No, you will stay with us."

He says to me, "You will find the medic, please."

I motion to Mac and we get back in the truck. Doesn't start right away so I have to get out and hand-crank it. What a racket. Enough to wake the dead, which is exactly what I want. Drive down to the bunkhouse, but park in front of the cottage where Lieutenant Voss kips. Knock, push open the door, go in. He's reading, drinking wine. Seems a bit dozy.

"Voss," I say. "We have a problem... is there a medic around?"

Tell him what's what.

"What a bore!" says Voss, groaning. "I really don't feel like moving."

"A bunch of armed men in our yard and you don't feel like moving?" I say. "Christ, Voss."

"Get Schmel to deal with it, Thorsen. You know how I spent my day? Writing a report on the deaths of von Schellenberg and Zero. And a letter to my mother. I'm really not in the mood for this."

"Schmel and Edler are in Blumenau getting loaded, Voss. This is serious."

"Take our Brazilian colleagues a first aid kit, then show them the gate. What do you want me to do?"

"Is Colonel Barasso back? No? Listen, Voss, they're holding one of my men."

Voss looks exasperated. "If he killed one of their policemen, they'll arrest him... obviously. Who is it?"

"Frank Gomez."

"The crazy fellow?"

I nod. Voss laughs, says, "Don't worry, *mein Freund*, he can just fly away to safety!"

Look at the bottle, see he's worked his way through most it. I'm just about through the door when Voss calls me back.

"You say they're State Military Police looking for some prisoners? What about those Targets you brought down from Rio?"

Now it hits me: this could be a breakout. The Professor... Paul, Rotten Rodrigo, and Kid Zombie.

"You might be right," I say. "There's something phony about these pricks. Look, we have to collect as many men as we can and get back to the yard."

Voss sobers right up, grabs his Luger and an MP-40 sub-machine gun.

"How many?" he says. "The Captain, three foot soldiers and the injured guy... if he really is injured. So four or five."

"Weapons?"

"Pistols, rifles... I don't know what they have in the truck. Why wasn't there someone on the lousy gate?"

Voss shrugs, says, "Base security isn't my detail. This is a Sigma operation. Ask your man Barasso."

I know what he's saying. Eden is more like a holiday camp than a commando training base.

Outside we find Mac returning with a couple of our Sigma guys. Brazilians. One is the big black guy who looks like that boxer Jack Johnson, and the other is a bit of an Indian. Good guys. No problems, always ready to dance.

"No Germans?" says Voss, disappointed.

"One guy is taking a bath, and another is washing his gonchies," says Mac. "The rest are in town."

"Let's get organized," I say. "What about the Zep crew?"

"The Zeppelin will be returning tomorrow," says Voss.

We lose five minutes or more getting the two SS guys, which is fatal, because when we get back to the yard, Moto and his squad are disappearing up the road. We try to catch up but they have a light machine gun on the tailgate and open up with that. A Madsen, judging by the casings we find on the road later. Chews up the front of our truck, wrecks the rad, knocks us off the road, and we're bloody lucky we don't crash and burn, so we just let them run.

Yeah, they were after the comrades alright, and they broke them all out and left Gomez locked in the cell with the other clown who was supposed to be minding them. The son of the gardener, the old Portuguese guy who used them as workers when they weren't being hunted as moving targets. Yeah, they all got away Scot-free (as they say). Obviously the commies are still pretty organized despite their failed revolts against the government in Rio, and they must consider The Professor an important asset to stage this rescue operation. Feel like a dummy because I didn't recognize it for what it was, but to tell the truth, I'd forgotten about those prisoners. They were around but I just didn't see them, same way you don't see the dust on the table unless the blinds are open and the sun is passing by.

And I don't care if they get away, just as long as we never meet again. Having them around was a drag, like hauling the body of a wife around in a suitcase. Unfinished business. Always felt guilty about Paul, his situation. Maybe he tried to kill me in the Tijuca forest, maybe he didn't. Maybe he would've stood by and let the Professor and Rotten cut me in two if Samba Girl hadn't said stop. They say there's no honor among thieves. Maybe so, but sometimes, y'know, we were almost friends.

O Florianopolis Palavra (The Florianopolis Word) In the early hours of Thursday morning heavily armed insurgents attacked the Eden ranch 50 kilometers west of Blumenau. The attackers are believed to be communists sympathetic to Luis Carlos Prestes, leader of the ANL (*Alianca Nacional Libertadora*), who recently escaped from prison in Sao Paulo. The Eden ranch is a property belonging to the Sigma Corporation and is used as a training facility by special units of the armed forces, including paramilitary units using foreign advisors.

A spokesman for Sigma said "casualties were light" and that "the attackers fled like dogs when confronted". When asked for a reason for the attack, Sigma suggested it was to steal weapons and to celebrate the escape of the "fanatic" Prestes.

"This is a time of unprecedented peril for Brazilian society from agents of the Comintern (Communist International) who are dedicated to the overthrow of democratic governments everywhere in order to establish international communism in the belief that a workers' paradise will follow. This delusion must be resisted at all costs in all quarters."

"*Deus, Patria e Familia!*"

Manuelo Barasso, who owns Eden and is one of Brazil's wealthiest businessmen, was unavailable for comment. Colonel Barasso is also a leading member of the Integralist Party, and is the likely frontrunner to succeed Plinio Salgado.

O Estado de Sao Paulo (The State of Sao Paulo) Editorial. The attack by communist gunmen on the Eden Ranch in Santa Catarina recently was not only an example of class sectarian politics but also an attack on the Estado Novo. That communists would attack Integralists is no surprise, and the timing of the attack should be no surprise either.

The Corporatist coalition that Getulio Vargas cobbled together isn't the all inclusive government that Brazilians were promised. The economy is stagnant and the poor remain poor. Literacy rates remain low while crime rates soar. Government bureaucracy remains mostly in Rio and in control of the elites who dine at the Jockey Club. The Estado Novo has proved itself to be no less totalitarian than the regimes of Italy and Germany with their secret police bureaus and crude control of the press. If the Estado Novo uses an amoral agency like DOPS (Department of Political and Social Order) to silence and control an emotive public, is it any wonder that socialists and other groups have resorted to violence in order to combat injustice? While everything from bank robberies to prison breaks and street riots are routinely blamed on Leftist groups, these crimes are often no more than political ephemera invented by the Establishment. The imprisonment of Luis Carlos Prestes was a shameful event in the political history of Brazil. The real crime is the National Security Act which was used to imprison him, not his words or deeds or even his recent escape from custody.

A lie has been perpetrated. It is said that Getulio Vargas gave Prestes a very large sum of money to ensure his silent support. It is said that Prestes gave a large part of this money to Antonio S. Campos to hide in Buenos Aires and now pretends that this money was lost in the aircrash that killed Campos. It is said that Prestes has escaped with inside help from Vargas agents and is now living in Miami.

(last paragraph redacted)(by Filinto Muller's office)

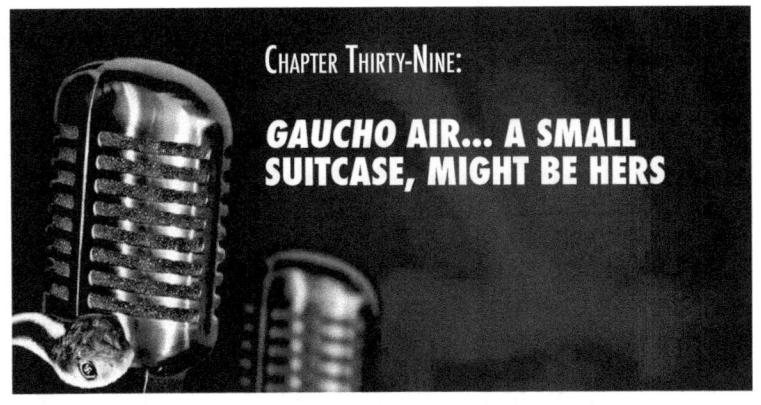

Chapter Thirty-Nine:

GAUCHO AIR... A SMALL SUITCASE, MIGHT BE HERS

I INTERCEPT THIS MESSAGE purely by accident. With short wave you never know what might come bouncing in, which is part of the attraction for me. You can hear your neighbours talking thousands of miles away, or as I like to say, thinking. Sounds like Roosevelt to me. My thought is he's on an American warship somewhere in the Atlantic and he's passing this message along to the Embassy in Berlin... to relay to you-know-who:

"Are you willing to give assurance that your armed forces will not attack or invade the territory or possessions of the following independent nations?"

The list includes Poland, Belgium, France, Great Britain and Ireland. No mention of Brazil or any of the islands in the Atlantic.

Normally something like this would be an encrypted message, so I do wonder if it's someone fooling around, some comedian who's heard one of FDR's fireside chats doing an impersonation or if I actually picked up a fragment of a CBS Roosevelt broadcast.

Go to the bunkhouse, look for Mac. He'd know. No one's seen him. Check around, find his gear is all gone. Go to the yard... one of the trucks is gone too. Mechanic says Mac "went to Blu for something" and won't be back until late.

Well, he's gone. He said he was gonna bail, head for Buenos Aires, but stuck around when he found out von Schellenberg was after me. I thought he might stay in for the Amazon mission, had hoped he would, but... he's gone. Might be limping, might be breathing hard, but he has the dough, a gun, and is one crafty sonofabitch. As canaries go, one of the best. He'll survive. Maybe we'll meet again one day. Could've gone with him but I'm not done with Brazil just yet. Sure, it's too hot for any white boys under 65 and Brats make up the rules as they go along, but I'm not done with Brazil just yet. No siree. Back home is monochrome, and here everything is in color. It's chaos, and y'know, I'm getting to like chaos.

Runway is lit with an avenue of kerosene tapers and the headlights of a truck positioned at the set-down marker. Rough, sure, but the Fiat can land anywhere there's a couple of hundred feet of easy space. It's not really dark but dark enough to mess with a pilot's depth perception. But Dani's good, just drops in like a nighthawk, no sweat. That big V-12 engine has a nice roar when throttling up or down, and I'm wondering why I didn't get into flying as she taxies back to the hangar.

Barasso must be reading my mind. He says to me, "How do you feel about a flight to Sao Paulo tomorrow?"

I'm watching Dani hoisting herself from the cockpit and stepping back to earth easy as a bird, thinking, I'd fly anywhere with her.

She's long and thin in her overalls, more like a boy than a woman. Good features but not a good-looker, not a dame. Yet... I'd fly anywhere with her.

I say, "Whatever you say, boss."

He's still looking tired, and he's not his usual macho self. Tense. Was tense when he got back yesterday, definitely preoccupied with something, maybe the escape of the prisoners or maybe the business in Asuncion. Haven't even told him about McDonald's bunk yet.

He says, "Leonora's very ill. I've had her moved to a clinic in Paulo."

Don't like to hear this. I'm very fond of Leonora. Dani approaches, flying cap and goggles in hand. Faint smile as she greets us.

"Hi boys," she says. "I reek of fuel... the motor was running a *muito* hot. Machine desires a bigger radiator for this hot world."

She nods at me, embraces Barasso.

"Were you successful?" says Barasso.

"Yes... it's behind the seat."

"Good, good. I want you to fly to Paulo tomorrow, Dani. Thorsen will go with you. Alright?"

"What about you?"

"I need a day to handle some business."

Seems we're getting ready to move on. The Zeppelin is here and the squad has been told to get ready to pack up within a day or so. The Germans are coming. The destination is Amazonia... exactly where

348

remains a mystery although Voss believes it's a research station of some sort the Germans are operating with the blessing of Rio. Could be. Or could be we're gonna be dropped off in some rubber plantation to keep the wild animals at bay or ride shotgun on ore transports from some precious metal mine. Anything is possible. Edler says we're looking for El Dorado. Fine. Just so long as we get paid.

Still don't know if Manuelo and Dani share a bed or what. Maybe it's all business. Maybe she's just an icon for Sigma. I'll find out, I guess.

Out on the airstrip at dawn there's a bit of dew, but you can feel the heat coming. Have all my stuff in my kit bag, as I won't be coming back to Eden. Barasso is carrying my M-1 rifle as we approach the plane. Dani's already there, doing the usual preflight inspection. The mechanic is topping up the tanks, so we get wafts of that special 5-2-2 mix... petrol, alcohol, benzole. Racing fuel. Also notice he checks the machine guns on the upper nose deck... is the magazine loaded? I don't ask. It's a mean machine when you're looking head-on at the prop, the shark-mouth rad and those streamlined spats on the wheels.

Dani rigs me up with a parachute which hangs around my ass like a diaper. Cockpit's extended for an observer cradle... guess if you want to sell one or train somebody, you have to have a two-seater model. She sold a few to the Venezuelans last year, word is. She's coy about money but you just know it's better than selling cars to accountants or hand guns to dope dealers.

"Eddie will pick you up in Paulo," says Barasso. "Give him the package."

I nod, say, "How long is the flight?"

Barasso looks at Dani who's checking her mouth in a small vanity mirror. Lipstick. Never seen her do this before... but then, of course, I hardly know her.

"Mmm?" she says. "Less than three hours... if we catch the sailor's wind."

"Bumpy?" I say.

"*Claro*... don't worry, Mister Viking, I can fly upside down if you need to be sick, o.k.? Just hold onto your horns."

Well that takes my balls out of the sack, doesn't it? See Edler in the distance, watching. Should've asked him for a 535. When I get myself strapped in behind Dani, Barasso steps up on the stirrup, hands me the rifle.

"You might need this, Safari Man," he says. "Got extra ammo?"

"Yeah."

"*Bom*... now listen, *senhor*, don't be surprised at anything you might see."

Wonder what he means by this, natch... but I might see a lot of surprising things in Sao Paulo.

"I'll see you in a couple of days, Thorsen. Look after Dani."

This makes her smile. She's looking after me, I'd say.

The mechanic grabs the prop, gives it a throw. Engine catches right away. O.k., goggles on and we're away, rolling over the grass onto the hard dirt of the runway. Dani holds back just for a few seconds to let the engine howl and then away we go, no pussying around... within seven seconds the wheels are off the ground and we're climbing at thirty, forty degrees, heading south briefly before banking east where the sun is like a bloated eye rising out of the distant ocean. A dip to the left, then to the right as we salute Eden. My stomach drops from my chest to where it should be and in no time we're flying up the coast at a thousand feet.

Some beautiful bays and chunks of sand, all sorts of hidden coves and sleepy fishing villages. Big gleaming ocean, stacks of cloud faces on the horizon. Some fishing boats down there, the occasional freighter. She drops lower over the coastal marshes at the mouth of a river. Flocks of flamingos rise in pink clouds and wheel away. Sea turtles sprawl on the sand bars and here and there you can see the coral sea bed and its blurry blood vegetation. The coastal mountains rise above us, sometimes tight to the beaches, sometimes falling back as jungle valleys to the interior.

Now we're climbing slowly, although I know this baby can go as high as Everest in fifteen minutes if you have oxygen. When we get to six thousand feet or so, we bank softly northwest, head inland. Lots of mountain wilderness, forests and alpine meadows on the altiplano. Fly along the ridges, scattering herds of wild ponies. Here and there the odd fazenda with some animals but mostly the high country is pretty lonely. Few roads, few people... lonely creeks and cloud shadows.

See a fast moving shadow ahead of us, starboard side, rippling over the ridges and gulches. Another aircraft, a mile ahead maybe, a thousand feet lower... probably in the commercial aviation ceiling of five thousand feet. Shoulder wing monoplane, could be a Ford Trimotor or maybe something smaller, hard to say at this distance. Dani points, then banks into the sun as if she's going to make a pass. We're faster, of course... a lot faster. See another shadow, think it's ours, but it isn't. Small biplane, a barnstormer or maybe a military pursuit fighter. Again, Dani looks back at me, motions. I see it, baby, I'm watching. Suddenly the sky has become awful busy for such an off-the-track area, but then, maybe for airplanes it isn't.

The biplane has dropped behind the mono like it's stalking it. Doesn't see us, cause we're a thousand feet higher, hidden by the sun. Yeah, it's military, as I can see the Brazilian green-yellow-blue bull's eye rondal on the fuselage. Must be practicing a combat manoeuver or escorting some V.I.P. Now I recognize the model, a Boeing P 12, about the same size as our Fiat CR 32, but with a fat round snout to accommodate its radial engine. Unmistakable with that ring cowl. Cat's ass in its day but way out-classed by our Fiat. We're much faster.

I'm twisting my neck trying to read the letters on the monoplane. Looks like "*Gaucho*", so maybe it's a commercial flight from Buenos Aires. We're just starting to pull away when the Boeing lets go with its machine guns and the next thing you know the mono is blowing a trail of dirty black smoke and dropping fast. Tap Dani's shoulder and point, but she's seen it anyway and is banking for a better view. The Boeing follows the mono down like an eagle who's just dropped a cat on the rocks. It's all mountain ridges and high plateau here, with snatches of forest and river valleys, the backside of the Serro do Mar coastal range. No gas stations, no airstrips, although the pilot of the mono is trying to land his ship anyway. Not allowed, apparently, and he goes in with a love moan, although the moan is mine, I guess. Hits some pines, takes off a wing, settles down in the boulders. The Boeing circles low over the crash, empties a few more rounds into the wreckage. Christ, this is murder, or if you wanna be pretty about it, an assassination. Someone important wants someone important dead.

We circle, watch as the Boeing circles, then departs, flying low to the north, apparently satisfied. Dani takes us down steeply and we make a couple of passes. Ugly. Gaucho's broken in two, the engine and cockpit burning, the tail and a chunk of fuselage hung up on a tree or some rocks and I can see three passengers on the ground, ejected like cigarette butts. Dani shouts above the wind, "I'm going to land." Where? Is she crazy? Of course I know someone might be alive, someone might need immediate help. But... aren't we on a priority mission to Sao Paulo? What about Leonora?

There's a bare spur on the side of a cliff. Not great, but seems to be the only landing spot close enough to the crash without having to mount an expedition. Can feel a bit of a downdraft pulling at us as we go in. It's unnerving as I'm blind to the landing track, looks like we're flying straight into a wall. Yet Dani sets her down like a wasp on honey, with some room to spare, spins her around, cuts the motor. The sky is blue, it should be calm except the wind is still roaring in my head like the ocean. Open cockpits do that to you. When you're not sticking your head into the gale, you're nursing the roar of the engine. Rip the leather helmet off, run my fingers through my hair, shake my head but the roar is slow in fading.

Voice sounds as distant and small as a memory: "Want me to make a radio call?"

Dani shakes her head, says, "Later... it might bring trouble now."

She's thinking about that flying assassin in the P 12. This is why I sling the M 1 rifle over my shoulder when we set out. What did Barasso say? 'Don't be surprised by anything you might see....'

"What's this all about?" I say. "The shooter was Brazilian airforce."

"There is no Brazilian Airforce," says Dani. "Air defence is under the army and the navy."

"So what's going on?" I say. "Dirty politics?"

"Let's find out," she says. "Better bring the aid kit."

Takes us ten minutes to get there through the Alpine brush. Probably about three thousand above sea level, not exactly in the clouds, just some wisps of morning mist and that evil black smoke which is blowing right at us. Clusters of small boulders, smooth as molars in the heather. You could run sheep here, or goats, but don't see any.

My head is quiet by the time we reach the crash. This was the worst spot on the ridge to come down on, with the biggest obstacles, and they hit 'em. Pilot's a piece of roast meat. And although the three passengers escaped the fire, they're dead.

"What do you think?" I say.

Dani just shakes her head, looks at the bullet holes in the wing.

"I think there is nothing we can do."

"Doesn't exactly inspire confidence," I say.

"In flying?"

"In life."

Two men and a woman. The woman was a looker if you could see past the mess she is now. South American for sure, just like the men. The fat guy on his back looks like a business man. Suit, modern moustache. Key chain from his belt to his trouser pocket.

"I think this man is Tony Campos," says Dani. "Big shot labour leader."

"You know him?"

"Just his picture. Communist. He was in exile in Argentina or Uruguay, don't remember which."

The other guy is a short distance away, face down. Rolled comic book stuck in his jacket pocket... what do you know? A Mexican Bible... *Senhor Prolific*, the classic with Vargas and Carmen Miranda. I lift him just enough to see—godamn, it's the Professor! A week ago he was in chains in Eden, today he's on a mountain ridge, dead. Stand up again, take another look at the woman. Could be Samba Girl, but I'm not sure.

Young, beautiful body, face ripped and scarred, part of her scalp missing. There's a small suitcase, might be hers. Nice blood leather. Strong, obviously, as the lock didn't spring with the crash. Remember the key chain on the fat guy's belt. Carry the case over to the body, go through the keys until one works. Goddamn, the case is full of dough, American bills, wads of fifties all stacked like they've just come from the press. Could be a half mil here. I whistle at Dani, who's taking a look at what's left of the fuselage.

She comes over, takes a look.

"What do you think now?" I say.

"I think we should get out of here pronto," she says.

"What about this?"

"What about it, *padrinho*? We take it, *claro.*"

We head back to the plane. My head is reeling with unexposed photos, memories of a lifetime. Plane crash. Shit. People I know. Shit. Someplace along the way, I pull up, say, "We keeping it?"

"Fifty fifty," says Dani, still moving.

"It's a lot of dough. Someone will miss it."

"Really? Let me tell you a secret: it takes a lot of money for a lady to be a flier. Fifty fifty, sweets, o.k.?"

"What about Manuelo? Shouldn't we be telling him?"

"You scared of the boss? I don't think so."

"Just sayin', doll."

"Fuck Manuelo... fuck them all. If you don't want your share, fine, I can use it."

Dani's a risk-taker, no question. She flies.

My turn to grab the blade, flip the prop. First time I fire a blank... second time too and I'm thinking we're gonna have to hike down this damn mountain, and then what? Surrender all this lovely loot? But third time is lucky and the engine catches, then roars like a reaper cutting corn. When we get airborne, we circle the crash for one last look. I spot a large animal approaching through the scrub grass. A jaguar. Dani takes notice, drops down and gives it a buzz but instead of running off, it just settles down on its haunches and snarls at us. I let go with a few rifle shots but I'm just pissin' in the wind. It pays no heed, resumes its advance towards the crash site. The big cat smells something and it isn't money.

WE ALMOST RUN OUT OF FUEL. Fortunately the Fiat has a 25 litre reserve tank so we make it to the Campo de Marte airfield on the north edge of Sao Paulo, a bit late, but not so late as to call out the scouts. As we taxi towards our parking area I notice a biplane sitting nearby exactly like the one that shot down the Gaucho Aviation monoplane. Makes me wonder, although Dani says the military have lots of these kites.

Eddie's waiting beside the Mercedes. Chucks a pair of binoculars onto the back seat, strides towards us.

"You're late," he says, "aren't you?"

"We took the scenic route," I say.

He looks at the red suitcase, says, "Is that the magic powder?"

"This? Nah, it's the lady's kit."

Dani's checking the plane... landing gear especially. That was a rough unscheduled touchdown in the mountains.

Eddie looks her direction, says, "Eh, so you fly with the famous Dani Boy...."

"Dani Boy?"

"Yeah. You know she's a lesbian?"

Another of Eddie's jokes. He hasn't changed.

"How's Leonora?" I say.

"Not good, man, not good. You brought the package?"

"We did. What is it?"

"Some special medicine, I don't know what. From the Inca or the

Coneheads... some jungle lizards."

So that's where Dani went. Can't imagine this is something from a laboratory. Paper bag, stuff that looks like tea leaves going to powder at the bottom, smells musty. Maybe a half pound. Hand it to Eddie, drop my rifle and kit bag in the trunk. Eddie's sniffing the bag.

"Wonder what it is?" he says. "People go crazy trying to get it."

"Juju?"

"Something like that. Hey, good to see you, *Senhor* Safari Man!"

"Miss me?"

"Yeah... the ladies miss you too. How was Eden? Great, huh?"

"Crazy place, Eddie. It's like Deutchland West... all Krauts. Hey, seen Uma?"

Eddie's still smiling, yet I detect a shift in his eyes.

"Not since the *Senhora* became ill."

I nod, say, "Work stopped, eh. No models required."

Eddie says, "Yeah yeah... it's bad, Thorsen. You won't recognize her."

Some airfield workers have gathered around the Fiat. Unusual aircraft, famous aviatrix.

I gesture towards the P 12, say, "See that military plane?"

Eddie looks, says, "Yeah... it landed about thirty minutes ago."

"It did? What direction did it come from?"

"Don't know, just saw it touchdown."

"See the pilot?"

"Sure. He walked right past me. Dog collar."

"What do you mean, dog collar?"

Eddie puts his hand to his throat, says, "Priest... army priest."

"You mean a Chaplin? They fly?"

"Why not? They're officers."

I'm trying to get my head around this when Dani arrives, greets Eddie effusively, you know, the way they do in Brazil, hugs and kisses.

"Eduardo... *sangue... que e pra sempre*...."

"Manuelo asked me to book you a hotel."

"*Bom*? I like to be close to the field."

"That's why I booked a room at the Santana, Dani *mina*. No reporters eat lunch there."

"Good boy. You think of everything."

"I just follow orders, *mina*. You're booked too, Thorsen. Boss says."

"Thorsen's my dog," says Dani slyly. "So watch out."

Sounds good to me. I like this job. Except... except, what am I doing stealing money from an aircrash? Get in the back with Dani and the red suitcase.

Sao Paulo is like Chicago from the air, or what Chicago might've looked like twenty five years ago in 1914. The scrapers are going up, the expressways, the factories, the suburban grids. Modern... well, modern in the middle, shanty on the outskirts. Million people anyway and who really knows with so many *indocumentados* around. They just drift into town from the jungle swamps, the *cerrado*, the flori, the sea... the stars.

"You're a Paulistano, aren't you, Eddie?" says Dani.

"Nah," says Eddie. "Minas."

"Same thing," says Dani. "All you southerners want the same thing... the thing that doesn't exist."

"You got that right. The divorce rates are soaring."

"You mean murders?"

"Yeah. Same thing. Boom boom."

"So if Brazil had the death penalty, would there be more love?"

"Eh, don't ask me. We need a political solution... but what? Don't ask me."

Dani says to me, "What does, um, Safari Man think?"

"Me? I dunno. Brazil has the death penalty, far as I can see. It's just off the books, like natural selection."

Road's bumpy and if it wasn't for that little red suitcase sitting between us, we'd be samba bumping.

"You mean, let the people decide who lives and who dies? Take care of justice? Hmm. Interesting."

"Problem is, it's the rich who get to decide mostly."

Give her a look, but she chooses not to take it.

"That's why we want to be rich," she says. "Right, Eduardo?"

Eddie looks at us in the rear view, chuckles, says, "When I was in the army the only thing I ever shot was dummies. In the second *tenentista* revolt here in Paulo our platoon had a bounty for every proven kill. I made nuthin', not a single reais. This is why I now drive you to a hotel where I will never stay."

"That's a horrible little story, Eddie," says Dani. We let this hang for a few seconds, then Dani adds, "How much is a dead communist worth?"

"That's just it," says Eddie gloomily. "Nothing."

Now we're laughing. Dani glances at me, says, "I have reason to believe that dead communists are now worth... oh, let's just say lots... lots of money."

Eddie isn't convinced. "No way. The Estado Novo is making love with the unions. Vargas invited Campos to return from exile."

Gotta hand it to Dani—she's one cool customer. Return from exile. Little does he know.

She says, "Antonio Campos?"

"Yeah... and they let Prestes escape. You must've heard about that."

"No, you don't hear much when you're up in the lonely skies as much as I am."

"Lucky you. You're not political anyway, are you, Dani?"

"If you work for Sigma, you're political, *sim*?"

"Wouldn't know, *mina*. I just follow orders."

"Oh what shit, Eduardo—you're the worst man I know for following orders. I know all about you."

"*O que*? The boss say things to you?"

"No, Eduardo. I read your mind. It's the first thing you learn in flying school: mind reading."

"Eh, is that like map reading? If it is, must be why I'm lost... what *rua* is the Santana on? Eh, *mijada! Estupido*!"

Dani laughs merrily. Notice she's resting a hand on the suitcase like it's a pet. Between dodging the mules and the autos, we see lots of construction going on. Paulo looks like it's full of ruins and holes in the ground but it's just a construction boom. Flagmen here, diversions there, dust in the air, the music of hammers. There's an ambulance... looks like workmen are falling from the scaffolds like shanked nails. We look but say nothing as we pass. It's a nice day and we're entering a nice neighbourhood with nice trees and nice shadows.

As if reading my mind, Dani murmurs, "We're here to make the best of a bad situation, not feel guilty about it."

Eddie grunts, focuses on his driving.

I say, "What's the highest building here?"

Dani says, "In Paulo? That would be the Martinelli... right, Eduardo?"

Eddie says, "Yeah, the Martinelli. Thirty floors. Avenida Sao Joao."

The Santana is colonial, looks like a museum with the arches and recessed windows and mythological nudes on the pillars supporting the balconies and roofs. At the taxi stand there's a horse drawn carriage. Eddie's greased our arrival so the registration should be short and sweet. Adjoining rooms, second floor, which might be the top floor the way this place is laid out. Quite posh, not the Ritz, yet a notch or two above what I'm used to. Lobby reminds me of the ocean liner... not the style, but the quiet comfort. Coffee, cigars, cathedral light. Birds in the atrium. Palms outside, palms inside. It'll do.

"Who am I?" says Dani as we approach the desk. "What are we booked under?"

She's still wearing her flying suit, you know, the coveralls and the natty tunic.

"You're Bianca Remington."

"Didn't I use that last time?"

"No no, last time you are Winchester."

"Same thing. People think I'm English."

I say, "What about me? The Count of Monte Cristo?"

"You are Schmitt, o.k.?"

"Thanks a lot. I got a first name? A title?"

"Whatever you want, *padrinho*. Your choice. I book you as Schmitt."
Eddie's itching to get going, make his delivery, which is the whole point of
us being here in Paulo. And I know I'm supposed to be acting as muscle
for Dani until the boss gets here, but I feel I must visit with Leonora.
Think of her as my patron, even though it's her husband who's paying me
the bucks. If her life is in peril, I should be there. Part of the deal. Dani
has no problem with me going with Eddie. She wants to take a bath, have
a siesta... maybe count the money... although, of course, I have the key.

The private clinic isn't far away. Looks like a villa converted and
modernized in a mature garden setting, facing east to catch the sunrise
and hold the illusion. Doesn't matter where these places are, they give
me the creeps. There's always a smell, y'know? Could be the floorwash,
could be the iodine... or it could be the uniforms. They say nursing is
the highest calling a woman can have, unless she's a nun and a nurse. No
nuns here. These people are technocrats. The Barassos don't pay good
money for voodoo. Or so Eddie says.

"Ahhh," says the doctor, her eyes glistening, "the weed that resists
putrefaction. You are Pegasus?"

She's talking to me, even though Eddie's the one who handed her the
bag.

"Pegasus? Yeah, I flew in with it. Hope it helps."

"We call it a weed although it comes from a vine... it's all a matter of
definition."

"There's no sure-fire drug for malaria?"

"Not really... soon, perhaps. The parasites adapt stubbornly, resist all
attempts at elimination. This just might work. Some Amazonian Indians
have a cult based on this stuff... expect you know all this."

She's talking to me like I'm the son or some special relative. The
aryan look, I guess. She's cast like a middle-aged contessa, bit of a double
chin and moustache. It's that black glossy hair and lipstick combination.

Eddie says, "How is *Senhora* Barasso today? Can we see her?"

Her black eyes deflect towards Eddie and she says, "*Claro.*"

First thing I notice is the sleep mask that conceals most of her face, and the way the blinds are partially closed to subdue the sunlight in the room. And the lupus spots on her arms. When she hears us, she raises the mask. Eddie was right—Leonora doesn't look good.

"Boys," she says. "How nice to see you."

The doc says, "They bring the medicine... *correio aereo* all the way from the Amazon."

"Where's Manuelo?" says Leonora. "Is he here?"

"Tomorrow," I say. "He sent me ahead, *Senhora*."

"Thorsen," she says. "I need to talk to you... Eddie, do you mind?"

"No, *Senhora*," says Eddie. "I'll wait in reception."

Gives me the what-did-I-say look as he leaves.

The doc says, "Do you want to get out of bed, Leonora? Stretch your legs?"

"Not just yet, Carlotta... I want to talk to my model."

"He's a model? I thought he was an aviator."

Leonora chuckles weakly. "He's many things, this young man."

The doc stops at the door, says, "Don't tire yourself talking, I'll be back soon with your new medicine."

When she leaves, Leonora says to me, "New? It's as old as the hills. Well, no matter. They say it works... I hope it works."

"How did you get malaria, *Senhora*?" I say.

"How? I suppose I was bitten by a mosquito the first day I arrived in Brazil... I don't remember. Anyway, I'm truly Brazilian now. Half the population carries malaria to some degree or another. Yes, malaria is essential for citizenship. Manuelo hopes to make a lot of money from malaria, did you know? He's invested a fortune in researching a new drug with some Germans. Probably just dressing up some jungle plant, some Indian remedy such as you've just delivered, put it in a pill, brand it with IG Farben or some other chemical company, sell it to the military. War's coming, isn't it?"

"Hope not."

"Be honest—what's going on down in Eden?"

Tell her about the Germans, which she knows about, of course.

"I read the papers," she says. "They say Santa Catarina is full of war fever."

"It's like Little Germany," I say. "Despite the distance, they stay close to the old country."

Leonora sniffs, says, "I don't like it. National Socialism. Is not Hitler a male without a female? National Socialism is for men only."

"Well you'll be happy to hear I killed a Nazi—well two actually—in a duel."

"You must be joking."

Repeat the story of the Major von Schellenberg fiasco. "Didn't actually kill him. He got blown up by a booby trap meant for me."

"And this Major said he was Uma's husband?"

"That's what he claimed but I think it was just an excuse. He arrives, picks a fight, then boom."

"What does Manuelo think?"

"He thought it was fishy. Have you seen Uma?"

Leonora sighs, says, "I've seen no one for weeks, never mind Uma. I hope you're not in love with her. Are you?"

"No... well, sort of."

"Poor Thorsen. Uma's a classic grass widow... she's always tied to someone or something. That's the feeling I get. Maybe she has or has had a husband... and of course she always has a boyfriend. She's a beautiful looking girl, so there's always someone in line for a heart ache."

Without giving me a name, rank and serial number, she's telling me Uma has moved along and I might as well too.

I look around, not really seeing anything, say, "This is a nice, quiet room."

"Yes... it's also a lonely room."

"Where's Lucy?"

"At home in Rio. Illness frightens her. Well I don't blame her. What can she do here?"

"Play piano."

"As a matter of fact she'll be here next week. Will you...?"

"Don't think so."

"Pity. She likes you, you know."

"If people really knew me, they might not like me so much."

"Oh... do you have a secret, Thorsen?"

I sigh, I sigh. Really need to unburden.

"You don't need to hear my troubles, Leonora," I say. "I'm supposed to be helping you...."

"Nonsense... out with it. I have the time... I can put off dying until tomorrow."

"I don't know...."

"Please, amuse me. Someone else's misfortune is the best cure going." So I tell her about what happened on the flight up, the aircrash, the money... Dani.

"I know Danielle... she's a famous woman in Brazil. Manuelo uses her as company advertising. He's selling Italian aircraft. She helps."

I'm nodding. She helps alright. Need a body dropped in the Atlantic?

No problem. Need some fast dough? No problem.

"She's a bit old for you, isn't she?"

"Oh, there's no romance."

"Really, Thorsen? The story you've just told me sounds extremely romantic. Yes, extremely. Just where is this partnership headed?"

"Damned if I know, which is why I'm asking."

"I'm the only one who knows? You haven't reported the aircrash?"

"Nope."

"Incredible. How much money do you say?"

"I don't know. Lots."

She thinks about this, then says, "And the plane was shot down by one of our military fighters? My god, the newspapers will be all over this."

"Crash site might not be found for days or weeks."

"Antonio Campos... President Vargas had forgiven him."

"Maybe not."

"My word, this is a pickle. Presumably the plane that shot him down could've landed and recovered the money if that's what they were after. He could've, couldn't he?"

"Dani was able to."

"Hmm. What does she want the money for? You know?"

"Old age? Don't know. She said something about flying around South America."

"No sponsor? Hmm. I'll ask Manuelo... if I ever see him."

"He'll be here a.s.a.p., I'm sure."

"Hmm. Keep your mouth shut about this. Don't tell anyone, not even Eddie."

Haven't given her the full picture, haven't mentioned the Professor and Samba Girl... if that woman was Samba Girl. The money doesn't bother me as much as the victims, even though I had a hate on for the Professor, who was as mean and ruthless as they come, another asshole with a book of instructions on life. The money might be union money, cash fleeced from the sheep, or it could be financing from Moscow. No, the money doesn't bother me.

"Help me sit up, there's a good boy," says Leonora.

Put my hands below her armpits and heave.

"Can you imagine?" she says. "One day you're full of confidence, the next... well, you're just bits and pieces."

"Do you want to get out of bed, maybe sit in the patio?"

"Not just yet. Dancing is out of the question today. Don't suppose you've been doing much."

"Dancing? No. Marching mostly."

"See those cigarettes? Please."

Get her a cigarette. Private clinic, can smoke if you want. Her first drag is full of longing.

"Imagine if smoking was good for you. Imagine if it could kill the parasites that eat you. But it isn't. All the good things in life end up killing you."

"So the key is to be bad...."

"Yes, Thorsen. But there's an art to it."

Obviously. And not everyone has the art.

"Tell me," I say. "None of my business, *claro*, but how did *Senhor* Barasso make all his money so quickly?"

This provokes a husky chuckle. "His father was a jockey and told him which horses to put his money on," she says. "No, he came upon a suitcase at an aircrash... is this what you want to hear? Nothing so romantic, alas. His family. His father had several coffee plantations and oodles of cattle, left it all to Manuelo, and he just keeps adding to the empire. Not everything he does makes money... he squandered a fortune in a failed aircraft project with Santos Dumont. What an ugly mess that was. But... he goes on, we go on."

Doctor Carlotta and a nurse return with the medicine, which is just like a glass of hot tea. Leonora takes a sip, grimaces. Good time for me to leave.

As we're driving back to the Santana, I say to Eddie, "With a car like this, you could pick up a lot of women."

Mercedes 540K, couple of years old. Leather, wood, rag top. Wouldn't say it was black, wouldn't say it was blue. Maybe night shadow.

"You should know, Thorsen. Didn't you drive Lucy around in this?"

"Yeah. Where is she?"

"In Rio, driving the Bugatti."

"What's gonna happen, you think?"

"With the *Senhora*? God, I don't know. She's sick, sick."

"But malaria comes and goes, doesn't it?"

"Yeah."

"I wanna get drunk."

"Yeah?"

"Yeah, but... listen, you know where Ida's mother lives, don't you? I want to see her."

"Ida? Eh, let the dogs sleep. You don't want to do this."

"Unfinished business, Eddie."

I don't tell him about her sister, Samba Girl, and that she might be dead too. "My conscience is troubled, amigo."

"You're in the wrong business, man."

"Eddie, if she was your sister—"

"I hear you. But there's no point. You gotta move along."

"I try to, Eddie, I try to. Remember Alfredo?"

"Of course."

"His handlers sent someone to kill me."

Takes his eyes off the road, almost clips a guy riding bareback on a pony. "*Quando*?"

Tell him about von Schellenberg.

"You blew him up?"

"Stroke of luck, man."

"Don't be modest, Safari Man. You took care of business. Fuck him."

We swing into the loop in front of the Santana, park below the long neck palms that form an island. A faint blow of warm drizzle in the air, coming up the valley through the *Serra do Mar* from the Atlantic. Makes everything look a little foggy.

My turn to shower, shave, clean myself up. Feel like I've been digging ditches, so much tension in my bones. Lie down on the bed. Take a look through the window, see a ruined yard, stone arches with grass and weed growing from the masonry dirt and sod. Back of a chapel? There's a priest in a long black cassock and wide brimmed hat standing near a wall, reading a book. Behind this there's a new building going up, a small scraper with empty windows and spikes of rebar. Different kind of ruin, one leaving, the other arriving, side by side... and does the priest notice? I'm thinking he's a statue until I see his hidden hand rise to his mouth with a cigarette. He smokes, he reads... my eyes close.

Knocking on the door, the one that joins my room to Dani's. It's already dark and the noise of the traffic is more sporadic. Door opens. It's her. She's wearing a dress. Too dark to say what color, although it's tight on the waist.

"I'm hungry," she says. "I have to eat."

I sit up, groan. "What time is it? Guess I snoozed."

"Time to eat. Let's go."

As I roll off the bed my hand gun gets swept onto the floor. Pick it up, transfer it to my jacket.

"Where's the money?" I say. "We can't leave it lying around."

"I agree," she says. "What's the plan?"

She's in the room now, close enough I can smell her scent. Lipstick, perfume, dress... must be the big city.

"You're all dolled up," I say. "Do I need a suit?"

"I just don't want to be recognized," she says. "You've no idea what it's like."

"Well I do as a matter of fact... once upon a time. We should get rid of that case."

"Yes... perhaps we should count it."

"Yeah, o.k."

Follow her into her room. Case is on top of the antique wardrobe. Not a great place, although better than below the bed, I guess. Recover it, chuck it on the bed, fish the key from my pocket, open it.

"You're very trusting, Thorsen," says Dani. "I could've flown away with it when you were visiting Leonora."

"Or your conscience could've gotten the better of you and you turned it in to the authorities."

"The authorities! Don't be naive—what do you think the 'authorities' would do with it? Deposit it to the State Treasury? It would be petty cash for some damn politico... just like the one we took it from!"

"Alright, I get it. No conscience. Guess that's why you didn't use your guns to rattle that jaguar. I know your ship's magazine was loaded... would've been easy to strafe that *gatinho*, save those dead people the further indignity... know what I mean?"

"It's not my business to anticipate the fate of others, child."

"No? You're catholic, aren't you?"

"I'm a flyer, is what I am. I leave guilt on the ground for others to deal with."

I nod, murmur, "Sure, lady."

Start counting the money. First the bills in a bundle, then the bundles.

Dani says, "If I shoot the *gatinho*, then I leave the possibility that someone will say I shot down that plane. *Entender*?"

She's right. Hadn't occurred to me but she's absolutely right. These modern fighter aircraft all use .303 calibre machine guns. Different countries, different models... but nearly always .303 ammo. Yes, she'd be setting herself up.

I say, "You think they've found it yet?"

"Not likely. They might never find it."

Finish counting. Thousand a bundle, four hundred bundles, give or take one or two... or three.

"Four hundred thousand dollars," I say. "These bills look new, so they might be counterfeit."

"Don't say that... well, who would know?"

"President Roosevelt? I dunno. Not our first worry... we need a secure stash."

"The hotel safe?"

"Are you kidding?"

Go to the window, look for a fire escape, but there isn't one. Two floors? You can jump, *hombre*. Well, I don't jump but I do find a back door. Obvious that the ruined yard behind the chapel is the best place to hide a red ox blood suitcase.

We eat in an Italian joint next door to the hotel. High ceiling with white stucco arches and clusters of wine bottles hanging from the rafters. Horizontal barrels holding up the counter and booze stacked into the sky. Small tables with red terry cloth. Candles, guy with a fiddle, another with an accordion floating about. Old guy waiter with a white jacket fills our wine glasses. Let Dani do the ordering. She has cannelloni, I have lasagna Bolognese. Fair to intermediate great, I'd say. Easy to get loaded without getting pissed.

"So how is *Senhora* Barasso?" says Dani. "You never said."

"You ever meet her?" I say.

"Once... oh, maybe another time."

"A great artist. It's a shame to see her so ill."

"You're a protégé of hers, are you not?"

"I work for Manuelo."

"He says Leonora took some photographs of you. Is this true? She wanted to photograph me... once."

"You must get photographed a lot."

"Newspapers... when I'm news."

She keeps her hair short. Guess it makes wearing a flying helmet easier. The young and cheeky look, even though she must be pushing thirty five or forty.

She says, "I confess... I saw that picture of you in Rio Life. Who is the girl?"

"A German model... Uma."

She pours herself more wine. "Major von Schellenberg was her husband... am I getting this right?"

"That's what he said. I don't want to talk about it."

"*Claro, claro...* forgive me. When Manuelo asked me to do this favor, he didn't explain the circumstances. One day the Major arrives in Florianopolis, we're introduced, drive to Eden... the next day he's dead. I know soldiers sometimes get shot... but this seemed fast, even for Brazil. Then he's in the ocean."

"Thank you."

"I didn't like him. How old are you?"

"Twenty-five."

"How many men have you killed?"

Just shake my head, suddenly wish I had a beer instead of wine. No, make that a double whiskey.

"I was married once," she says. "But that's another story. Cheer up, Thorsen... er, Schmitt. Keep your back straight, eyes straight ahead."

"Yes, mam."

"Brazil is full of girls."

"In the jungle?"

"The jungle... is that where they're sending you?"

We're interrupted by a Brazilian officer—short and stocky, boots, britches, tunic and dog collar.

"Forgive my interruption," he says in Portuguese. "*Senhora* Danielle d'Anza? I am Captain Vaticano. I believe you are giving a demonstration to my unit the day after tomorrow."

Dani smiles.

"I will be flying ACM with you."

"Really, Captain Vaticano?"

"Yes, the combat exercise. We're all keen to see the C 32 in action. It's a superb aircraft."

"You will be flying...?"

"A P 12... a bit old now, naturally. But agile."

"Well I'm no combat pilot, Captain. Stunts, perhaps... endurance, certainly."

He turns towards me, chuckles, says, "The *Senhora's* modesty is charming, don't you agree, sir?"

"This is Lieutenant Schmitt," says Dani.

"*Alemao*?" says Vaticano.

"Waffen SS Jungle Brigade," I say smoothly.

"Ah, the *Schutzstaffel*," says Vaticano. "How interesting. What brings you to Brazil, Lieutenant?"

"The jungle," I say.

This springs a laugh from Dani, although Vaticano just smiles politely.

"Training?"

"Training and instructing."

"How interesting. Where is your unit?"

"Santa Catarina. Just a few of us."

"And what brings you to Sao Paulo?"

"Well, the architecture... *claro*... and the *frauleins*... *claro*."

He grins but keeps his teeth concealed. If this sonofabitch is who I think he is, he eats his meat raw.

Vaticano draws his heels together, bows, says, "Perhaps I will see you at the demonstration. *Boa noite, senhor, senhora.*"

We watch him leave, join some other officers at the bar.

"He's the bastard who shot down *Gaucho* Aviation," I say. "Dollars to donuts."

"That's crazy," says Dani. "There are dozens of P-12 fighter pilots in Brazil."

"You saw the P 12 at the field," I say. "Eddie says it landed twenty, thirty minutes before we did. And the pilot was wearing a dog collar."

Dani looks towards the bar. Vaticano seems to have moved on.

"Eddie says the pilot was a priest?"

"That has to be him, Dani... how many flying priests you got in the Brazilian military?"

Can see she's weighing it. Taps a spoon against an empty plate. Like a clock approaching the hour.

"There's one way to find out," she says. "Check the aircraft's machine gun magazine."

"Let's do it."

Dani's looking into my eyes... sternly, like a school mistress. "Does it matter?" she says. "Does it matter who did it or why? We have the money."

"I think it matters," I say. "And I'm not catholic."

"If Vaticano did it, what would you do? Blackmail him?"

"Colonel Barasso might."

"Colonel Barasso might've commissioned him, chump. You have no idea of the politics in this country."

"Somehow I doubt the boss has anything to do with this. Why use Vaticano when he can use you?"

"Thank you. You know I wouldn't shoot down an unarmed aircraft. In fact, I wouldn't shoot down anything."

"What about this 'demonstration' Vaticano talked about?"

"We're trying to sell some Fiats, that's all."

"But you're engaging Vaticano in a combat demonstration, aren't you?"

"Simulated ACM. Just a few moves, that's all."

"Sure, sure... wouldn't you like to know who you're up against?"

She thinks it over, then says, "Alright, let's go to the *Campo*. Where's our driver?"

Look at my watch, say, "He was meeting me in the lobby for a beer at 11 pm."

"Good," says Dani. "Let's go. I need to change robes anyway."

CHAPTER FORTY-ONE:

THE DEATH OF ANTONIO CAMPOS IS SUSPICIOUS

EDDIE HASN'T GOT A CLUE. He thinks he drove us to the field because Dani is worried about her plane, forgot to do something or left something behind. Guards I.D. us, natch. No problem—we're with the famous aviatrix. We're at another part of the field, away from the tower and the commercial bays. No lights. Problem is, when we find her plane and expect to find Vaticano's P-12 parked nearby, there are a dozen P-12s parked in a line, the whole damn squadron. Must've come in some time in the afternoon after we went to the hotel.

We're standing beside the Fiat.

"What do we do now?" I say. "Can't open them all up."

"I'll find it," says Dani. "You boys make yourselves busy."

She slips into the jagged shadows cast by the aircraft. I climb into the cockpit of the Fiat.

Eddie says, "What's going on, Thorsen?"

I say, "Schmitt, man. I'm Lieutenant Hans Schmitt, remember?"

"Yeah yeah, Schmitt. What's she looking for?"

"Got a cigarette?"

He holds up his box, lets me pull one, then takes one himself. Have my lighter, so fire us up. Turks. Strong, rich... nuts.

"Why do you smoke these damn things?" I say. "Gotta be nuts."

Eddie's eyes are lit. Must be the moonlight.

"What's she looking for?" he says.

I tell him about the sales demo that's coming up. "She's trying to get an edge, y'know? For when she has to go up against the army pilot."

"Dogfight?"

"Yeah. So the Generals can see just how good this little Italian plane is. A few maneuvers, stunts... boss wants to sell as many of these babies as he can."

"Eh, I don't know... can a woman really fly an aeroplane? Tell me, *mano*... did you feel safe?"

"No."

"So why you do it? Chariots of fucking death, ask me."

"She's a good pilot."

"Then she must be a man. When you look at her, do you see a woman?"

"What do you want? A cow? You want she go moo, *senhor*?"

"I want samba bells on my women, something you can shake, hear things go ring-a-ding!" He laughs short and hard, finishes with a shiver. Bawdy.

"Eddie, let's take a walk around the plane, make like we're serious in case some security folks are watching."

We do that. Eddie clips his shoulder on the propeller, curses. He seems a tad loose to me, careless happy like he's been drinking. He forgot to turn on the headlights when we drove away from the hotel. But then, maybe I'm in double-focus myself. Half a litre of *vinho tinto*... maybe more, don't recall. We tap the wings, the fuselage... stroke the smooth parts like we're dreaming of modern women made of aluminum and fabric. A searchlight near the tower snaps on and the beam probes the sky. Lots of stars, some cloud. Can hear an engine, a plane coming in from Rio maybe, or Buenos Aires... anywhere. A runway lights up—electric, not your usual kerosene bins. Modern, like this city. A trimotor lands. Could be a Ford or a Junkers, difficult to say.

"Might be the boss," says Eddie.

"Tomorrow," I say. "Isn't that what he said?"

Dani returns, rubbing her hands on a rag, gives me a nod and the semaphore eyes. Assume she found the plane, assume Vaticano is guilty. Once again Eddie drives, and we're sitting in the back.

"Well?" I say, low.

"He fired about a hundred and sixty rounds," whispers Dani. "That's what it took."

"Bastard. Sure it was the right plane?"

"He has a Latin cross below the cockpit... and the word 'Credo'."

"Credo... what does that mean?"

"It means 'I believe'. Could also be his callsign, *sim*?"

"They got radios?"

"Yes."

"Bastard. Who's he working for?"

"God, *claro*."

God, sure... in the name of, sure. In the name of DOPS, the secret police... or some rogue military cadre. The 1930 revolution was really rooted in the so-called Lieutenant's Revolt of 1922 when the old guys fell out of touch with the new and the young officers went ape with the blessing of the urban professionals. Trained by Germans, believed in technology and art. The oligarchs—meaning the coffee growers and the cattle men and anyone who still believed he was royalty—were their targets. This was the start of it all. Then Prestes picked it up... labour, the unions, the rural *camponeses*... and a lot of it was coming out of Sao Paulo, so the government bombed the shit out of them. Bit like Spain, same sort of thing. Bit like a lot of places in the world these days. And where does Manuelo Barasso and Sigma fit into all this? The new nationalism. They call it fascism some places, other places communism. Yeah, communism too, the imperial face of Stalinist Russia. The nuances are in the old religions and the new machines.

I'm starting to figure it out.

Voce Sao Paulo, morning edition. Wreckage of a downed aircraft has been spotted in the Highlands west of the Serra do Mar. It is believed to be that of a Gaucho Aviation charter flight from Montevideo which failed to reach its destination in Rio de Janeiro two days ago. The flight manifest lists three passengers as well as the pilot. It is reported that the passengers include the labour leader Antonio Campos, who was living in Buenos Aires following his exile in 1935 for his part in the failed communist coup d'etat.

Sources say Campos had been invited back to Brazil for talks with President Vargas and a possible position in the government in keeping with the Estado Novo's recent shift towards reconciliation with old foes. A rescue mission is underway, although an aerial reconnaissance saw no survivors in the wreckage. Weather conditions in the region have been described as "excellent".

O Florianopolis Palavra (The Florianopolis Word) The crash of the Gaucho Aviation plane and the death of Antonio Campos is suspicious. Unconfirmed reports say the fuselage contains bullet holes. An unnamed witness claims to have heard gunfire before the passenger plane caught fire and crashed on a rocky ridge killing all on board. The witness, who is a local shepherd, says two military aircraft were involved and made repeated strafing runs even after the target had crashed. The witness was unable to confirm identification markings or have an opinion on the origin of the attackers.

Antonio Campos was returning to his native Brazil following four years of exile in Argentina. *Senhor* Campos was a leading left-wing figure, although he always denied he was a communist. His two companions remain unidentified. One is said to be a woman. Identification is difficult because the bodies were mutilated by the violence of the crash and the foraging of wild animals.

No senior government official has been available for comment.

The flight is said to have originated in Montevideo.

O Estado do Sao Paulo (The State of Sao Paulo) The motive for the murder of Antonio Campos is now complicated by the rumour that he was carrying half a million dollars when his plane crashed. The origin of this money is said to be the Estado Novo, who transferred the funds as part of the deal to ensure his safe return to Brazil. Government sources deny this.

"This is fantasy," said an official close to the President. "President Vargas would never countenance a deal that involves bribery."

Others say the money comes from the Brazilian unions or the Communist International.

Investigators at the crash site say no money has been found. It is possible it was burned or scattered by the crash. It is also possible that there was no money.

But the evidence that the plane was shot down appears solid. Therefore it is unlikely that money was the motive. There was a conspiracy, that is certain, as it takes a conspiracy to marshal the resources needed to carry out an assassination of this nature. Was the act carried out by a rogue element in our armed forces? The suggestion is there, but it is too soon to pass judgment.

Or was it an act of aerial piracy? Half a million dollars appeared and disappeared.

Earlier reports say the crash victims were partially eaten by a mountain cat. Perhaps the money was eaten too.

CHAPTER FORTY-TWO:

THE MARTINELLI IS THE TALLEST IN PAULO

INTIMACY... WHAT IS IT? Friendship? Love? Trust? Shared illusion? Dani and me are getting pretty tight. She likes having me around. Sharing a suitcase of money can bond a couple of people, of course. Partners in Fortune, partners in crime.

Barasso phones while we're having breakfast with the birds in the pergola. Follow the bellhop to the desk, pick up the phone.

"I can't get the hold of Eduardo," says Barasso. "I'll be at the Campo in a couple of hours."

"He's stopping by here shortly," I say.

"Good. I need him. Business to take care of that needs a car. Looking after Dani?"

"Of course."

"Enjoy your flight?"

"Yes."

Barasso picks up on my hesitation, laughs, says, "She scare the shit out of you, Safari Man? Listen, I think you're a good match. We can do good work together. Leonora thinks so. She has ideas... hopefully, when she gets better we can carry them out. You deliver the package?"

"The medicine? Yeah."

"Never get married, Thorsen. Times like this, worry can kill a man."

"She's strong... I'm sure she can pull through this spell."

"I pray she will. That medicine... it cost me more than a couple of tanks of aviation fuel. Pra caramba... it's just money. May it never run out!"

"You want to speak to Dani?"

"No, I'll see her at the airfield. I have her mechanic with me."

Bertuzzi, the Italian guy claims he was with the *Aviazione Legionaria* in Spain and I'm sure he was. Comes with the plane, the official Fiat Aviation mechanic all the way from Turin, Italy. He wasn't happy when he had to stay behind, let me take his place.

Eddie arrives when he's supposed to, and on the way to the Campo de Marte he says, "Know that plane crash? Newspaper this morning, she say it's murder, the plane was shot from the sky by a bandit. You guys see anything?"

Dani says, "Don't believe everything you read in the newspaper, Eduardo."

Eddie says, "They say Campos was carrying a million dollars and the bandit lands, gets the money."

I look quickly at Dani. She puts her hand on mine. "Who says, Eddie?"

"*O jornal...* some *gaucho* say he see it all."

"Fascinating. They say what kind of plane?"

"Brazilian military... eh, this is ugly politics. Why be a communist? Get on the winning side!"

I won't deny my asshole is drawing tight, a little electric shiver going up my spine. A witness? How long before the tabloids get it right? How long before Cyclops is on my trail again, or some guy in jack boots knocking on my hotel door?

Little bit of a breeze as Barasso's plane comes in, enough to make it drift sideways, look awkward. Junkers Ju 54 trimotor, Brazilian green. Aeros Condor flight from Florianopolis. Surprised to see Edler disembark with Barasso and the mechanic. He's wearing combat fatigues, no jacket, shirt sleeves rolled up for the heat. Kit bag over his shoulder. Barasso and Bertuzzi are wearing suits. As they confer with Dani, I exchange greetings with Edler.

"*Was für eine Uberraschung!*" I say, shaking his hand. "How goes it, Edler?"

He smiles his crooked smile, says, "Better than last time, Thorsen... see?"

He points at the insignia on his collar, the two lightning bolts on one side, and—significantly—the three diamonds on the other.

"I've been reinstated," he says. "*Obersturmfuhrer*, no less!"

"First lieutenant?" I say. "How come?"

"I have to thank you, *mein Freund...* von Schellenberg's death is my good fortune. The command chain was weakened, so now they had to reinstate me. Voss is now Captain."

"He's in charge of your squad?"

"Things change fast in the Third Reich. Can't you feel it?"

Again, that cynicism. Edler is no believer. Right now he's along for the ride.

"So, why aren't you with your squad?" I say.

Again, the smile that makes women weak, pisses men off.

"Why, I am here to liaise... the squad will be following in a few days. Then we go to the Amazon, ja?"

Before Barasso drives off with Eddie, he takes me aside, says, "Stay close to Dani, make sure she doesn't get hassled, o.k.?"

I nod.

"And amuse Lieutenant Edler. He's a different sort of German. I think he can be useful to us."

He looks towards the city, says, "Paulo... you never know what the weather will be. Not like Rio. Here you can have four seasons in one day."

"You're going to the clinic?" I say.

"Did you see her? What was your impression?"

"She's strong. But... well, hell, what do I know about malaria?"

"Malaria is a fucking vampire, Thorsen. It's sucking the life out of Brazil. I mean to do something about it."

It's funny, though. Whenever he drives off with Eddie, that Mercedes looks like a bloody big mosquito. Don't know why, because it's a nice car, a comfortable car, a safe car, but that's what it looks like, bug eyes and all.

Doesn't take long to get the Fiat installed in a hangar and leave Bertuzzi to get on with his trade. Yeah, he'd rather be at the horse races, but he has to look after "the wife", right? He loves that plane. It's amazing how a machine can get a hold on a person. Perhaps it's Dani. Perhaps it's the package, the woman and her machine, like she's some sort of modern warrior princess and he's her squire. He's not married. You couldn't have a job like his and expect to have a family. Not now, anyway. The only time I talked with him at length was at Eden over a game of horseshoes behind the bunkhouse. He's been around. Ethiopia? He's been there. Mussolini? Got his vote. Italy is now the Land of the New Man, the Land of the Airmen. Italian aircraft rule the world. Old Rome is rising once again. Just give me some vino primitivo and some smokes signor and I'll fly anywhere. Just don't put me in one of those German gasbags. *Salut!*

Of course he's heard of the Martinelli Building, and what's more he's been up it, and we should check it out as Italians also know how to build a real tower. Pisa? Forget that. Old man Martinelli was a stone mason from the old country and personally got involved in the construction, laid a few stones himself. Might be a millionaire shipping mogul now and all that but he wasn't afraid to get his hands dirty. See the Martinelli Building, sure, take the elevator to the top, see Sao Paulo as an Italian count sees it. His pad is up there, he might invite you in. Salut!

Good idea. I don't mind seeing the city and Edler has no objections. Dani seems keen, so we grab a taxi from the front of the terminal.

"*Centro*," says Dani. "*Edifico Martinelli.*"

Taxi is a fairly new Ford humpback, a 37 or 38 model. No offence intended but the cabbie is so black he looks like he just escaped from the plantation. Says he's originally from up north, Salvador, or, if you want the whole mouthful, "the city of the Holy Saviour and the Bay of All Saints".

"You can't make any molucca in that place," he says, waving his hands. "Nobody works, it's a carnival every day."

When we get away from the agriculture and embrace the concrete, it's crazy. Loads of construction, rock drills and jack hammers and trucks backing across the street without warning. Everybody's got a car or a motorcycle or a bike or a horse, even if the horse has no saddle and fears for its life. It's crazy. Sidewalks are loaded with people, all sizes, all colors. The word is 'cosmopolitan'.

"You must drive a lot of different people," I say. "Nationalities, I mean."

"I do," says the cabbie. "I see them all."

He sighs, as if it's all a drag.

"Who's the worst?" I say. "Who are the real bastards?"

He shrugs, shifts gear.

"The French?" I say. "You drive them?"

"Not many, sir."

"How about the Anglos?"

"The English? They can be arrogant. They have an empire, so they be arrogant."

"What about the Germans—they arrogant?"

"Lately, yes."

"Americans?"

"Ah, you never know with them. The worst and the best. I hope you're not American, sir."

"No, I'm just a bastard from nowhere in particular."

My companions laugh, although Dani is puzzled, almost perturbed. She says, "You need to calm down, child. Be more *tropicalismo*."

"You mean, like these crazy people? Worse than New York!"

"Eh, Paulo takes a while. You have to learn it, like you learn to speak, to walk, to fly."

That puts me in my place. Can only do two on the list.

Most of the buildings are about five stories or less.

Edler points to a low gothic, says, "The German Embassy?"

Dani almost cackles. "That's the Saint Bento Monastery!"

Lots of billboards... Italian magnesium tablets, American Life Saver candies, American movies, Portuguese olives, German photo film... piles of newspapers and magazines on rude tables or stacked on the sidewalk... legions of men wearing fedoras, women with flashy earrings and business suits. It's wild. Here's a man with a herd of goats, selling milk as you ask for it. A man selling multi-lingual parrots. Machines digging holes, black men swinging sledge hammers. Open face emporiums and cafes. Cops patrolling in pairs. Elevated streets and sunken gardens and the confusing smell of petroleum fumes and exotic cooking. It's wild, yeah.

The Martinelli is built like a four hundred foot wafer. Looks new, looks old... everything's a rectangle... windows, floors, even the tiles. Granite, lots of marble, ceramics, crystal... buttresses, terraces and above the penthouse, a Coca Cola sign. Batman could have a suite there. No big deal in New York or Chicago, but definitely quality class here or there. As we come off the street I notice it has a movie theatre, Cine Rosario, and a swank kip joint called Hotel Sao Bento, like the monastery. We ride the elevator to the top or near the top, find the public terrace has a few tourists taking the view... although the view isn't the first thing I notice.

There's an anti-aircraft gun on a small terrace behind and above us. Sandbags. Can't see if it has an on-duty battery crew or not. Edler notices it, looks at me and nods.

As for the rest, well it's great... but I've seen it better when we were coming in to land the other day.

Someone recognizes Dani, even though she's wearing shades and a floppy hat. A young girl, maybe eleven or twelve years old. Asks for an autograph, and Dani obliges. While this is going on I notice two men leaning on the parapet deep in conversation, far end of the terrace, forty or fifty feet away. One of them is Captain Vaticano. He's wearing a charcoal suit and one of those brimmed priest hats. That's no surprise, really. The big shocker is the other man in the white linen suit: Colonel Powell.

I know instinctively Powell shouldn't see me, so I use Edler as a blind. Thinking, what the hell business has Powell got going with this creep Vaticano a.k.a. Credo? Was the assassination of Campos and his colleagues a US operation? Men like these don't meet in places like this for the view. Powell slips him an envelope. A payoff? Information? Or the recipe for his granny's apple pie....

Then, of course, the US might be trying to sell the Brazilians some new fighters and the Colonel is just trying to grease the skids. Fair enough, and certainly not as heinous as commissioning the shooting down of a civilian passenger plane. Whatever it is, it smells. It smells because Credo is a killer. He's not a soldier who kills but a killer who soldiers. Line of duty? Dirty politics?

When I boarded that ship in New York months ago I figured I knew most of what I needed to know. But, y'know, I was just one young naive sonofabitch.

The kid's mother has a box camera, wants to take Dani's picture. Dani's right into it, playing the good natured star. The lady takes a photo and then Dani suggests I join her for another, removes her hat and sun glasses, puts her arm around me. When the lady gets that she's emboldened enough to ask if Edler would take one of her and her daughter with the famous aviatrix, and sure, why not?

By now I notice Colonel Powell has departed. Hope to God he didn't see me. Doesn't matter about Vaticano. He has his back to us right now, looking towards the blue domes of the Metropolitan Cathedral. There's a sizable crowd gathering on the steps and the concourse between the palms. Could be something, could be nothing.

Chapter Forty-Three:

VATICANO, THE CROSS OF FIRE

"TENSION WITHOUT COSMIC PULSATION is the transition to nothingness."
Spengler. Amazing what I can get out of this book despite the hole cut
through the pages to make it into a gun case. Whole sentences, sentence
fragments, and sentences that have disappeared. It's like life: you see a
little, imagine a lot, know you're just something stuck between nothing
and nothing.

Sitting by the window in my hotel room. See that priest come
into the ruined yard behind the chapel, light up a cigarette, assume his
position at the wall, start reading his book, whatever it is. A humming
bird buzzes him, hovers provocatively, then zooms away. Priest pays it
no heed, just sticks to his reading, now and then taking a drag on his fag
without taking his eyes off the page.

Little does he know there's a small suitcase jammed with dough
hidden not far away.

Tap on the door joining my room to Dani's. Opens, and she sticks
her head in, says, "I'm going to take a nap... mind if I use your bed? I just
can't relax in my room for some reason. Too much sun."

"Close the blinds."

"Makes no difference. You're meeting Eddie anyway, aren't you?"

"Right now."

"It's crazy but I get the feeling some reporter is going to burst in on
me. It happens."

"Hey no problem, Dani. I understand. Probably a wise idea."

She comes in and lies down on the bed. Shimmies to get comfortable.

"You're a considerate man. You're not greedy and arrogant."

"Thank you."

"You've been influenced by a woman. Your mother?"

"Maybe."

"You're not married?"

"Would I be here if I was?"

"No, probably not. You trust that German?"

"You mean Edler? No reason not to."

"I find his appearance strange."

"He's doing business for his unit. Right now he's at the German Consulate, getting some money for his men. They have to eat, you know. Other stuff too, like renewing visas... like picking up mail from Berlin. Stuff, Dani. They're breaking camp in Eden, will be here soon."

"You like him? He made a pass at me."

I grunt, say, "Sure... he's a ladies man. That's why he got sent here."

"Oh? Whose heart did he break?"

"How would I know? Anyway, they demoted him and banished him to Brazil. Now he's been reinstated and everything's copacetic. He's got a problem with discipline, is all. Doesn't give a shit."

"I know. The hunger that is never satisfied."

"You get proposals from strangers all the time, don't you?"

"Proposals in the mail, propositions at the bar."

"Gonna go for it? *Obersturmfuhrer* Edler?"

She emits a low, scornful groan, says, "I don't give a damn about men and romance. All I care about is flying."

"Is that so... once upon a time you must've used a man or two to get what you want. All women do, if they can."

"Men and women... women and men. It's simple. A good mother will have a good son... and a good son will honour a good mother."

Amusing. I say, "This a catholic proverb? The nuns teach you this in Sunday School?"

"My father. He wanted a boy, so he insisted I was a boy."

Look into the yard. The priest is still at it, book raised, eyes glued. Can hear music coming in drifts, horns, cymbals, drums. Marching band, probably practicing for the Cinco de Mayo or whatever the next holiday is.

I say, "Who was your father?"

But she's asleep... or pretending to be.

Naturally, the Brazilian P 12 pilots are all interested in the Fiat and give it close attention, although they give Dani even closer attention. Old news now but she was the first female to fly solo from Paulo to Rio, and from Rio to Recife, then on to Belem at the mouth of the Amazon. Her flight up the Amazon to Manaus in '34 earned her a gold medal, presented by the famous Brazilian aviator Santos-Dumont just before he committed suicide (if it was suicide, not murder). Yes, she's done a few things. Better pilots out there maybe but she's got chops. To some extent she's out of the public eye, as these sort of publicity flights to faraway places have become common. "These days I'm just a taxi driver with a fancy aeroplane," she says, meaning her gig with Sigma. But these guys know who she is and she doesn't mind playing to them, I notice.

Basic instinct. Sell me, sell the plane.

We're clustered around the plane in front of the hangar. Suddenly there's a roar and we all look up. It's a monoplane approaching fast from the North. The roar is incredible as it banks, dives, then goes into a steep climb above us. Keeps on going until it rolls over onto its back at 12 o'clock high, swoops down towards us as it finishes the loop, then passes overhead with a raw ghost whistle. Brutal. Like storm rain on the face.

"What the fugg is that?" I say.

"Bad news," says Bertuzzi, the mechanic.

"What is it?" I say. "You seen one before?"

"I've seen it," he says. "Spain. You want to know what it is? It's Adolf Hitler, is what it is."

Saw the German cross, sure, but the event was so fast, it was just a smear. He's landing now, the retractable undercarriage unfolding like paddles, the big engine crackling as it down throttles. Gray blue underbelly, sand coffee everywhere else. Black markings. Small swastika on the fin. Touches down, taxies over the grass to our location, parks maybe a hundred feet away, part of the party, sure, but hanging back like an uninvited guest who just dropped over the garden wall.

As the cockpit canopy pops, flips to the right, I see Edler ambling over. He raises his hand in that half-assed Waffen SS salute. Obviously none of this is a surprise to him. The pilot is unbuckling.

Several Brazilian officers are heading that way. Others remain back, gawking and bemused.

I say to Bertuzzi, "How fast is it?"

He waves his hands in defeat, says tragically, "Twice as fast... twice everything. Twice the climb, twice the range... with a drop tank, it can fly a thousand kilometers... twelve hundred, maybe more... our little princess, eight hundred, tops."

"It's a Heinkel," I say. "I've heard of these. Four hundred k flatline."

"No no," says Bertuzzi. "The model is Messerschmitt... a 109. They call it 'The Knife'. What I wanna know is, how is it here?"

Dani's standing in her flying suit, hands on her hips, elbows out, what the hell. Upstaged but not fazed.

"You know anything about this?" I say.

"It's a racer," she says. "Long nose, three blade propeller, small wings, small tail. Did it fly from Europe? Impossible."

"Got guns," I say. "See? In the wings."

"Is that your friend Edler greeting the pilot? I told you he was up to something."

Turns out Edler knew nothing. Says he was only told about it when he went to the Consulate late yesterday. *Campo de Marte*, 11 am. Be there, arrange for the refuelling and whatever else Hauptmann Kessler might need. The Messerschmitt was freighted to Rio and is being flown to Buenos Aires to take part in an air race at the Rio de la Plata. Just why it wasn't shipped directly to Aires isn't known, although Barasso has his ideas.

"They're trying to sell it," he says. "This is a publicity run. Or some *filho da puta* is trying to piss me off."

He's chewing an unlit cigar.

Captain Vaticano has another opinion. "It's a toy," he says. "There's a race at San Isidro next weekend. The Germans want to show the world how fast their new planes are. It's fast, we can see that. But how does it handle? Low wings have no lift, and they can't do tight turns. Believe me, for combat you can't beat a biplane. And that undercarriage... do you trust that? It's like a folding table... eh, sooner or later you're eating the dirt!"

He's got a big sheet of paper spread on the lower wing of the Fiat, is diagramming some moves to Dani. He seems perfectly normal. Maybe we have him pegged wrong.

I say to Bertuzzi, "In Spain, which plane was best?"
Bertuzzi says swiftly, "The CR 32! No plane had more kills, more victories!"

I say, "The 109 can't turn, right?"

Bertuzzi looks sad, says, "You think so? It has slats on the forward edge of the wings... they open, give more lift. Clever, eh? I tell you, that aeroplane is very clever. Don't be fooled."

He lowers his voice to a whisper, says, "The biplane is yesterday. That ugly creature is tomorrow."

Sounds like he's talking about a woman. Got to have a closer look, so I wander over. They're already gassing her up. Notice the pilot has an oxygen mask hinged to his chest harness. Blond guy, thirty something. Handsome... I guess. Has the aryan look... I guess. Catches my eye briefly like he recognizes a member of the cult. He's listening politely to a couple of Brazilian fliers as some guy in a suit translates. Consulate diplomat. Sidle up to Edler, say in German, "Germany's secret weapon, eh?"

Edler grins, says, "He's flying to Buenos Aires."

"Who is he?"

"Captain Kessler. A pet of Ernst Udet. Udet's in charge of technical development for the Luftwaffe... under Milch, of course. People I have no cause to mingle with... except today."

"Is this plane any good?"

"I have no idea, Thorsen. Why don't you ask Kessler yourself?"

Edler waits for a pause in the conversation, then calls to Kessler, says, "*Kapitan... sagen hallo zu meinem Freund von Sigma!*"

Kessler steps forward. We shake. The diplomat watches, fake smile in place.

"What's this... Sigma?" says Kessler.

"Sigma is like Condor," says Edler. "Lieutenant Thorsen is coming with us to the Amazon."

"Yes?" says Kessler. "The 109 needs some tropical trials... high temperature, high humidity. It's a different game. Wish I could join you."

"Why not?" says Edler. "I'm sure RLM would approve."

"Beautiful aircraft," I say. "Would you let a woman fly it?"

A few uncertain laughs.

"Not today," says Kessler. "There is a woman who flies?"

I wave to Dani but she's in conference with Vaticano. Kessler gallantly suggests we walk over to the hangar, even though he's dragging his parachute gear. He looks at his watch, says something to the diplomat, unbuckles his chute, dumps it on the wing. He hasn't much time, but he always has time for a woman.

Dani seems shy. She's met a lot of airmen but it's like she senses this guy is special.

I introduce them.

Maybe he's lying but Kessler says, "Danielle d'Anza? Yes, I have heard of you. This is your plane?"

"Yes," says Dani. "Are you familiar with it?"

"Superb aircraft," says Kessler. "Possibly the best biplane ever made. In a spin there's nothing like it. Very forgiving."

The Brazilians exchange looks. Bertuzzi smiles.

Dani nods towards the 109, says, "What's that? A racer?"

Kessler says, "Not specifically... it's an interceptor, just like the Fiat. A Messer 109. Would you like to fly it?"

Dani smiles, says, "Given the opportunity, yes I would."

Kessler says, "I will see if it can be arranged. Who knows? I might return this way soon."

Vaticano steps forward, says, "Hauptmann Kessler, you took part in the Spanish conflict. Fifteen kills, I believe. And several probables."

Kessler nods, says, "You were there?"

Vaticano says, "Yes. I am Credo."

Kessler is impressed. "Credo? You are Credo? The Cross of Fire? The Republicans had a bounty on your head."

Vaticano seems uncomfortable. "Some atheists, possibly."

Kessler says, "Naturally. The Catholic Church is fascist."

Vaticano says, "The true church, yes. There are some dreamers who think it can be socialist. You, sir—you believe?"

Kessler makes light of this, laughs. "I am a German, my dear Credo. I am a technocrat. I believe in algebra and brandy."

Vaticano laughs politely, says, "We are waiting for General Locusto. You should meet him, *Kapitan*."

Kessler says, "Generals I can meet any time. But an elegant aviator like *Fraulein* Danielle... my mission is complete."

Right... this makes my eyes go slitwise and my nostrils flare.

Dani says, "Why don't you stay for the show?"

The diplomat signals Kessler by tapping the dial of his watch.

Kessler looks around the group, says, "Perhaps I will have an occasion to visit with you again. I see my plane has been refueled, so now I must continue my journey to Argentina. *Auf Wiedersehen*!"

Edler and the dip in the suit guide him back to the Messer, where he does a quick visual inspection, locks on his parachute harness, climbs back into the cockpit. Fast, no messing around. Electric ignition—a few whirrs and the engine coughs, then kicks in and away he goes. What does it take to get airborne? Less than three hundred feet and he's gone. No showboat flyby, no collegial salute. In less than a minute he's a dot in the southern sky.

Auf Wiedersehen!

Now Edler tells me what Kessler told him all about 'Credo' during their walk back to the Messer. That Credo was responsible for some of the worst atrocities against civilians during the Civil War as part of the Nationalist intimidation and pacification strategy. Blitzkrieg? He was Deathkrieg. "He calls himself an observer," said Kessler. "Nonsense. He planned and participated in many bombings and strafings of villages. Esprit de Corps? Honest combat? This man is no gentleman. And he's no officer in the sense that we in Luftwaffe understand it. He's a killer. Just how he gets away with calling himself a priest is beyond me. The rumor was around that he was a member of a Catholic cult called The Cross of Fire and perhaps this had something to do with the way he could carry on. You tell the charming Danielle to watch out for this man—certainly do not use him for confession!"

Well, no surprise. This just reinforces what we already know. The only thing we don't know is who exactly is he working for... if it matters. Barasso is extremely pissed off. He's been cooling his heels waiting for the General in the hangar office. Apparently the General has been held up at the casino, where he likes to take breakfast most mornings when in Sao Paulo. And now a phone call comes in telling Barasso that there's an emergency at his coffee plantation some twenty miles west of the city, a place called San Mateus just off the old Bandeirantes slave trail. Manager says several service buildings are on fire, including the main shipping barn. Looks like arson. Looks like part of a coordinated plan to mess up Barasso's dreams, although who knows, could be some unhappy worker with a box of matches and a few tar balls.

"Eddie," says Barasso. "Take the car, go to the *fazenda*, see what the hell is happening. Take Thorsen with you."

"What about you, boss?" says Eddie, jangling the car keys.

"I'll stay here. Phone when you know the situation. I'll be here or at the clinic."

I want to let Dani know I'm leaving for a while but that look on Barasso's face says it: *Vamos!*

We're driving around the perimeter road when we see the Boeing P 12s roll onto the field and take off in pairs. They're not sticking around for the show. They must know something we don't, like, the General ain't coming. Alert Eddie. He ducks down 'til his head is kissing the steering wheel so's he can see past me. Grunts. Planes are heading south. Guess they're stationed somewhere towards Minas.

Heading northwest more or less through plantation country, large hilly fields of coffee bushes in sweeping geometric rows, swerving with the rises and dips. See Barasso's fedora and a bottle of brandy on the back seat, reach back, try on the hat for size. Sits a bit low—guess the boss has a bigger head. Pop the cork on the brandy, offer Eddie a swig. Couple of shots each and we're ready for whatever.

I say, "What sort of coffee they growing?"

"Arabica. Nobody grows more, nobody grows better."

"When's the harvest?"

"Soon... June. Is beautiful here when they flower... like snow, *mano*."

384

"How many *fazendas* has Barasso got?"

"Ten... fifteen... twenty, who knows. He has partners."

"So what do you think the problem is at Mateus? Arson?"

"Yeah, probably. Things are getting crazy. Who do you trust?"

He's got that right. Traffic is lazy. The odd truck, car, horse, donkey... *campones*, some sitting in the ditch, chewing grass, spitting tobacco, wondering what the hell. Times like this I get the feeling things aren't real. One minute I'm in the high life, next I'm travelling into flames.

"Eddie," I say. "From what I've seen, this country is controlled disorder. At best."

"Eh... like I say, who do you trust?"

"Everyone is trying to cut a deal with the Devil."

"Yeah..."

"What if Leonora dies?"

Eddie scoffs, says, "No way. That medicine, that juju you bring, it's the ticket. She look better already."

"Really?"

"The *Senhora* will be going home soon. So... Danielle... *panfleto bebe*... she's your new girlfriend?"

"Nah... you know she's the boss's mistress."

"People like to think... but Eduardo, he think no. She's a lesbian who fool men."

"You're guessing, man."

"Yeah? You know different? You 'ave your hot tongue in her cold mouth, *senhor*?"

We turn onto a dirt road, pass through a grove of old trees full of roosting yellow tail warblers.

"Is that smoke?" I say. "How much further?"

"Not far... a kilometer, maybe two. I haven't been here for a year."

Road levels off, rolls through rolling fields.

Eddie says, "That hat look good on you... you look like that gringo movie man... what is his name?"

"Humphrey Bogart?"

Large shadow crosses over us like someone just dumped a big bucket of black paint. Then we're raked by a machine gun burst, the bullets shredding the tires and port running board, tosses us into the ditch. Just glimpse the biplane pass over before I'm pulling bits of the windshield off my face. Eddie's hanging out of his side moaning, the door exploded from the crash. Can I move? Yes. Can you believe it? The fedora's still in place, chunks of glass falling from the brim. Boost myself out of the wreck, crawl into the ditch as I hear the plane circling back for another run.

Can see it. Sonofabitch P 12 coming low and slow like it's dusting a crop. Shout at Eddie to get clear but the plane's already spittin' fire and lead, like a welder trying to seal us into a steel coffin. Can feel the downdraft as he passes over with the dirty snarl that I'm getting to know too damn well. Pull myself onto the road, crawl around to Eddie but he's gone, almost cut in two. Real grotesque the way he's hanging upside down, feet caught in the car pedals, head almost bouncing on the dirt, face to the sky, eyes wide open.

Plane's coming back. I know who it is... you know, we know, everyone in hell knows. Stumble to the trunk, drag it open, recover my rifle, roll back into the ditch, try to get a bead on him but he's already strafing... short burst, long burst, a pattern like he's mocking me in Morse code. I'm eating dirt as the bullets tear up sod like the ripping roots of a falling tree and thunk into the soft shoulder of the ditch. Roll over as he passes, see his head pivoting above the cockpit as he tries to see what's left to do, mission accomplished or what. I get off three, four rounds but he's already out of range.

Look around, try to see if there's a better place to be. He's climbing but he's not going away. This time he uses a diving attack, which doesn't leave much cover in the ditch. So I run and weave, head for some trees. Wish I had another clip. He's dropping straight at me, firing like he's drilling a hole. By the time I get into the trees he's so close to the ground I figure he'll never pull up in time... but of course he does and I just can't get a good, clear easy bead on him. He starts cruising the strip, looking for me. Good. He's level, and I might get him. He tries pitching back and forth, wings left, wings right, looking for me. Still have the fedora on and I'm wondering if he thinks I'm Barasso. After all, what am I to the Brazilian military? The government?

Interesting development. Another aircraft appears, one I know very well. Dani's yellow Fiat CR 32. Credo sees her too as he turns away to escape as she closes. He climbs, and she follows. At the top of his loop he stalls and goes into a flat spin, tries to catch her from behind. But the Fiat is too fast and powerful, just banks out of the climb and pulls into a wall circle. Credo follows but as the circle gets tighter, the wall steeper, finds he is too slow and becomes the prey. Dani opens up with a deflection shot which catches the lower wing and the engine. He's done. His motor dies in a dirty flood of smoke and his plane drops.

Yet the arrogant bastard has the nerve to try and save himself from the 'cross of fire'. As his plane goes down, he bails, deploys his chute. By the time his plane hits the ground and explodes, he's drifting towards my position like a dandelion husk. Floss... nice but fragile. Wait till he's close enough to see me. One bullet, that's all. One bullet for Eddie and everyone else.

The Fiat lands on the road. Turns out Barasso is with Dani. Meet them running towards the Mercedes wreck.

"Eddie?" says Barasso.

I shake my head.

Barasso bites his knuckle, groans, "*Ahh! En nome de Deus!*"

Dani steps forward, touches my face. "You o.k., Thorsen? What happened?"

"Ambushed," I say. "We'd no idea. Eddie was driving."

Barasso stares at the car, then at the burning aircraft in the field.

"They were after me," he says. "Vaticano is their assassin."

"Was," I say.

"What?" says Dani. "We saw him bail out."

"Yeah, he bailed," I say. "But he's D.O.A."

Barasso's jaw is clicking. Seems to have recovered. "Alright, what's done is done," he says. "Let's deal with this mess."

Voce Sao Paulo (Voice of Sao Paulo) The body found early morning on Rua Líbero Badaró behind the Martinelli Building has been identified as that of Captain Demetrius Vaticano of the 2nd Aviation Regiment's Pursuit Squadron, Sao Paulo. Police say the poor condition of the body suggests that he fell from the observation terrace on the 31st floor. Suicide has not been ruled out.

Captain Vaticano, who was also an ordained priest, has been described as the leading Brazilian combat ace. He flew missions in both the Chaco War and the Spanish Civil war, seconded to Paraguay and then to the Nationalist forces in Spain under General Franco.

Major General Locusto who leads the 2nd Aviation Regiment says he is both shocked and saddened by the news of Vaticano's death. "Captain Vaticano is a true hero and will not be forgotten by his comrades or the people of Brazil. Credo was a personal friend of mine. There are stories to tell, but now is not the time. Our motto is *per ardua ad astra* (through adversity to the stars). His soul is now with God."

Avante Oeste! (Onwards West) (banned but distributed by street volunteers) People, do not be fooled by the propaganda statements of the authorities concerning the death of Captain Demetrius Vaticano, who is known as "Credo" to his buddies and his victims alike. He death is not a suicide. He was shot and his body dumped from the roof of the Martinelli Building, that hateful symbol of Brazilian Corporatism.

Rejoice, people. The execution of this fascist is a small recompense for his involvement in the murder of comrade Campos.

We have not finished. There will be more justice.

O Estado do Sao Paulo (the State of Sao Paulo) The story of Captain Vaticano becomes more like a detective novel conspiracy every day. First we are told he fell from the top of the Martinelli Building, possibly as a suicide. Then we are told that he was pushed, that his death is murder. Further to this, it is now said that he was shot through the heart.

As if this isn't enough, there is a suspicion that he didn't fall from the Martinelli at all, that he was killed at another location, and his body was then ejected from an aircraft over downtown Sao Paulo. A witness or witnesses claim to have seen or heard a low flying aircraft flying down the Rua Libero Badaró around 2 am on the morning the body was found.

This much is known. Captain Vaticano and his squadron flew out of the Campo de Marte aerodrome on the 26th just after noon. Sometime during the short flight to their field south of the city, Captain Vaticano and his aircraft disappeared.

Now there are suggestions that Vaticano was the person who shot down the Gaucho Aviation plane carrying the popular labour leader Tony Campos home from his exile in the Argentine. Proponents of this view say Vaticano was liquidated to cover the tracks of his handlers, the real perpetrators of this political murder.

Is it little wonder that many people have lost faith in the current government? President Vargas and the Estado Novo promised a new approach to the inequities that plague our beautiful nation, to reconciliate the dreams of the left and the right, the worker and the boss, yet every dawn seems to bring forth another murder that will remain unsolved and fester on the garbage dump of political mysteries that eat the soul of this nation.

JULY... OR MAYBE AUGUST, Amazon Time. This place is so stinking hot and humid, you forget about days of the week, just try to stay away from the sun, the eye of the hunter. The sound of the bugs is constant, like a mower coming and going, except at night when there's a different kind of mowing going on. Telegraphing monkeys, migrating pigs, bulldog bats (fishing), leopard cats on the hunt and the odd toucan with insomnia rasping like he's got a toothache. Sleep? Yeah, you can sleep if you've got a mosquito net and a bayonet below your pillow. Eat or be eaten—Darwin said it.

Right now, where's the sun? Heading down into the forest canopy, so must be four o'clock anyway. The lagoon is changing color. Three river otters on the bank, big buggers, pretty relaxed considering the hungry caiman population that fake dead logs in the roots and reeds... never mind the fresh jaguar pug marks in the mud. Must be those big incisors you can see when the otters yawn... bug-eyed like a Martian, whiskered mouth like a staple gun. They're relaxed, sure, cause they can look after themselves.

Which is more than I can say for some.

Hear the motor, that wanky huh huh that blends in with the bugs like the beat behind Artie Shaw's Beguine. Not that I feel like dancing. Nobody's been dancing since Edler went missing.

Boat comes into view, a shallow bottom that Traven uses to explore the rivers and lagoons looking for rubber tree groves. Traven's an old cholo from Manaus, meaning Indian mother and German father. He speaks the lingo—Tupi, Arawak, Carib... even the thought-magic some of these mumbos use instead of language—and he knows every tributary and pig trail in the area. And the area, brother, is pretty big. When we flew into camp weeks ago on the Zeppelin, the forest was like an ocean. No horizon, just an endless haze of earth and sky. Time without space... or space without time, depending on whether you're on patrol or not, or maybe just lying in your bunk reading the Mexican Bible or writing poems to whores.

Nine millimeter mosquitoes, thirty millimeter ants. Drive you crazy if you don't take precautions, like waxing up with carbolic soap. Traven sells it, makes some nice poker float from the guys.

When I first met Traven, I said to him, "Where's El Dorado?" Wise guy idiot question and he knew it. But he was patient, used to young guys with guns and limited geography. He said, "El Dorado is a man, not a place." What the hell did he mean by that? Anyway, this is why some of us took to calling him 'El Dorado.' He looks it. Somewhere between yellow and brown, stained by the sun and the narcotic coca he's always putting in his coffee. Or maybe it's the whiskey. He looks it. Soaked.

Well, here comes El Dorado, and the otters slip into the water and submerge as he passes, draws into the slough where we're waiting. Red 9 Mauser machine pistol with stock attached hanging from his shoulder. Never leaves home without it. Also keeps a chopped double barrel shotgun handy for close encounters. Like he says, in the jungle, if it isn't close, it doesn't matter.

"Tell me some good news," I say, as I grab his hand, pull him onto the bank.

"Marlene's available," he says. "She got a divorce."

Shake my head, say, "That was two years ago. Don't read the papers from Berlin, they're out of date. Listen to the drums. They tell the truth."

"I can dream, can't I?" he says. "She'll wait for me."

"She's in California... doesn't like Hitler."

"Who?"

"Never mind. Have you found our boy?"

Shakes the sweat from his hat, runs some fingers through what's left of his hair.

"The Nabs have him upstream," says Traven. "You understand how they work? They move around, village to village. Big flood one place, they go another. Game moves, they move. Another tribe comes raiding, they fall back. Kinda nomad, but not really. They follow the sun."

"The sun...?"

"Ja, right now, the sun is north so they go north."

"Cannibals?"

Traven finishes his rollie, puts it in his mouth. I light him.

"Ja."

"They shrink heads?"

"Ja... when they need to."

So these sons of bitches are hard core, no acculturation. Probably wear straw suits and dance off the beat.

"You know where exactly they're holding him?" I say. "A hut? A hole in the ground, a cage in a tree?"

"No, sir. Best I can do is take you boys to the location... rest is up to you."

Got Gomez and one of the Germans with me, a Corporal called Bekker, who doesn't really like taking orders from me, an Irregular, but this is the way we're playing it. He's really here because Voss wants it, wants his own boy in there. Voss is still confused after the von Schellenberg incident, doesn't trust me... at least when it comes to the welfare of the SS. One for all, all for one doesn't work in this situation. Sigma squad doesn't have the blood tattoo.

We get into the boat, first Traven, then us. Gomez has his M 1 rifle plus the latest Telefunken man-pack *Eule* radio, a very nifty portable. Limited range, of course, five to ten miles max but still very nifty cause he can carry it in an ammunition pouch on his belt. Separate pouch for the battery but in all, no big burden. This way we can keep in touch with the Zeppelin or our backup. Been good in our tests. Fully tropicalized, using 38 to 42 Mghz FM frequencies. Radio has come a long way last couple of years. The Stockhausen loop circuit helps. Less solar noise, sensitive enough to raise the dead.

But Gomez complains about the weight, says he's no better than a goddamn mule.

I say, "You know Dick Tracy, the cop in the comics who talks into his wrist watch? Does he complain? This unit is lighter than his, so be thankful."

"I'd rather be packin' extra ammo," he says. "I'm no Dick."

"Be thankful, soldier. You want action, don't you?"

"Yeah."

"We want to find Edler, right?"

Looks at Bekker, then at me. Bekker doesn't speak English, so he doesn't know what we're talking about. But he's got those Master Race snake eyes, so you just never know. Might be a mind reader.

"Big hassle for a dumb Fritz," says Gomez. "Let them die if they wanna."

Not exactly sure how Edler got bagged but he had fallen into the habit of taking long walks in the forest. The thing is, we haven't been farming any of the Nabilat for the drug trials. We've been stitching some of the more docile Indians to the south. Easy. See us coming, think we're gods.

But the Nabilat, they're a different breed.

Nod to Traven, and he starts the motor, and we hunker down, head across the lagoon through the lilies, float grass, and mangrove stilt roots into the varzea. It's an unbelievable maze, dense with reflection and fatal objects, so it's like navigating over a mirror of death. But old El Dorado, he knows where he's going, even if we don't.

Week ago or so I was with Edler on the veranda, having a smoke, watching some workers stacking drums of fresh tree gum on the dock for shipment down river. Raw rubber latex. Used to be big money in it, been slow for a while, but lately the price has been going up because of renewed demand. War? Everybody is rearming, it seems.

Edler says, "Amazing country, isn't it? Prehistoric."

I say, "Yeah, it's pretty brutal."

"This morning I saw a jaguar kill a caiman. The caiman was lying on the mud and the jaguar just crept up on it and pounced. It was a hellish fight. One of my men wanted to shoot the cat."

"Yeah? Who was that?"

"Bekker."

"Oh yeah... Bekker. He's *untermenschen*, he is."

Edler appreciates the joke.

"I wanted to see how the fight would turn out," he says.

"What were you guys doing?" I say.

"Mapping... looking for clear channels."

"Waste of time. Next big rain, they'll move someplace else and your maps are shit."

He sighs. "Ja well, orders, Thorsen. I serve a country, you serve a company. There's a difference."

"Is there? I wonder."

"Are you suggesting the SS is a corporate entity of the National Socialists?"

"Looks like it to me. The SS is just a security business."

An old rusty crane is swinging back and forth, lifting the drums onto the stack. But a lot of the real lifting is being done by the coolies. Shit job. Reminds me of back home.

Like he's reading my mind, Edler says, "You're Canadian... what are you doing here?"

"I dunno. What're you doing here?"

"I was sent here."

"So was I."

"Yes... but I had no choice. Did you?"

"Maybe."

"Ach, no one comes here by choice."

Then he gets to the meat and potatoes, says, "That day I went to the consulate in Sao Paulo... remember? I met a man, supposed to be a trade commissioner, but he was really an Abwehr agent. I was waiting for some instructions when he came into the office for a glass of water, started talking to me, you know, the usual stuff. I told him I'd just come from Santa Catarina, and he became very interested, asked me if there were any Canadian radio operators with the Brazilian irregulars."

My heart starts thumping, no lie.

Edler continues: "Well yes, I said. There was a Canadian who deserted. We think he went to Montevideo."

"McDonald," I say.

"Was that his name? Anyway, the description sounded more like you. Nordic, fluent German, armed and dangerous."

"Could be me, sure. But is it?"

"Of course not... that fellow went to Montevideo. But you can see how someone could be confused, ja?"

"Ja."

"Amazing story. A Canadian recruited by the Abwehr to set up a radio network who turns out to be a doppelgänger working for British Intelligence."

"Canadian, wouldn't it be?"

"British Intelligence, he said. Because of this Canadian, an Abwehr agent was compromised, ended up in prison."

"The Black Cathedral."

"What was his name? Anton Vanderzalm, wasn't it? He died."

"Tortured. He was a paedophile."

"Ah, you know all about this. Who told you—McDonald?"

"Anton Vanderzalm's code name was 'Alfredo'... sometimes 'Lisboa'. He was supposed to be setting up a radio network to enable the different German cultural associations to stay in touch, mainly in Brazil, but also with the rest of South America, with plans to expand into North America."

He laughs, says, "German culture clubs... who would believe that?"

"No one, Edler. Private ownership of a transceiver in Brazil is illegal."

"So it was an Abwehr spying operation. Are you a spy?"

We're at the point in the conversation where I either have to trust him or shoot him.

"I'm a sucker," I say. "I came here believing it was legit, ended up as a sucker."

"You don't strike me as naive, Thorsen... sorry."

"You know what a canary is? A canary is a bird who lives in a coal mine. I'm a canary."

He nods, says, "I get it. A tourist could be a canary... anyone. I could be a canary. But tell me, how did you end up with Sigma?"

I tell him. Looking for work, found it, here I am.

"Here you are indeed... armed and dangerous. I should have you arrested, Thorsen."

"This is Brazil, Edler. The Waffen SS is here by invitation. And I'm under the protection of Colonel Barasso."

Edler makes a dismissive gesture, says, "I really don't give a damn. The Abwehr are just a bunch of trouble makers. They spy on us too, you know."

"Yeah, and you spy on them... the Gestapo, isn't it?"

"Gestapo, ja. Specifically SiPo... the Security Police. You wouldn't believe what's going on in Berlin. The Nazis reorganized everything after creating their own cadres. Major von Schellenberg was SiPo."

"So why was he doing favors for the Abwehr?"

"I don't know. Why were you doing favors for the British?"

"Was I? I thought it was the Germans."

Edler laughs. "What a mess! Confess, *mein Freund*—it was a woman who got you into this."

"No, it was a Nazi called Klaus Gerwing. In jail now, but it was him."

"Nonsense. It was a woman. It's always a woman. Tell me, which do you prefer? German or Brazilian?"

"Right now I'd take the first one who comes up those steps, no difference."

Edler takes a swing at a mosquito as he laughs, looks at his palm. No blood, no luck.

"What about Danielle the aviatrix? She likes you."

"Lesbian."

"I don't believe it, sir. That's very unworthy of you. She's a woman of remarkable character."

"You don't take a remarkable character to bed, Edler."

"You think not? It's all fantasy. You enter a woman through her eyes, not a hole in her body."

He's a poet, I think. Told me his story once, yet how he ended up in the military is beyond me.

"Has Voss said anything about why exactly we're here?" I say.

"You think kidnapping Indians for medical experiments isn't enough? Why—has Colonel Barasso told you something?"

"No. But face it, they don't need us to grab some Indians."

"It's training. Counter-insurgency, jungle acclimatization... punishment for assholes. Christ how I hate it here!"

"What about the others—they feel the same?"

"They love it, the fools. *Sieg heil!*"

"What about *Kapitan* Voss?"

"He's o.k. Does his duty for the Fatherland. But he should be in the Wehrmacht, not the SS. He has the discipline but lacks the nihilism. I know where all this is headed, Thorsen. I've seen it."

Alluding to his concentration camp duty, I guess. Round 'em up, move 'em out, rawhide. Farming. Farming people, farming culture... farming the meaning of life itself. Himmler.

I say, "Do you know that half the people in Brazil have malaria or will have malaria?"

He says, "What do you expect? It's a shithole."

I say, "It starts with the chills, then you have a temperature way over a hundred... hundred and three, I think... then deliriums. It's not pretty."

He says, "So we will find a cure. Soon there will be a drug for everything. Then we will be normal."

"What's *normal*, Edler?"

He flicks a bug off his sleeve. "What's normal? Normal is when you can walk into a butcher's shop without thinking that could be me hanging up there, then go home and write an essay about The Rights of Man."

Such faith for a cynic! And I'm wondering if he would take the place of an Indian. And those workers, those guys stacking the drums for shipment on the flat bottom steamer. Seem to work day and night, like leaf-cutter ants. How do they do it? Coca leaves? Money? Not like the coast, where they walk around like zombies on holiday. No union, I guess. These coolies work.

Traven cuts the motor and points. Bunch of black vultures doing lazy eights above the forest canopy. Must be something, cause those flying priests don't waste time. We land, we investigate, we find death.

Three mules, two with packs, standing in the gloom, ears twitching from the flies. The lead mule bays timidly as we approach, leaves falling from its mouth as it stops chewing. The muleteer lies on the side of the trail, a short distance away.

"Bolivian," says Traven. Bugs are crawling all over him, but there are no wounds. Bad teeth, animal eyes. Bekker turns the body front and back, then allows it to resume its original position. Checks the pockets. Tobacco, shuck knife, some coins, a small rosary made from dried seeds.

"Know him?" I say.

Traven shakes his head.

"What do you think happened here?" I say.

Traven is kneeling, examining the neck, sees no dart wound or other suspicious marks.

"Maybe a boa got him," says Traven. "I don't know... very strange."

"Heart attack," says Bekker in German. "What else?"

Gomez is checking the mules, says, "Look at these crates... this hombre is a gun runner, hey!"

So he is... or was. We break open a crate, get a big surprise—these are not your basic surplus Enfields or Mausers. These babies have conventional wooden stocks and short barrels, with open bolt blowback action. Machine pistols, or if you prefer, sub-machine guns. We call them Burps.

"German?" I say, looking at Bekker. "Mausers?"

"Nein," he says. "Soviet copies of our Bergmann 28."

"Well these aren't for hunting boar," I say. "You ever seen these before, Traven?"

He shakes his head, looks around to see if we have company.

"These are combat weapons," says Bekker. "See? Round magazine drum, holds 71 rounds. 25 millimeter, same as the Mauser."

"Could he be selling to rubber prospectors? Miners?" I say.

"I've never been offered one," says Traven. "No, prospectors like rifles. Except me."

"The Nabilat?" I say.

"Why?" says Traven. "Unless they're going to war."

Turn to Bekker, say, "They fire singles?"

"Ja, single shots or automatic," he says. "Cheap, reliable, easy. They call them Daddies. Ja, it's a copy."

I'm thinking, what the hell, does this mean the Nabs have gone commie? Or the Bolivians have guerrillas in the neighbourhood? Yet if someone killed this Bolivian, he wasn't after the weapons.

I say to Traven, "How long has this man been dead, y'think?"

"He's already gone through rigor mortis," says Traven. "This be his second day in paradise."

"How far to the Nab village?"

"Three kilometers."

"Was he coming or going?"

Traven's eyes travel the trail, look for hoof marks.

"Coming."

"Does this trail go anywhere else? Could he have been just passing through?"

"Sure. You know, these guns are worth money. A lot of money."

We check the other crates. Three of them have Russian Moison-Nagant 91/30s, the standard Russian military rifle for years and years. Twelve per crate. With the twelve Daddies, this makes forty-eight weapons, enough to start a revolution. Lots of ammo too. Is our discovery pure chance or the inevitable odds of our presence, meaning, if you go looking for trouble with the SS, you find it.

I know I have to radio this in.

Chapter Forty-Five:

KALLINGRAM

IT'S GASPARI, the 3rd Officer on the LZ 131 who tells me about the first raid. The Sigma squad wasn't involved. It was just the SS unit, led by Voss and Edler. Was just a few days after we all arrived in Amazonia. There were heavy rains for a couple of days, then the sun returned and the jungle steamed like the oceans of hell and mosquitoes were everywhere. And those small black-stripe frogs that can kill you if they need to. One nip, that's all it takes, and you swell up like a piece of rotten fruit.

"I don't know how the village was selected. The Captain opened an envelope, gave us the coordinates, and we flew there in less than an hour just before sunset. I supposed they were forwarded from Rio.

"The flight was routine. As it was late before the rains subsided and the cloud dispersed, there were no tricky updrafts pushing from the jungle floor, so it was smooth sailing with good visibility. At times I thought I could see mountains on the horizon. Illusion, of course, as the Andes are at least three or four hundred kilometers away.

"*Salut*, sir. You like this? It's a Negroni, a very popular drink in Italy. Campari—which is good by itself—with equal amounts of gin and vermouth. There should be a slice of orange peel but we don't have any left. Christ, I need this. I'm all tense.

"You know some of these Indians have never had contact with the white man? That's what they say and I believe it. Short stature, look Japanese, except the Japanese wear clothes... and have no tails. I can't believe we evolved from this. I can't.

"We approached at 200 feet. We could see a long straight track through the jungle all the way to the horizon, straight as a surveyor's pencil line on a map. It wasn't an open road, although it was open in places, notably at the big circular space occupied by the huts of the village. I assume it leads to another village or series of villages although I didn't see any other open spaces further along. The symmetry of it all suggests civilization, doesn't it? Perhaps they were civilized once and then forgot it. Their huts are round too, framed with sticks and branches, thatched with some sort of straw. Hunters. Cannibals, although this is limited, as they're not always at war. I talked to some missionaries at Fortalez Maria when we stopped there last week and they claimed cannibalism is now ceremonial, just for special occasions. Special occasions, *merda*!

"Our elevator man did a really nice job of holding the ship steady, I must say. About fifty feet, with only a small drift. Our arrival caused quite a stir, naturally. Many of the women ran into the jungle with their children. The men threw a few spears, fired a few arrows, all futile gestures. Then their stregone came out of his hut wearing a yellow straw suit and a black spirit mask. He was dancing on the red dirt and waving his magic stick at us, shouting spells or something. Had two apprentices with him, wearing the same sort of straw suits. It was quite funny.

"Next thing, one of the Germans shot the witch doctor with his rifle from the open cargo bay. Killed him. The two apprentices dropped to the ground, imitating the witch doctor. Obviously they didn't realize he was dead, thought their prostration was part of the *cerimonia*... pathetic, and futile. The soldiers descended from the ship using a couple of ropes... what do you call it? Discesa in corda doppia we say in Italian. Commando style. All of them... Captain Voss, Lieutenant Edler... most of the squad. Very efficient, very professional. These men are fit, *il mio amico*. I went down too and it nearly killed me.

"Any of the Indians who tried to run away were shot. A couple of huts were burned just for intimidation purposes... or practice, I suppose. After we rounded up twenty or thirty of them, we picked ten of the best, put them in the cargo cage which had been lowered from the ship. As you know, weight considerations are important in flying a Zeppelin and any mistake can be fatal. We dumped some ballast, then winched the cage up up up into the bay. All in all, the mission went without a hitch. Well... *plus minusve*... more or less.

"I took a look around before we left. Unfortunately one or two of our German colleagues took advantage of the situation and forced themselves on the women. For me, it's a breach of discipline, but perhaps not for commando work. It's a pacification technique, I understand that, I was in

Ethiopia... but for me it's nasty and unwarranted. Edler intervened in one situation, fired his pistol as a warning. Sounds absurd, but the girl was quite pretty, and she was allowed to escape. Others weren't so lucky.

"You know the Sergeant? Schmel, I believe. He was looking for treasure. I looked. I didn't see anything worth taking.

"'The strength of a culture is measured by its capacity for violence,' said Il Duce. I saw him once. He came to speak to the cadets at the Academy in Modena. I don't know about Mussolini. When he's good, he's good, certainly. The evidence is clear. He got us an Empire. But... I don't know. Violence in small amounts, fine. Otherwise it's an illness, don't you agree?

"Another Negroni? Yes, let's have another, Lieutenant. The taste makes me think it's just another hot summer day in Bologna. Not too sweet, not too dry. Ah, *la bella vita*!

"You know what I'd like to be? A painter. I was good at it in school. But who can make money at it? It's not easy. This is why I decided to study aeronautics at the *Politecnico di Milano*. Here I am. Want to see the world? Learn to fly.

"Aren't the birds here magnificent? The macaws especially. If it wasn't so fucking hot I could spend my life here painting them. The kingfishers... the blue-eyed orpos... the herons... all of them. God's little beauties in hell.

"I say, Thorsen, have you been to the dispensary yet? Seen the clinic, the lab? It's quite the operation. The people in Rio really must be serious about the work here. There's Belo, the young Brazilian from Copacabana... I think he's an anthropologist. Not certain. He might be here to monitor Dr. Litmus. Litmus is from Dachau, wherever that is. German. A specialist in tropical diseases, knows a lot about chemistry, they say. Chemists... they speak a private language. I wonder what they want these Indians for?"

"Malaria."

"Oh, malaria. I can support that. I expect the drugs are too experimental to test on real people."

He lowers his voice, says, "We were lucky. On the return we realized we had a gas leak, a small hole in one of the lower gas cells. A bullet. Can you imagine? We're not appropriate for these low level missions, I say. Was it a stray from one of the commandos? Or do these Indians have guns? It raises questions, doesn't it? We came close to disaster. I love that ship, I do. But it's not ready for war."

Wasn't expecting this: the hanging sack-nests of the blue-eyed blackbirds, a whole grove of them mixed in with a few bulging wasp nests. I figured it was a herbal drying den, coca leaves or something, until Traven set me straight. They mingle with the wasps for protection from the cowbirds, who like to kill the nestlings and take over the nests, force old blue-eyes to look after their young. Sound familiar? Unholy alliances, slavery, and the fight for survival. I think of Darwin: "Improvise or perish," he said (or something like that).

But for our purposes, it's a good spot to recon the Nabilat village. Bunch of huts set back from the river, smoke from fires and what looks like a big pot cooking away in the communal area.

"Don't suppose Edler's in that pot," I say to Traven, handing him the binoculars.

He chuckles grimly, takes a look. "Cooking Moonflower juice most likely," he says. "They're getting ready for something."

"Moonflower... what's that?" I say.

"Keeps you going for days, don't need no sleep," says Traven.

"A plant?"

"Ja, it's difficult to find. Blooms once a year during a full moon. For the Nabilat, it's sacred. They kill you if they find you stealing from their territory."

"You ever steal it?"

Traven rubs his whiskers, has a foxy look.

"The Germans pay big money for it... you know that, don't you? Dr. Litmus. He buys all he can get. It's almost impossible to find without help."

Very interesting. A chemical that induces insomnia. Yeah, I can see the value in this.

"Is this how Edler got captured?" I say.

Traven is doubtful, says, "Why would he go into the forest alone? He wouldn't know where to look, senhor."

I'm thinking, well he might, as he's a bit of a drug connoisseur by my standards. He might take risks for something like the Moonflower.

The thing is, where are the Nabs holding him?

They got a floating town on one of the tributaries about sixty kilometers from here as the crow flies. Further by boat or canoe, almost impossible by foot. Plasmos. Used to have a lot of Europeans when the rubber boom was big and now they're drifting back, excited by the lure of American money. Started out as a single floating barque moored by the Jesuits and used as a mission, and as time passed, other boats were tied up there and huts built on them, and Plasmos became a trading post. It's actually a set of artificial islands joined by wooden bridges on stilts and docks built on floating *cedrela* logs.

Lot of rough customers there. Everyone's armed and you often hear gunfire. The bars never close. There's a River Police detachment but they're corrupt. You have to be to survive in a place like this.

The water is so silted up it looks like milk coffee, especially after the rains. They got whore houses and would you believe it, a theatre.

This is where I encounter Comrade Kallingram once again. Imagine my surprise when I see a crude poster in the market exhorting people to see 'Penguini, the Master Magician' saw a woman in half at the Majestico. Penguini, he's now calling himself. My gut tells me it's Kallingram and I have to see the show. Word is he's a stand-in for Beniamino Gigli, the Italian tenor who recently knocked 'em dead in Rio. Gigli, alas, has fallen ill and has cancelled. Sounds b.s. to me. Why would he want to sing in this godforsaken hole? Mussolini's favorite singer? I don't think so.

No refunds. See Penguini instead or eat the loss.

Barasso arrives in the afternoon on a white flying boat. Twin engine, looks German, might be American. Some outfit called '*Panair*'. Eight people get off, but he's alone, dressed like Safari Man. Doesn't have the height of the original. Or the aryan look.

Take him to the flat bottom sternwheeler which I rode from the camp with a cargo of rubber that's being transferred to a larger boat for shipment to Manaus. Get him settled in his cabin.

"How's Leonora?" I ask.

"Much better," says Barasso. "In fact, she's working again. She sends a message, says your money is safe."

Obviously she hasn't told him about the suitcase with the cash.

"She's looking after my money," I say smoothly. "Y'know, just in case something happens to me. She has my mother's address."

"Ah," says Barasso. "She asked me to bring you back to Rio with me."

"You going back right away, boss?"

"No no... think I'll get drunk first. Plasmo has so many first rate bars, *sim*?"

We laugh.

He adds, "I'll go with you to the camp, check things out. I want to talk to Dr. Litmus. Everything going o.k.?"

"No problems. No bandits, no accidents."

"*Bom, bom*... our German friends?"

"Fine. They train, they sweat, they swear, sing German songs."

"Our boys?"

"A bit bored, maybe. We're not included in the, um, harvest missions. But they like doing the rubber run to Plasmo. Have a drink, have a woman. So far, so good."

He has a recent Rio newspaper, sees me looking at it. He nods, says, "Go ahead, take it with you, I'm going to have a nap."

"President Vargas still in control?" I say.

"Maybe... it's a mad world, *meu amigo*. Guess what? Hitler has signed a non-aggression pact with Stalin. Can you believe it?"

"That makes no sense."

"Exactly... until you consider what's at stake. They'll divide Poland up between them, that's what they'll do."

The whole European farrago has sorta drifted out of sight, out of mind for me. All these countries, some with names I can't pronounce, let alone tell you exactly where they are. Poland... yeah, I know where it is, have run into a few Polacks back home. My mind tells me it's just a big flat field between Germany and Russia without definite borders.

He reaches for the paper, says, "Here... let me show you something."

A photo of Dani and some guy who looks familiar. Noivado.

"Remember Major Kessler?" says Barasso. "Flew into Campo de Marte with his Messerschmitt 109, spoiled our show? That's him. He and Danielle are engaged to be married."

Engaged... I'm speechless. Shouldn't care but I do. Unfinished business and I don't mean just that suitcase full of dough... which I've already given to Leonora for safe-keeping.

"Actually, she sends her love, Safari Man. And she's another woman who asked me to bring you back to Rio pronto."

I just bet she did. I say, "Didn't this Kessler fellow go back to Germany?"

"Turns out to be a piece of good luck for us," says Barasso. "He's been attached to the Brazilian Command Headquarters as an advisor. Our military have bought some Stukas and are interested in the 109. Sigma can get a piece of the action. Danielle seals the deal."

I just bet. That lady certainly knows how to seal a deal.

Light up a fag, say, "There's a magic show at the Majestic tonight."

Barasso yawns, says, "Thought there was an opera singer. That's what I read on the flight up."

"A man saws women in two. I think we should take it in, boss."

We do. Place is more like a saloon with a stage, so you can eat and drink while you watch the show or ignore it, cause the seats don't always face the front and the customers don't always sit. Very strange crowd. Prospectors, miners, fishermen, sailors, merchants, government agents, bar flies, dwarves, painted women... some Brazilian Marines in uniform... and the weirdest of all, a bunch of Bolivian Coneheads. Name fits.

Indians who practice skull mutilation in their infancy, so they look like aliens from another planet. Hard not to keep staring at them, although there are plenty of other exotics cruising around. Well, who am I to pass judgement? I suppose I look pretty weird too for some of these folks.

Yes, sir. This is my third visit to Plasmos and it never seems normal. No one leaves his machete at the door. Men just piss where they want, as the river is always near.

Lady who runs the Majestico might have been a countess somewhere sometime. Big woman, body like Mae West, face like WC Fields. Has her own box over the stage, which is just a small balcony extending from her office. Now and then she appears, smiles, launches a paper airplane into the crowd. Advertising for the brothel or something.

"How did Eddie's funeral go?" I say.

Barasso's eyes avoid mine, stay on his meal.

"Quietly," he says. "I told his mother, we got a priest, buried him at night."

My piranha sandwich or whatever it is doesn't taste so great. Guess I'm not hungry.

We're interrupted by a Brazilian Marine in uniform. Young guy, short, black hair, white, or vaguely mestizo.

"*Coronel* Barasso?" he says. "*Desculpe a minha intromissao...* I am Captain Furtado of the Pedro."

The Pedro is the Navy gunboat visiting Plasmos.

"*Capitao*," says Barasso. "What can I do for you?"

The Captain smiles, allows his gold tooth to shine. "I have heard so much about you, Colonel. It's indeed fortunate that our channels cross this evening. I am hoping to visit Camp 'M'."

Not sure that Barasso is wild about this idea.

"Instructions from Rio," says Furtado, apologetically. "For our maps, you know."

"Sit down, please," says Barasso. "Would you care for a drink?"

He smiles again, sits, glances at me.

"This is my security chief, Lieutenant Thorsen," says Barasso.

We nod to one another. Furtado looks over his shoulder, snaps his fingers. One of his officers steps forward with a chart.

"If you could suggest a route," says Furtado.

Barasso sighs, says, "Eh, you need a shallow draught to take a boat to Camp M. What do you have? A corvette?"

"All we need are two fathoms, Colonel."

"Four meters? Very dangerous."

Fresh drinks arrive. The Captain raises his glass, says, "Vargas!"

We jerk our drinks, murmur 'Vargas'.

Barasso studies the chart, then traces a possible route with his finger. "This would be the best way," he says.

"This is the route your rubber transports take? We can follow you, *sim*?"

"For half the distance, maybe. The last stretch is impossible for you."

"We will take soundings."

"Don't waste your time, Captain. These channels were surveyed before Camp M. was established. In the early days we travelled overland, used mules. The research station came only after we found a channel deep enough for our boat."

"Hmm. But this forking channel, you say... possibly?"

"Possibly. We don't use it because it's longer and narrow in some places. You need to be vigilant, Captain Furtado. You might find yourself trapped."

The Captain confers with his Lieutenant briefly, then says, "We'll try the last leg by the route you suggest, Colonel. Does this tributary have a name? Our chart has nothing... or has forgotten it."

"The Iso, I think... like the Indians, *sim*?"

"Hmm. The Iso. Are they docile?"

"Far as I know. You have guns, *sim*?"

"Yes, we have guns. You have German army personnel at Camp M.?"

"Indeed. The research station is a joint German-Brazilian project."

"Private, though, isn't it?"

"No, Rio has some investment."

"Malaria, isn't it?"

Barasso nods.

Captain Furtado drains his drink, rises, bows. "You have been most gracious, Colonel. Our visit at Camp M. will be a short one, a mere formality. *Ate mas tarde!*"

He and his officers withdraw to another table.

"He'll never make it," says Barasso. "Sheer lunacy. But, eh, that's our navy for you."

"You think it's an official visit, as he says... or is he just ambitious?"

"Probably both. Eh, maybe he think he can find a passage to the *Rio de la Plata*, do the big circle."

The three piece orchestra strikes up, the way they do when a fight breaks out. But no, the show is starting, Penguini the Magican... who is none other than Kallingram. The brute baby face, the gleaming inky eyes, the hands that grow birds and aces. Same tux, same tricks, except the sawing routine has been changed. Instead of sawing the woman in half and then putting her back together again, he saws her in half and produces, presto, two women! The crowd loves it, goes ape, want more women. Men offer up their wives and whores. He repeats the routine, same woman, same result but declines all volunteers and sacrifices. His models aren't bad, look like local recruits—meaning downriver, Manaus or Belem—although they're kinda coarse compared to the incandescent aryan, Uma.

Notice the Coneheads are particularly impressed.

"I remember him from the ship," says Barasso. "But not the party at our casa in Rio."

"He was dressed as a German officer," I say. "I was introduced to him. You, boss—you introduced him."

Barasso is puzzled, looks towards the stage.

"I? Let's talk to this *feiticeiro*... let's find out who he really is."

But by the time we finish our drinks and go back stage, the Maestro Magician has already departed. He must've gone straight out the back door, maybe onto a boat, maybe to another bar, or maybe swallowed by that invisible world only magicians know.

We cut a deal. Traven will go with me into the Nab village, translate... in return he gets the Nagent rifles. We keep the Daddies, the sub-machine guns. He'll be the Bolivian and I'll be the European interested in selling lots more guns if the Nabs and their buddies want them. Gomez and Bekker will remain positioned for covering fire if need be. Bekker will keep the radio open in case we need reinforcements.

We unload the guns, just go with two mules and empty crates, with a couple of Nagents for show. I have my M1 anyway and Traven has his Mauser. Now he's wearing the Bolivian's fedora, and y'know, they don't look that different in the twilight.

A few monkeys set up the alarm, dropping from the trees and running through the village as we enter the open area with the fire and cooking pot. Notice a couple of long sacks hanging from poles, just like the orpo nests, only much bigger. Big chunks of raw meat too. Pig by the looks of it, as some heads are stacked up like witnesses to their own execution. Some rough pots with flowers floating in them, big white beaded pistils that look like little people, which maybe explains why these folks like eating missionaries. Yep, moon's up, big and low, just a day or two past full phase. Creepy. Enough to make a white man haul out the weed killer and start spraying... to quote SS Sergeant Schmel the other day when he was cleaning his MP-40. Thought he was being a tad harsh but now that I'm getting to see the Nabilat heartland for myself, maybe not.

They don't wear any clothes, unless paint and tattoos be clothes. They turn their skin into camouflage, can be damn hard to pick out in the jungle. The men have long hair and beards, even the little kids. They shave a track across the skull, don't know why unless it's to channel the rain or make it easier to wear a spirit mask or an animal head. Puffy cheeks, puffy bellies, small assed, walk like apes. Don't know what branch of the human tree these guys fell from but I hope it isn't mine. Good for autopsies, says Dr. Litmus. Yeah. They look at us, say, good for eating.

Thing is, they're not black, they're almost white. Depends on the light, like they're photo-sensitive. There's a lizard like that, isn't there? I know there's a bird that looks like gray tree bark. Amazon is full of them, sleep by day, hunt by night. The Nabilat can look like anything if you're trying to draw a bead on them. Save your bullets, man. Negotiate.

That's what we're doing.

This guy steps out of the shadows, tattooed face and a dong as long as his arm. Artificial, whispers Traven. Pig's bladder. Looks real enough to me except nobody, not even a Nazi, has a dick like that.

He's alone, although we know he isn't. The others are in the shadows with their dart guns, spears and second-hand machetes.

Traven seems to be able to talk to him, make sense.

"We're looking for a white man," says Traven. "Young and stupid, because he trespassed on the world of the Nabilat. He is important to us, as he is a magic man, even though he is young and stupid, and we are willing to give you a magic rifle in exchange for his return."

Words to this effect.

Big Dick seems interested, wants a demo of the rifle. We're ready for that. I take one of the Nagents, show him how to load it, then show him how it's done. Let go a round, put a nice hole between the eyes of a pig's head. Naturally, he wants to try. But the kick sets him on his ass, and his bullet goes to the moon. In the shadows, his people are laughing, just like music from a hidden radio. Even the monkeys are in on it.

Well, it's a deal, except he wants both rifles. Then, it isn't a deal. Two aren't enough.

Traven says, "He says he wants 'special magic.'"

I say, "What, he wants a machine gun?"

"They like glass... got any beads?"

Oh yeah... like I have my necklace below my shirt. Put my hand in my pocket, feel for a coin, find the glass eye, the *mau olhado* I took from that bastard cop in Rio.

Pull it out, jam it in my left socket, stare at Big Dick. This gets his attention. He wants it. Give it to him, and he tries to fit it in his eye. It falls to the ground. He picks it up, cleans it carefully against his stomach. Heavy magic. Deal, stranger.

I follow him to a hut. Traven remains with the mules, finger on the trigger of his Mauser. Everything seems cool but you don't know.

There's a white man in the hut alright, wounded, damn near dead and it isn't Edler. He's lying against a wall, his unshaven face as gray as the moon in the ghost light.

"Kallingram," I say.

He sees me, takes his time, says, "Have we met?"

"Sure," I say. "I used to saw Uma in half... after you, of course."

He's looking at me with interest now. "You're too late," he says. "If you can't smell me, you will soon."

"That bad?"

"I've been shot. Gone to septicemia, I think. Where's the Bolivian?"

I jerk my head like he's just outside. "Too late," says Kallingram. "He's arrived too late. They have my head, I'm afraid."

They have my head... what does he mean? It's then that I notice the hut is full of shrunken human heads. Various sizes. Some look like dolls, others, devils... even book ends. Yeah, you could sell these back home. It's an art form, I guess.

"You seen a German kid?" I say.

"The young Nazi? Yes, they have him. Perhaps they've eaten him."

"Why are you here, Kallingram? What happened to you?"

"Why? I'm studying magic, of course... exchanging ideas."

"How'd you get shot?"

He groans, says wearily, "My Bolivian friends and I were ambushed by some mercenaries... are you one of them?"

So he and the Coneheads wasted the Pedro and its crew. And then later they got wasted by the SS squad.

"You're Russian, aren't you?" I say. "You're trying to spread the revolution."

"I prefer the term 'Magic'... bourgeois reactionaries have appropriated the term 'revolution'... can mean anything these days. Hmm... is the Bolivian really out there? You're not here to rescue me, are you. No matter, it's too late. The moon is already in decline...."

He slips into some mumbo here, like he's with the spirits.

"Did you kill the Zs?"

"The two greedy Jews? You think I put them in my box, cut them in two? I could, I could."

"Did you?"

He coughs, groans. "What are you, sir? Another bourgeois moralist expecting a death bed confession? Leave me alone."

"B 49," I say. "The Jew's move was too good for you."

"Was it? I don't remember."

"The thing is, it wasn't his move, it was Hitler's."

He slips into Russian briefly: "*Sto vyy znayeetay*? What do you know? Oh, perhaps you do. Perhaps you are an American agent. So, you want to kill me? Too late... I'm already dead."

He's right about that. Information? It's like extracting memories from a dead man. The head's still hot but the body's cold.

"Directive 49 is Hitler's plan to grab the Atlantic Islands and then Brazil. It was in the chess piece, right under your nose."

"Don't be silly. The chess piece? The micro-film was in his stomach. The greedy bastard wanted too much. He said his wife had it."

"Now who's being silly."

There's a vibration, followed by a quickening roar which I recognize as the 12-cylinder Dailmer-Benz engines of the Zeppelin. Step outside, look up. The airship is descending above the village with its landing lights on, which flash like lightning strikes. The Nabs are shitless, prostrating themselves as they cry out like children. Several SS are sliding down ropes, sub-machine guns low and ready on their chests. Bekker must've called them in, figured we were taking too long. Or maybe this was the plan all along.

Last thing I see is Big Dick ripping one of his eyes out and plugging the glass voodoo in the bloody socket. What a mess. Some fellas will try anything to stop the onslaught of civilization.

Chapter Forty-Six:

SUSTAINED INSOMNIA

CAMP M. HAS THIS HUT which I suppose you could call a bungalow that Litmus and his assistants use to relax in. Got bug screens and fans, and a radio that works best at night. Not too far from the lab and the dormitory of the prisoner pen. Some electric too. Camp generator runs in cycles, feeds the batteries.

Litmus (or Klaus to his intimates) is in good form tonight. Interesting guy, been around, but I wouldn't say he was fun. Berlin is always lending him out in the name of science. Did malaria research for Mussolini before coming here, used patients at an Italian loonie asylum as test subjects. Lots of Italian soldiers back from Abyssinia have the parasite. Wouldn't say he's doing this for the money but there's money in it, and there's a bit of urgency behind the search for an antidote, so they cut corners. It's like torture—highly unethical but if you wanna get results, sometimes you have to do what's necessary.

Guess you could count the graves if there were markers.

Litmus: "You macerate the flower, extract the compound to an organic solvent using water, so you can partition the compounds, get the one you want. We discard the depleted flower, although some people might want to try the raffinate as a flavoring agent in, well, whatever you want, moonshine perhaps. The extract is a powerful amphetamine by itself but we can make it more powerful. Instead of three or four days of functioning insomnia, how about a week or two weeks... imagine a workforce that can function without sleep for two weeks... imagine an

410

army... imagine... imagine an entire culture. To break the conventional 24 hour cycle is to master Time. Imagine! Yes, he who dares to imagine rules the world!"

He waves his cigar, stretches, gets comfortable in his chair, crosses his legs.

Voss: "What about the malaria antidote?"

He waves this off, says, "I've already dealt with that. Chloroquine. Berlin has the information or should have it soon. Copy to Rio, of course. Now our research must be focused fully on the moonflower. Imagine— insomnia, the secret weapon!"

"But how can it work? Sleep is necessary for rejuvenation, isn't it?"

"Not so. Our tests suggest sunlight is more important."

"Sustained insomnia... then everything becomes a dream?"

Litmus laughs awkwardly, tugs at his ragged goatee. "There is nothing metaphysical about it, Hauptmann Voss. Pain remains, fear has its purpose, the strong are rewarded."

"Then does it follow that sleeping itself is a sickness?"

"Interesting, ja? I studied the condition in East Africa... it's my contention that the parasite is carried by everyone."

"Everyone? Malaria too?"

"No... not yet. It's possible that Brazil is being genetically transformed by malaria... a silent, invisible migration within the cells... followed by gene mutation. My experiments in Italy first gave me the idea of malarial madness, a cultural deviation or sublimation. We see it in the tropics, everywhere we look."

"What about cholera, Doctor?"

"What about it? Don't drink shitty water!"

All this is in German. Voss thinks Litmus will win the Nobel Prize. Sure. Either that or someone will hang him.

Don't like his taste in music, though. Like a lot of Krauts he sucks Wagner like a fly, plays it on his windup in the evenings. Sounds like a drunk running a cement mixer, ask me.

Still, I yawn. The technicals don't interest me much, refined cruelty even less.

Dawn. Some of us are in the washroom freshening up, getting ready for another day. Schmel is shaving, hogging the mirror. He looks like Father fuggin' Christmas the way his face is all lathered and his belly is in the sink. Well I exaggerate. His belly is as hard as a medicine ball and he's got shoulders like a bull elephant. He can bend iron bars. I've seen it. Once when we were training in Santa Catarina one of the trucks hit a pothole and bent a two inch tie rod and he just crawled below and straightened it out with his bare hands.

He's a happy camper this morning. The mission yesterday against the Coneheads went textbook. When we picked up the Pedro's distress call on the radio, the Waffen SS squad responded with a Zeppelin drop.

"The Bolivians blocked the channel by dynamiting some big trees, so when the Brats tried to back out, they dropped some more trees and trapped them. These monkeys have themselves some serious weapons, Soviet stuff, MGs and sniper rifles. We have some serious communist trouble here, kumpel, no mistaking it. These Coneheads are Red. The War of the World is on, better believe it. They got training, they got leadership, they got weapons. Weakness? They ride donkeys.

"Ja, that Pedro gunboat had a twin 50 MG, but they didn't know which way to shoot so they got chewed up pretty bad. They also had a Becker 20 mm but you know, they were caught like fish in a barrel. Grenades did them in. She caught fire and the Marines panicked, jumped in the water, so if the snipers didn't get 'em, the crocs did.

"When we did a fly over to scout the situation, the boat was half under water. Even the river was on fire from the fuel. The Captain ordered the crew to open the valves. Maybe he opened them himself. Last thing he did because he took a bullet in the throat.

Schmel draws his razor across his throat with a flourish.

"Did any of them survive? Not many. Maybe some still hiding in *der Dschungel*. Good luck to them. Hey, maybe the Sigma squad can go looking, do some mop up. Maybe you can find a Marine or two hiding up a tree. Eh fucking bimbos... *arbartige*... they got what they deserved, maybe."

"But they were ambushed, Schmel! They weren't expecting trouble!"

He pauses, leers at me in the mirror. "Well, if you take a canoe up a sewer, what do you expect?"

Has a point. Barasso warned Captain Furtado.

"We dropped Bekker close with the portable, so when the Coneheads retired he was able to radio in their position and direction. We were waiting for them. What goes around, comes around, ja?"

"No prisoners?"

"The officer got away. White man."

"So you killed all the insurgents?"

"Let it be a lesson to Red Coneheads everywhere."

"How come the white man got away?"

"He's white, isn't he?"

Schmel taps his head with a finger, adds, "He won't get far... *dachschaden*."

Dachschaden. Head wound.

"Seems to me you want that white man, Sergeant. Intel."

"You want to go after him? Waste of time. He's already kaput."

"He could be carrying important intel. Be good to find him."

"Be my guest. Hey, you think this mirror is accurate?"

He's clean shaven, and his cropped hair is fuzzed like a boot brush. Fat, hard face, brutal without redemption. His smile is never a smile, even when admiring himself. Some of the squad have been using their bayonets to etch crosses on the wooden frame. Swastikas too. Crude.

"It's flawed, Sergeant. See? Your head is square."

He's clenching his teeth, his eyes locked on mine. Seems he's the only one allowed to make jokes.

"I can kill you, faggot."

"I'll forget you said that, soldier. I outrank you, remember?"

Said it before and it's going through my mind again: Schmel is a criminal masquerading as a soldier.

"We're the Armed Protection Force, Herr Thorsen. We're the chosen few, don't you know? What are you? You belong to nothing. So fuck off."

Couple of SS soldiers in the room, none of my boys. One of them is grinning like idiot, head like a hatchet. The other is more sober, but paying close attention. They still have blood fever.

For me, the odds aren't good.

"Why don't you find yourself a donkey, Leutnant?" Schmel sneers. "Then I can shoot you."

I nod, say, "O.k. Schmel... we'll settle this later."

I leave. Can hear them laughing as I walk swiftly towards nothingness. Corner of the rec hut, I black out briefly. My face is all wet with sweat. Could be anger, could be fear, but seeing as I have a temperature, it could be something else.

Chapter Forty-Seven:

THE MIRROR

HEADING OVER TOWARDS the lab hut where the Zeppelin is moored. Voss has been using a cabin on the airship as an office, for obvious reasons. Meet Barasso coming down the gangway. He's using a stick.

"Thorsen," he says. "I have to go back to Rio pronto."

"What's wrong?" I say. "Crisis at home?"

"My back... I did something, don't know what," he says. "Yes. One of my managers has a problem that needs fixed."

"Serious?"

"Political."

I tell him about the 'white man' who escaped the SS policing action, express my dissatisfaction with the way the Germans are carrying on. "They just shoot everyone, take no prisoners. And they don't give a fuck about those marines."

"Yes, I've just been talking to Captain Voss about that. It's delicate."

"Rio is gonna go nuts, surely."

"I will handle it. Come, walk with me."

We go the rec hut, passing the prisoner compound where the sad, dead eyes of the Indian test subjects watch us pass by through the razor wire. Strong fecal smell. Someone's crying.

"Good news about the antidote," I say.

"That's another thing," says Barasso. "We haven't received any information about it. Litmus is being evasive."

"No formula? He says he copied Rio with the results. I heard him say that to Voss."

"He's a liar or else it got lost in the mail. You might have to shoot him for me... eh, maybe I joke. His mind seems to be somewhere else."

"Moonflower."

"Ah, yes, the moonflower. If there's money in it, fine. But frankly it's illogical. Insomnia? No one wants to be awake. It sounds, eh, religious. We want sleeping pills, better booze, cheaper happiness."

"He's talking about a military application."

"Fine. Prove it. But I want my malaria drug."

He hobbles up the steps and we go into the rec hut. Radio is on, whistling off the station.

"You know, boss, if we could find that officer, we could find out what the Bolivians are up to."

He lowers himself into a chair, groans. "Communists. Part of an insurgency in the Andes. Since the Chaco War nothing has been right. Bolivia thinks this part of the basin is its territory... Peru... even the fucking Colombians. Meanwhile Moscow is stirring up trouble with the Indians. Frankly it's a mess. But believe me, amigo, this land is Brazilian. The people, the resources, the rivers, the forest—Brazilian. It's a real problem for the Estado Novo because Indians don't give a damn about borders. It's delicate. What happened to the Pedro is bad, but Rio won't want it publicized. They have reasons... we all have reasons."

"Lot of bodies out there... like they say, the gunshot fades but the body remains."

"Bodies? Eh, this is the Amazon. You won't find any bodies today."

He's right. Here, existence is just the blink of an eye.

"Listen, Thorsen. I want you to stay here another couple of weeks. You're a good man. I can trust you."

I nod. Wish I was going back with him. The jungle isn't for me. Been thinking about Uma too, some unfinished business. But a job's a job, so I guess I can hack another week or two.

"If Leonora knew what was going on here, she'd cut my balls off. Listen, I appreciate what you did for Eddie. Justice, amigo."

Vaticano. Justice, sure. What Barasso doesn't know is that when I shot Vaticano it was not only justice for Eddie but also four other victims who died on a mountain ridge when Vaticano a.k.a. Credo the Cross of Fire shot down their plane. Unless, of course, Barasso was the guy who commissioned Vaticano in the first place. I'll never know... unless the four hundred grand isn't around when I call my banker Leonora to collect.

"Keep an eye on Dr. Litmus. See if you can acquire some of this Chloroquine. Could be some insurance."

"Better have that back seen to."

"I will. Litmus offered to give me an injection for the inflammation."

"Did he?"

"I suggested he give me some pills instead. Let him stick a needle in me? Fall asleep, arise tomorrow as a monkey."

Yeah... Litmus is more like a vet than a doctor, and he's neither. He's another Nazi farmer like his real boss, Heinrich Himmler. Edler told me that Himmler was a chicken farmer before he went into politics.

The mirror went missing the same day Edler did, although there didn't seem to be a connection. Somebody said the mirror committed suicide because it couldn't stand Schmel's ugly face, just cracked and someone tossed it. I didn't say it but it sounds about right to me. Maybe they ran out of space on the frame to carve their kill crosses. Maybe somebody fucked up, put his bayonet through it. Anyway, it's gone.

If you want to shave or squeeze some zits at Camp M. you're on your own. Better have a good picture of your face in your head or you might do some serious damage. Schmel cut himself. Looks good on him.

As for Edler, no one paid any attention until he didn't show up to lead a patrol at eleven. And they made jokes about that too. He'd sneaked off to Plasmos for a piece of ass with a monkey or a boa got him. Or he took some of that combat drug 5-3-5 and is on his way to Peru. Stuff like that. But of course Voss took the disappearance seriously, sent some people looking. And they came back empty. Lieutenant Edler had disappeared without a trace.

Couple of days later we talk to El Dorado, our river guide. See what you can find out. Money in it.

By the way he shifts his eyes, I figure he knows something. Sure as hell, next day he shows up, says the Nabilat have their boy.

Never occurs to anyone to ask if he knows what happened to the mirror.

There's a party for Edler at Camp M. after the rescue. Well, he's the excuse. These boys want to let her rip anyway after annihilating the Coneheads and humiliating the Nabilat. They didn't kill any of the Nabs, although they razed a few of their huts. Excuse was, they were looking for Kallingram. I pointed to the exact hut where the Magician was, but they said he wasn't there. Must've crawled off during the ruckus. He won't get far with his wounds. Too bad. He has more questions to answer.

Edler was in one of the cooking sacks, all trussed up. His girl Moonflower was in the other. One of the SS—Corporal Bekker, I think—dragged her off for a little *untermenschen* fun and games... and he came back alone. Nothing Edler could do about it, even if he wanted to, as he was out of it. They just put him in the cargo cage and took him up into the Zeppelin when they left *sehr schnell*. They got this search and destroy blitzkrieg thing down to an art... but I notice they don't include Sigma in much of it. More and more we're doing things separately. Guess we're just the rubber mules, and they're the warriors.

Me and Gomez return the way we came, help Traven pack the Russian rifles to the boat. He keeps the Nagents, we take the machine pistols. Well, we let him keep one Daddy, as he says his Mauser is getting a bit old. Deal's a deal.

By the time we get back to camp, the Germans are already going at it, drinking beer and schnapps and singing German songs. Well, everybody's into it, our squad, their squad, Litmus and his lab assistant... some of the Zeppelin crew. Edler is pale, to say the least. Snake bite. Not sure if it was an accident or part of a Nabilat ceremony before they stuffed him in the cooking sack. Litmus shot him up with something, says he'll be o.k., he'd already be dead if the bite was fatal. He looks like he's shell-shocked, his mind tossed someplace else. He drinks, but it doesn't make a difference. The others get merry, get drunk, get stupid, but he stays sober. Captain Voss proposes a toast, raises his glass, declaims, "*Leutnant* Edler!"

Others respond with respectful murmurs, "Edler...."

Someone—sounds like Schmel—shouts "*Sieg Heil!*" and the room explodes with a chorus of *Sieg Heils*. Edler looks a bit dazed.

Later, he wanders outside to get away from it, have a smoke. I'm there with Gomez and the Brazilian guy from our squad who's telling us about his days as a samba dancer.

Edler listens in, then says, "Wouldn't you rather be doing that than this?"

"Be no money in dancin," says Juno (that's his name).

Juno's black, and I notice he looks at Edler suspiciously. The SS guys have treated Juno with special scorn. Not Edler, but the others.

Edler says, "I have a confession: I am the one who took the mirror from the washroom."

Juno shrugs, says, "No difference to me. Your men wouldn't let me use it."

I say, "That's why Lieutenant Edler took it, Juno."

Everyone laughs, even Edler. That loosens things up. Gomez and Juno go looking for more beer.

Edler says, "I gave it to her."

This surprises me. "The girl you let escape? The Nabilat woman?"

"Moonflower. She's, she's not Nabilat. She's from somewhere else, a hostage taken from another tribe who might've taken her from someone else before that, some people in the Andes. I'm guessing, because I don't speak her language, but she's different, certainly not an Amazon Indian of the sort we've been kidnapping.

"The Nabs considered her special, and were holding her as a sacrifice. They do that."

Yes, they do that. Don't ask why. Like dogs bringing back the rabbit to Master.

"One day I went into the forest by myself. I wanted to see what it would be like to be in a primal place like this alone, not part of a patrol, not part of a group. Be by myself, understand? Others do it. Prospectors, like old Traven. You never start out learning anything as part of a group. You start out alone... and at times we forget that in our haste to belong to civilization. You are alone. To know the face of your father doesn't change this. You are alone, even if your mother sends letters after you've enlisted.

"In Germany we have a painter called Friedrich who painted our forests the way they were more than a hundred years ago, wild and primitive, full of solitude and ancestral memory. We have to study him in school. Romantic. But the European forest is very different from the South American equatorial forest. In Europe, life and death are cyclical... here, they are coincidental, always present. One is passive, the other is volatile. In Europe, the demons are in the mind, here they are everywhere to be seen.

"Maybe it's a form of suicide, walking alone in the Amazon. Nature is so powerful you become blind from the noise of it all. It becomes the silence that roars. Am I making sense? Expect not. Germans are idiots without a book in their hands. Bach... you know Bach wrote music to combat insomnia... literally. He wrote harpsichord patterns to put you to sleep. Yes, consider it: using hammers to make lullabies. That's the special German madness, using hammers to make lullabies.

"Mad. I've been mad since birth, I think. I've certainly been mad since I arrived here at Camp M. I was mad to show mercy to that girl, let her escape... and I was certainly mad to go looking for her again. That's why I went into the forest alone. I didn't admit it at first, but the second and third time my disappointment wasn't that I'd escaped death but that I hadn't found her. Well, I was searching not only in the wrong place, but also at the wrong time. I had to go at night. Yes, night, when the moonflower blooms and the ghosts of the forest manifest."

I'm saying nothing, just letting him ramble. Maybe it's the snake bite or he's taken some of that 535 combat drug again.

"I found her. Or should I say, she found me. As they say, the forest has eyes.

"She was being groomed for sacrifice. Just how this unpleasant realization came to me, I don't know. I'm not a mind-reader and I'm not an anthropologist, yet when someone draws a picture in the dirt, I can read it, just as I can read a woman's eyes. Her story is this:

"God is dead. Otherwise we would see him. Therefore in order to appease him, we must sacrifice beauty. Beauty must be sent to the Afterlife for his pleasure. If he is pleased, then he will make the moonflower bloom.

"Cruel and fantastic, isn't it? I'm not sure if I fell in love with her or the way of understanding she led me to. I tried to tell her how beautiful she was but she refused to believe it. Now I think I understand why. If she thought of herself as ugly, then she might avoid death.

"So I stole the mirror from the washroom, took it into the jungle so she could see herself, recognize the magic of her beauty. And she did. She saw a stranger—herself. And saw me.

"We kissed until sunlight caught the glass and blinded us. She cried out, then, as her sight came back, she realized she could use the mirror to illuminate places of darkness, reveal the hidden eyes of the forest. It was a new game... she could make the sun move wherever she wanted, urged on by celestial forces we recognize but never understand. But I have to say, she was an animal, and I succumbed to the animal. The distance between her and I wasn't language, the idiot bond of babblers, it was a million years of dust and dreams. As I lay in her arms, I realized the waking man is the dream of the sleeping woman.

"So they caught me. The Nabilat. They caught me in her arms and that's fair, because I wanted to die anyway. They put me in a sack with a snake. It wasn't a big snake and its bite wasn't quick death, it was more like a living death. Real death would come with the moonflower feast and my head would be shrunk to mark the year.

"What happened to her? To Moonflower? I wonder. Was she dead or was she killed in the raid? No one seems to know. Do you? No?"

"I owe you my life, Thorsen. I understand you led the rescue group. I know my squad is taking the credit but they're so infatuated with their idea of themselves, so arrogant, so bereft of charity they can't give credit where credit is due. Well, they lie. Of course they took a risk, endangered themselves, but... National Socialism produces its share of arseholes.

"Perhaps I can return the favour one day. Cigarette?"

Cigarette, sure. I take one, and we smoke in silence. The moonlight is splashing silver flares on the dark skin of the zeppelin moored in the distance. Looks like a sleeping dinosaur humped against the tree-line of the prehistoric wilderness. Bursts of drunken revelry and the odd unknown creature signalling. Stars, the vast twinkling of the Milky Way. In one sense we're hopelessly lost, in another we're completely safe and secure in a place called Camp M.

Chapter Forty-Eight:

HIS EYES ARE OPEN AND HE MUST SEE SOMETHING

MALARIA. I'm scared that it's got me. Sweating buckets and if my temperature isn't a hundred and three, it's close enough. Now the chills. I crawl free of my mosquito netting, head for the dock, see Traven.

"You're pretty bad, boy," he says. "Looks like you got the fever. Here, chew some of these."

Gives me some coca leaves. What the hell, nothing to lose. Seem to help.

"You see *die Amsel* yet?" he says.

"No."

"You're not really sick. When the blackbird hangs around, you got a problem. Some folks on the big river call it *O melro*."

Really talking about black spots here. When everywhere you look you see bugs dancing.

"Maybe you should make a sacrifice to the *Mami Wata*," he says.

"What?"

"The river god, *senhor*. The Candomble cure."

"Uh, no more voodoo, thanks."

"No? Well, you can try a bottle of rum."

See he's got one sticking out of his bag, which he now drops in his boat. Shotgun, Mauser, ammo and grub. Watch him start the motor, head onto the main channel, disappear in the blur. Going to Plasmos, probably. Once asked him if he had any dreams for the future, and he said, "Ja... Marlene." He always says that. Think he's actually talking about his boat or his bag of coca leaves or maybe one of the monkeys that hang around the dock that he sometimes feeds. Certainly isn't any kind of woman in the Nazi sense of the word.

Edler comes to see me. He's cheerful, has some new capsules.

"Chloroquine," he says. "This will make you a man again."

"Where'd you get it?" I say.

"The lab," he says. "I know what it is. It's new."

"You stole it?"

He shrugs, says, "We can't wait around until Berlin decides who can have what. The SS has the right of first access, and I'm SS."

I take some... couple more days of craziness and the next time I wake up the storm in my head has passed. I get up, go for a piss. Prefer to piss outside because the smell of the lavatory is bloody awful. Even so, the flies show up right away. My piss is like gasoline -- smells bad at first, then smells great, clears the head in a crazy kind of way.

First day of September everything changes. The only reason I know the date is because of the magnitude of the event: Hitler invades Poland and the shit hits the fan. The Zeppelin crew pick up the news on their radio and that evening everyone in Camp M. is drinking a little heavier than usual. Of course it takes a couple of days before the wheels really fall off and Britain and France declare war on Germany but it's happening. Everything changes. One day you're brothers, the next you're enemies.

Voss comes to see me. "We have new orders, Lieutenant Thorsen," he says, kinda formal. "My squad has to leave."

I nod, say, "The Zeppelin too?"

"Ja. Captain Weisbaden has orders to fly to Recife."

The City of Reefs, on the coast, due east.

"Then Berlin?"

"I expect so. We'll know when we get to Recife."

Recife's on the bump, where Brazil sticks out into the Atlantic, is closest to Africa. It's the route home.

Can't say I'm going to miss these guys but I lie, say politely, "It's unfortunate, isn't it?"

"Have you been in contact with Colonel Barasso?"

"Not yet."

"Why don't you come with us?"

I'm thinking he means catch a ride to Recife.

"Can't," I say. "Got to take a cargo of rubber to Plasmos."

His face goes sour, as if to say what a waste of time. He says, "Think it over, Mackenzie King. We leave this afternoon."

He raises his hand, gives me the salute, leaves.

Voss. He's changed. When I first met him on the boat coming to Brazil nearly a year ago he was an agnostic. Now he's a believer. Guess it's the responsibility. Make a man a captain and you got yourself a slave.

I am thinking now. Dr. Litmus is packing up, leaving too. Doesn't want to but the orders include him as well. So what happens to the Indians? What happens to the test subjects? When I get to Plasmos, I can phone Barasso, or send him a telegram. He must be aware of the European situation, and the implications for Camp M. Sigma should have its own radio but for some damn reason it doesn't.

There's a ruckus at the prisoner hut. Shots. Sounds like a burp gun, little bursts. I get out of bed, go the window, see some Indians running into the jungle. Warning shots? Get-the-hell-out-of-here shots? Execution shots? I get dressed, grab Oswald, head for the pen... and then I realize I'm still in my bed, dreaming. The fever has returned, and I'm half-in, half-out. Not a good place to be. Sweat like a pig, dream like a devil.

It's brief. Wake maybe an hour later, feel pretty damn good. Get up, thinking I'm done with this place. I'll find the boys, make some arrangements.

Step behind some barrels near the extraction shed, have a normal piss, light a cigarette, have a normal smoke. Then I hear angry, brutal voices. German. It's Schmel and Bekker and they've got Edler, are kicking and punching him. Edler drops to his knees and Schmel pulls out his Luger and shoots him in the head. Boom. That's it. One shot and Edler sags, rolls over dead. Schmel looks down, pushes the body with his boot, then fires another shot for good measure.

It's fast, and the shock of it leaves me frozen. They don't see me and it's a damn good thing, as I'm sure Schmel would shoot me too. Why did they execute Edler? The other day they were celebrating his rescue, and now they've shot him. Well, it's not too hard to figure. Edler didn't fit. His liaison with the *untermenschen* was beyond the pale for a fanatic like Schmel... especially if he knew about the mirror. Did Voss sanction this? Doesn't matter. Edler has a record of going a.w.o.l. and in the haste to depart Camp M., who will miss him?

Wait until they're gone, then I go through Edler's pockets, find a capsule of 535 pills and another that looks like Chloroquine. Well, I won't be sending these to his mother. Look at his face. His eyes are open and he must see something I can't, because he's smiling.

CHAPTER FORTY-NINE

SEPTEMBER 1939: *UNTERMENSCHEN*

"JOIN THE WAFFEN *SS,* *mein Freund.* We take foreigners, no problem. Serve honorably and you will receive citizenship in the 3rd Reich. Your mother is German? Then you are already a citizen. Join with your natural comrades with whom you are bonded in blood. The Fate of the world is in the balance. Stalin and Jew Bolshevism... or Hitler and National Socialism—which is it to be? We are expanding. Now we are just a few thousand, extensions of Hitler's bodyguard. There will be new brigades, new divisions. Opportunity awaits. There will be a Foreign Legion... French comrades will join, Belgian, Dutch, Spanish... Hungarian, Croatian... I can tell you, there will be a Viking Division, pure aryan volunteers from Denmark, Norway, Sweden... ja, the future is the SS."

As a recruitment pitch, it's pretty good. Sergeant Schmel is standing nearby, pretending to admire the view through the gondola window, smirk on his fat face, but I know he's listening. Just as I know Corporal Bekker is gripping the handrail a bit tightly cause he's scared of flying.

I look at Voss, jerk my head at Gomez, say, "Sounds good. Him too?"

Voss looks at Gomez for a sec, says, "American or Mexican?"

Gomez says, "Whatever you want."

Voss says, "Perhaps... are you really interested in joining the Waffen SS, Corporal Gomez?"

Gomez says, "What's the money?"

Hear Schmel murmur fucking *untermenschen* just as the airship 2nd Officer comes up, says Captain Weisbaden would like to see Captain

Voss. Voss excuses himself, follows the 2nd Officer to the bridge. Us, we have a beer. There's an unmistakable feeling of optimism in the air, like the prospect of returning home and joining a real war is a good and honorable thing. Even Dr. Litmus, who's sitting at another table drinking schnapps and smoking his cigar, has a big smile as if the Fuhrer has summoned him personally. Maybe so. Maybe Schmel is gonna get a medal in Berlin or something, although not if I get a chance to drop him through the cargo hatch before we make Recife.

Smile at Gomez, clink glasses. Cheers. He'll help me. The best weapon against an enemy is another enemy. Nietzsche.

The engines are purring, happy in the cooler air at two thousand feet. A few whiffs of cloud scud past, nothing serious, could be exhaust or vapor off the hull. The only cloudbank is in the far distance, like a range of phantom mountains rising up from the jungle. Beautiful. Too beautiful to describe. You can only feel it, y'know? Start mouthing on about it and you only mess it up.

Thinking about Uma and her keyhole body. I need a woman and she's a woman and maybe I'm getting tired of being a gun for hire. Maybe. Maybe it's that stash of money and I'm thinking I could go someplace romantic with the right woman, just get lost.

Someone's pointing, and we look down through the observation lens. A long red track through the forest, straight as a dye. At intervals, circles, could be villages, might be just clearings.

Voss has returned. He says, "Remnants of a lost civilization?"

Schmel laughs, says, "*Es ist eine Schwein Spur!*"

It's just a pig track... yeah, he should know.

Voss comes to our table, says to Gomez, "Could you excuse us, Corporal? I need to speak to Lieutenant Thorsen alone."

Gomez grunts, gets up, takes his beer, takes a walk. Voss sits down, speaks low.

"You know what happened to Edler, don't you?"

I just hold his eyes, say nothing.

"He went back to that Indian girl, didn't he? Damn fool. The Nabilat will kill him. Well, he deserves it. My report to Berlin will say they kidnapped and killed him, which is partially true. I can count on your discretion, can't I, Thorsen? Otherwise I might not be able to follow through on my offer...."

To join the SS. I sort of nod. He sort of smiles, more sad than relaxed.

"We're not going to Berlin," he says. "We're going to a small island in the Atlantic. Can you believe it?"

I'm amused, or as amused as one can be after seeing a man executed a couple of hours ago. Edler, poor bastard. I'm tempted to confront Voss about it.

Instead, I say, "Directive 49."

Voss, naturally, is surprised. "How do you know about Directive 49, Thorsen?"

"Everyone knows about Directive 49, Voss. Even the Estado Novo."

Schmel is guffawing again, calls, "*Kapitan*, look!"

There's a cohort of Indians marching towards us in two parallel lines on the track. Of course these guys don't march, they shuffle, half-way between a trot and a dance. At the front, there's a flash, like the sun has caught a shield or a mirror. The flashing continues, and the light dances around the walls of the gondola the way sunlight sometimes bounces off running waves at the beach. As we look, the flashing stops and the light swells into a blinding super nova. Everything goes silent as we go both blind and deaf and the Zeppelin suddenly rolls over towards hell. No explosion, although there's got to be an explosion. No chaos, although there's got to be chaos... awareness is just the brute roar as we destruct.

Next thing I see is the jungle canopy spinning towards me. I'm in free-fall, stomach sucked in like it's touching my spine. See Gomez, his arms and hands extended in a cross, like he's trying to pull out of his dive. See bits and pieces of tumbling debris, smoking, burning... see spinning bodies bent into grotesque shapes... smoking, burning. Hear the whisper of the wind as I black out.

When I come to I'm flat on the ground with someone lying beside me and first thing I see is the shredded keyboard of the lounge piano hanging from a tree. Can't believe I'm still alive and maybe I'm not. Just lie there, shocked, afraid to move anything, even a finger, in case nothing works and I should be dead. Could be paralyzed with fear or just plain paralyzed. The body beside me is very warm, and it's alive too, the breathing heavy and hoarse. Feel it shift position, and as I realize my companion is a black pan jaguar, my eyes close again.

Pass in and out of consciousness, and between swoons, see the jaguar drag a body into the underbrush, start feasting. Looks like Schmel and everytime I open my eyes there's less of him. He's just like a carcass in a butcher shop getting smaller and smaller as the shadow moves down the wall.

Now it's dark. I'm on my back, stars glittering through the gaps in the canopy. Turn my head... where's the cat? Eyes gleam, but what are they? Who? The dead? I can move but just as soon as I realize this, there's the jaguar stretched out beside me again. God Almighty, what am I? Food, a pet, a trophy—what? Can feel the hot rough tongue lick my hand... and then it's like a sheet being drawn over my face.

Goodnight.

Awake again. Day, but what day? Must be mid-morning as the sun's getting up there.

The jungle is chattering like a radio. First I think it's music, then someone talking, full of noise and drift the way you hear it on short wave. '*Dies ist lhr Führer... Dies ist lhr Führer...*' Repeats over and over, repeats 'this is your Leader... this is your Leader'. But all I can see is a beautiful yellow bird on a branch, a big canary or something getting into the solar pulse. Just noise, just Brazil, where everything sounds like a damn radio, samba and fried eggs.

Roll over, get to my feet without thinking. Left arm aches from a bad festering wound. No sign of the jaguar. But I almost fall into the stack of cadavers in his food dump. Do I recognize anyone? Do I want to? Pieces of wreckage here and there... some guy stuck head first in the ground like a fence post, another impaled on a tree branch... hands... feet... a swastika flag... I just want to get away from it all, lurch blindly through the junk weed until I come to a stream, drink, then follow that until I hear the low roar of a river. Takes a long time to get there and I sense I'm being followed by the cat... not stalked, but escorted like a prisoner to the Gate. Yes, I know: fatalism is for trauma victims and dummies.

Yet I find the river, get there, collapse on the bank, pass out again for the nth time.

Wake up when I hear a motor, see a *barca* coming up stream. Wait till it gets closer, raise my right hand. Chest feels like it's been clamped and compressed, so I can't shout. Or maybe I've forgotten how.

It's not Traven but it might be the real El Dorado, if El Dorado is indeed a man. White but tropicalized. Older, bearded, thin and packing a Lee Enfield. Ranger hat and linen jacket that's seen better days. As he glides onto the muddy beach below the bank, some kingfishers swarm excitedly over the fast moving part of the channel. Might be a fish. Might be the limb of a tree or the body of man. Might be sweet bugger all but some confusion about life and death. I don't want to know.

"Hello, sir," says the man. "Are you lost?"

Toffy English accent, like a Lord or something. Mind you, skid row is full of actors with accents like this.

I nod, have no words, just spittle.

"Name's Fawcett," he says. "Colonel Fawcett. Yes, you look like you need assistance."

He's looking me over. Gives me a cigarette, makes me sit down, gets some gasoline from his spare tank, pours a few drops on my wound which is full of maggots. They don't like that. I start picking them out one by one, then jab them with my cigarette like I'm mental. But hey, it's either them or me, right?